THE POSSESSION

Arabella's fists were pounding him, her nails scratching him in her frenzy. Slowly he moved against her, watching her eyes darken.

"Tell me you want me, Arabella," he commanded.

"I want—" Her words stopped as she reached out to him. He lowered his head and began to nibble and kiss her belly.

"Wrap your legs around me," he said, his control dissolving. She gasped.

So wildly was he caught up in the swirling passion that he ceased to be apart from her. Kamal felt as though his very soul had been torn from his body. "You are mine, Arabella," he said softly, but he wondered if afterward she would pull away from him, denying again the love between them. . . .

DEVIL'S DAUGHTER

DEVIL'S DAUGHTER

CATHERINE COULTER

A SIGNET BOOK

NEW AMERICAN LIBRARY

NAL BOOKS ARE AVAILABLE AT QUANTITY DISCOUNTS
WHEN USED TO PROMOTE PRODUCTS OR SERVICES.
FOR INFORMATION PLEASE WRITE TO PREMIUM MARKETING DIVISION,
NEW AMERICAN LIBRARY, 1633 BROADWAY,
NEW YORK, NEW YORK 10019.

Copyright © 1985 by Catherine Coulter

SIGNET TRADEMARK REG. U.S. PAT. OFF. AND FOREIGN COUNTRIES
REGISTERED TRADEMARK—MARCA REGISTRADA
HECHO EN CHICAGO, U.S.A.

SIGNET, SIGNET CLASSIC, MENTOR, PLUME, MERIDIAN AND NAL BOOKS
are published by New American Library,
1633 Broadway, New York, New York 10019

First Printing, May, 1985

5   6   7   8   9

PRINTED IN THE UNITED STATES OF AMERICA

TO GREG
May you enjoy all the success you so richly deserve

Prologue

Mediterranean Sea,
Coast of Sardinia, 1802

Hamil El-Mokrani,
Bey of Oran, stood beside his captain at the helm
of his *xebec*, his powerful legs braced against the
rising wind that whipped through his black hair.
He looked toward the bulging storm clouds rolling
toward them and folded his arms tightly across his
chest, a devil-may-care grin curving his lips.

"The ship is sound, highness," Aben said. His
eyes darted up to Hamil from the wheel that lurched
beneath his callused hands.

"Do you convince yourself or me, Aben?" Hamil
asked, still scanning the horizon. "You will have to
do both. The storm has caught us off Sardinia. The
waters will be treacherous."

The *xebec* dipped into a deep trough, throwing
Aben to port. Hamil grabbed the wheel and righted
their course. His deep laugh resounded across the
deck, drawing the eyes of the sailors toward him.

Aben, grim-faced, took the wheel again. More

quickly than it seemed possible, the black clouds were upon them, gushing torrents of rain. He yelled orders to his men, his voice a thin thread in the wailing wind. He watched Hamil stride toward the mizzenmast, as if he hadn't a care in the world, and help the sailors furl the heavy, sodden rigging to protect it from the tearing wind.

The *xebec* floundered on the crest of a wave, and heeled sharply to port, its timbers groaning. Aben knew they must lighten the ship, cast off the precious goods they had captured from an Italian merchant ship three days before. He shouted the order and watched his men scurry belowdecks.

Hamil's dark eyes narrowed as they heaved casks of precious wine and heavy cords of rich velvet cloth over the side. It was a pity, he thought, that Lella would not see the rich material. He had pictured her pleasure as she stroked the soft velvet, her eyes smiling up at him. His gaze passed to the group of sailors from the *Reale*, the Italian ship, crouched together near the rain barrels, cowering in fear. Sniveling fools, he thought, we are not murderers. He shook his head like a large mongrel, throwing his thick black hair back from his face and strode toward the railing to help a young sailor hoist a cask of wine over the side.

"Highness."

He turned to see Ramid, his self-effacing Moorish slave, struggling toward him, his head bowed against the roaring wind. Hamil knew Ramid hated the sea, and was foully ill whenever the Mediterranean was anything but calm as glass. Even now the man's thin face was pinched and pale, his eyes wide with fear.

"What is it you want, Ramid? By Allah, man, go belowdecks! One look at you and the men will think we are all fish bait!"

"Please, highness, you must accompany me. You are needed."

Hamil frowned at him, wondering where Ramid had found the courage to come for him, but he followed the man aft. Ramid's lips moved as if in prayer as he walked carefully over the treacherous deck, Hamil striding impatiently behind him. At last he stopped and leaned over the railing, gazing raptly into the churning water below. Hamil wondered dispassionately if he was retching again.

"What is the problem?" Hamil shouted at his slave over a crack of thunder.

Ramid pointed downward and moved quickly aside. Curious now, Hamil took his place at the railing. He heard Ramid say in a thin, wailing voice, "Forgive me, highness, but I will be free and rich at your death!"

Hamil turned swiftly, and the dagger aimed at his back struck deep into his shoulder. He struck out with all his mighty strength, but the dagger plunged again, into his side. He gave a howl of fury and staggered against the railing. "You swine!" he yelled toward Ramid.

Ramid seemed to shrink at his rage, but a second man, a swarthy Nubian, shoved him aside. "It must be now!" the man shouted. They were upon him, lifting him, though he struggled, his pain forgotten. Hamil felt his back bending over the railing, and then he was hurled outward. He gave a howl of fury and locked his arms about the Nubian, squeezing the writhing man to him as they plunged, locked together, into the sea.

1

Clare Castle, England, 1803

Arabella rushed down the great oak staircase, a whirlwind of velvet riding skirts pelting her legs, only to draw up short at the sight of her brother entering the hall. She watched him negligently strike his riding crop against his thigh in thoughtful rhythm to his booted step. It was on the tip of her tongue to chide him, for he was late, but he paused a moment, his eyes drawn to the rich medieval trappings of the great hall, and she stood silently watching him. She knew his thoughts, for she had stood many times gazing in awe just as he was doing. It was an impressive chamber with high timbered ceilings that boasted a cavernous fireplace large enough to roast a boar, fifteenth-century suits of armor, both Italian and English, and myriad well-dusted Flemish tapestries. Silver sconces designed for ancient rush-light torches of mutton fat, empty now, but highly polished, were fastened to its stone walls at six-foot intervals.

She watched Adam stop below the painting of the long-dead first Earl of Clare, who had lived not in the thirteenth century, but in the seventeenth, under the reign of William and Mary. She smiled, thinking about Roger Nathan Welles. That earl had been fascinated by the ruins of a Norman castle on a gentle rise of his newly purchased land, and had its great hall reconstructed to its former grandeur according to his own vision. Then, caught up in his own handiwork, and inspired by dubious legends of King Arthur, he had expanded his fancy into a four-towered edifice of soft gray stone dug from a Chicester quarry. The result was perhaps a bit unusual for its time, but nonetheless a home that all subsequent Earls of Clare would have protected with their lives. Happily, their vows were never tested, for the time of civil wars in England was past.

Adam Charles Parese Welles, Viscount St. Ives, had indeed been thinking about the beauty of his home. He was ready for a rest now after two hectic months in Amsterdam, dealing with recalcitrant Dutch shipping merchants, ready for nothing more trying than riding his stallion, Brutus, through the rolling hills that surrounded his home. But he was to leave again, to journey to the Villa Parese, in Genoa. Images of Italy flowed easily into his mind, for there was Ligurian blood in his veins. Whenever he set foot there, he shucked off his English trappings as easily as he did his clothes.

"Adam," Arabella called to him in her exuberant voice, "where the devil have you been? I've been waiting for you an age! Quickly, love, we are to meet Rayna very soon."

"Rayna?" Adam repeated, his mind still on the letter from his father in his waistcoast pocket.

Arabella frowned at her brother's obvious preoc-cupation, wondering what he was thinking. She tugged at his coat sleeve and said with exaggerated patience, "We are supposed to ride with Rayna Lyndhurst, Adam. I told you last night she is visiting her aunt, Lady Turbridge. And she isn't a silly little schoolgirl any longer. She is nearly eigh-teen and most interested in seeing you again." Arabella paused, wondering yet again if Rayna would recognize her darkly handsome brother. It was six years since they had seen each other. Rayna's family, the Lyndhursts, lived a good sixty miles to the west of Clare Castle, and Viscount Delford, Rayna's father, rarely sought her own father's company. Arabella smiled impishly, not doubting for an instant that Rayna would lose her young heart to her dashing brother, for he was no longer a gangly boy, but a man, a very handsome man. She had been planning this meeting for two months now, for she had decided after long and profound thought that Rayna and Adam were well-suited. She frowned at him, wishing he would show a bit more enthusiasm. He resembled their father so closely it was uncanny, save for his velvet blue eyes. Only she had inherited her father's black eyes and dark brows, in startling contrast to her fair complexion and honey-colored hair.

"Quickly, Adam!" she chided again.

Adam clasped his sister's gloved hands. "I fear I am unable to oblige you, Bella. Please give my regrets to Rayna Lyndhurst. I must leave soon. The *Cassandra* is sailing on the evening tide, and I must be on her."

The look of dismay in Arabella's dark eyes quickly turned to excitement. So that was it! She felt her blood quicken, and her eyes sparkled. "You've had a message from Father? He wants you in Genoa?"

"Aye, and I'm off as soon as I've seen Mother. Rayna Lyndhurst will have to wait another year or so. Do give the child my regrets." He smiled ironically at his sister, guessing that she had been spinning matchmaking fancies. It amused him, for Arabella was about as subtle as a firing cannon. The two girls had been friends since their years at a young ladies' seminary in Bath, and Adam wondered what tales Arabella had spun about him to Rayna.

"Oh, no," Arabella said. "I will write her a note. I must pack! I will be ready in an hour." First things first, she thought, lifting her heavy riding skirts above her knees and dashing up the stairs.

"Bella!"

Adam shook his head and followed more sedately after her. He had been on his way to his parents' bedchamber, the room where he was born twenty-six years before. He passed a pert chambermaid who had offered him more than his breakfast since his return to Clare Castle. He gave her a slight smile, knowing it would never do to enjoy the favors of a serving maid in his parents' home. His father thought the *droit de seigneur* as distasteful as did he.

His mother, Lady Cassandra Welles, was sitting at her dressing table with her maid, Betta, standing behind her. That stern-faced retainer, a woman of indeterminate years, was arranging the countess's hair. "If only," Betta was complaining, "Lady Bella could sit still for but five minutes! That one's more roisterous than a boy!"

"We are lucky that she is so naturally lovely," the countess said. "She scarce needs more than five minutes of your assistance, Betta."

"Mother, I must speak with you."

Lady Cassandra heard the tension in her son's voice and swiveled about in her chair. "You may leave us now, Betta," she said pleasantly to her maid.

Betta, curious as always, sniffed and took herself off.

Adam strode to his mother and leaned down to kiss her upturned cheek. "You must tie Arabella down, Mother," he said, frowning. "I've received a message from Father. I am to leave for Genoa within the hour, and Bella is doubtless in her bedchamber hurling her clothes into a valise. There is trouble. What it is exactly, he doesn't say." He grinned crookedly as he handed her a thin envelope. "Perhaps he tells you."

The countess gingerly spread the single sheet of paper before her on the dressing table. "My love," she read, "I have asked Adam to come to me. We have lost another ship, perhaps to the Barbary pirates. I hope to know the truth of the matter by the time he arrives in Genoa. If I know my son, he is likely at this moment inching toward the door, ready to be away. Keep Arabella safe with you. With any luck, I will be back in England by the summer, with this damnable business over."

The countess read the letter again more slowly. She smiled at Adam, who was striding impatiently about her bedchamber, just as Anthony had known he would. She dismissed Arabella's most persistent suitor, Vincent Eversley, from her mind as if he had never existed. If Arabella had any interest in the viscount, her feelings would last, and no man, she knew, would ever forget Arabella.

"Well, Mother, does he explain?"

"He says another ship has been taken, perhaps by the Barbary pirates."

"Ah," said Adam, his brilliant blue eyes, his mother's eyes, narrowing thoughtfully. "It makes no sense. We have paid tribute to those damned pirates for more years than I have been on this earth. Were all our men lost? No survivors?"

"Your father doesn't say, my love. We will find out quickly enough."

"We?" Adam repeated, eyeing his mother with deep foreboding.

"Have your valet pack for you, Adam. Arabella and I will be ready for your escort in an hour's time. Who is captaining the *Cassandra*?"

Adam stared, nonplussed, at his mother. "Surely, Mother," he began, disregarding her question, "you will reconsider. Our treaty with the French is tenuous at best at the moment. It wouldn't be safe. Father would be none too pleased if—"

"You are wasting time, Adam," the countess interrupted. "There is much to be done, if we are to make the evening tide."

"But what about Eversley? He is due to arrive tomorrow from London, and he will want to see Arabella."

"I know, dear brother," came Arabella's drawling voice from the doorway. She eyed her brother with open challenge. Really, she thought, Adam was behaving like an anxious father who wished to be rid of his daughter! "And I am all of twenty years old, and on the shelf, growing longer in the tooth by the month, waiting for dear Eversley to pluck me off. Forget him, Adam. He is not at all like you or Father, and I have decided I won't have him."

"Eversley appears to fill all the requirements," Adam said sardonically.

"I want a man, Adam, not a sniveling Carlton House fop!"

"I doubt you know what you're saying, love."

"That is quite enough from the both of you," the countess said coolly, rising to shake out her skirts. "If you will keep down your gorge, Adam, we can all get ready to sail for Genoa. I understand, Arabella," she continued, turning to her daughter, "that Edward Lyndhurst is to visit his sister, Lady Turbridge, tomorrow, to escort Rayna back to Delford Hall. I will write him a note and let him deal with Viscount Eversley."

Adam saw his sister's triumphant smile, and knew he was beaten. He was pulled from the pleasant fancy of throttling her by the touch of his mother's fingers on his sleeve. "I miss your father, my love. It is time we were all together again."

Adam gave her a crooked grin. "Just when I thought to be free of petticoats, ma'am, you've saddled me with a sister who does not know her place and tries to take mine!"

"Like father, like daughter, dear brother," Arabella said.

2

Villa Parese, Genoa

Arabella breathed in the warm flower-scented air and sat back against the plush black leather squabs in the open carriage. She felt glad to be home again. She shook her head, bemused at the thought, for she felt the same way when she returned to England from Italy. She swiveled about to gaze back at the glistening blue Mediterranean, dotted with tall-masted ships, like limpid glass under the bright afternoon sun. The city glittered white, rising from the shore like a beautiful woman, her father was wont to say, with the sea before her and the glorious snow-capped mountains pressing against her back. Genoa—*La Superba*.

Though she searched for changes, she saw none in her beloved city now that it was a French protectorate. The peasants trudging beside their donkeys along the dusty road were going about their business, as had the determined shopkeepers in the city. But she feared for them, for she knew

Napoleon would not allow them this semblance of freedom for much longer. There was no unity among the Italian states, and Napoleon was drawing them into his insatiable maw as it pleased him. He had already proclaimed several free Italian states the Cisalpine Republic, an excuse to loot their treasuries and quarter French troops in their cities. There was little anyone could do to prevent the French from drawing Genoa into the empire, and if that happened, Genoa could no longer be her home. She dreaded that day. Though with her honey-colored hair she could never pass for an Italian, as could Adam, she was proud of her heritage, proud when her mother chided her, with a twinkle in her eyes, about her passionate Ligurian blood whenever Arabella lost her temper. She was intrigued that she was supposed to be passionate, for she knew nothing about it. She knew only that she had a temper.

The thought of being confined to England did not appeal to her. No, the Proserpine arrangement of the past twenty years suited her just fine. Englishmen, Arabella had decided, when she was old enough to draw their masculine attention, were not at all to her taste. They were too civilized, too affected. They probably didn't know about passion either.

"Smell the oleanders and the olive trees," she said to Adam, who was blissfully resting his chin on his chest. "Adam?"

"Let him sleep, love," her mother said, lightly

patting Arabella's sleeve. "He spent all his time on deck during the storm."

"It was a beautiful storm," Arabella said.

"I wouldn't have liked it if we had ended up on the rocks at Minorca," her mother said wryly.

"Or in the hungry arms of a Barbary pirate?"

"Trust you to think of those barbaric savages as romantic princes," Adam said, stretching and shading his eyes with his hand.

"You're a stuffy stick," Arabella said. She leaned back and closed her eyes. "Smell the wild carnations, Adam. There is nothing like them in England."

"Don't forget the hyacinths, jasmine, and roses in your raptures," Adam said dryly.

Their mother sat forward. "Ah, the Villa Parese! Home at last!"

Adam and Arabella straightened as the carriage neared the huge scripted iron gates. The gate boy, Marco, was beside the carriage in a flash, grinning widely up at them.

"Buon giorni, contessa." He beamed, flourishing his woolen hat.

"Come sta, Marco?" the countess asked, smiling down at the impish face of Sordello's son.

"Molto bene, contessa, molto bene, grazie."

"Is *il signore* here, Marco?" Arabella asked.

"Si, signorina."

The carriage passed through the tall gates on the graveled drive. Arabella gazed at a white marble fountain, dominated by a statue of Neptune, that stood in the middle of the lawn. She sighed happily at the rush of memories it brought her, of hours spent as a child spinning stories beneath that beautiful bearded god.

She started to say something of the sort to Adam, but noticed that he was frowning. "Whatever -is the matter now, brother?"

"Father," he said shortly. "He wasn't expecting a parcel of females."

"A sister and a mother hardly constitute a parcel. Besides, you can leave Father to us. He will soon come around, Adam, you will see."

It was likely true, Adam thought. His father and mother were appallingly loverlike. And as for Arabella, the minx could usually wrap their father about her slender finger.

"Well," he said gruffly to Arabella, "if he takes a strap to you, don't say I didn't warn you."

Arabella was certain that her father wouldn't do anything so violent, but she did worry that he would be none too pleased with her arrival. She tossed her head. If she couldn't convince him of his delight, her mother most certainly would. She smiled impishly at Adam and patted his arm. "So heartwarming, your warning, brother dear. We shall see."

Their father's Scottish valet, Scargill, an ancient relic after thirty years of service with the Welleses, his carrot head of hair now a shock of white, met them in the entrance hall of the villa.

"Well, ye scamp," he wheezed, looking Adam up and down, "I see ye canna deny the ladies any more than yer father can. It's hardly pleased the earl will be, I can tell ye."

The countess gave a trilling laugh. "You grow pessimistic in your old age, Scargill! My lord will be delighted, once he is over the shock."

"Ye forget his lordship's temper so quickly?"

"You're an old fusser," Arabella said, and kissed him soundly on his wrinkled cheek.

"Little twit," Scargill muttered fondly. "It's in the library ye'll find him."

Though the Villa Parese could have housed a staff of fifteen servants, there were but six, a sop, their father told them, to the Genoese gospel of thrift. Thus only one housemaid peered down at them from the top of the stairs as they stepped through the entrance hall. As if by tacit agreement, Adam and Arabella let their mother precede them through the library doors.

They found the Earl of Clare staring thoughtfully down into the empty grate, his fingertips drumming softly on the cool marble mantel. When he saw them all standing in the doorway, a mighty frown drew his dark brows together.

"What the devil!"

To Adam and Arabella's embarrassment, but not their surprise, the countess launched herself at their father, threw her arms about his shoulders, and kissed him fully on his mouth. Arabella stared raptly at a vase of fresh-cut flowers on a table, until she heard her father say softly to her mother after a moment, "Little fool, can I never trust you to obey me?"

"So, my lord," the countess said impishly, "have I mistaken your disapproval for enthusiasm?"

They heard her laugh as their father murmured something they couldn't hear. Then he straightened and said, "Well, Adam, I see you have as much difficulty controlling our women as do I."

"Sir," Adam said, "I would as soon face down a hurricane."

His father merely smiled, his fingers tightening about his wife's hand. "With two such women, Adam, I am only surprised you were not delivered to me trussed up like a chicken."

"You see, Adam," Bella crowed to her brother, "I told you Father wouldn't mind."

"That I did not say," the earl said, beckoning his daughter into his arms.

"Behold your women, Father," Arabella said, bestowing upon him her most brilliant smile. "We are here to solve your problems for you. Surely you did not expect Adam would be your sole support."

"Indeed," the earl said, smiling lazily toward his son, "I suppose that even the best of us occasionally have need of a woman."

"Bella," the countess said, "I do not know if we have been complimented or insulted!"

"Bella I will insult, my dear," the earl said. "You I will appreciate. So, daughter, you left a bereft Eversley to come adventuring?"

Arabella shrugged indifferently. "I forgot him, Papa, our second day out."

"It is just as well. Eversley, for all his noble

antecedents, would likely not do for you, I'm afraid. He is, I think, rather too . . . tame in his tastes."

"That is what I told Adam, but he is such a priggish stick."

Adam watched his father's dark eyes meet his wife's over Arabella's head. "Have you no control over these two when I am not about?" he asked blandly.

"I grow more concerned, my lord," the countess said, "when they are not bickering, for it means they are likely plotting something outlandish. And I fear they are both too old for a strapping."

"Father," Adam said abruptly, "have you discovered what has happened to our ships?"

"Perhaps, indirectly," his father said calmly. "I will tell you about it after you have settled in."

Adam seemed impatient, and his father added, "It has been over five months since I have seen your beautiful mother. Keep your sister out of mischief until dinner."

Arabella watched her parents walk arm in arm from the library, her fair head raised to his dark one. "They are likely going to be silly and make love," she said.

"What would you know about that, little chit?"

"I know a thing or two, Adam," she said, grinning knowingly.

"Bosh," Adam said shortly.

"For instance," she continued, her eyes downcast so he wouldn't see the wicked gleam, "I know it begins with taking off one's clothes." She wrinkled her nose and paced about the library for a moment. "Eversley kissed me once. I hated it. His lips were all wet, and he tried to make me open my mouth." There, she thought, quite pleased with herself, now he wouldn't believe her such an ignorant miss!

"Is that all?" Adam asked carefully, controlling his anger at the viscount's presumption with his sister.

"It was quite enough, thank you. I stepped on his toe." Arabella saw a dangerous glitter in his midnight-blue eyes, and narrowed her own, deciding she had goaded him enough. "Really, Adam, I wish you would stop acting like a silly, overprotective man. I can quite take care of myself." She was thoughtful a moment, then added in a spurt of candor, "I shouldn't like to have taken my clothes off with Eversley."

"Thank God for that!" Adam said fervently, a crooked grin on his mouth. "There's quite a bit more to love than just kissing and quoting poetry, Bella, and taking off your clothes, for that matter. You should be careful of men who would try to take advantage of you."

"And you know all about them?"

"A man learns some things early in life."

"Well," she said indignantly, her hands on her hips, "I believe I shall learn all about it too! The world is half women, Adam."

"To my everlasting pleasure," Adam said, grinning at her.

Arabella gazed upward, a quizzical frown puckering her forehead. "Do you think you'll still want to do all that sort of thing when you're older, like Mother and Father?"

Adam burst into laughter. "I will be older, but I will not be dead!"

Rosina, the housekeeper, appeared in the doorway, and Adam finished under his breath, "This isn't proper talk, Bella." He turned swiftly to Rosina and gave her a big grin. "You are more beautiful than ever, *signora*," he said in Italian.

Rosina flushed, her black eyes flashing with pleasure. Arabella, used to seeing females of all ages flutter at Adam's attention, yawned elaborately.

"Welcome home, *signore, signorina*," Rosina said. "It is your *sorella* who is the beautiful one. All that golden hair, just like her mother's."

"My sister, beautiful?" Adam murmured, as if amazed.

"Beast!" Arabella hissed at him in English, poking his ribs.

"Ah, and spirited as ever. It is good that you are all here. *Il signore* has been lonely, I think. And so much trouble, always trouble. There is no peace in the world, what with that *diavolo*, that Corsican monster, pillaging." Rosina sighed, and patted strands of her peppery hair back into its severe bun at the back of her head. "When Scargill told me you had arrived, I sent that lazy Marina to prepare your rooms."

"I hope Marina doesn't wander into our parents' room," Adam said under his breath. To Rosina he said, "May we have some of your delicious lemonade? Arabella and I will be in the gardens."

Rosina curtsied and left the library, her stiff black skirts rustling over the marble floors. She would probably grant Adam anything he wished, Arabella thought.

"Come, Bella, we will sit for a while," Adam said. "I, for one, am a bit blown."

"If you had shared the helm with me during the storm, you would not be so weak-kneed now," his sister retorted. "You probably just want to look at the naked statues in the garden, not the flowers."

Adam gave his sister a lazy smile and took himself off, knowing she would be at his heels. He strode through the entrance hall, an airy and spacious room hung with Alexandrian tapestries, to the back of the villa. All the rooms were filled with more flowers than furniture, and the scent of fresh jasmine hung in the air. He stepped into the three-tiered gardens, immaculately tended, and gazed up at the Palladian structure of whitewashed stone, thick circular columns, and flower-covered balconies that ran along the entire second floor. Three gardeners worked in the Parese gardens, and the result of their efforts was a barely contained wilderness of flowers that abounded with color. He wandered about a bit, glad to be away from the trimmed and corseted gardens of England, and sat himself on a marble bench beneath a rose bower.

"When do you think we shall dine?" Arabella asked when she joined him, spreading her white muslin skirts gracefully about her.

"It may be a long wait," Adam replied. "Perhaps too long, since I have only you, sister, for company."

Arabella chose to ignore his drawing remark. "I am worried for this place, Adam," she said aloud. "We have given everything away with the Treaty of Amiens. How could the king and Addington allow it? By God, all the English have left is Trinidad and Ceylon. And Napoleon can take back Naples and the Papal States whenever he wishes. We may not have an Italian home much longer, Adam."

"True," Adam said, stretching his long legs in front of him. "We must think of it as a respite, both for England and, unfortunately, for France. At least we knew enough not to hand over Malta to the Knights Templar. The czar has begged us to stay. Alexander, thank God, is not the fool his father was."

"Do you think Genoa will end up like Switzerland and the Cisalpine Republic?"

"Undoubtedly. Napoleon will not rest until we bury him."

Arabella chewed thoughtfully on her lower lip, gazed up at their parents' bedchamber, and said unexpectedly, "Since I've gotten to know Rayna, I've wondered what we would be like if mother had married Edward Lyndhurst instead of Father."

Adam cocked his head at her in amusement. "Even though they grew up together, I somehow can't help but think that Mother would have been a sore trial to the staid Viscount Delford. As for us, Bella, we wouldn't exist."

"Thank God," Arabella said fervently, "that she discovered Father in time!" A perplexed frown drew her dark brows together. "Do you suppose Lord Delford still loves Mother?"

"I can't think he would be pining, not with five sons and a daughter! His viscountess isn't a dull mouse either."

"No," Arabella said pertly, "and neither is her only daughter." As she got no particular reaction from her brother, she pursed, "But why doesn't the viscount like Father?"

Adam shrugged. "I get the impression the viscount doesn't particularly approve of any of us, Bella. Remember, he's a staunch Englishman. He would likely deplore the thought of his children having foreign blood."

Arabella, whose thoughts had flittered to Vincent Eversley, said suddenly, "Adam, do you have a mistress?"

At his narrowed eyes, she quickly amended, "You are, after all, twenty-six now, and you haven't married. Surely you aren't celibate."

His dark blue eyes twinkled. "I will tell you, Bella, only that I am as fastidious as Father," he said obliquely.

"But Father doesn't have mistresses!"

"No, of course not, not since he married Mother."

"When?" Arabella demanded, not mincing matters.

"You should be married. Then I wouldn't have to suffer your improper questions."

"Ah, but I'm not, and so you must. Mother won't ever tell me anything, and Father just looks forbidding."

"I really don't remember, Bella. Near to seventeen, I suppose."

"Good heavens! I'm twenty! I don't like it at all, Adam, that you know things that I don't. It isn't fair."

He cocked a black brow at her. "Why this sudden interest, Bella?"

"I began to wonder what all the fuss was about after Eversley kissed me. Don't be such a prig, Adam. You're the only one I can ask. I mentioned lovemaking to Rayna Lyndhurst once, and she just stared at me as if I were babbling about some black mystery. With five older brothers, you'd think she'd know *something!*"

"Doubtful, given her father. And her brothers probably treat her like a fragile little flower." Adam was thoughtful for a moment. "I feel some sympathy for the man who must take Rayna to wife. Most English girls, for that matter. He'd have to spend his time pulling her from under the bed and drying her tears."

"But you haven't even seen her for . . . what is it, six years?"

Arabella ignored his disinterested nod and said stoutly, "Rayna is very pretty now, not a skinny little girl any longer. But you're right," she added on a sigh, "she is wrapped in wool. Perhaps what she needs is a very understanding, gentle man to teach her about . . . things." At Adam's look of disbelief, Arabella retrenched. "Odd, but now that you say so, I think her father may not like her to be in my company. He's always exquisitely polite, just as he is with Father, but distant. Her mother, Lady Delford, well, she's different. Full of fun and all."

"Edward Lyndhurst is probably nervous of your influence on his daughter. And you asked the poor girl about lovemaking? For shame, Bella!"

"We shall see," Arabella said obliquely. She glanced toward a white marble statue of one of the Greek gods—which one, she couldn't remember. "Men are quite lovely, I think. Yet I can't imagine Eversley looking like that. You probably do, Adam."

Adam flushed. A mistress talking thus was one thing, but a sister, quite another. "So I've been told," he said blandly, not looking at her.

"Adam, I don't suppose you would consider—"

"Bella!"

"Well, I was just curious, you know. And I am twenty, a veritable spinster now. And you are beautiful."

Adam grinned despite himself. He wagged his finger at her. "You must learn not to be so . . ."

"Honest?"

"So . . . forward, Bella, and keep your curiosity behind your teeth. If you spoke this way with a man, he would think you the loosest of creatures and treat you accordingly, whether you are Lady Arabella Welles or not."

"I am not such a fool," Arabella said, indignant. "I would butcher any man who tried anything with me!"

"I do not disbelieve you," Adam said wryly. "Eversley was lucky, only to have his foot stepped on for his impertinence." Adam glanced up at the balcony of his parents' bedchamber. The golden brocade curtains were still drawn.

"Surely it must be time for dinner," he said.

"I suppose we should change, else Father will give us one of his withering looks."

"After you, madam," Adam said, and rose.

Rosina served dinner on the rear veranda. The earl sat, resplendent in black velvet, at the head of the table, and his countess, arrayed in gold-threaded silk, at its foot.

"I have missed this light, fruity wine from our vineyards," the countess said. "I propose a toast. To a family united once again."

The earl amended her toast gently. "Let us drink to our being together and this beautiful evening, my dear."

Adam sipped at his wine, watching his father's tender glance toward his mother, and wondered briefly if he would ever find a woman who would be the center of his life. Arabella, he noticed, seemed to be barely controlling a fit of impatience. He knew well enough that his father could not be rushed, and was content to sit back at his ease and watch the half-moon ascend over the Mediterranean. Arabella suffered through an interminable meal, scarcely tasting the flaky scallops and the fresh garden salad. When the covers were removed and ripe orange slices and nuts set upon the table, she could no longer contain herself.

"Father, will you please tell us what this is about?"

The earl cracked a nut between his long fingers, a slight smile on his lips. The small, scruffy little girl had become a lovely young woman. What had not changed, and it pleased him inordinately, was her straightforwardness, her exuberance, her utter honesty. "Certainly, Bella," he said pleasantly. "We have lost two ships to date. I must presume that all hands were killed or taken captive, and the ships burned. I have discovered that the cargoes have appeared in Naples—at the court of Naples, to be exact."

"But the Barbary pirates do not burn captured ships," Adam said.

"Yes, it is most odd, I think."

"At the court of Naples," Adam repeated, staring at his father.

"So Daniele Barbaro has discovered. It appears that the bulk of the goods from the *Bella* have made their way from someone in the court itself to the French. If the Barbary pirates are involved, their motive escapes me."

"But surely Khar El-Din's son Hamil would not betray your agreement," the countess said.

"No, Hamil would not. But I received word some time ago that Hamil is dead, drowned in a storm."

Arabella, who was gazing intently at her mother, said abruptly, "You sound as if you know this pirate, Khar El-Din."

The countess flashed a quick look at the earl.

"Your father knew him for many years before he died. He was the Bey of Oran, in Algiers."

"One who died not with a scimitar in his hand," the earl said, "but in his bed, with his wives surrounding him. Hamil was his son by his first wife, Zabetta."

"And who rules now, Father?" Adam asked.

"Another of Khar El-Din's sons, Kamal, a young man whom I have yet to meet. Of course, after I verified that the ships were lost, I wrote to him. I received a reply not long ago in which he denies he is involved, and assures me he will look into the matter."

"Surely, Father," Arabella scoffed, "you don't believe the word of one of those people!"

"I assure you, Bella, that I have, at least in the past. It would not have been wise of the Barbary pirates to break a lucrative tribute agreement. Nor, as Adam pointed out, is it their way to burn valuable ships."

"The court of Naples," Adam said quietly. "The key lies there."

"Yes, Adam, I believe it does. It was my intent to travel to Naples myself, but upon reflection, I did not think it wise. I am too well known there, and my presence would likely send the men responsible into hiding. That is why I asked you here. I believe that you, acting not as the English Viscount St. Ives, but rather as a wealthy Italian nobleman, would have both the entrée to the court and the anonymity you need to discover who has this unaccountable desire for our goods."

"Could Adam be in any danger, my lord?" the countess asked.

Adam smiled grimly. "Not unless I were to wear a placard stating my purpose, Mother."

"I believe it unlikely in the extreme, *cara*. Even if Adam were to shout that he is my son, the thieves would likely take to their heels. Still, Daniele and three of his men will be at hand, should the need arise. Adam, are you familiar with the situation in Naples?"

"I know," Arabella said, leaning forward with her chin cupped in her hands, "that the queen, Maria Carolina, holds power, and that King Ferdinando is a buffoon without much of a brain."

"Not uncommon," the countess said.

"Perhaps it is the way of the future," Arabella said, grinning toward her brother.

"You are interrupting us, Bella," Adam said. He leaned forward like his sister to rest his chin atop his folded hands. "The queen was Marie Antoinette's sister, was she not?"

"Indeed yes," the earl said. "Thus, in large part, the reason for her hatred of the Jacobins, and Napoleon. The murder of her sister and Louis profoundly affected her, and she vowed that the French would never take the Two Sicilies. But she stands alone. The Spanish Bourbons are helpless and the Austrians dither first one way and then the other. Only the Treaty of Amiens keeps Naples from French hands, and it will not be enough. Even now, Maria Carolina and Ferdinando must dance to Napoleon's tune to survive."

"This is all well and good, Father," Arabella said abruptly, "but there are so many people at court. Where is Adam to begin?"

"Your sister," the earl said with a smile to Adam, "terrifies me. She never loses sight of the mule's destination. Well, Bella, Daniele has discovered that one of the many French émigrés to the queen's court is the Comte de la Valle, a young man of rather questionable morals and loyalties to the crown, who perhaps knows more than he should about our Caribbean rum. He plays the role of the displaced French émigré and is accepted at court, very much in the queen's good graces. There is something else about him you should know, Adam. Do you remember the Hellfire Club in England some twenty-five years ago?"

Adam snorted. "A group of satanic revelers, weren't they?"

"An affectation Naples does not seem to have yet discovered. But it appears the Comte de la Valle may be involved in a similar group, Les Diables Blancs, the white devils, they call themselves. He has managed to draw some young Italian nobles in with him."

"It appears," Adam said thoughtfully, "that I shall find myself equally drawn to this charming Comte de la Valle."

"Adam, a white devil!" Arabella crowed. "You will fit marvelously well, brother."

"I doubt I will be bored," Adam said.

"There is a problem, Father," Arabella said suddenly, one dark brow arching upward, "but also a solution, I think." She felt her heart begin to pound with excitement, for she knew what she wanted. Go slowly, my girl, she told herself.

"What is, *cara*?"

"The Lyndhursts will soon be journeying to Naples. Rayna told me the queen's minister finally succeeded in convincing Addington to send her father to the court of Naples as a military adviser and aide to England's ambassador, Sir Hugh Elliot."

"Rayna is accompanying her parents?" the earl asked. At his daughter's nod, he murmured, "I can't imagine why Delford, of all people, would want to take his daughter to a foreign court."

"Why did you not tell me this, Bella?" Adam demanded.

Arabella shrugged. "Mother knew, but you, Adam, did not seem interested. Now they are a problem to you."

"That is an understatement, Bella! Good God, sir, the Lyndhursts have known me since I was born, and would recognize me in an instant."

"Can you not simply write to Edward, my lord," the countess said, "and request his presence here before he travels to Naples? You can explain the situation to him and ask that he keep mum about Adam."

"Aye, I can." The earl cocked a sardonic brow. "Though I doubt that Viscount Delford will be greatly pleased."

"But you've forgotten Rayna," Arabella said, quite pleased with her timing. "She too might recognize

Adam, though she hasn't seen him for years. For her, I have the perfect solution."

"Oh?" the earl said carefully.

"Yes, indeed, Father." She drew a deep breath and plunged onward, crossing her fingers in her lap. "I will journey to Naples with the Lyndhursts, as their houseguest. I so long to see Naples, Father, and if Rayna even suspects Adam looks familiar, why, I could well convince her otherwise!" She shrugged elaborately. "And who knows? Perhaps I can help Adam discover who is behind all this." And, she added silently, very pleased with herself, I will ensure that my best friend meets my brother.

"Like hell you will!" Adam burst out.

"Just because you are a man, Adam—"

The earl raised a stilling hand. "I, for one, wish to think about all this. The both of you can argue to your hearts' content once your mother and I are gone." He lightly tweaked his daughter's chin. "A holiday in Naples, daughter? I am not certain if the gentlemen at court could survive such a whirlwind. We will speak of it tomorrow."

The earl rose, smiled thoughtfully at Adam and Arabella, then offered the countess his arm.

No sooner had their parents left the veranda than Adam said firmly, "Arabella, I do not want you in Naples."

"And why not, may I be so bold as to ask? I have more chance of charming information out of a gentleman than would you, brother."

"This is not a game, Bella."

"Ah, ye never change," Scargill said, emerging

from the shadows onto the balcony. "All ye do is scrap." He took a puff from his pipe and blew a thoughtful cloud of smoke upward.

"Adam," Arabella said firmly, "is being overbearing, Scargill."

Adam grinned wickedly. "Do sisters have uses, Scargill?" he drawled. "Since this twit is my sister, I must protect her despite herself."

Arabella threw her napkin at him, jumping to her feet. "It will not be your decision, dear brother. Father is not so unreasonable. And I will go to Naples with the Lyndhursts, you will see."

Scargill blew another cloud of smoke, and shook his grizzled white head. "Do ye want yer dueling pistols now?"

"I would prefer a foil," Arabella said. "I could skewer him easily!"

"Lord," Adam said in disgust, "I pity the man who has the taming of you."

"Taming! And what of the poor women who must bear with your ridiculous whims?"

"Now, lassie," Scargill said, waving his pipe at her, "ye must at least make men think they are getting their way."

"Men," Arabella said, squaring her shoulders and staring at her brother, "should all be lined up and shot."

"Men, my dear sister," Adam drawled in a mocking voice, "also have their uses, which you will learn if you ever decide to grow up and be a woman."

Eversley's face flashed in Arabella's mind, and

she flushed. "I don't want men, or their uses," she snapped. The wretched flush spread down her neck, and she knew Adam saw well what was in her mind.

"I think, Scargill," Adam said, leaning back in his chair, his arms crossed over his chest, "that this time I've had the last word."

"Then ye'd best take yerself off now, lad, afore yer sister finds her tongue." He banged his pipe against his palm, chuckled, and disappeared into the gardens.

3

Oran, Province of Algiers

Alessandro di Ferrari, known in Algiers as Kamal El-Kader, Bey of Oran, stood in the front courtyard of his palace, resting his bronzed hands on the mosaic tile of the garden wall. He raised his eyes from the formidable fortress below him to its sister that straddled the sloping hill across the valley. Together, with their guns trained upon the harbor of Oran, they were a warning to Europe and a promise of protection to the ships nestled in the harbor below. At least a dozen *xebecs*, the deadly swift three-masted ships favored by the corsairs, were moored there, and a heavy Spanish trading vessel, its captain come to arrange tribute. The drill commands of Kamal's Turkish troops, over five hundred strong, floated up to him. It was a fine day, the cloudless blue sky overhead mirrored in the smooth surface of the Mediterranean.

A warm breeze ruffled his wheat-colored hair and dried the thin sheen of sweat on his forehead.

He heard the soft tinkling sound of bells, and a smile flitted across his tanned face. They reminded him of Elena, a new concubine to his harem, a gift from the Dey of Algiers. He remembered her lying soft and languid in his arms, her silken ebony hair flowing over his chest. When he had learned she was captured as a child by *rais* Hamidu in a raid on the coast of Italy, he asked her if she would like to return to her home. She had opened her dark chocolate eyes in astonishment, and when she realized he was serious, she had burst into tears. She had little memory of Italy, and even less of her parents. She was a sweet child, he thought, but like the others in his harem, she was unlettered and ignorant, save in the art of pleasing him.

Kamal frowned at his uncharitable thought and turned to rest his back and stretch his tense muscles. He knew the death of his half-brother Hamil was still raw in his mind, and he was tired, having just returned the evening before from Algiers, where he had served as the dey's *wakil al-kharidj*, or foreign-affairs minister. Because he had lived for many years in Europe and spoke three of their languages, it was he who dealt with European councils. They would begin with expressions of surprise that he, a Muslim, spoke their language, without a Jewish interpreter, and then the usual honeyed complaints about the pirating Algerian *rais*, the sea captains. He answered in phrases as smooth as their own, knowing full well that the privateering would not be halted, not until the Europeans opened their ports to the Barbary trade. Perhaps not even then, he amended to himself. It was a way of life to the *rais*, and it brought too many men, the dey included, substantial wealth. His people were raised to accept and pass on traditions, and they would not easily embrace abandoning this one. It troubled him, for he understood the Europeans as well. They would soon be forced to war with Algiers, Tunis, and Morocco, indeed the whole world into which he was born. His Turkish blood rebelled at the thought, yet he knew that the western powers could not for much longer abide the Barbary corsairs, not in the modern world.

He had listened to the foreign councils, and directed them as always to the *khaznadar*, the dey's treasurer, a wily old man, who, if they didn't pay the tribute the dey demanded, would merely smile, noting those who refused.

As his half-brother Hamil had before him, Kamal dealt more openly with private merchants such as the Italians, who could not afford the protection of a navy. They understood each other, and their business always ended with a banquet, and music, and nightly gifts of slave girls to warm their beds. The wealthy merchants knew that their tribute would buy their ships safety in the Mediterranean, safety even from the Tunisian privateers, for their sovereign, a bey just as was Kamal, would take his share of the tribute.

Kamal's thoughts turned again to his half-brother Hamil, who had been more like a father to him than had Khar El-Din. It was Hamil who had helped his own mother, a former Genoese contessa, to convince Khar El-Din to have him educated in France and Italy. To help him understand the foreign devils, Hamil had said. And it was Hamil's death in a storm off Sardinia that had brought him back to rule his people. Hamil's first wife, Lella, was swollen with Hamil's child, and Kamal intended that the child would never forget his father had been a great and powerful ruler, a man of courage and strength.

"Highness."

He turned at the soft voice of Hassan Aga, his minister. "Is it time?" he asked.

"Soon, highness. Today you have but four judgments to render." Hassan paused a moment, negligently smoothing his white wool sleeve. "One of the men, a wealthy spice merchant, wishes to pay you his respects, in the form of *piastres.*"

"Was the man subtle in his bribery, Hassan?"

"Not at all, highness."

"You will point him out to me so that I may look upon the man who would seek to buy justice."

"Yes, highness." Hassan, a smile on his leathered face, started to turn. His eyes shadowed a moment as he said, "Your esteemed mother wishes to speak to you, highness." He bowed and left Kamal to prepare for his entrance into the large formal chamber reserved for greeting visitors to the bey.

Before Kamal turned to his mother, he straightened his full-sleeved shirt and his leather vest, and adjusted his wide, soft red leather belt.

"Mother," he greeted her.

"Yes, my son."

He dutifully bestowed a kiss upon her upturned cheek, and switched easily to Italian. "You are well?"

"Ah yes," she said. "I heard that fool Hassan tell you of the merchant's offered bribe."

"Hassan a fool?"

His voice was carefully neutral. He had learned quickly upon his return to Oran that his mother was jealous of anyone who could influence him. Her possessiveness surprised him, for she knew him as little as he did her.

Giovanna Giusti, formerly of Genoa, now the mother of Oran's bey, shrugged her slender shoulders. "He could simply have accepted the bribe and filled your coffers, my son. There was no need for you to know, and if your judgment had gone against the merchant, he could have said nothing. There is Jewish blood in his veins, after all. He is beneath your notice, or should be."

"There is no justice in that, madam," Kamal said. "If I did not render honest judgments, where would the people go?"

Giovanna shrugged again, impatiently. "Does it matter so much to you?"

Kamal found himself thinking like a Muslim for a moment, believing that he could not expect a woman to have any notion of honor or duty. He studied her silently for a moment. She was still a remarkably fine-looking woman, still possessed of much of the exquisite beauty that had captured his father's roving eyes so long ago. She was slight, reaching only his shoulder, and as slender as a girl. Her hair was inky black—dyed, he suspected— with no trace of gray. But despite the care she took, there were lines on her face, bitter lines that deepened when she spoke of anything or anyone Muslim. He had given her a measure of power when he became Bey of Oran, power at least over the women, until he discovered she had placed Hamil's widow, Lella, in a small, airless chamber fit only for a slave. When he had taxed her with it, she had lifted her narrow black brows in astonishment. "Lella is nothing, my son. She deserves to be sold, indeed, I think it would be best. It should be done before her belly swells."

"By God, Mother the woman carries Hamil's child! Her son will be my nephew, and my heir until I take a wife and breed my own son!"

"Your heir!"

He had realized suddenly that she considered Lella and her unborn child a threat. To her or to him? he had wondered, staring at her. "Yes, my heir," he had told her. "Nothing will happen to Lella, Mother. Nothing. She and her unborn child are under my protection. Do you understand?"

Her face had smoothed out, as if by magic, into submissiveness. "Of course, my son," she had murmured, bowing her head. "Forgive me. I will see that Lella is housed as befits her station. I am only concerned that you, Alessandro, be given what is due you."

"Is there something you wanted, Mother?" he asked her now, a hint of impatience in his voice. "I haven't much time. Hassan awaits me."

Her dark eyes studied him before she lowered her head before him and murmured in a soft voice, "Perhaps later we can speak again, Alessandro."

"Yes," he said. He watched her pull her veil back over her face and walk gracefully toward the women's quarters.

The ceremony that attended the bey when he rendered judgments to his people had been nearly the same for over two hundred years. Kamal strode into the large sunlit chamber, its only furnishings his high-backed chair set upon a dais and a narrow table where his scribe sat, taking notes of the proceedings. He was flanked by Hassan Aga and a half-dozen of his Turkish soldiers, more for show than for protection. Their faces were expressionless, and they wore flamboyant red-and-white uniforms and highly polished scimitars fastened at their waists.

Kamal turned to face the afternoon's supplicants, and sat stiffly in the heavily ornate chair, brought from Spain by his father, Khar El-Din. He nodded to his minister, Hassan, who began to recount the first case, that of the spice merchant Hajj Ahmad, a fat man of middle years, the man who had wished to bribe Kamal. When Hassan gravely told the merchant to begin, Hajj Ahmad moved to speak before Kamal, his hands folded before him. His beard was liberally threaded with white and his nose was bulbous and reddened from too many years of good spirits. His voice, somewhat to Kamal's surprise, was soft and cultured. Kamal studied him carefully as he spoke.

"This man, highness," Hajj Ahmad said with immense dignity, turning slightly to point to a slight, swarthy man older than he, "cheated me of payment. I had spices delivered to his store, and he refused to honor the terms of our agreement."

Kamal looked intently into the man's eyes, as his half-brother, Hamil, and his father, Khar El-Din, had taught him. *Unless a man is the greatest scoundrel on earth, you will see the way to justice in his eyes.*

"Why, Hajj Ahmad," Kamal asked politely, "did you allow the delivery of the spices if the man did not pay you?"

"One of my sons arranged it, highness. He returned to me with the news"—he nearly spat at the other man—"that this insect refused to pay."

The shopkeeper took his turn. "I paid, highness, but the son of Hajj Ahmad refused to give me a receipt for my payment."

"A lie, highness!" Hajj shouted.

Kamal raised his hand for quiet. He gazed closely at both men, then turned to speak softly to Hassan, who stood beside his chair.

He said nothing more, and Hassan directed the two men to wait in the antechamber. Kamal rendered his judgments on two other cases, both involving matters of personal status, and thus under the Our'anic law. He then turned to Hassan and nodded to him.

A sloe-eyed young man, with the beginnings of a paunch as noble as his sire's, strode into the hall of justice with Hajj Ahmad. Kamal turned to Hajj Ahmad. "This is the son you sent to deliver the spices to the shopkeeper?"

"Yes, highness."

Kamal looked closely at the young man and smiled. "Tell us what happened," he said.

The young man glanced briefly toward his father, and told the same story that Hajj Ahmad had recounted, embellishing upon it at the seemingly sympathetic smile from the bey.

Kamal said quietly when he had finished, "And you serve your father so well that you would leave his goods with another, without payment?"

"The shopkeeper said he could not pay me, highness. He said he would send payment the next day to my father, but he did not."

Kamal stared down at the huge emerald ring upon his third finger. "Hassan," he said at last, "the bastinado for the son."

"Highness!" Hajj shrieked. "He is my son! He is of my flesh! All his life he has served me faithfully."

"Your son has stolen from you, Hajj Ahmad. If under the bastinado he does not admit where he has hidden the shopkeeper's payment, I will still consider that justice has been rendered. It appears that you are not a good judge of men. You misjudged your son and you have misjudged me. Do not again attempt to bribe me."

Hassan clapped his hands, and two of the Turkish soldiers, their scimitars glittering silver at their sides, dragged the young man away. "Do not let them beat the fool to death," Kamal said to Hassan. "He is a coward. When he tells his father what he has done with the money, release him. Hajj Ahmad will treat him then as he should be treated, I would wager."

When Kamal had finished with the last case, a dispute over a young bride's dowry, Hassan's wizened face crinkled into a smile of pride. "I feared, highness," he said softly, "that a man who has spent so many years away from us would not see truth among us as would one born to it."

Kamal laughed. "But you still pray that I will grow wiser as the years pass, do you not, Hassan?"

"Yes, highness. It is inevitable." Hassan paused a moment as a slave handed Kamal a glass of fruit juice. "There is another matter, highness," he said softly.

Kamal cocked his head in question, dismissing the slave with a wave of his hand.

"The reply you made to the English earl some weeks ago, highness, the Earl of Clare."

"The missing ships. I told him that I knew nothing of it, Hassan, as you know. You have since discovered something?"

"Yes, highness. One of our captains, Bajor, was responsible."

"We have broken tribute," Kamal said after a moment, his voice tense with disbelief.

"Bajor claimed, highness, that your seal was on the order he received to destroy the ships."

"The man lies," Kamal said flatly. "Only you and I use the seal."

"There is another, highness, if you will recall."

Kamal could only gaze, appalled, at his minister. When he had gathered his thoughts, he said in a calm voice, "Please have Raj inform my mother that I will dine with her this evening in her chambers."

"As you wish, highness," Hassan Aga said.

Kamal left the hall and walked thoughtfully through the ornate passages and chambers that led to his suite of rooms in the west wing of his palace. The two spacious chambers had belonged to Hamil, and Kamal had not disturbed the memories of his half-brother. Precious tapestries from Egypt, spun in brilliant colors, fell from ceiling to floor on the whitewashed walls. The floors were covered with Persian carpets, each woven with swirls of blue, gold, and crimson. Low sandalwood tables, inlaid with ivory, elegant and simple, were surrounded by thick embroidered cushions. A long, narrow sofa stood along one wall, one of Kamal's few concessions to his own comfort.

He shrugged out of his clothes as he walked into

his bedchamber and tossed them into the waiting hands of his personal slave, Ali. He was a slender, black-eyed boy of seventeen whose origins were Moorish. Kamal had seen him in the slave market some five months before, and knew that the boy would likely be castrated by his new owner. There was such hopeless terror on the boy's face that Kamal could not help himself. Ali was fanatically loyal, and his whimsical personality usually brought a smile to Kamal's face.

"It is warm," Kamal said to Ali. "I hope the water is cool." He walked naked from his bedchamber to his bath. Its walls and floors were set with hand-painted mosaic tiles, each tile depicting individual scenes, some of battles, some of splendid banquets, and a few of men with their female slaves. The bath was a sunken pool, some three feet deep and eight feet wide, set between marble tables covered with white linen cloths. Kamal stood quietly as Ali soaped his body and rinsed him with warm water from a painted urn. He slid into the cool pool and let the clear water close over his head, until he felt the tension in his body begin to ease. He thought lazily that the Europeans could benefit from this Muslim custom of the daily bath.

After a relaxing fifteen minutes, Kamal stepped out of the pool. He allowed Ali to shave his jaws smooth, then stretched on his stomach on one of the marble tables.

"When do you go out with the *rais*, master?" Ali asked him as he massaged warm, scented oil into his back.

"You think I grow too soft as bey, Ali? You want me to brandish my scimitar and capture infidel ships?"

"No, highness, you are not soft," Ali said honestly, glancing at his master's lean, fine-honed body. "I only fear that you will grow bored, and relieve your boredom by beating me."

"I will give you warning, Ali," Kamal retorted.

As he massaged Kamal's broad back, Ali kept up his usual stream of chatter. "There is a representative from the Sudan come to see you before your evening meal, highness. I hear that he brings a girl for you, a virgin of great beauty captured near Alexandria, a gift from his master. Perhaps you will find her more to your liking than Elena."

There was a hint of contempt in Ali's voice when he spoke Elena's name, but Kamal chose to ignore it. He stretched and turned over on his back. "Just how do you know the girl is a virgin?" he asked.

Ali held up two fingers. "The Sudanese—I heard him talking to that old graybeard Hassan—he tested her."

"Hassan or the other man?"

"Hassan, that licentious old goat!"

"Careful, Ali," Kamal warned softly, the laughter gone from his voice.

Ali cast a furtive glance at his master, knowing he had said too much. Hassan and his master's witch of a mother were two people no one could insult, even in jest. "Ah, master, will you have me bastinadoed?"

"Perhaps," Kamal said easily. "Or perhaps I shall repeat to Hassan what you said, and let him decide your punishment." His eyes remained grim until he saw fear in Ali's eyes.

"Young fool!" he said gruffly, and rose from the marble table. He continued in disgust, "I feel as oily smooth as a girl!"

"Ah, master, but you do not smell so sweet!"

"You have a quick tongue, Ali," Kamal observed as his slave dressed him.

"It serves me well with the women, highness," Ali said, grinning widely.

"So you would like to have tested the new slave yourself?"

"I would have done as well, highness."

"I should have made you a eunuch," Kamal remarked, but Ali merely smiled, secure in his master's goodwill.

Kamal allowed Ali to finish dressing him, then sat on a bench to have him brush his thick hair. When Ali was done, Kamal rose, resplendent in a white wool tunic and full-cut white wool trousers. A soft blue leather belt hugged his narrow waist, and from it hung a curved jewel-handled dagger. He wore light blue leather shoes with curved toes and a long golden chain about his neck.

"I am told that you greatly resemble your father," Ali said with satisfaction.

"Yes, though I am even more fair than was he. There must have been a Norse princess in our lineage years ago."

"I am also told," Ali continued irrepressibly, "that the famous Khar El-Din delighted in favoring more than one of his harem girls at the same time. It is said that their cries of pleasure could be heard all over the palace." Ali shook his head, as if confused. "Odd, master. Could he have had more than one tongue?"

"Perhaps I shall have your tongue removed, Ali," Kamal said, and buffeted the boy on his slender shoulder. Even his light blow sent Ali tumbling to the floor.

"Dammit, boy, when are you going to grow some muscle?" Kamal leaned down and dragged Ali to his feet.

He grinned down into Ali's face. "A man has full measure of pleasure for a woman between his legs."

"You more than others, master," Ali said.

"Impertinent young fool," Kamal said without heat. He was silent for a moment, then said without enthusiasm, "I will see the representative from the Sudan first, before the evening meal."

Ali nodded in agreement. "A man should have his pleasures, highness. You must, after all, put your women to use, if only to let the people know that you are potent as your father was. You have not yet even taken a wife!"

Kamal only shook his head. He did not wish to take a Muslim wife. He thought briefly of the virgin it would be his responsibility to take to his bed tonight. Another addition to his harem, another woman to reflect his power and wealth. He wondered idly how a European man would react if he suddenly found himself with a willing virgin in his bed. He would likely think he had gone to his heaven.

He dismissed Ali, and his thoughts quickly returned to his mother. When he had arrived in Oran, he had given her freedom no Muslim woman could have dreamed of. By all that was holy, what had she done with it?

4

Kamal walked through the huge central courtyard that set off the harem from the main palace. The evening was warm, but not unpleasantly so. A quarter-moon, just beginning its ascent, lit the darkening sky with a few of the brighter stars.

Guards were placed discreetly along the perimeter of the harem walls, and two eunuchs stood at its double gate. The harem walls were nearly twelve feet high, to prevent anyone from seeing in, and the women from seeing out. The two eunuchs bowed low to him and opened the gates.

A central courtyard opened before him, lined with full-branched willow trees, their narrow leaves and tassellike spikes of flowers drooping downward. A fountain and pool stood in its center, decorated with flowers, marble benches, and at least a dozen of his harem girls. They were all young and lovely, dressed in a rainbow of color. Their tinkling conversation and laughter blended with the lapping of the fountain. Directly beyond the courtyard through high-arched doorways were the harem suites.

The courtyard was suddenly silent. The women had seen him, and were watching him in awed, wide-eyed consternation. He was not expected. He nodded toward them, and they dropped their eyes from him. Several of the girls were unfamiliar to him, girls who had likely shared Hamil's bed.

"Highness!"

Raj, his head eunuch, waddled toward him, shooing away the girls. Kamal was not displeased to see them disperse.

"You should have told me when you intended to come," Raj chided him gently.

Kamal smiled at Raj, an older man of mammoth girth, baby-smooth cheeks, and a head as bald as an egg, shaved, Kamal suspected, to lend him more dignity. He knew Raj to be as intelligent as he was loyal. He ran the harem with a minimum of fuss, and dealt well even with Kamal's mother.

"I know my way, Raj," he said. Still, Raj walked at his side toward his mother's suite of rooms, rooms as royally appointed as were his own. Raj stopped in the doorway and bowed deeply toward Giovanna.

"His highness," the huge eunuch murmured.

Kamal glanced about at his mother's apartment. She had made many changes in the last six months that had left the chamber an odd mixture of Arab and European. The far wall was hung with a dark green velvet tapestry, ornamented with colored silk damask flowers. The doorway was inlaid with the finest Italian marble. Choice china and crystal encircled the room on a molding near the ceiling, with large looking-glasses framed with gold placed beneath. The floor was matted and covered with thick woolen carpets. Familiar loose cushions were on the floor, but his mother had added several curved-armed Italian chairs. On another wall there were numerous paintings, anathema to Muslims. His mother was seated in one of her chairs, but quickly rose when Kamal strode toward her.

"My son," she said softly. "I am delighted you wished to join me for my evening meal."

"It is my pleasure, madam." He lightly kissed her proffered cheek.

"You are kind to your lonely mother."

"You have no reason for loneliness," Kamal said dryly.

His mother did not reply, but nodded to Raj, and he, in turn, clapped his hands softly. Three slave girls carried in covered silver dishes and laid them gently on the low table. Fine bone china, napkins, forks and knives were already set upon the table, another European custom Muslims disdained.

The meal was a refreshing change to Kamal. He enjoyed the rare steak and the stewed potatoes, but drank the fruity red wine sparingly. They spoke little until he sat back, his belly comfortably filled, and accepted a cup of coffee served in a small cup from China, placed in a gold filigree bowl. A slave handed him a peeled pomegranate on a silver plate. He watched his mother wave dismissal to the slaves and daintily sip at her wine. Muslims were forbidden to drink wine, particularly women. But his mother was Italian, after all, even though she had accepted Islam to become his father's second wife.

Giovanna eyed her son over the edge of her crystal wineglass. She regretted that he looked like his father, that rutting old stud! But Alessandro was her son as well, and she had ensured that he would be every bit as Italian as he was Muslim. But she did not know him well.

"Alessandro," she said in her soft Italian, "I must ask you for a favor."

Kamal held up his hand. "Before you ask me anything, Mother, there is a matter I must broach with you. You will tell me why you used my seal and instructed my captain, Bajor, to destroy two of the Earl of Clare's ships."

So he had at last learned of it. She had hoped he would not until she was ready to tell him, but it made no difference now. She would appeal to his man's honor, as a helpless woman. She smiled a bit to herself at the thought, but answered him seriously enough, "It is a vendetta, my son. I have had to wait over twenty-five years to have . . . justice rendered. Now that you are the bey and a powerful man, I ask that you help me."

His thick brow remained arched. "Vengeance, Mother? You are responsible for making me a liar and breaking tribute with a powerful English nobleman. By God, madam, do you know what you have done?"

Giovanna lowered her eyes to her smooth hands, for Alessandro, like his father, was talented in reading people's eyes. She frowned a moment at the several small brown spots.

"Yes," she said quietly, "it was I, and I know what I have done." She raised her eyes and saw cold, disbelieving anger on his face. "Alessandro, before you judge me harshly, please listen! Twenty-five years ago I was captured by your father and brought here to Oran as a slave for his harem. A slave, my son," she said, her voice rising, "and I was a contessa, a noblewoman, in Genoa!"

"I listen, madam, and as yet I do not hear anything I do not already know. You have spent half your life here, as my father's second wife. You have given me no reason to assume you were displeased with your station in life." He gazed about the richly furnished chamber.

"But a slave nonetheless. You have lived many years in Europe. You know that European women live with their men, eat at the same table, go out with them in society. They are not shut away, their faces covered with veils!"

Kamal heard trembling anger in her voice. "You digress, madam. I trust this vendetta in some way gives meaning to your foolishness."

"I will tell you what happened, my son," Giovanna said, seeming more controlled. She saw Raj from the corner of her eye, standing silently near the doorway, and drew to an abrupt halt. She had no idea how much the eunuch knew, but she did know he disliked and distrusted her, though he had never shown her any overt disdain. She dismissed him with an angry wave of her hand.

She stretched her slender hand over the small table and clasped her son's wrist. "Twenty-six years ago, I was to wed a wealthy man, half Italian and half English, a man who was a peer of the English realm. His name is Anthony Welles. His title, the Earl of Clare. He is a man of substance in banking and shipping. He spends half his time in Genoa and half in England. It is he who was responsible for my capture."

Kamal frowned at her unexpected words, but his voice was calm. "And why did the Earl of Clare do such a thing?"

Giovanna drew a convincingly shuddering breath and forced a furrow of pain to her brow. "It was not actually he, my son, but rather the harlot he had brought from England with him. You see, I was to wed him, but this little English slut, one of his mistresses, knew of it, and offered a great sum of money to your father to remove me permanently. The earl wed the woman, while I languished here, a slave."

Kamal's frown did not ease. "This Earl of Clare, did he know what his wife had done?"

"Yes, but only after he had wed her. Your father told me that."

"The earl made no inquiries? Made no attempt to right the wrong done to you?"

Giovanna sniffed pitifully. "The little harlot had spun her web about him by that time and was to bear his child. He did nothing."

"How was an Englishwoman able to contact my father?"

"I do not know, but the fact remains that I am here, and have been for more years than I care to count. Both of them merit my hate, Alessandro, and yours, as my son. They must be punished for what they did."

Your hate has already plundered two ships and brought me dishonor, he thought. "Continue," he said flatly.

"They are responsible for something horrible, Alessandro. You see, I was with the earl's half-brother at the time of my capture. He was an innocent young man, and he was swiftly put to death. I believe that the earl distrusted his half-brother and was glad to be rid of him. Cesare Bellini was his name, and he was a brilliant man, a man who possibly could have taken over the earl's holdings in Genoa."

"The Countess of Clare—is she still living?"

"Yes. And they have two children, grown now, just as are you. They have become but richer with the fruits of their deceit."

"Why did you simply not tell me this? Why did you act behind my back? Does it please you to have made me a liar and a murderer?"

"No one, my son, will ever know that the earl's ships were taken by Barbary pirates. No one will ever suspect you. I have protected you."

"Protected me!" He gave a furious bark of laughter. "This is beyond reason! If you wished vengeance, Mother, why did you not ask Hamil to help you?"

Hamil would have laughed in my face! Giovanna was expecting this and answered readily enough, "Alessandro, it is your responsibility, as my son, to avenge me. Your father saw me as naught but a plaything for his bed, and Hamil saw me only as his half-brother's Christian mother, not worthy of his exalted notice."

But Hamil hadn't been that way at all, Kamal thought, staring down at his coffee. He said slowly, "Now that you have . . . toyed with the earl, do you wish me to have him killed? Is that the favor you ask, Mother?"

Giovanna leaned toward him, unable to contain her excitement. "I want them to suffer, as I suffered. I want them both brought here so that I may face them with their treachery. Perhaps the harlot could be sold in the slave market and spend the rest of her days treated as the miserable slut she is. As for the earl, I would see him in the mines."

"Your reason is poisoned with your vengeance," Kamal said, feeling distaste at the venom in her voice. "When the Earl of Clare discovers that we did indeed destroy his ships, do you think he will not take action against us? Do you not realize what the English could do to us with all their warships?"

Timely tears glistened in her eyes, and she stammered, "I . . . I promise you, my son, that not one man escaped to tell what happened. The earl cannot be certain it was the Barbary pirates who were responsible. I was most careful. Indeed,

I have let his men discover that most of the goods from his two ships have appeared in Naples. Soon, my son, the proud earl will travel to the court of Naples to discover the truth. Then I will have him!"

Kamal stared at the woman who was his mother. "Then you wish me to send men to Naples to capture the earl when he appears? We could do that just as easily in Genoa."

"No, Alessandro. I myself will travel to Naples, not using my real name, of course, for the earl would recognize it. When he appears, I wish to confront him myself. He will be away from his armed fortress in Genoa, away from all his friends, and all his men. I will bring him here to you, for justice."

"You have planned this for a long time, have you not?" Kamal asked her, his blue eyes steady on hers.

"Oh yes," she said, again lowering her eyes. "For a very long time. A woman does not have much to do, after all, in a harem, even the bey's mother. Even my choice of Naples works beautifully, for there are many French dissidents in the court itself, unknown to the king and queen. I am using one of the more . . . dishonorable young noblemen for my purposes. You needn't worry, my son. He will do exactly as I wish once I am there to control him. When the earl arrives, his disappearance will be blamed on the French dissidents. There will be no taint of dishonor on your name."

"What of the earl's children?"

Giovanna knew Kamal would shield the earl's children, who were innocent in his mind. He was damnably soft, not nearly as ruthless as his father had been, and she was more cunning and ruthless than Khar El-Din had ever imagined, the old fool!

She said softly, with a touch of compassion in her voice, "After the earl is gone, his son will take his place. The daughter will doubtless wed an Englishman. They are both grown; they will survive."

'I asked you once if you wished to return to Italy, to Genoa, and you refused. You refused because in Italy you had not the power to act against the Earl of Clare, is that not true?"

"Yes, my son, I wanted it done."

He sat back in his chair, his arms folded tightly across his chest. "If you were not my mother, you would die for what you have done. You have broken trust with me, and dishonored me. I will send Hassan to take back my seal. I will inform you tomorrow of my decision. But when it is over, you will no longer live in my household."

She sucked in her breath, unable to believe his words. Her hand fluttered, and her eyes pleaded with him, but Kamal rose quickly.

She gave a small sob, realizing how much she had won and what she had lost. "Please, Alessandro . . ."

"Thank you for the dinner, madam," he said, and turned on his heel.

Kamal looked with annoyance at the young girl who approached him, until he remembered who she was. His gift from the Sudan. She wore a soft yellow silk harem jacket that fastened under her high, pointed breasts, and silk trousers bound at her ankles. She was really quite lovely, he thought dispassionately, with her thick chestnut hair and green eyes, and very young. She peeped at him from beneath her lashes and smiled.

"Master," she whispered, and knelt before him, touching her lips to his leather slippers.

"You may rise," he said abruptly. The smile faded from her face, and he saw she was trembling. He sighed deeply, knowing she was afraid she displeased him.

He gentled his voice. "Your name is Maya?"

"Yes, highness."

"You are lovely, Maya." he lightly caressed her silken hair. "How old are you?"

"Fifteen, highness."

He heard a tremor in her voice. She was not to blame that the last thing he wanted this night was a fifteen-year-old-virgin in his bed.

"Shall I disrobe, highness?"

"Yes." Hoping she would not see the flat disinterest in his eyes, he added, "It would give me great pleasure, Maya."

He reclined on his fur-covered bed, pillowed his head on his arms, and stared a long moment at the ceiling. He heard the rustle of clothing, and forced his eyes back to the girl.

She was undressing slowly, with great skill, her every movement meant to whet his desire. He found he was unstirred by the sight of her pale breasts and dark pink nipples. Her woman's mound was shaved, her nether lips lightly rouged with henna.

She stood uncertainly, her young body gleaming in the pale candlelight, staring toward him. Kamal knew he did not have to treat her gently, though she was a virgin. She was likely as skilled as any courtesan in Europe, her maidenhead merely a technicality. For a moment he was angered that this girl had known little of childhood, that her training had likely begun before she had even begun her monthly flow. He knew his anger would change nothing. He must take her, else she would be shamed.

"Come here, Maya," he said.

She walked seductively toward him, her hips swaying, and sank to her knees beside him. He rose from his bed and allowed her to undress him. He was relieved at her skill, relieved that her fingers were well trained to heighten his senses. When he was naked, he discovered to his chagrin that his thoughts were still on his incredible conversation with his mother, and not the anxious girl who hovered over him.

"Tell me of your home, Maya," he said, drawing her down beside him on the bed.

She stared at him in dismay. "Alexandria is a large city, highness," she managed after a few pained moments. "I did not live in the city. I do not miss it. I want only to make you happy, master."

Kamal sighed and reached for her. She mewled and whimpered softly as he caressed her. He did not know whether she feigned pleasure at his touch. He knew she did not expect him to care what any of his harem girls felt. She was here for his pleasure, and not her own.

He kissed her soft mouth and let his hand rove over her breasts and belly. She parted her thighs as he gently stroked her. He knew a moment of surprise that she was warm and moist, until he realized that her maiden's passage had been oiled. It was a reminder she wasn't a woman who desired him, but a slave whose body belonged to him. He stretched out on his back, knowing she would know how to arouse him. He closed his eyes and let himself respond to her gentle fingers and soft mouth. He was at the point of taking her when he chanced to look into her eyes. They were wide with fright. I am being a pig, he thought, treating her as if she had not a thought or a feeling.

"I will try not to hurt you, Maya," he said softly. He gently opened her thighs and lifted himself above her. He wanted to get it over with, but he slowed to stroke her, to tell her in a quiet voice of her beauty, of her softness, of how much she delighted him, until he felt her ease. Slowly, as gently as he could, he pushed into her. He felt her taut maidenhead, and stilled, waiting for her to absorb the feel of him inside her. To his surprise, she suddenly thrust up her hips against him, drawing him deep within her. He heard her cry out. He had the cynical thought that she had likely been taught to cry out. She started to writhe beneath him, and he said sharply, "Maya, hold still. You but hurt yourself needlessly."

He began to move gently within her. He felt her stroking his back, felt her hands curling about his buttocks, and he let himself respond to the girl beneath him. He thrust again, deeply, and spilled his seed into her. He lay on top of her, his head resting beside hers on an embroidered pillow. He realized she was stiff beneath him and reared up on his elbows.

"Thank you, Maya," he said, and lightly kissed her lips. He saw that she was staring at him uncertainly, and said in a weary voice, "You gave me great pleasure. You may go now, Maya, and rest. Hassan Aga is waiting outside. He will give you a token of my pleasure."

"Yes, highness," she said, and quietly left him.

His body was eased somewhat, but his mind was not. Maya was like all the other women in his possession. Even Elena would only pretend to listen to him, lower her lashes seductively, and tell him that she didn't understand him. He remembered with vague regret the European women he had known. Though they lived by rules as rigid as any in the Muslim world, they knew freedom that neither a Muslim man nor a Muslim woman could conceive. They spoke their minds, loved with discretion, and had spoiled him with their willful and entrancing freedom.

Kamal sighed and rolled over on his belly. He knew he must take a wife soon; it was expected of him. It was his duty to his people and his position. If he did not marry and produce a son, his half-brother, Rissan, now nearly twenty, would be his heir. Until Lella's child was born. Rissan could never cope with the complexities and the responsibilities that would face him as Bey of Oran. Rissan was happiest among the *rais*, captaining his own ship, preying on the hapless merchant vessels that had not paid tribute to the Dey of Algiers.

"The girl, Maya, highness. She did not please you?"

Kamal looked up to see Hassan Aga standing uncertainly in the doorway. "Enough, old friend. I trust you gave her a jewel or something to compensate her for her maidenhead."

"Indeed, merely a small token."

Hassan turned to leave, but Kamal stayed him. "No, Hassan, remain with me a moment. Come, sit down."

Kamal pulled on a bed robe of soft crimson silk and joined Hassan beside a small table surrounded with soft embroidered cushions.

"You do not act like a man who has just relieved his needs, highness. You are thinking about Europe, perhaps, and the Corsican who keeps England's eyes focused away from us? Or perhaps"—his voice deepened—"you dwell on the two ships taken under your seal?"

"Yes, and ordered, as you suspected, by my mother." Kamal rubbed his fingers over the knotted muscles in his neck. "At the moment, I think about honor. There is little of it in any of us, it appears. Do you know that I stopped years ago telling anyone in Italy and France that my home is in Algiers, indeed that I am half-Muslim, for they made me the butt of jokes and treated me like a rabid barbarian."

"Intolerance is bred into every culture, highness," Hassan said quietly. "A man, it appears, cannot be content with himself and his station unless there is another man he can disdain."

There was silence between them for several minutes before Kamal recounted to Hassan, his voice expressionless, the story his mother had told him. "Do you know anything of this, Hassan?" he asked when he had finished.

"No, highness, I know nothing of what your mother told you. I have met the Earl of Clare . . . the Marchese di Parese, as he is known in Genoa. Your father and your half-brother Hamil knew him better. I met him but once, in Algiers, shortly after I arrived here, some ten years ago. He has paid tribute for many years." He paused a moment, his eyes on his crooked fingers that pained him when the weather changed. "It is distressing," he said finally, "that your mother took action against him without your knowledge or consent."

Kamal's lips tightened into a thin line. " 'Distressing' is a mild word, Hassan. It scarce touches my feelings in the matter."

"What do you intend to do, highness?"

"I have not as yet decided. As I told you, if I

allow her her revenge, she will no longer be welcome in Oran. She will return to the life she forfeited over twenty-five years ago. This English nobleman, the Earl of Clare, what do you remember of him?"

Hassan spoke slowly, dusting the years off his memories. "I remember him as a man who understood his power, as a man of ability."

"An honorable man?"

"I would have said so, yes."

"Did he deal well with my father?"

"As I recall, there was a certain . . . coolness between them. But they were two vastly different men. He dealt quite well with Hamil."

"Anyone with half a notion of honor dealt well with Hamil. Hassan, your eyes tell me there is something more you would say."

"There are many motives, highness, that men may not understand. A motive of vengeance can be clear in one man's mind and a tangle of confusion in another's. I understand vengeance, highness, but in this matter I am not sure. I ask you to tread carefully in this."

"I shall, old friend."

"Your learning is important for our people," Hassan continued after a thoughtful moment. "They live as they lived a hundred, nay, two hundred years ago. When I think of Cairo, my home, and its vast libraries, I would weep for what we have lost here. The Moors no longer hold learning above all else; the Turks are content to spit on the Jews and Christians and slaughter anyone who intrudes upon their sport. The Europeans loathe and fear us, and want only to crush us. I fear for the future, highness. The Grand Turk cannot help us. Your half-brother Hamil sought change for our people, but more than that, he sought honor."

"I did not wish to become the Bey of Oran. You know that, Hassan. And never at the sacrifice of Hamil's life."

"Hamil was proud of you, highness. Each letter he received from you, he read proudly." Hassan paused a moment, then added quietly, "I do not think he was a man to be governed by a woman."

Kamal met Hassan's wise old eyes. It was a bold statement for Hassan, who usually spoke obliquely, in the Muslim way.

"Nor am I, Hassan," Kamal said, "though women in Europe are vastly different than they are here."

"Women who understand guile are the most dangerous of creatures, here or in Europe. To trust a woman is folly."

"Even if the woman is one's mother?"

"Ah, that is different, and yet not different. I am pleased that you are bred to two cultures, highness. It gives you wisdom that is mysterious to a Muslim. I feared you would not be accepted by our people. Yet I see you, a young man, rendering justice that men twice your age accept without question."

"Sometimes I feel very old, Hassan. Not particularly wise, just weary from what I have seen."

"You are a young man, highness. I pray that your life is not cut short as was your half-brother Hamil's. He was an excellent sailor, at home on a ship as he was on land. I still cannot believe that he fell overboard during that storm."

"The Koran teaches us to accept such tragedy as Allah's will, Hassan. You are tired, old friend. And I weary you with useless talk."

Hassan waved a bony hand, and stared toward the heavy tapestry that draped from ceiling to floor on the opposite wall. "Remember that vengeance is for men, highness. A woman's vengeance knows no honor."

Kamal grinned suddenly. "I should have reminded my mother that if it were not for this hated earl and his countess, I would not be on this earth."

"Such logic is not convincing to a woman, highness." Hassan rose slowly to his feet and bowed deeply. "Do you wish to retire now, highness?"

Kamal sighed. "Yes. There is much to consider."

"May Allah guard you," Hassan said, and walked silently from the chamber.

5

Naples

A wispy fog swirled from the bay, curled over the docks, and crept through the narrow streets of Naples. Three men, shrouded to their feet in thick black cloaks, huddled against the side of a building in a crooked alley, waiting. One of them, by far the oldest of the three, eased his narrow shoulders around the corner of the building and stared through the murky fog down the street.

"Quiet, lads," he hissed. "He's coming, but not alone. There's someone with him."

"Give us some sport," another of the men said. He spat neatly toward a mangy cat that was pawing a pile of refuse.

The Comte de la Valle negligently twirled his beribboned cane as he listened to his friend Celestino Genovesi.

"*Gesù*," Celestino growled, "it's as black as a pit in hell. You tempt fate, Gervaise. I'd feel uneasy walking here during the day, what with all the riffraff hanging about."

"Stop whining," Gervaise said. "As for its being a black night, it will give you practice for when you leave this earth."

"You're a cold-blooded bastard, Gervaise. I still don't like it."

"Why not think about that lovely little morsel you shared in tonight?"

Celestino, a paunchy young Italian nobleman with crispy chestnut side whiskers, shuddered in distaste, knowing Gervaise could not see his expression. He said only, "With four of us taking the little whore, she quickly lost her desire to please."

"Perhaps next time you will be first," Gervaise said, sounding bored. "She did whimper quite prettily. That must have pleased you, Tino." He shrugged his elegant shoulders. "She was paid for her services. The gold I placed into her grimy little hand was the amount her father demanded. It was overpayment, I think, for her maidenhead."

The silence was suddenly rent by coarse shouts. "Get 'em, my lads! Break their heads!"

Three black shadows flew from the alleyway. Celestino howled in startled fear. Gervaise, Comte de la Valle, quickly drew the dagger at his belt and tossed aside his useless cane.

"Fight, you fool!" he shouted at Tino. "You cannot run from the scum!" He lunged at one of the men, his dagger slicing downward toward his breast. He felt his arm suddenly wrenched behind his back in a grip that made him gasp. The man who held him had twice his strength. He struggled in silence, Celestino's howling cries ringing in his ears. Like a damned girl! He closed his eyes when he felt the point of a knife touch his bare throat. *Merde,* he thought very precisely. To die at the hands of wharf rats bent upon robbing his purse.

Gervaise heard another yell from the gloom. He whirled about to see a man hurtling toward them, his sword glistening silver in the swirling fog. For an instant he was held immobile, watching the figure lunge toward one of the thieves. The man dodged his sword, then shouted at the top of his lungs, "Away, my boys! Away!"

The three thieves disappeared into the darkness as if they had never existed. Gervaise calmly sheathed his dagger and brushed off his sable-lined cloak.

"For God's sake, Tino," he growled toward his friend, who was leaning against the side of a derelict building, vomiting into the street, "get hold of yourself!"

"Are you all right?"

Gervaise strained his eyes to see more clearly. He heard a young voice, smooth and educated, speak in Italian. He saw a flash of silver as the sword slipped back into its scabbard.

"*Si,*" he said easily. "Your timing was exquisite, my friend. Christ, Tino, pull yourself together!"

"He is shaken," the man said. "The thieves are gone. There is nothing more to fear."

"Who are you?" Gervaise asked him.

The figure before him bowed elegantly at the

waist. "The Marchese Pietro di Galvani," the cultured voice said.

Celestino, feeling more a man now that his belly was emptied of food and fear, straightened and strode toward them.

"What were you doing down here alone?"

The man shrugged. "I was bored. I thank you both for the excitement. The scum didn't put up much of a fight," he added with scorn in his voice.

"Bored!" Tino shrilled. "*Dio*, man, you could have been killed!"

The man gave a low, amused laugh. "Then I would have again escaped boredom, would I not?"

Gervaise said suddenly, "I wish to repay you, sir. Celestino and I were on our way to my house. Join us for a drink."

The marchese seemed to hesitate.

"Do," Tino seconded. "Can't see your bloody face in all this dark and fog."

He appeared to shrug. "Very well."

"I am Gervaise, Comte de la Valle, and this is Celestino Genovesi—Conte Genovesi, I should add. Perhaps it will help him regain his balance and his bravery."

"You are French," the Marchese Pietro di Galvani said easily in that language. "I am new to Naples. You have provided me my first taste of sport."

"*Oui, je suis français*," Gervaise said. "Unlike you, *mon ami*, I have been here for more days than I care to count."

The three men began their walk in silence, except for occasional blasts from the foghorns and the clopping of their boots on the cobblestones.

"You are a royalist, *enfin*," Pietro said.

"Speak Italian," Tino complained.

"He asked me if I were a royalist," Gervaise repeated. "Yes, you could call me that. There are many of us here at the court of Naples, outlawed from our country by the miserable Jacobins and that upstart Napoleon."

"Then I will say good night," the Marchese Pietro di Galvani said, and spun about on his heel.

"But why?" Celestino said, grabbing his sleeve.

Pietro said slowly, shaking off Tino's hand, "I am, as I said, new to Naples. I have no desire to consort with"—he nearly spat the word—"with . . . supporters of the Bourbons or Capets!"

"Ah," Gervaise said softly. "Wait, my friend. Perhaps you should withhold your judgment, if just for tonight."

"Yes, do come with us. Gervaise is not what he seems—"

"Shut up, Tino," the comte said pleasantly. "*Monsieur?*"

"The night is young," Pietro said.

"And you wish to escape boredom, *n'est-ce pas?*" The marchese shrugged. "Very well."

"Where do you come from?" Celestino asked, puffing slightly to keep up with the swift stride of the two other men.

"Sicily," the marchese said shortly. "Yet another part of the Bourbons' kingdom."

"Then why, my friend," Gervaise said, "did you come here to Naples?"

"I came for business reasons, and . . ."

"And?" Celestino prodded.

"To see that harridan of a queen and her lecherous fool of a husband fall to Napoleon. It cannot be long now."

"Ah," Gervaise said. "No, I suppose it cannot be much longer. The Treaty of Amiens that keeps Naples safe will fall soon." He shrugged as if bored. "Then we shall see."

The three men turned onto a lighted street, wide and surrounded by tall, elegant houses. The stench of the dock was behind them.

"My humble abode," Gervaise said, pushing open a wrought-iron gate. He withdrew a key from his pocket and unlocked the narrow oak front door. "My servant is asleep, or at least the fool should be," he said over his shoulder. He led the two of them through a narrow entrance hall and stepped inside an adjoining room to light a branch of candles.

"Quite cozy," the marchese said, gazing about. The drawing room was long and narrow, and furnished with cherrywood pieces of delicate beauty. He watched the comte walk to the sideboard and lift a decanter.

"Brandy?"

The marchese nodded and unfastened his cloak.

Gervaise watched him unbuckle his sword and place it with careful precision by his cloak on a tabletop. He eyed his rich clothing and his tall, powerful frame. When the marchese turned, he stared into his black-bearded face.

"You look like a bloody pirate," Celestino said.

The marchese shrugged. "I am from Sicily," he said, as if that were explanation enough.

"Your brandy, sir," Gervaise said, handing him a crystal goblet.

"A toast," Celestino said, raising his glass. "To the rescue of two of Naples' best young noblemen!"

The marchese arched a thick black brow, but said nothing. He sipped his brandy and moved to seat himself on a brocade sofa.

Gervaise continued to drink his brandy, studying the young man. "You have odd coloring, *monsieur*. Your eyes. Never have I seen an Italian with blue eyes."

For the first time, the marchese smiled, displaying even white teeth. "That is what I told my father," he said, smiling still.

Celestino gave a shout of laughter. "I've heard much about the Sicilians!"

"And you speak French well, *monsieur*," Gervaise continued, disregarding Tino's comment.

"Of course. What man of education does not?"

"See here," Celestino sputtered.

The marchese's smile alighted on Tino's face. "You did not allow me to finish, my friend. A man of education who wants above all to free the rest of Italy must be able to speak the language of its liberators." He saw that the Comte de la Valle had stiffened, and added pleasantly, "But I insult you, *monsieur*. Tonight that is not my intention. Had I realized that you were a royalist, I would still have joined the melee."

The Comte de la Valle proffered the marchese an elaborate bow. "You are honest, if nothing else," he said in his soft, hoarse voice.

"Don't be too certain of that," the marchese said, tossing a smile, as if it were a careless bone, toward them. "You, *monsieur* le comte, are blessed with fair looks. I have never seen a Frenchman with hazel eyes and light hair."

"*Touché*," Gervaise said.

"Do you plan to go to court?" Celestino asked, depositing his bulky frame in a wing chair opposite the marchese.

The marchese looked bored. "What else is there to do in Naples?"

"There are many beautiful women at the court," Celestino said.

"Ah, that is something, I suppose. Can one be assured they will not give a man the pox?"

The comte, who had been standing negligently against the mantelpiece, straightened and smiled. "They give their favors freely. I have heard it said that when the queen was younger she kept as many as three lovers at the same time. Of course she is a raddled hag now."

"I think," Celestino said with a sharp glance toward the comte, "that a man is only safe taking virgins."

"Ah," the marchese sighed. "If I were to pay a gold piece for every virgin I could find, I would still be a rich man at the end of a week."

Celestino chortled and opened his mouth to speak, but swallowed his words at a frown from Gervaise.

"You are doubtless right in part, *mon ami*," the comte said. He gazed down into the amber liquid in his goblet and said slowly, "I would suggest, marchese, that you do not speak so openly of your French leanings in the court. The queen has more secret police than most imagine. More than one innocent man has been butchered because of her hatred and fear of Napoleon. Your exalted rank and your wealth would not save you, I fear." He paused for a long moment, and added, "Why, even Celestino and I could be in the pay of her majesty. Yes, you must be more careful."

The marchese stretched his long legs out before him. His dark blue eyes were hooded, almost as if he were nodding off to sleep. "I thank you for your . . . advice, comte," he said, not looking up. "I trust whatever my father did, he did not raise a fool."

"Do you play cards?" Celestino said, leaning forward in his chair.

"What gentleman does not?" the marchese said blandly.

"The night is still young," the comte said. "Name your game, marchese, and Tino and I will contrive to amuse you."

Adam did not awaken until noon. When he left his room, Daniele Barbaro was awaiting him in the drawing room.

"Well?" he asked without preamble.

Adam yawned. "You and the men did excellently, Daniele. I did not stagger home until dawn. I allowed the Comte de la Valle to relieve me of a bit of gold," he added, smiling ruefully.

Adam's valet, Borkin, entered the drawing room bearing two cups of steaming coffee and a tray of rolls.

"Will you join me, Daniele?"

At the older man's nod, Adam seated himself in front of a small circular table and began to eat. He said nothing further until Borkin had bowed himself out of the room and pulled the door closed.

"It is not that I doubt him in any way," Adam said, more to himself than to Daniele. "I don't want him to know anything that could place him in danger. I trust none of your men were harmed last night?"

"Nay, your feint with your sword was impressive, no damage done to Vincenzo. Did you learn anything?"

Adam stretched, took another bite of a flaky roll, and sat back in his chair. "Not much, but then again, I didn't expect to. But I expect that the comte's friend Celestino Genovesi will sooner or later divulge the game. I accompany them to court tonight. There is a ball, or some such thing. The comte will present me to the queen. The king, I hear, is at his palace at Caserta, hunting and whoring."

Daniele grunted. "Have you heard from the earl?"

"Aye, yesterday." He raised a mocking black brow. "My damned sister will be arriving shortly with the Lyndhursts."

"A rare handful is Lady Arabella," Daniele said, grinning shamelessly at his master.

"I look forward to seeing the minx. But I cannot like the fact that Rayna Lyndhurst is coming with her parents. The chit's only eighteen, and from what Bella tells me, she's so innocent she blushes when a rose opens."

"She shouldn't recognize you. With that beard, you don't look the English gentleman—more a damned pirate."

"Exactly what Celestino observed last night." Adam chuckled. "Father wrote that Viscount Delford was appalled that he was allowing Arabella to come here because it was *her* wish to do so. Claimed he wouldn't allow his daughter to gainsay his wishes, to which my father replied in that satirical way of his, 'But, my dear sir, I want my daughter's character to be as strong as her mother's.' "

"Ah," Daniele said comfortably, "there is that. You needn't worry about Lady Arabella, my lord. She's safe with the Lyndhursts. The only danger she'll know is keeping the young noblemen at court at arm's length. No different from London." As he stood, he added, "What harm can a girl come to attending parties?"

"You, Daniele, don't know my sister!"

"Did Viscount Delford agree to cooperate with us?"

"He had no choice. Lord Delford will keep mum about me. Father can be most persuasive."

"Aye, I've been with your father since before you were born. I wouldn't want to cross him. Now, my lord, I must go. Vincenzo will be near, and you can send a message to me anytime of the day or night at my lodgings."

Adam rose and shook his hand. "Thank you, Daniele. With any luck at all, we'll have this wretched mess resolved and be back in Genoa before too much time. My only real concern is that Napoleon will descend with one of his armies and take Naples."

"Nay," Daniele said, "it will take time to break the treaty. If it should come to pass, my lord, you will simply bundle your sister out of here before she can catch her breath to protest."

6

"How am I supposed to feel like a princess with my slippers pinching my toes so dreadfully?" Arabella whispered behind her white-gloved hand to Rayna Lyndhurst. Rayna was staring wide-eyed at the sprawling magnificence of the Palazzo Reale. The palace was lit with scores of flambeaux, held high by royal liveried servants outside the palace and secured in golden wall sconces within.

"It was your idea to wear my slippers, Bella! I cannot help it if my feet are smaller than yours."

"How kind of you to point that out!" Arabella said on an unladylike snort. "Oh, I just heard, Rayna," she continued in a conspiratorial whisper, not wanting either Lord or Lady Delford to hear her, "that King Ferdinando has returned from his favorite retreat, Belvedere, and will make an appearance tonight! I understand he is sated with his latest mistress and with hunting deer in his private preserves. I also heard it said that he did not pay much attention to the game, but more to Lucia, his overblown mistress."

"Is she here tonight?"

"No, I think she is being protected from other gentlemen's sight at Belvedere."

"Bella, where do you hear all these spicy things? No one tells me anything!"

"This person or that," Arabella said airily, and returned her attention to the vast reception hall. Soaring white marble columns, carved with eager cherubs, divided the huge hall into smaller salons. What seemed to be miles of crimson velvet draperies fell from ceiling to floor along two entire walls. And so many beautifully attired people! The men, she noted with a crooked smile, appeared every bit as flamboyant as the ladies, many of them still wearing wigs, some dyed in dazzling colors.

She was excited about meeting the King and Queen of Naples, but she was anxious about Adam. She scanned the brightly colored throng for him, but could not see him. She glanced at Rayna, who was standing quietly beside her mother, seeming quite nervous. She was sorry Rayna could not understand the lilting Italian, or smile, as she could, at the chattering nonsense she heard, no different from the nonsense spoken at the fashionable balls in London. She looked back to the hall where the bewigged musicians began playing at the far end of the chamber, and many of the gentlemen and ladies stepped out to dance the minuet. She finally saw Adam in the distance, in conversation with a tall young man. Was it the

Comte de la Valle? He certainly didn't look particularly debauched, with his blond good looks.

"Come, ladies," Lord Delford said. "We are about to be graced with the royal presences."

Arabella followed in the wake of Lord and Lady Delford. Lord Delford, tall and severely lean, was immaculately dressed in formal black velvet with frothy white lace at his throat and his wrists. His only jewelry was a large emerald signet ring on his right hand and a diamond stickpin in the folds of his cravat. His viscountess looked a bit pale, Arabella thought, as if she hadn't yet fully recovered from their voyage from Genoa. But she held her head proudly high, her auburn coloring set off by a rich gown of green satin. Rayna was wearing a gown of old ivory satin, with a strand of creamy pearls about her throat. Arabella thought her young friend looked exquisite, but of course, she wouldn't tell her that again, not after the insult to her feet! As they neared the royal presences, Arabella patted Rayna's hand.

"Head up, Rayna," Arabella whispered. "You are far more beautiful than the queen's two daughters. I vow they'll hate you within minutes!"

"If only I were as tall as you, Bella, instead of squat!"

"The old satyr has returned to the queen to rest for a while," the Comte de la Valle was saying to the Marchese di Galvani on the far side of the salon. "Do you know that he was ready to leave for Palermo several months ago for hunting? Sent ninety of his hounds over by ship. Acton convinced him it wasn't wise to leave Naples, with Napoleon breathing down our necks. How the old fool cares for his throne!"

"A pity," Adam said obscurely. He kept his gaze fixedly on the queen, not wanting to glance toward Arabella. The queen sat upon a high-backed chair, flanked by her two daughters. She looked pale and painfully aged, Adam thought, with her crimped gray hair and the wrinkles obvious on her face, even from a distance. The Princess Amélie was a tall, quite lovely young woman, but her sister, Christine, some three years older, had unfortunately inherited her father's rather bulbous nose and his rounded shoulders. The king had not yet made his appearance, and Adam had heard that the prince royal, Francesco, and his young Bourbon princess, Isabel, were at his farm near the palace at Caserta. He did not particularly care. He would not have come to the reception in any case if it had been his choice, but the Comte de la Valle had baited him, insisting in his hoarse voice that he must see the lion in his den surrounded by all his cubs and keepers before deciding if he deserved to rule.

"Such a pity that the *lazzaroni* starve," Adam said in a sneering voice, "while that fat king fills his belly."

"Ah, but the *lazzaroni* adore King Ferdinando, *mon ami*. He is one of them, you know. Despite his royal Bourbon blood, he is as ignorant as a pig, talks in the most vulgar parlance I've ever heard, and enjoys himself most when he is selling fish in the market."

"You sound most critical for a royalist, Gervaise," Adam said.

The comte shrugged. " 'Tis but the truth. Prepare to compose your pirate's face into a more accepting expression, Pietro. Here is his royal majesty."

King Ferdinando, closer to sixty now than to the fifty he proclaimed, strolled into the vast salon, nodding to his right and left, acknowledging bows and curtsies. He wore rich purple Genoese velvet, adorned with thick gold braid at the shoulders and over his breast, that fell loosely over his heavy frame. He greeted the queen and his two daughters when he reached them, and heaved his great bulk into his chair beside the queen's.

Adam watched him greet Edward Lyndhurst and his wife, his guests of honor, and then bestow his most beguiling stare on the two rather taken-aback young ladies with them. When at last he had looked his fill, he waved toward the musicians to begin their music again, and strains of the minuet filled the huge chamber.

"Would you look at that lovely little morsel."

Adam turned and saw that the comte was gazing fixedly toward the Lyndhurst party. Adam's eyes fell upon Arabella, breathtakingly lovely in a gown of pomona-green satin with rich embroidered gold binding the material beneath her breasts. Her honey-colored hair was braided into a high coronet, with thick tresses falling over her shoulder.

He said in a dismissive voice, "If you like her washed-out coloring, I suppose the girl is passable."

"Washed-out? Really, *mon ami*! That beautiful auburn hair and those exquisite hazel eyes? And she is so very young and . . . untouched."

Adam's eyes followed the comte's to Rayna Lyndhurst, who was standing slightly behind Arabella. He started at seeing her. The scraggly little peahen of a girl he remembered had emerged as a young lady of glorious plumage. She was standing very close to her mother, gazing timidly about her. He had the unaccountable urge to tell her not to be afraid. It was all show. Adam tried to subdue the uneasiness he felt at the comte's words.

"She has the look of a convent," he said indifferently.

"And I have the look of a man who will scale the convent walls!"

"I believe," Adam said thoughtfully, ignoring the comte's jest, "that she must belong to the Lyndhurst family. He is the new adviser to Sir Hugh Elliot, I hear."

"How convenient that I am such an ardent royalist," the comte said. "After they have paid their respects to their raddled majesties, I will contrive an introduction. I wonder if that other lovely girl is also a daughter. I did not know the English bred such exquisite females."

Both females were curtsying deeply to Queen Maria Carolina, having endured the king's ogling.

"Welcome to Naples," the queen said, proffering

her hand to Viscount Delford. "You have made Mr. Acton's acquaintance, have you not?"

"Indeed, madam," Edward Lyndhurst said. He nodded formally to Acton, who stood beside the Princess Amélie. He felt a tug of liking for the most powerful man in Naples. He was tall, portly, and heavily jowled, but his eyes were a light gray that seemed alight with amusement at some untold joke.

"My wife is shortly expecting a baby, else she would be here to greet you, my lord," Acton said.

"Please offer our congratulations to your wife, sir," Lady Delford said. "This is my daughter, Rayna, and her friend Lady Arabella Welles."

"Charmed," the queen said, bestowing a royal smile on the two young ladies.

"As am I, your majesty," Arabella said with a brilliant smile.

"I will agree," Acton said, his smile widening. "Ladies," he continued after a moment, "I will leave you with Sir Hugh, the English ambassador. He knows everyone and will give you splendid introductions. Lord Delford? Have you a moment?"

To Arabella's surprise, the queen rose and led Acton and Viscount Delford through a narrow door behind the dais. The king did not appear to notice their leaving, for he was in conversation with an older woman who was flirting outrageously with him from behind her ivory fan.

Sir Hugh noticed Arabella's raised brows and followed her gaze. He said in a lightly snide undervoice, "Please ignore his majesty, my dear.

He takes little notice of the running of his kingdom. The lady is his lastest flirt, a newly arrived contessa from Genoa or Milan, I am not certain which."

"But she is old," Rayna blurted out.

Sir Hugh smiled gently at her. "Indeed, nearly my age, I suspect. No, my dear, do not blush. I was merely teasing you. I suppose I must introduce you first to Alquier, Napoleon's ambassador. He, at least, is not a crass bore like his predecessor."

"This is a splendid gathering, Sir Hugh," Lady Delford said.

"And the palace is most impressive," Arabella added.

"Indeed, ladies," Sir Hugh agreed. "It is a pity the queen dislikes it so much. You see, the French held Naples back in 1797 for some five months, and used the palace for their own diversions. It holds some bitter memories for the royal family. They now do most of their entertaining at the palace at Caserta. But Monsieur Alquier is approaching."

Arabella thought the *monsieur* a slippery snake when he finally allowed them to escape. Her thoughts were so clear in her expressive eyes that Sir Hugh chuckled.

"Do not, my dear," he chided her quietly, "let Alquier know what you are thinking. He is unbelievably powerful. For the moment, he is content to allow their majesties to reign."

"It is a fault of mine, Sir Hugh," Arabella said. "I will contrive to keep my lashes fluttering."

Sir Hugh turned to Rayna. "What did you think of Monsieur Alquier, Miss Lyndhurst?"

Rayna did not hear the ambassador. She was occupied in staring at a tall young man who was standing on the opposite side of the salon. He was dressed elegantly in black velvet evening clothes, with frothy white lace at his throat and wrists. His eyes were a startling blue, and he sported a full black beard on his lean face, as dark as she was fair. A man shouldn't be that beautiful, she thought, shaking her head at herself. Maybe she was wrong about his eyes; after all, he was some distance away. Maybe he had bad teeth. She remembered her father telling her "foreigners have nothing worth hearing to say and their manners have no dignity," or some such thing. In this man's case, she doubted her father's pronouncement.

"Rayna, my love. Are you all right?"

Rayna blinked. "Yes, Mother?"

"Sir Hugh is speaking to you, my dear."

"Oh! Yes, Sir Hugh, I agree with you fully," she said, gazing up at him with wide hazel eyes.

"Excellent!" He laughed and tossed a smile to Arabella, as if sharing a secret. He led the ladies through the salon, seemingly indefatigable in his introductions. And he appeared to know everyone. Arabella was beginning to think her face would freeze into a permanent smile before they were through. She met Adam's eyes as they approached and winked at him. A brief frown crossed his forehead.

"*Monsieur* le comte," Sir Hugh said. "Allow me to present Lady Delford, her charming daughter,

Rayna, and Lady Arabella Welles. Ladies, the Comte de la Valle."

Rayna murmured something, unaware that the comte was regarding her closely. She barely noticed him.

"You will have to introduce your friend, *monsieur* le comte," Sir Hugh said.

Gervaise bowed. "Ladies, my friend the Marchese Pietro di Galvani, newly arrived from Sicily."

He has lovely teeth, Rayna thought, extending her hand to the marchese. Adam smiled down at Rayna Lyndhurst, carefully avoiding Arabella's eyes, and brought her slender white hand to his lips. He gently turned her hand over and lightly kissed her palm.

Rayna knew the marchese was taking liberties, but still she felt her pulse quicken at the gentle touch of his lips. She did not snatch her hand away as she most assuredly would have if any other gentleman had been so outrageous.

"*Signore,*" she said, raising her eyes to his face. She blinked, thinking for an instant that he looked somehow familiar. But that was surely impossible. She had never been in Italy before, and he was a Sicilian nobleman. For a long moment he held her gaze and she noticed that his eyes were an even more vivid blue than she had first thought.

Adam released her hand and looked into his sister's face. He saw a silent warning in her eyes, and a measure of amusement. And something else, he thought. Smugness. That was it. The chit looked smug!

"*Signorina*," he said politely, bowing to her and then to Lady Delford.

"Do you speak Italian, *signorina*?" Adam asked lightly, turning back to Rayna.

"A little," she said. Indeed, she thought, she would pay more attention now to Arabella's lessons.

"French?"

"*Oui, monsieur, je parle français.*"

"Her French is far more fluent than mine," Arabella said, sounding mournful. "Indeed," she added with a covert glance at her brother, "now that you have discovered a common language, why do you not dance?"

Adam cast her a wry smile, but quickly turned back to Rayna. "An excellent idea, *mademoiselle*. Your permission, my lady?" he directed toward Lady Delford.

Lady Delford was in a quandary. Her husband had assured her they would not see much of Adam Welles, yet here he was, looking for all the world like a bearded buccaneer, asking her permission to dance with her daughter. There was no reason she could think of to refuse him, and she nodded, albeit unwillingly. She saw her daughter smiling up at him, her eyes sparkling outrageously. She was not blind to Adam Welles's attraction—what woman could be? And it was but one dance. "Enjoy yourself, my love," she said to her daughter.

"If it pleases you, my lady," the Comte de la Valle said, staring for a moment after the marchese and Rayna, "I also would like to dance with your lovely daughter, after the marchese."

"Certainly, *monsieur*," Lady Delford said.

"I will wait with impatience, my lady," the comte said, his eyes on Rayna's retreating back.

"So you are left high and dry," Sir Hugh said to Arabella.

"I am quite sunk!" Arabella said dolefully. "I ask you, ma'am," she continued to Lady Delford, "is it fair that Rayna receives all the masculine attention? Perhaps I am fated for a convent."

"You are not a Catholic," Lady Delford said, obviously distracted by the sight of Adam and Rayna together.

"No," Arabella agreed. Things, she thought, fluttering her lashes so her thoughts wouldn't be clear on her face, were going quite well. Yes, all in all, very well. Adam and Rayna seemed quite taken with one another, as she had thought they would be.

"It is a pity," Adam said to Rayna as he took his place opposite her in the dance.

"What is, *signore*?"

"The dance leaves little time for conversation."

They were immediately separated to perform their steps with the others.

"I have never before been to Italy," Rayna said, pleased that she had managed to think of a sensible comment before they stepped back together. They touched hands lightly, Adam bowing and Rayna curtsying. Rayna's attraction for him was not lost to Adam, but what he did not understand was why he had asked her to dance. He saw her flush deeply, and cocked his head to one side in silent question.

"Have you ever been in England?" Rayna pursued valiantly, wishing she could fan her burning cheeks.

"I? Why do you ask, *signorina*? What reason would I have to travel to that cold, distant country?"

"It is not that cold, *signore!*"

"And the English," he said, a wicked light in his eyes. "I have heard it said they are as cold and aloof as their wretched weather."

Rayna could feel the color surging again to her cheeks and cursed herself. She blushed too easily. It was embarrassing, like the sprinkling of freckles that dotted her nose during the summer.

"I . . . we are not cold, *signore!*"

They were separated again, and by the time he was close to her, Adam was wondering why he was drawing the little chit. He repressed any more teasing comments, and said only, "That will doubtless please your husband, *signorina*."

"I do not have a husband."

"A lady as beautiful as you will not long last without one, I think, *signorina*."

"You speak very smoothly, *signore*," Rayna said somewhat stiffly. She thought he was indeed an accomplished gallant, who was flirting with her simply because it was his habit to do so.

"Yes, I suppose that I do," Adam said.

"I wish you would not. I do not like gentlemen to say pretty things. It is not honest."

"Just because I spoke smoothly," Adam said,

studying her upturned face, "does not mean I am not honest. It simply means that I am intelligent enough to be able to admire a beautiful woman . . . suitably."

"I am but half English," Rayna said on a sudden inspiration.

She has no guile, he thought. It both intrigued and worried him. "Ah, a skeleton in your sire's closet?"

"Oh no," she assured him earnestly. "My mother is an American. They met in New York when my father was a major in the English army during the war with the colonies. I am the youngest of six children, and the only female."

Adam managed to look appropriately surprised. "Then I must be careful not to offend you, *mademoiselle*. Five brothers! I am blessed with but one sister to protect me."

"They are overbearing at times," Rayna said. "They teased me unmercifully when I was a child."

"It must be the fate of younger sisters," Adam said. "I too am a mixed breed."

"You are from Sicily, *monsieur?*"

Adam found he did not wish to lie outright to her, and said easily, "You are wondering perhaps about my blue eyes?"

"They are rather startling," Rayna said with thoughtless honesty. "I was waiting to get closer to you to see if they were truly such a deep blue."

Adam stared down at her for a long moment. He realized with a start that the music had stopped.

"I thank you for the dance, *mademoiselle*. Perhaps you will dance with me again this evening?"

"Yes, *monsieur*, I should like that."

"You dance as sweetly as you blush," Adam said, immediately wishing he had kept quiet.

Rayna's hands flew to her cheeks. "I cannot help it! It has nothing to do with you, *monsieur!*"

"A pity," Adam said, grinning. He knew that flirting with Rayna Lyndhurst was the height of folly. But she was so damned refreshing, and so unlike the flippantly sophisticated ladies of his acquaintance. "I will take you back to your fond parent," he said, offering his arm. He felt her fingers tighten about his sleeve, and cocked a thick black brow at her.

"You will not forget our next dance, will you?"

He started at her wistful tone. He was not particularly pleased to see the Comte de la Valle striding confidently toward them, ready to take Rayna back to the dance floor.

He said in an even voice, "No, I shan't forget. Your friend . . . Lady Arabella is her name?" At her nod, he continued, "I should like to dance with her."

She had bored him with her silly conversation. She knew the laughing, teasing Arabella would never bore anyone, this gentleman included. "Arabella is a most graceful dancer," she said only.

"If she is as graceful as you, *mademoiselle*, then my evening . . . well, it will not have been a futile exercise in smiling."

"Oh, I felt the same way! It is so difficult to think of amusing things to say to perfect strangers!"

"Yes, and all of them foreigners."

The Comte de la Valle was standing impatiently beside them. "Gervaise," Adam said shortly to him. He bowed and strode away toward Arabella, who was standing alone, fanning herself.

"Why don't we get something cool to drink?" Adam said to his sister, and without waiting for an answer, caught her arm and bore her away.

Rayna watched the marchese and Arabella walk to the far end of the salon, where refreshments were laid out on long tables. She felt something like what she thought was jealousy, and was surprised at herself. She had just met the man, and he was, after all, a foreigner, as he himself had laughingly pointed out. She noticed that her dancing partner was watching her closely.

"I have not stepped on your foot, *signorina*," the comte said gaily.

"No," she said shortly. "I suppose that I am not used to the heat."

"Heat?" Gervaise raised his brows.

Rayna realized that the vast room was really quite cool and quickly retrenched. "I meant cold."

"Ah, I see," he said pleasantly enough. So the little chit is taken with the marchese, he thought. He would quickly change that.

"We mustn't spend too much time together, Bella," Adam was saying to his sister.

"Better with me than with Rayna," Arabella

mocked him gently. "Lady Delford had a mild fit while you two were dancing."

Adam was on the point of telling her that she had started it, but refrained. After all, he had most willingly asked Rayna for a second dance.

Arabella sipped at the sweet wine punch and said in her blandest voice, "I think you've made an impression on Rayna."

"She has changed," he said easily.

Arabella laughed and touched her hand familiarly to his arm. "Ah, brother, can it be that you are equally taken?"

"With a child fresh from the schoolroom?" Adam asked. "Really, Bella, strive for a little sense. Now, tell me what you have been doing."

Arabella frowned an instant at his daunting words, but answered readily enough, "Well, we moved into a charming villa last Wednesday. It is on the outskirts of the city, set upon a hill overlooking the bay. Sometimes I can almost imagine that I am home in Genoa, with the smell of the water and all the flowers." She saw that Adam's eyes had strayed from her face to the dance floor, and added wickedly, "Soon you won't have to speak French with Rayna. She is quite fast with languages, and will be fluent in Italian in no time at all, much to her father's disapproval, I might add."

"I am relieved she didn't recognize me. Lady Delford, as you said, was rather put out. You shouldn't have engineered the dance between us." He negligently flicked a puff of lint from his sleeve and added blandly, "Her father will not like it when he finds out she danced with me twice."

"Twice?" Arabella asked. "Methinks, brother, that you tempt fate!" But she was smiling at him delightedly.

" 'Tis but a dance, Bella," he said sharply. "But I also told Rayna I would dance with you. Come along."

"No," Arabella said firmly. "You are only my brother, and I don't have to suffer through a dance with you. You see, I am wearing Rayna's slippers, and alas, they are dreadfully small! But tell me what you have learned. Has the Comte de la Valle anything to do with what father told us about?"

"God, yes," Adam said. "I am in his good graces now, having saved him and one of his friends late one night from three vicious brigands. Daniele's men, of course. No one was hurt, thank God. Keep Rayna away from him, Bella. And don't you tread near him either."

"Yes, my lord," she said demurely, giving him a mocking curtsy. Big brothers, she thought, couldn't seem to help themselves when it came to giving orders to their little sisters.

Adam frowned down his nose at her and said, "As to learning anything, no, not yet. The comte has let slip that he has a mistress, an older woman who is in the court circle—near to the king, I might add. His friend Celestino let drop that the *old hag* is making Gervaise richer than he has a right to be."

"Rich with our cargoes?"

"Possibly. As for this society he has organized, I haven't yet been asked to join. But I think I've met most of the other members at Gervaise's lodgings. They are, for the most part, young noblemen bored and primed to be wicked. Gervaise is undoubtedly their guiding light."

"Well, I shall have very attentive ears and eyes. If the woman is here in the court, I am bound to meet her."

"You will take care, Bella." He nudged his knuckle against her jaw.

"You know I will, bully!"

Rayna forced a wide smile to her lips. "It is all so exciting!" she said in an overly bright voice to the comte.

"Indeed," the comte agreed dryly.

Rayna was thankful the music came to a stop. She dipped a curtsy to the comte. "I must return to my mother, sir. I see her waving to me."

Gervaise bowed and proffered her his arm. "How long will your illustrious father stay in Naples, *mademoiselle*?"

Was there a tinge of sarcasm in his voice? "I am not in my father's confidence. I suppose that much depends upon what happens in the king's negotiations with the French."

"I shouldn't like you to be in Naples when or if the Treaty of Amiens is renounced. I have heard it said that Napoleon is displeased with Acton. The pot is nearing the boiling point again, I'm afraid."

"I sincerely hope it will not boil over, *monsieur*.

I pity any country that is conquered by another, and its people enslaved."

The comte arched a fair brow. "There are many in Naples, *mademoiselle*, who view Napoleon as a liberator, many who would throw the city open to him."

"I fear they are deluded. Napoleon has looted every country he has taken, and tried to destroy the traditions that bound their people together."

"And some say these people have never known greater freedom since his arrival, and less corruption."

"For an ardent royalist, *monsieur*, you seem rather open-minded."

Gervaise smiled down at her serious young face. "I have lived more years than you, *mademoiselle*. Perhaps I have become a cynic."

"I thank you for the dance, *monsieur*."

Before he could ask her for another, Rayna curtsied to him and turned to her mother.

"*A bientôt, mademoiselle*," he said softly.

7

Sardinia

Old Antonio Genovesi scratched his wiry gray beard as he pondered the slow progress of the man on the beach below him, the man he had pulled from the churning waters of the Tyrrhenian Sea some six months before. He was not a young man, but his features, gaunt from months of fever and pain, made him appear older than his years. That he had survived the stab wounds and hours spent in the storm-tossed water clutching a piece of driftwood testified to an extraordinary strength. As his wife, Ria, had said as she nursed him, "This one will not let the devil have him, not before his time!"

Ria had hardly left his side for months, hovering about him as if he were her son. Not that Antonio minded. Ria's grief over the son they had lost to the sea years before had aged her too. She called him Dono, for to her he was a gift from the sea. There was a fierce light in her rheumy eyes now, and they held purpose again. During the months of fever, he had raved of odd and strange things, and places so bizarre that Ria and Antonio could only gape at him. "He is no common sailor, our Dono," Ria had whispered to him.

He watched Dono turn slowly back up the beach toward their thatched hut. He raised his head, and even from the distance brilliant black eyes met Antonio's gaze. Dono raised his crutch and waved it toward him. "Who are you?" Antonio whispered. He waved back and made his way down the crooked path to the beach.

Hamil had just seen his reflection clearly for the first time in six months in a limpid sea pool. A wide strip of shock white hair flowed from his temple through his black hair, as if painted there. His full beard was threaded with white, and there were lines etched about his eyes. He had stared at a stranger.

His once powerful body still trembled from weakness whenever he walked the length of the rocky beach. It was his fury that kept him doggedly exercising, fury at his betrayal that had kept him clinging to that piece of wood when other men would have let go. He still asked himself: Who had paid Ramid to betray him?

Hamil smiled to himself as he watched the old man carefully tread down the path toward him. Antonio would say nothing, but would walk beside him, ready to shoulder his weight should he falter. Soon, he thought, he would not need the crutch; soon his strength would return.

He waited for the old man to reach him, leaning

heavily on the crutch Antonio had carved for him several months before.

"Dono!" Antonio said in his soft, scratchy voice. "I watched you. You walked the whole length of the beach without halting. Soon, my son, you will be as you once were."

My son. Hamil smiled at the grizzled old man who barely reached his chin.

Antonio saw a grimace of pain through Dono's smile and pulled the younger man's arm over his shoulder. "Ria will have our lunch ready," Antonio chattered, wanting to spare Dono the embarrassment of leaning on him, an old man. "Fish stew today, but it's tasty, as you know, Dono."

"I know," Hamil said, allowing Antonio to support some of his weight.

As they neared the hut, Hamil said abruptly, "I wish to fish with you, Antonio. I have done nothing save take from you. I must repay you if I can for your kindness."

"Yes, you will fish with me, perhaps next week," Antonio agreed. "But you are not a fisherman. I would not wish to fish you out of the sea again."

"No," Hamil said. "I am not a fisherman, but I am a good sailor. I will learn."

Ria appeared in the doorway of the small hut, waving her faded apron at them. "Dono! Look at you, boy! You have had enough exercise for this day . . . leaning on that old man. You walked too far! Come, you must rest now and eat. It's a thick stew I've got for you today. Potatoes from that old witch who lives beyond the hill."

Hamil, used to Ria's scolding chatter, allowed her to lead him into the one large room and settle him on a chair beside the rough-hewn table. In truth, he was exhausted. He attacked the stew as if his life depended on it.

He laid down his spoon beside his empty wooden bowl and leaned back in his chair. Unbidden, the image of Lella rose in his mind. Had she been killed as he was to be, six months ago?

For the first time in his life, Hamil bowed his head and let pain-filled sobs break from his throat. He felt burning tears streak down his cheeks. He felt Ria's arms close about his shoulders, and without thought, he buried his head against her scrawny bosom.

"Dono, my son," he heard her whisper softly to him as her fingers stroked through his thick hair, "it is all right. No one else will hurt you again."

"Lella," he whispered.

"Your sweetheart, Dono?"

"My wife. Perhaps she is dead now, even as I was meant to be."

Ria's eyes met her husband's over Hamil's bowed head. Gently, her fingers still stroking his hair, she asked, "Who are you, Dono?"

Hamil stilled. He felt a great shame at his weakness. A man did not weep like a woman, not even a skeleton of a man. He raised his head and looked into the wrinkled face he had come to know well.

"Ria," he said sadly, "I have shamed myself."

"Men," Ria grunted. "Do not be a fool."

Hamil had never before been called a fool by a woman; indeed, only his father had dared. Yet he wasn't angered; rather, he felt strangely comforted.

"My name," he said slowly, looking from Antonio to Ria, "is Hamil." At their blank looks, he gave a mocking laugh. "Until six months ago, I was the Bey of Oran."

Ria sucked in her breath and gazed at him, appalled. "A pirate? You're one of those men who raid ships and make slaves of people?"

"I rule them. Rather, I ruled them. I am now supposedly dead."

Antonio stared at him as if he were a creature with three heads. "You are a . . . king?"

"Something like that. The Bey of Oran rules at the whim of the Dey of Algiers, who, in turn, owes his allegiance to the Grand Turk in Constantinople."

"You're a heathen," Ria said.

"No, but I am a Muslim." He saw Ria mouth the foreign word. He asked softly, "Do you want me to leave? I must go soon in any case, to Cagliari. I have friends there, powerful men who will help me regain what is mine."

"No!" Ria said, tightening her arms about his shoulders. "I don't care if you are one of . . . them. I'll not let you go until you are well. We will speak of this again. Eat the stew, Dono."

"Antonio?" Hamil inquired.

"Eat the stew, boy."

8

Naples

Edward Lyndhurst greeted his daughter pleasantly when she stepped into the sitting room with her mother. "This wretched climate appears to agree with you, puss," he said. "You are looking quite lovely."

"Thank you, Papa," Rayna said, eyeing him a bit askance. It was not yet teatime, and she had not lived with her father for eighteen years without learning to recognize the gleam of purpose in his eyes.

"Sit down, my dear," Edward Lyndhurst said. "Your mother and I wish to speak with you."

Rayna obligingly sat on a blue brocade wing chair, smoothed her narrow skirt, and smiled up at her father. "I have always enjoyed speaking with both of you, sir."

"Yes, well . . ." her father began. He paused a moment, fiddling with his watch fob. "You have always been a good-hearted girl, Rayna, and a pleasure to your mother and me."

Oh dear, Rayna thought, sitting up straighter. Her father's tone, though gentle as it always was toward her, was becoming weighted. "I trust so, Father," she said.

"We are not in England, my dear."

"Indeed, Papa. I have freckles on my nose, and it is still spring. That would never happen in the fog of London."

Edward Lyndhurst's smile was perfunctory at best. Rayna watched him glance toward her mother, then back at her. "What I mean, puss," he continued stiffly, "is that we are in a foreign land surrounded by people we are not used to. Their ways are different and their customs are much . . . looser."

"Good heavens, Papa," Rayna said. "Of course we are not used to them. But I am trying to learn a bit of Italian, and I am finding that they are not so very different. And as for their being loose, Maria, our housekeeper, told me but last week that if I were an Italian young lady, I would have just come from the convent!"

"That, my dear," Jennifer Lyndhurst said sharply, "is not quite what your father meant."

"Indeed," Edward Lyndhurst said. "You have always been protected, Rayna. You know nothing of gentlemen who are not really . . . well, gentlemen. We are concerned for you. In the future, my dear, when we attend balls or court functions, I would prefer that you not fraternize overly with the gentlemen."

Rayna's usually sweet expression darkened and

she shot her mother such a reproachful look that Lady Delford's eyes widened.

"Fraternize, Papa?" she asked candidly, turning her eyes full on her father. "Do you mean that I am so naive and lacking in judgment that I should cling to your coat or to Mother's skirt? Or would you prefer that I pass what is left of my time in Naples in a convent?"

Lord Edward stared at Rayna in surprise. "I beg your pardon, miss?" he asked calmly, in the tone he used for his sons.

"I asked you, Papa," Rayna continued, undaunted, "if you would prefer a convent." Rayna was aware that her heart was thumping in her breast, but for the first time in her life, she thought her father's pronouncements sounded positively gothic!

"Perhaps I should have been more specific, Rayna," Lord Edward said coldly. "I should have said that I will not have you *flirting* with any of the young men you will meet here."

Rayna could scarce believe her ears. Her mother had betrayed her to her father, all because she had given two dances to the marchese! She looked down at her lemon kid slippers and said mildly, "You have nothing to worry about, Papa, for the young man in question did not find me particularly to his liking."

"And who might that be, pray tell?" the viscount demanded, knowing full well whom she meant. It galled him to ask, but he wanted to hear from his own daughter's mouth that Adam Welles had found her wanting. Damned young puppy!

From what his wife had told him, he was just like his father.

"The Marchese di Galvani," Rayna said softly.

"And just what about the man attracted you, if your *father* may be so bold as to ask?"

Rayna looked directly into her father's face. "He is the most beautiful man I have ever seen."

"That says little for his character," Edward growled.

"And the kindest."

Lady Delford stepped into the breach, seeing that her husband was about to stray woefully from the point. "Rayna, my love, a man is not beautiful. That is a very odd thing to say about a man."

"The marchese is," Rayna said firmly. "He is from Sicily. Perhaps that is why he has such incredible blue eyes."

Edward Lyndhurst knew exactly where Adam Welles had gotten his blue eyes. He selected his sternest voice. He'd be damned if he would let her throw herself at Adam Welles! "You will perhaps see the . . . marchese at court, but that is the only place, miss."

"Perhaps you are right, Papa," Rayna said. "Although he was quite polite to me, he also seemed to enjoy Arabella's company." She cocked her head to one side. "I do not understand. He is, after all, a marquess, of noble blood—"

"Bah! Every Italian carries a title. He could easily be a goatherd's son!"

"He does not smell at all of goats."

"You would not have spoken so smartly to me

before Lady Arabella Welles came to us," the viscount said. "Arabella is a beautiful young woman, but I find her manners too bright, too open. If this marchese prefers her, it is just as well." He firmly repressed a twinge of guilt at the false impression he was creating.

"Perhaps," Rayna said, regarding her father straightly, "when my Italian is more fluent, I can be as witty and beguiling as Bella. And, Papa, whatever you may think, the marchese is an honorable gentleman. He would never take advantage of me."

He already has, her father thought angrily. "I have told you my wishes, Rayna. That will be an end to it. Now, if you will both excuse me, I must meet with Acton and Sir Hugh. I will see you at dinner."

It seemed to Rayna as if her father were escaping. It both surprised her and amused her. She supposed he had grown used to her being as pliant as a puppet. He usually had merely to gently tell her what he wished, and she applied herself to please him.

"My dear," she heard her mother say, "I pray you to attend your father. We both want what is best for you. The . . . marchese appears a very worldly man."

"Yes, Mother, I am quite certain that he is." She rose suddenly and walked to the door.

"Worldly men know how to impress young girls," Lady Delford called somewhat desperately after her daughter.

"I may be innocent, Mother," Rayna said, her hand on the bronze doorknob, "but I am perfectly aware of what goes on around me."

How could her mother have told her father! Had she been so obvious about her attraction to the marchese? A small secret smile appeared as she climbed the stairs to Arabella's bedchamber. During their second dance, he had teased her unmercifully. She would have thought he was showing a sisterly affection for her had she not glanced up at him in an unguarded moment. What she had seen in his eyes had nothing to do with brotherly feeling. She frowned on the heels of that thought. He had spent a great deal of time with Arabella. Well, not a great deal, perhaps, but nearly as much as he had spent with her. When she gained the bedchamber, she found Arabella pacing to and fro.

"Well?" Arabella demanded the moment Rayna had closed the door. "Whatever did your father want? I don't expect he was angry because you ripped a flounce on your gown."

Rayna sighed. "Perhaps I am a most undutiful daughter," she began, only to glance up angrily at Arabella's gay laugh.

"You needn't make fun of me, Bella!"

"Oh, you silly goose! I'm not making sport. 'Tis just that you are the most dutiful daughter I have ever known. Come, what happened?"

"Well, you would not believe it, Bella, but all that fuss was over my two dances with the marchese! Papa ordered me not to *fraternize* with the young gentlemen, particularly the marchese. Indeed, he accused me of flirting with the marchese, and, well, I couldn't let that pass, could I, Bella?"

"Of course not," Arabella agreed stoutly. "You are eighteen now, Rayna, and no longer a child." And I do believe, she thought, that Adam will shortly be drawn to every undutiful bone in your body.

Rayna fell into a brooding silence, then blurted out, "I also told Papa that he didn't have to worry. The marchese is more likely interested in you than in me."

"Ah," Arabella said, turning her face away so Rayna would not see her amusement. "Appearances," she continued, her back still to Rayna, "are sometimes deceiving. I beg you not to be cast down, love. We will see what happens. Perhaps you will see the . . . marchese again at the queen's reception for Lady Eden on Friday." Indeed they would see each other, she thought. She had made certain that Adam would be attending the reception. She turned to face her friend. "I am glad you defended the marchese to your parents. He seems a most handsome and nice man."

"It seems that the queen is always receiving somebody," Rayna said, disregarding Bella's blatant opening. Her feelings for the marchese were too new and too fragile to discuss, even with her best friend. And, she thought, sighing, she wasn't certain that the marchese didn't prefer Arabella to her.

"Well, I for one am delighted. I want to meet

everyone! Now, Rayna, it is time for your Italian lesson."

"Very well," Rayna snapped, "though I sometimes wonder why I bother!"

A quarter-moon lit the night sky, its light reflected from the wispy fingers of chill fog that stretched along the narrow streets. Adam flung off his black cloak as he entered his lodgings. He strode into his small sitting room and nodded silently to Daniele Barbaro, who stood near the fireplace, stretching his hands out over the flame.

"I expected you sooner. Here, drink this." Daniele stepped forward and handed Adam a snifter of brandy. " 'Twill seep the cold out of your bones."

Adam tossed down the brandy and stared blankly into the empty goblet.

"What happened?" Daniele asked. "You saw the comte and the club members? 'Tis the narrow house set in the cul-de-sac at the end of the Via Rozza?"

"Aye. I thought I had seen almost everything, Daniele," he said at last. "But I was wrong. Don't mistake me, they are not really satanists, but their notion of amusement is disgusting."

Daniele moved back to the fireplace and waited for Adam to continue.

"Their house, so nondescript from the street, has been furnished like a medieval hall, complete with a trestle table and high-backed chairs. There were eight of them, all charming noblemen one meets at court. Very bored, I fancy, to be drawn into Gervaise's influence. In any case, I watched through a narrow window while Gervaise showed them some sort of map. I couldn't hear what he said, more's the pity! There seemed to be a lot of discussion and a lot of drinking. When Gervaise left the room, I thought it was the end of their evening."

Adam rose and poured himself some more brandy. "It was but the signal for their amusement to begin. Gervaise came back into the room with a young girl, a peasant girl, I would imagine, quite pretty and likely very poor. They didn't rape her. No, I fancy that she and her parents sold her virginity to the group of them. After the fifth man was through with her, I do not imagine she relished her bargain."

"Jesus," Daniele said.

"Do you know they drew numbers to determine the order?" He shook his head. "That's how I know she was a virgin—that, and the look in her eyes when the first man finished with her."

"We must return, my lord."

"Aye, we must, Daniele, later, after they have all left. The house is three stories and only the bottom story was lit. Perhaps the upper floors hold our cargoes." He fell silent, his long fingers tightening about his empty glass. "When I become a member of Les Diables Blancs, I do not know what I will do. Taking young girls seems to be their distraction after they've discussed their treason against the king and queen."

"All of us do what we must," Daniele said.

Adam raked his hand through his hair and began pacing. "They are not evil men, save perhaps for the Comte de la Valle. Once he is stopped, I imagine they will disband and search elsewhere for their amusements."

"I and my men will help you, my lord, when the time is right."

"Aye, Daniele. I think that time is not too far distant."

The Contessa Giovanna Giusti, known in Naples as the Contessa Luciana di Rolando, felt the king's hooded eyes upon her, and forced a smile to her lips. Old fool, she thought as she smiled at him. But she was used to rutting old goats, and she knew how to treat them. This evening it was particularly easy because her blood was coursing through her veins in anticipation.

The proud Earl of Clare's daughter was in Naples and she would see her again tonight. She had never dreamed of such a plum falling so easily into her lap. She had sought no introduction to her during her first night at court, content to watch her. The girl was the picture of her mother, though her eyes were her father's, clear, intelligent, and black as night. She had watched the girl's easy, confident manner with gentlemen and ladies alike. The girl had grown to womanhood, doubtless beloved of her parents, while Giovanna had languished in Algiers, a black veil over her face. Tonight, she thought, forcing herself not to draw away when the king's age-spotted hand covered hers, she would meet Lady Arabella Welles. She didn't know why the girl was in Naples. Surely her proud father would not have sent her, a mere woman, to find out who had stolen his ships' cargoes. She smiled. The earl would come, sooner or later, to join her.

Giovanna became aware of the queen's eyes upon her. When she met her gaze, the queen smiled, then turned to speak in a low voice to her daughter Amélie. Amélie laughed and said something back to her mother behind her gloved hand. Let them gossip about her, the cold bitches!

When the king's attention turned to Sir Hugh Elliot, the English ambassador, Giovanna gracefully moved away, and smoothed down the wrinkles in her green taffeta gown. She knew she still looked attractive, despite her fifty years, and her figure, at least through her gown, appeared slender and firm.

"*Madame*, you look radiant this evening." Her young lover, Gervaise, Comte de la Valle, was standing in front of her. Was there amusement in his voice? she wondered.

"Thank you," she said, her eyes narrowed on his handsome face. There were tiny lines about his eyes. He was young, but the life he led would age him prematurely, if he lived that long. The thought pleased her. He thought he was using her, an older woman, grateful for a young man's lovemaking. He was a fool, like most men, and it would be too late for him when he at last realized she was using him instead.

"I am hungry for you, *madame*," the comte said, his voice softly hoarse, the way he knew women liked it.

"There will be a banquet in but an hour," Giovanna said in a tart voice, "and I am not one of the courses!"

"Ah, you are being cruel."

"You must know, comte, that it is unwise for me to speak to you here at court. Come to my villa tomorrow night, and I will provide you with food and talk."

Gervaise's smile did not fade. She was older than any lover he had had, but at least she didn't repel him, and the rewards he reaped were making him rich.

"As you wish, *madame*."

Giovanna watched him step through the inevitable crowd. He stopped near the daughter of Viscount Delford, the Englishman here in Naples as an adviser to Sir Hugh Elliot. He seemed to be waiting for someone, she thought, somewhat amused. Had the little red-haired chit appealed to him? Her gaze shifted to Lady Arabella Welles, who was talking to Lady Eden. The girl seemed to draw people to her side, with her warmth and her tinkling laughter. I was once like her, Giovanna thought.

"You should not wear white, *ma mie*."

Rayna's obliging social smile became radiant at

the sound of the marchese's voice. "*Monsieur!* I had hoped you would be here!" She looked into his twinkling eyes and grinned charmingly. "As for the color I am wearing, marchese, I believe my white and your black announce our respective characters."

"An angel and a devil? You wound me, *mademoiselle*."

"But why, *monsieur?*" Rayna asked with mock seriousness. "As a devil, you would be most exciting and wicked, whereas as an angel I would most assuredly be insipid and boring. It is you who wound me."

A black brow winged upward. "You are no angel, Rayna, but a minx."

Rayna was pleased that he used her name. He said it as the English did, and she wondered at it for a moment. "Are you wicked, marchese? A rake, perhaps?"

"No," Adam said rather curtly. At her questioning look, he added on a lazy smile, "My dress and my black beard are misleading. I am the mildest of men, *mademoiselle*, I assure you."

"That is what I told my parents," Rayna said, pursing her lips.

"What?"

Rayna flushed slightly. "Well, you see, my parents believe that you are a very worldly man, far too sophisticated for me."

"So you informed your fond parents that I, far from being a rake, am a gentle soul?"

Rayna gazed raptly at the gold buttons on his

waistcoat. "Not precisely," she said. "I told them I think you are kind."

Adam stared at her for a long moment. "In England, young girls go to London for a Season, do they not?"

Rayna nodded. "Yes, and it's very silly, I think. They go to balls and routs and all sorts of things, just to find a husband. Fortunately, I came to Naples instead."

"Then you have not met many gentlemen," he said gently, thinking of all the debutantes he had observed over the years in London. He had found several of them interesting enough, he supposed, but none like the glowing girl standing in front of him. "You have been . . . protected."

"I have never understood," Rayna said thoughtfully, "why girls are so hemmed in, whereas gentlemen are so very free. No one cares if they are not chaparoned. I am thinking, of course, of my brothers."

"A man wants a wife who has been properly chaperoned," Adam said, "and thus kept pure."

"Well," Rayna said sharply, "a girl wants a husband who is equally pure!"

Adam broke into rich laughter. "I fear if that were the case, there would be no more marriages!"

"I think," Rayna said, "that you are every bit as gothic as my father."

"Perhaps, *ma mie*, you have been influenced by your friend Lady Arabella."

"That is what my father said, but I assure you it is not true. Bella may be half-Italian, but after all,

I am half-American. That, surely, is more adventurous. I can tell you quite as many tales about New York as she can about Genoa."

Adam gazed down at her, silent for a moment. She is enchanting me, he thought. "So you can tell me all about red Indians," he said, not really attending his words.

"Bloodcurdling stories," she said. "Of course," she added on a sigh, "all the Indians I have seen were quite kind, actually. But it was not always so, particularly when my father was a young man during the revolution."

"I thought all good Englishmen called it a mere uprising."

"Perhaps," Rayna said tartly, "but look at the result! My mother and her father were Tories, but even she believes England was most unfair in her treatment of the colonies."

"I believe, Rayna, that your father has noticed our conversation. He has the look of a thundercloud."

"I know," she sighed. "Sometimes I feel like the colonists must have felt. I wish I were free to do as I please, without my parents suffocating me with restrictions."

"Perhaps," Adam said very softly, "you will not always want to be free."

"Would I not be free as a wife?"

"Not all of you," Adam said, fascinated, as he watched her pink tongue glide unconsciously over her lower lip.

"Then neither would my husband."

"Men," Adam said, wondering how the devil he had gotten himself into this discussion, "are different."

"Do they not want a family, a lady they can love?"

Adam flung up his hands. "Enough, *mademoiselle!* I am undone. Will you dance with me later, Rayna?"

"Perhaps I will, marchese." She lightly touched her fingers to his black sleeve as he turned away from her. "I find you most persuasive."

Rayna's smile was still hovering when the Comte de la Valle blocked her view of Adam's retreating back. "Good evening, *mademoiselle*," Gervaise said smoothly, bowing over her hand. "I hope you do not mind my saying that you look exquisite this evening, like a spring rose ready to unfurl its petals to the sun."

Rayna's smile faded. "Good evening, comte," she said, choosing to ignore this flowery compliment. Arabella had mentioned to her that the comte might not be the honorable young man he appeared to be, and Rayna agreed with her. There was something about him, something elusive, that struck her as false.

"Your gown is lovely," The comte persisted, despite her unenthusiastic greeting. "The green silk matches your eyes, and your beautiful hair is like spun flame."

"*Spun flame?*" Rayna eyed him in amusement, and said lightly, "What a dreadful thought!"

Gervaise grinned through the flash of anger he felt at her. "Give me but the time, *mademoiselle,* and I will find the words to suit you. Would you allow me to bring you a glass of punch?"

Anything to get rid of him, Rayna thought, and quickly nodded. "Thank you, *monsieur*."

Where was the marchese? she wondered, searching the faces in the huge salon. She felt her mother's watchful eyes on her, and turned to smile at her. It was then she saw him, speaking with Arabella, not six feet away from her.

Lady Delford followed her daughter's gaze, and felt her heart plummet to her toes. She had watched her daughter speaking to Adam Welles, and it had looked innocent enough. Now the look of naked longing in Rayna's eyes smote her. It was the look of a woman, not a girl, a woman who could no more help what she was doing than breathe. She knew well why her husband disliked Adam Welles, indeed all the Welles family. She had told him of her concern only because she had believed that Adam Welles was trifling with her daughter, perhaps just to provoke her husband, something Adam's father would have smoothly done. Now she was not so certain. She suddenly felt old, and angry with her husband. He was stiff-necked and overly protective of his daughter. She wished now they had never come to Naples, never agreed to the Earl of Clare's deception. But it probably would not have mattered. Rayna would have met Adam in England, and the result would likely have been the same.

"Have you discovered anything?" Arabella was saying in a low voice to her brother. She laughed before he could reply. "It seems that is the only thing I ever have to say to you!"

"True," Adam said. "Actually, I have discovered what is left of our cargoes. Obviously the comte has been selling the goods, likely to the French for a sizable profit." He paused a moment, his eyes going toward Rayna, for he saw the comte approaching her. "I cannot yet face Gervaise down until we find out who is providing him with the goods."

"Well, I haven't been much help," Arabella said with obvious disappointment. "Perhaps," she continued, her eyes following Adam's toward Rayna, "I should flirt with the comte—that is, if I can draw his attention away from Rayna."

"He is as I suspected, Bella. You will stay away from him."

Arabella arched a fair brow at his vehemence.

Adam sighed. "His amusements, when he is not spying for the French, are rather despicable."

"How would you know? You are not a member of his club yet."

"I followed the comte a couple of evenings ago to their meeting place. I will thank you to accept my word in the matter."

"You are no fun at all, Adam!"

"Perhaps, but that is all you will hear from me, little sister." His gaze wandered back to Rayna, who was now in conversation with Gervaise, a glass of punch in her hand. Arabella saw a look of black fury cross his face. "As for Rayna, it appears I will have to speak to her personally. I thought you told her to stay away from him."

"Rayna doesn't care for him at all, Adam," Arabella said reasonably. "It is difficult for her to cut him at a function such as this."

"Nonetheless . . ." Adam said fiercely.

"It is you, marchese," she said dryly, though her dark eyes twinkled, "that Rayna's father objects, to, particularly after Rayna told him she thinks you something of a paragon."

A fleeting smile touched his lips. "Yes," he said, I know. She told me."

"She did, did she! Then Rayna is not so shy as I had thought. I, of course, tried to convince her you are nothing at all out of the ordinary, but still she persisted in the most dogged fashion imaginable."

"With you for a sister, I . . ." He broke off suddenly. "Jesus," he growled, "the little fool is dancing with him!"

"Rayna must be polite, Adam. Her father is a guest here, and his family mustn't ruffle any feathers. The Comte de la Valle is considered an ardent royalist."

Adam merely grunted, and left Arabella's side to move closer to the dance floor.

The comte was trying to make conversation with the stiff girl, whose eyes roamed about the salon whenever she was separated from him in the dance.

"You speak French beautifully, *mademoiselle*," he said to her.

Rayna merely nodded, tight-lipped.

"I am of the French aristocracy," he told her with a touch of anger in his voice.

"My felicitations, *monsieur*."

Gervaise ground his teeth at her aloofness. He held himself silent, and by the end of the dance he had maneuvered her near the windowed balcony.

"You look overheated, *mademoiselle*," he said firmly. "We will enjoy the evening air for a moment."

Rayna felt a shiver of fear, and chided herself for being a ninny. The comte was persistent, but there were literally a hundred people nearby. She tried, nevertheless, to gently pull her arm free of his hand.

"I am not overheated," she said. "Please release me."

"In a moment, *ma chère*, in a moment."

The comte gave her a light shove through the door that gave onto the wide balcony, smiling at the back of her head.

Rayna, seeing no immediate hope of escaping the comte without creating an abominable scene, raised her chin, walked to the edge of the balcony, and clasped the wrought-iron railing.

"It is beautiful, is it not?" the comte said in his hoarse voice. "Look yon, you can see the English ships in the bay. It is comforting to know that we have protection."

"It is lovely," Rayna said coldly. "But I find it rather chilly. I would like to return now, *monsieur*."

"Look down into the gardens," the comte continued, disregarding her. "The scent of the spring flowers is most pleasant." He took her arm and gently tugged. "I would like to stroll in the gardens for just a moment, *mademoiselle*."

"It is not at all proper, sir!" Rayna gasped, unaware for the moment that she had spoken in English. "I don't wish to," she quickly amended in French.

"There is no need to be prudish," the comte said smoothly, and pulled her with him. Rayna looked back at the balcony door. Someone had closed it.

"You have no reason to be uncomfortable, *ma chère*," he said softly, close to her temple. "A few minutes of your charming company—'tis all I ask."

Rayna considered screaming. It seemed like the thing to do, but it occurred to her it would be something of a scandal, and her father would be most displeased. Perhaps he would forbid her to leave the villa, or give her no chance to see the marchese again. She shook her head. This comte angered her, but he could hardly harm her, not in the royal gardens!

"Very well," she said in a tight voice, "but only for a few minutes!"

The comte smiled. He knew women well. Only the English, it appeared, had to make some sort of coy fuss before giving themselves enjoyment. He supposed she was a virgin, and overly valued that commodity. Perhaps he would have to marry her. The thought was not appalling. She was lovely and likely would bring him a sizable dowry.

Rayna walked stiffly beside him down the short flight of steps into the gardens. She was beginning to think herself seven kinds of fool, for the only light came from above, from the salon, and she was alone with this man.

"The flowers fade into insignificance when you are present," the comte said in a ridiculously seductive voice.

"Hardly," Rayna said, striving for calm. "I am a quite indifferent specimen."

"There is no need for playacting," he murmured. He smoothly clasped her arms in his hands, pulled her toward him, and kissed the cluster of curls over her ear.

"Let me go! I am not playacting, *monsieur*! If you are a gentleman, you will cease this nonsense!"

The comte's response was to hold her wrists with one hand and close the other over her chin.

She felt him press her body against the length of him, felt him glide his tongue over her mouth. For an instant she felt paralyzed with fear, and then she felt ferocious anger.

She struggled against him, trying to pull her arms free of his hold. "You miserable beast!" she gasped. She pulled her hands free and hit him as hard as she could across his mouth with the flat of her hand. "You insufferable cad!"

The comte drew back, surprised and angered. He lightly touched his fingers to his cheek. "You will pay for that, little dove," he said in a soft voice, and reached for her again.

Rayna suddenly remembered her brother Thomas telling her, with embarrassment clogging his normally steady voice, that if a man ever went beyond what was proper, she was to kick him . . . with her knee. She remembered wondering why that would make a man cease being improper, but she brought up her knee nonetheless, and slammed it with all the force she could muster into the comte's groin.

He fell away from her as if she had shot him. She saw his face contort with pain and his hands clutch convulsively at his groin.

"You damned little bitch!"

His voice sounded as if he were strangling, but she did not wait to hear any more. She dashed toward the steps that led back to the balcony.

Her fear returned in full measure only when she halted just inside the salon, trying to calm her raspy breathing. She felt certain that anyone who saw her would know what had happened. She edged around the side of the salon and ducked into an antechamber. It was a small private receiving room, a room, she supposed, for diplomatic discussions. She fanned her burning cheeks, discovered that her legs had somehow become weak as water, and sank down into a stiff-backed chair.

"Why the hell did you go outside with the comte?"

Rayna raised her flushed face and found herself staring up at the Marchese di Galvani.

"Have you no sense at all?" Adam snarled, his anger flamed by her silence.

"A great deal, I daresay," she managed in a thin voice. "I . . . I did get away from him, after all!"

"Yes, I saw you kick him in the groin. Most enterprising. Did you learn that trick from one of your brothers? No, don't tell me. You were a fool to go outside with him."

Rayna rose somewhat shakily to her feet. "I have no intention, *signore*, of remaining here and listening to your insults! Perhaps I wasn't altogether . . . wise to allow myself to be placed in such an intolerable situation, but it is over."

"The comte is not a man to forget that he was bested by a silly little chit! Damn, you have pulled the tiger from his cage."

"Perhaps," Rayna said, trying desperately to stiffen her back, "you and my father see more eye to eye than I imagined. You are just as unfair as he is!"

Adam heard the slight break in her voice, and felt his anger ease. She looked pale and beautiful and immensely vulnerable. "Rayna," he said in a more temperate voice, "I am simply worried for you. Promise me that you will not again allow him to be alone with you."

"You mean as we are now, marchese?" She pictured him suddenly in laughing conversation with Arabella, and hissed at him, "I am not a fool, *signore*, nor am I blind. Did you come in here because Arabella is otherwise occupied and you couldn't be with her? Or perhaps Arabella sent you after me."

"Stop ripping up at me, little shrew! I came after you to be certain you are all right!"

"Shrew! Just because I will not tolerate your arrogance, you have the audacity to call me names!"

Adam realized the last thing he wanted was to trade insults with her. Without thinking, he clasped her shoulders in his hands and pulled her toward him. To his besotted surprise, she did not try to fling away from him. She seemed to melt against him, her slender arms inching around his neck. He kissed her gently, and she parted her lips to him naturally, with a soft moan.

When the marchese's lips caressed her mouth, Rayna felt as if a door had opened and she had sailed through it. He suddenly released her, pulling her arms from his neck, and she stared up at him, her expression stunned.

"I . . . I don't understand," Rayna whispered, unable to look away from him. "Please, Pietro, I want . . ."

He dropped his arms to his sides and took a quick step back. "You don't know what you want," he said harshly. "And stop looking at me like that! Is that how you looked at the comte?" He could have cut out his tongue when he saw the bewildered look in her eyes.

"For God's sake, go back to your parents," he nearly shouted at her.

Rayna choked back her tears. "I hate you!" she yelled at him in English, and without thought, slapped him, just as she had the comte. She picked up her skirts and raced from the room, not looking back.

Adam stood still, staring after her. He turned around slowly, his head slightly bowed, and walked to the fireplace.

"We both failed, it would appear, *mon ami.*"

The comte's silky voice made Adam stiffen with anger. But when he turned to face the comte, there was a small smile on his lips. "Oh?" he said carefully.

"I saw the little English bitch fly out of here like a rabbit from a trap. The girl needs a lesson."

It was all Adam could do to stay where he stood. "I misjudged the girl," he said coolly, negligently flicking a speck of lint from his black velvet evening coat. "She is an innocent."

The frown suddenly left the comte's face, and he smiled widely. "Yes," he said slowly, "I believe you're right. A cold virgin."

"It is probably best that we both keep our distance," Adam said, trying to repress a feeling of dread at the comte's smile. "There are other fish to be caught, after all. I don't intend to waste any more of my time with that one."

"True," the comte said obliquely.

"I suggest that you do the same," Adam said more sharply.

Gervaise tilted his head to one side, his full lips in a grin. "Methinks you still want the little fool," he said. He turned and said over his shoulder, "We shall see, my friend."

9

Mediterranean Sea

The *xebec* skimmed the calm surface of the sea, its speed steady in the southerly wind. Kamal pulled his white full-sleeved linen shirt over his head and tossed it to his grinning servant, Ali.

"You have grown too pale in your palace, highness," Ali said. "Now the sun will bake your back."

Kamal grunted and flung back his head, closing his eyes against the bright afternoon sun. He felt his muscles relax in its soothing heat. He had been too long ashore, he thought, too tied up with all his administrative duties as a bey. He opened his eyes when his *xebec* veered to port, and saw its sister ship pull closer to starboard. A third *xebec* lay in an inlet a mile or so to the north, waiting.

"A sighting?" he shouted to Droso, his captain.

"Not yet, highness," Droso called back. He was a mammoth man, who looked the part of a savage corsair with his black beard and shaggy long black hair. But despite his looks, Droso was one of the gentlest captains of an Algerian privateering ship Kamal had ever known, and it was for that reason Kamal had selected him.

They were not privateering, Kamal corrected himself silently. Not this time. What they were doing was sheer piracy. He remembered his anger at reading his mother's letter from Naples. He had left his bed to think, clothed only in his white wool trousers, his bare feet making no sound on the marble floor of the great reception hall, and walked into the walled garden. He had breathed in the sweet scent of hyacinths, jasmine, and roses, and stared up at the quarter-moon that cast silvery shadows on the stone walls. He had sensed Hassan's presence without hearing a sound. "Who is there?" he asked softly.

"An old man, highness, merely an old man. But you are young, and should be abed."

"You could not sleep, Hassan?" He turned to face his minister, whose white hair was as silvery as the gentle moonlight.

"If an old man sleeps, he but shortens the time left to him. I prefer to savor every hour, highness, knowing that I breathe and think, even when the moon is high."

"Ever the philosopher," Kamal said, quirking a fair brow at him.

"You are thinking of your mother's letter," Hassan said gently.

"Yes. She tells me the Earl of Clare is not in

Naples, and she wants the viper pricked closer to his nest."

"I cannot think it is wise, highness."

Kamal heard a reproof in his minister's gentle voice. "She asks me to lead a raid on another of the earl's ships." Hassan was silent, and Kamal, as if in argument with himself, said loudly, "I have promised her vengeance. See that we discover the next Parese ship to sail."

"It is your judgment," Hassan said quietly.

Kamal stared down at his hands, not raising his head to Hassan. "We will bring the men aboard here and keep them until the Earl of Clare shows his hand."

"You mix wisdom with folly," Hassan said. "The Earl of Clare will know within the week that the Barbary pirates took his ship."

"Yes, he will know."

"And he will have to act. It is possible, highness, that he will come here."

"Perhaps. If he does, I will hold him for my mother's return."

Hassan plucked a bit of lint from his red brocade robe. "A woman's vengeance. It is a terrible thing, and yet so much can provoke it, things that none of us understand."

"You speak in riddles, Hassan."

"It is not my intention, highness. Your mother's letter said that the Earl of Clare had not arrived in Naples. I do not believe that can be true. A man does not allow his possessions to be seized without taking action."

"Still, he is not there."

"Another must be, another acting for him. A man as powerful as the earl is not foolish or stupid. He would not walk into a trap."

"You believe my mother is in danger?"

"No, and neither is the earl, at least for the moment. I wonder if the captain of the ship you will seize will know what happened twenty-five years ago to your mother. Treachery has a way of staying alive."

"As does the desire for vengeance."

Hassan turned away, stretching his stiff shoulders, and plucked a red bloom from an oleander.

Kamal smiled, watching him sniff in the sweet scent. "A woman smells sweeter, Hassan. You are not that old."

"I am too old for a woman's sweet scent and her wiles. A woman's mind dances in circles that confound me. A woman's lust makes me shrivel now."

"Lust?" Kamal shook his head. "Sometimes I wonder if their lust is not but pretense, meant to make our own minds dance in circles."

"What else can a woman do? If she does not have the skill to control a man, she has nothing. I have seen a man's lust rule him, but never a woman's. A man feels lust; a woman uses it to her own advantage. A man walks a fine line."

"Be he Muslim or European?" Kamal asked dryly.

"Your blood and your European education did not prepare you to treat women as would a Muslim.

You find them boring, their minds and conversation childish. You must accept what they are, highness, not what you would like them to be. Your Elena would make you an acceptable wife. And if she displeased you, you would simply divorce her. It is what a Muslim would do."

Kamal sighed. "It is not easy for me, Hassan. You see, I do not trust Elena."

"Trust a woman? Only a fool would do so, highness. What has trust to do with a man's children? A woman gives you sons, and it is their trust that is yours. No, highness, no woman is to be trusted . . . even a mother."

The moon dipped suddenly behind a cloud and Kamal could not see Hassan's eyes. He heard movement behind the walled garden. Soon three of his Turkish soldiers came into view. He turned from Hassan to speak to them. "Good night, old man," he had said over his shoulder.

"Ho, highness!" Droso called down now. "The watch has spotted a Parese ship, the *Heliotrope*. She's heavily loaded!"

The *Heliotrope* was sailing from the West Indies, Kamal knew, carrying sugar, rum, and tobacco. He caught his shirt from Ali and pulled it over his head.

"Is she alone, Droso?" Kamal called up as he fastened his wide leather belt about his waist.

"A babe for the plucking!"

And her captain thinks himself safe from the Barbary pirates, Kamal thought. He climbed the wooden steps to the wheel. The *Heliotrope*'s sails billowed white and full in the wind, and even from this distance Kamal could see her troughing deeply in the waves, her hold filled with cargo.

"Remember, Droso, no killing." He had prepared to take an outgoing Parese ship, and thus had brought two other *xebes* with him. But the *Heliotrope* had been away from the Mediterranean and did not know of her danger.

Droso regarded the young bey with a mixture of affection and doubt. He was breaking tribute, but he was not planning to destroy those who could tell of his deed.

"My men will only protect themselves, highness," he said.

Sordello, captain of the *Heliotrope*, swung up onto the quarterdeck at a yell from his first mate, Mr. Dibbs.

"What is it, Allan?"

"I don't believe it, sir," Allan gasped. "Barbary pirates, and it looks like they are closing on us!"

Sordello wheeled to starboard. Two *xebecs*, each boasting three masts with the black flags of Algiers flying at their peaks, were slicing smoothly through the water toward them.

"Jesus," he muttered under his breath. "It must be a mistake, Allan. Aye, perhaps a new *rais*". Sordello shouted to his cabin boy, Marco, "Fetch our passage papers from my strongbox!"

"We can't outrun them, sir," Allan said, fighting a knot of fear in his belly.

"I don't intend to. We will allow them to board us, and present our papers. No heroics, Allan, and raise a white flag quickly. We are too close to home to risk the fools firing at us."

"Aye, captain," Allan said, releasing the wheel to Sordello.

Sordello hoped his feelings did not show on his face. One bloody week from Genoa, and this! Never in his five years as captain of the Earl of Clare's ships had he been approached by *xebecs*. The earl's ships were well known. *Am I and all my men to end up stinking slaves in Algiers?* He shook away the image of his wife, Maria, her soft lips smiling at him in tender farewell. He gazed toward the far horizon, away from the swiftly approaching *xebecs*. There was another Italian ship, sailing as impudently as the *Heliotrope* had but five minutes before, secure in the safety of tribute. But both *xebecs* were heading directly toward him, seemingly oblivious of the other merchant ship. He felt hair prickle at the back of his neck.

He saw a huge man standing at the railing of the closer pirate ship, his coarse black hair whipping about his heavy face. Another man, tall and fair-haired, dressed in white wool trousers and a full-sleeved white shirt, appeared to direct him from the upper deck near the wheel. A score of privateers, armed with scimitars, lined the rail, ready to board his ship. Sordello felt the ship heel to starboard as the grappling ropes thrown from the *xebec* caught the railings. He took a sheaf of passage papers from Marco, straightened his shoulders, and strode down from the quarterdeck to meet the captain. His sailors were milling nervously about, their faces drawn with fear. He waited for the two ships to draw together.

The giant man gave a shout, and a score of men swarmed onto the *Heliotrope*'s deck.

"We fly the white flag!" Sordello shouted as one of them lunged toward him.

"Hold, you fool!" Droso snarled.

Sordello felt like a stunted child when at last the captain stood before him, his legs spread wide on the tilting deck.

"You are the captain?" Droso asked.

"Yes," Sordello said in as calm a voice as he could manage. "There is a mistake. We sail under safe passage. We are under tribute."

Droso shrugged. "You may discuss that with his highness." He tossed his black head toward the fair-haired man in white still aboard the *xebec*.

"I have our papers!"

"Show them to his highness," Droso said shortly. "You will tell your men to behave, and no one will be killed. Most of us will remain aboard to bring the ship into port. You, captain, will come with me."

His highness? What the devil did the Dey of Algiers want with him? Or was it one of his beys? Had the earl not paid tribute? The thought was too appalling to consider. He clutched the papers tightly in his hand and followed the giant captain to the *xebec*.

"Captain!"

Sordello turned at Mr. Dibb's voice. "There will be no harm done to anyone, Allan! I will straighten out this mess. Do as the corsairs bid you!"

"His highness is below," Droso said when Sordello stepped aboard the *xebec*, and gave him a light shove in the back.

He made his way through the hatch and down a narrow companionway. The huge man stopped before a closed door and rapped lightly. At the sound of a voice calling, "Enter," Droso opened the door and pushed Sordello inside.

Kamal rose from a sofa of pillows and furs and silently studied the *Heliotrope*'s captain. He was a man of Hamil's age, Kamal thought, and he was frightened. He said to Droso, "I want you to captain the ship into port. Ensure that there is no violence."

"Yes, highness," Droso said, and bowed himself from the cabin.

Kamal switched from Arabic to Italian to reassure the man. "There will be no harm done to your men, captain. Will you be seated?"

Sordello drew himself up to his full height. The man he faced was young, a good ten years younger than he, with sun-bleached blond hair and eyes as blue as the Mediterranean. He looked to Sordello more like a Viking than a corsair.

"Who are you?"

"I am Kamal, Bey of Oran and foreign-affairs minister to the Dey of Algiers."

"Hamil is dead?"

"Yes, my half-brother died some seven months ago."

The new bey did not realize he had taken a Parese ship. "There is a mistake, highness," Sordello said. "I travel under tribute." He thrust his papers toward Kamal.

To his astonishment, Kamal waved the papers away and said gently, "Yes, I know. Unfortunately, my friend, you must be detained, you and your men, and your ship. Your cargo will be confiscated, for the time being."

Detained! What the devil did that mean? Sordello thought again of Maria, waiting for him, of his two sons, and of a future as a slave. Would he be gelded or sent to the mines for the rest of his years? "I don't understand," he said, choking on the words.

Kamal guessed his thoughts. "Have no fear. It is not slavery that awaits you. You will be held at my palace in Oran until . . . all has been settled with your master, the Earl of Clare."

Sordello gaped at him.

"Join me for a glass of wine, captain. It is quite sweet, from Tunis. It will relax you."

Was the wine drugged? He shook his head as Kamal held out a glass of the red wine to him.

Slowly Kamal raised the glass and sipped the wine. "You see, captain? I do not seek to harm you."

Sordello accepted the glass with trembling fingers and downed the sweet wine. "Tribute is never broken," he said. "I do not understand."

"There is much you do not understand, captain. Ali will show you to your cabin. Do not worry about your men. They will not be mistreated."

Both men whirled toward the door at the sound of a piercing scream. Kamal cursed under his breath and rushed from the cabin, Sordello at his heels. He gained the deck in time to see Droso strike one of his men, Sard, with the flat of his scimitar.

"Marco!" Sordello yelled. "Your word, highness," he spat at Kamal. "He is just a boy!" His cabin boy was weaving where he stood, his blue shirt rent at his shoulder, his blood rushing down his arm. In his other hand he clasped Sordello's strongbox.

"The boy tried to break away, highness," Droso said to Kamal.

Sordello raised anguished eyes to Kamal. "He had not given me all our papers. He was afraid you would kill me."

Kamal knelt beside Marco. He removed his wide leather belt and fashioned a tourniquet to slow the bleeding. The boy raised wide eyes to Kamal's face. "The papers," he whispered between pinched lips. "I have papers for you."

Hassan was right to say he had mixed wisdom with folly, Kamal thought. What he had done might mean this boy's life. "Take him below, to my cabin," he told Droso. "Ali will see to him." He rose and stared long at Sordello. "If the boy can be saved, my physicians will do it. Do you wish vengeance on the man who struck him?"

Sordello said in a voice of deadly calm, "Unlike your pirates, highness, we are not butchers."

"No," Kamal said, "I did not think so. Come, captain, you may stay with the boy until we reach Oran."

Kamal spoke with Ali, who had been watching the exchange, walked slowly to the railing of the *xebec*, and stared down into the rippling water. The *xebec* heeled sharply to port, its black sails beating loudly in the wind. He raised his head and met Droso's black eyes.

"Sard is dead, highness," Droso said calmly.

10

Naples

Arabella sat in the middle of her bed, her arms clasped around her drawn-up knees, watching Rayna pace back and forth in front of her. "Rayna," she said finally, "it is after midnight. I wish you would cease acting like a caged tiger and tell me what happened. Come," she continued, patting the bed, "sit down and warm yourself, and talk to me." Surely, she thought, Adam could not be the cause of Rayna's upset.

Rayna looked a specter swathed from neck to toe in a white lawn nightgown, her luxurious auburn hair loose to her waist. She wrapped a blanket around her and sat on the edge of the bed.

Aha, Arabella thought, realizing the likely truth of the matter. "It is that wretched comte, is it not?" she prodded gently.

"Yes," Rayna said, not looking up. "I was such a fool, Bella! I went for a breath of air on the balcony with him. I didn't want to, truly, but before I knew it I was in the garden. So stupid of me! Someone closed the balcony door and he became . . . disgusting. Well, I kicked him between the legs, just as Thomas told me to do if ever a gentleman went beyond what was proper."

Arabella's eyes widened. "Oh, Rayna, how I would have liked to witness that! Sent him to his knees?"

Rayna shuddered at the memory. "I am not certain, Bella. I was running too fast to notice. But I think I did hurt him."

"Well, he deserved it. And here I thought you needed protecting from that bounder." Arabella leaned forward and shook Rayna's limp hand in congratulation. "I am proud of you, Rayna. He will likely keep his distance from now on."

"The marchese wasn't proud of me!" Rayna blurted out.

"What do you mean?" Arabella asked carefully. So Adam did fit somewhere in this mess after all.

"After I escaped the comte, I found a small antechamber. The marchese came in." Rayna's fingers fretted with a pleat in her nightgown. "He was . . . arrogant and gothic, Bella. He had the audacity to rail at me for being with the comte, as if it had been I who wanted to seduce that beastly man!"

Arabella stared, mesmerized by this information. "Did you not explain to him what had happened?"

"Yes. Indeed, he had seen most of it. He went on and on about my being a fool. And then he . . . kissed me!"

"I see," Arabella said. Good Lord, she thought, trying desperately not to laugh. Things were moving quickly, very quickly indeed.

"I slapped him," Rayna said, raising her chin.

Oh dear, Arabella said under her breath. Aloud she said, "Very proper of you, love. My, two gentlemen after you in one evening. You must give me advice, Rayna, on how to interest men. I vow that I haven't had one nibble since our arrival here."

"You are just trying to make me feel better, Bella. And you know it is not true. I think the marchese was merely . . . toying with me. It is you he is interested in. I have seen how he laughs with you."

Oh dear, Arabella thought ruefully. How can Rayna be so very blind? She said carefully, "He does laugh with me, Rayna, but it is only friendship of a sort that we share."

"His beard scratched me when he kissed me." Rayna suddenly jumped off the bed and began her pacing again. "I hated it when the comte kissed me, but when the marchese did, I felt the most marvelous feelings. It was he who pulled away from me, as if I were a loose hussy."

"Nonsense, Rayna," Arabella said sharply. "He undoubtedly felt guilty for taking advantage of you. He pulled away because he did not want to compromise you."

Rayna whirled around toward Arabella. "Do you think so, Bella? Do you think he cares for me, a little?"

"I think that he must. There is another infernal

court function on Thursday. Likely the marchese will be there. You must talk to him, Rayna. He is probably just as concerned as you are."

"Perhaps you are right, but he seems so certain of himself, so . . ." She waved her hand expressively.

"So arrogant?"

"Not really that. He seems a man who gets what he wants. I would not want to be his enemy."

Neither would I, Arabella thought. "You told me he was all that was kind, Rayna."

"That is true. And he is gentle with me, and teases me. But still, I saw his anger tonight. I do not believe I could love a . . . violent man."

"The marchese violent? Come, Rayna, that's absurd!" Arabella would have liked to explain exactly how absurd it was, but she could not. "He was angry because he was afraid for you, not particularly *at* you."

"Nonetheless," Rayna said, "he is not at all like Papa."

"No," Arabella quickly agreed, "he is not. I think he is used to being in control," she continued with a sister's loving objectivity, "and perhaps he can be ruthless. But I do not believe he would ever be cruel to someone he loved."

"I do not care for ruthless men," Rayna said.

Impatient with Rayna's prim tone, Arabella retorted, "Likely the marchese doesn't care for girls who are too timid or too proper to stand up for themselves."

Rayna sucked in her breath. "I am not too timid! And of course I am proper. I am a lady."

"I would imagine," Arabella said thoughtfully, "that the marchese would not particularly want a lady in his bed."

"Oh!" Color flooded Rayna's cheeks.

"But," Arabella continued, "it seems to me you forgot all your prudish propriety when he kissed you."

A sudden smile lit up Rayna's face. "I think I did," she confessed. "Bella," she said after a moment, "have you ever been in love?"

"No. And as for gentlemen who would steal kisses, I don't care for them at all!"

"But you're twenty, Bella!"

"My brother tells me I'm on the shelf, but I am content to wait. Perhaps there isn't a gentleman who will kiss me and make me want to forget I'm a proper lady."

"You are silly, Bella," Rayna said.

"And you, Rayna, what are you?"

Rayna pursed her lips thoughtfully. "I don't know. Sometimes I feel afraid, and other times I feel so light I think I could float!"

"Well, don't let your parents see you floating. You know how they feel."

"Yes, but they will come to see reason," Rayna said with great confidence. "Good night, Bella."

"Good night, love."

"You are English, yet you speak Italian like a native."

Arabella answered with her open smile, "I was most blessed in my parentage."

"Your accent, if I am not mistaken, is Genoese?"

The older woman seemed genuinely interested, and Arabella, overly heated from too much dancing, was ready to relax.

"You are very perceptive, *signora*. We have a home in Genoa," she said readily, sitting back in her chair. "My father is the Earl of Clare, and my grandmother was Antonia Parese."

The Contessa Luciana di Rolando drew her dark brows together as if in thought. "I believe I have heard of your illustrious father. Is he not one of the few English aristocrats who indulge in business? Shipping and banking?"

"Yes, he does," Arabella said eagerly. "And he is terribly proficient at whatever he undertakes."

The contessa smiled indulgently. "He is your father, so I suppose that makes him something of a paragon to you, his daughter. My father, on the other hand, was a failure at anything he attempted."

"A paragon?" Arabella knitted her brow. "No, I do not think I am such a fool as to believe him that. But I do love him very much, and find him ever so splendid."

"And your mother? Is she still living?"

"Indeed! I am told that I resemble her greatly, save for my eyes and eyebrows."

"Are you their only child?"

"No. I have an older brother. Our other brother, Charles, died when he was very young."

"Ah, so very sad."

"Enough about me and my family, *signora*. I have been trying to place your accent, but I confess that I cannot."

"I have . . . traveled a great deal."

"Do you live in Naples?"

"For the time being, yes. The world is so very unsettled. I really do not know where I will be in, say, three months."

"That is what my father says. He is concerned that Napoleon will soon make Genoa part of his empire. I should hate that, for we would have to return to England, and likely remain there until Napoleon is overcome."

The contessa reached over and lightly patted Arabella's hand. "It is a pity that you, so young a girl, must worry about leaving her Italian home."

Arabella's dark eyes twinkled. "I am not so very young," she said, chuckling. "I turned twenty last month. Alas, I fear that I will become a spinster."

"Your parents want to keep you with them, then?"

"My parents," Arabella said firmly, "only want me to be happy. Unfortunately, I have yet to meet a man who can measure up to my brother and my father."

The contessa lowered her eyes and let her fingers curl into her palms. "Is your brother here with you?"

Arabella gave a start, but said smoothly, "Oh no, Adam is in Amsterdam. I am merely a guest of the Lyndhursts. Their daughter and I went to school together in England."

The little chit Gervaise wants. "And will your parents come fetch you soon?"

Arabella didn't mind questions, truly she didn't, but the contessa seemed almost too curious, too insistent. She said carefully, "My parents, for the time being at least, will remain in Genoa. I am here only because my father thought it would benefit me to see more of the world."

"How wise he sounds."

It seemed to Arabella that the contessa's tone held a touch of sarcasm. She did not understand it, but thought: I will put the shoe on the other foot—and said brightly, "Do you have children, contessa?"

The contessa smiled blandly. "You think I am a nosy old woman. It is true. When you reach my age, there are few pleasures left. But to answer your question, *signorina*, I have one son, Alessandro."

"Is he with you in Naples?"

"No, Alessandro, like me, enjoys travel."

"Is he married?"

"He is only twenty-five years old, *signorina*. Too young, I think, at least for a man, to consider marriage."

"I have always thought it unfair," Arabella said seriously, "that women are considered to be beyond the pale if they are not married at an absurdly young age, whereas gentlemen can do just as they please for as long as it pleases them."

The contessa frowned. How often she had thought that when she was younger, married to a man old enough to be her father when she was but eighteen. At least the old fool had died and left her rich. She firmly repressed the tug of liking she felt for the lively Arabella Welles. "Life is not always fair," she said aloud, knowing she sounded inane.

Arabella smiled suddenly and rose to her feet. "I have been monopolizing you overmuch, contessa. Forgive me. My father is always telling me that I am sometimes too exuberant."

"Allow me to disagree with your father," the contessa said. "But you are young and ready for more dancing, I daresay. Let us speak again, child. There is a handsome young man who appears eager for your company."

Arabella smiled at her in her friendly way. "I should like that, contessa," she said, and offered the older woman a slight curtsy.

She greeted Adam with an impish grin and whispered behind her gloved hand, "Have you spoken yet with Rayna?"

"Aye, and I have something of a favor to ask you, Bella."

She arched a smooth brow at him. "Something ennobling, I trust, brother!"

He looked for a moment somewhat hesitant. "I wish to speak to Rayna in a more private place. At her parents' villa, to be precise. Perhaps in the garden."

"Adam Welles! My brother, nothing but a cad!"

"Bella, dammit—!"

"And after all my efforts to have you meet Rayna

in England, and you, I daresay, not the least bit interested at the time."

Adam gritted his teeth. "I pity the man who must break you to bridle! Now, will you shut up and listen? I have no intention of compromising Rayna in any way, so dismiss all your lurid fantasies, Bella. Your role, my dear, will be to play chaperon and guard dog. Unseen and unheard, of course."

"Naturally!" Arabella paused a moment, then said quite seriously, "Do you intend to tell Rayna who you are, Adam?"

"No," he said sharply. "Not until this business of ours is finished. I will take no chances with her safety."

"Reasonable," Arabella said with stark disapproval, "but disgustingly unromantic. And here I had thought you—"

"A dashing rake?" He laughed. "Come Bella, this, I believe, is quite different. Will you do as I ask?"

She squeezed his hand. "Of course. Now, Adam, I suggest you take yourself off before we become an *on-dit*"! A meeting alone, she thought, somewhat put out that Adam had thought of it and not she.

Arabella had started to make her way toward the Lyndhursts when she was hailed by Lady Eden, a friend of the notorious Lady Hamilton and now an intimate of the queen. She had no choice but to stop and smile politely, even though her small chance of escaping the ever loquacious and equally indiscreet lady within the next half-hour gave her rueful pause.

"Poor Princess Antoinette," Lady Eden sighed, willing to share her perturbation with anyone, it seemed. Arabella had heard from Lord Delford that the queen would confide her concerns, even state secrets, to anyone she liked, without regard to judgment. Though Arabella did little more than cock her head to the side in question, Lady Eden continued with great verve, "The poor princess was married to the Prince of the Asturias. She is treated with the greatest contempt by the prince's mother and her lover, Godoi. Can you believe that the queen thinks Antoinette a threat? And all because the dear queen is Austrian and hates Napoleon. It is too sad, really."

"I daresay," Arabella said in a neutral voice.

"And there are poor Charlotte and Amélie, quite old now and still held close to the queen. Do you know that Napoleon had the audacity to offer an alliance between his stepson and one of the princesses? The queen sent him to the right-about!"

"Very proper of her. Oh dear, ma'am. I see Lady Delford waving to me. I must go now!"

"Oh, my dear, and that simply dreadful French ambassador, Alquier! You would not believe what I heard him say to our dear queen!"

Arabella's retreat was instantly checked, and there was no remedy. She sighed inwardly and searched the ballroom beneath lowered lashes for Adam. She saw him performing the boulanger with the Princess Amélie, his midnight-blue eyes twinkling down at her with devastating charm. And she saw the Conte Celestino Genovesi, plump, good-natured, with brains enough to fill a walnut, dancing with Rayna. She knew he was a friend of the comte's and likely one of his intimates in Les Diables Blancs. He appeared to be much enjoying himself, preening under Rayna's sweet smile.

". . . And you simply wouldn't credit the story I heard just this morning about that silly creature Lady Alice Devereau . . ."

To Arabella's inuterrable relief, Lady Delford actually waved to her. "Oh, my dear ma'am," she exclaimed, "Lady Delford, you know! I will be in the suds if I do not attend her!"

Rayna, for her part, was enjoying her dance with Celestino, for she had already managed to speak to the marchese. If Celestino believed her tinkling laughter the result of his wit, there was no one to tell him otherwise. Indeed, he chortled his conquest some hours later to both Adam and Gervaise as they sat in the comte's narrow drawing room sipping brandy.

"Ah, yes," Celestino crowed, "the girl obviously has taste. Prefers me to the both of you!"

Adam thoughtfully sipped silently on his brandy. Gervaise, his fair brows raised, said in his hoarse drawl, "Any girl who prefers you, Tino, has need of glasses."

"You're jealous, Gervaise," Tino said with some satisfaction. "I made her laugh."

"She was likely laughing in anticipation of your waistcoat buttons popping over your fat belly."

His eyes went toward the marchese. He swirled the amber liquid about in the snifter for a long moment, as if in silent comtemplation. "I think the time has come," he said finally.

Adam stretched his long legs before him toward the fireplace, hoping his excitement did not show on his face. "Oh?" he asked, looking bored.

Celestino leaned forward in his chair. "Really, Gervaise?"

"Yes," the comte said shortly, his eyes still on Adam. "I believe I have a rather enticing answer to your boredom, *mon ami.*"

"I hope it is enticing, Gervaise," Adam said easily. "I am considering joining the French troops in Calabria. I grow weary of the court and of paying compliments to that hag of a queen and her simpering daughters."

"How severe you are," the comte chided, dry laughter in his voice. "Before you decide, marchese, I ask you to attend me. I believe you will find my diversion far more pleasurable and far less harrowing than the French Army."

"Then I shall wait," Adam drawled.

11

Arabella stood in the shadow of the villa, a bemused smile on her face at the sight of Adam. He was leaning against an oak tree watching Rayna pace about the garden. She would retreat, she told herself, the moment Adam approached Rayna. Even though the evening shadows had lengthened, she could still see the expression on his face. He looked hungry, she thought, startling herself at such an odd notion. No man had ever looked at her like that. She felt a spurt of jealousy and longing. Stop it, she told herself firmly. She glanced toward Rayna, and imagined that Adam, who had never seen her with her hair loose, was thinking of rubbing his hands in the thick tresses that flowed nearly to Rayna's waist. How strange it was that Rayna, two years younger than she, did not look at all virginal in her simple white muslin frock. Indeed, her every graceful step seemed a promise. Was Adam's pulse quickening at the gleam of excitement in Rayna's hazel eyes? Arabella felt an elusive, faint pain. Someday, she thought.

Finally Adam dusted his hands on his black breeches and walked silently toward Rayna. Arabella grinned, for the wall surrounding the garden at Lord Delford's villa was not particularly high, but it was filthy.

Arabella knew she had to leave them and turned to walk quietly back into the villa, her thoughts turning to Lord and Lady Delford. She didn't want to imagine her consternation when they learned of their daughter's attachment to Adam Welles. She told herself fiercely that it wasn't their lives or their decision. It was Rayna's and Adam's. She only wished that Rayna knew who Adam really was. What a shock that would be! She smiled when she heard Adam say Rayna's name softly, obviously not wanting to startle her.

Rayna whirled about to face him, and for a moment they stared at each other. "I am glad you waited for me," he said.

"Pietro," she said, splaying her hands toward him. "I was afraid you would not come."

"So little faith in me?" he said lightly. He switched from French to Italian. "Where is our guard dog?"

"I am not certain. Bella just told me she would be about and we were not to worry. I imagine she is keeping an eye on Papa's study, and Mama and her cooking.

Her starchily accented Italian brought a smile to his lips.

"But we are alone. Bella promised she wouldn't interrupt unless she had to. How did you get into the garden?"

"Over the wall," he said, grinning. "Actually, I would have swum a moat to see you."

"I am glad that wasn't necessary. You would have smelled dreadful, I would imagine."

He chuckled at the impish laughter in her voice. "We will speak quietly, even though your papa is in his study and your mama is immersed in her cooking."

"Yes, and Papa is very involved studying some papers, very serious papers, he informed Mama and me, and must have absolute quiet. As to her cooking, Mama is busy showing our Italian cook how to make Yorkshire pudding!"

"And Arabella is listening at keyholes?"

Rayna dropped her eyes to her hands. "About Arabella . . ." she began in a tentative voice.

"I should prefer it if you look at me when you speak, *cara*."

"You would not have asked her to be our . . . guard dog if you had cared for her."

"Ah," said Adam. "Arabella Welles is a charming girl, Rayna, but she would never consider herself a rival, at least for my regard."

"You certainly became friendly with her quickly," Rayna said, willing to be convinced.

"Did I? I do not know if I would necessarily call her a friend. But I do trust her. Do you not?"

"Yes, only . . ."

"Only what?"

"I . . . well, I was concerned that perhaps Bella had a *tendre* for you."

Adam looked amused. "Can you really believe she would have offered to be our guard dog if she had a *tendre* for me?"

"No, it wouldn't make any sense, would it?" she asked with a trusting smile.

Adam remembered the women he had admired, the women he had been infatuated with as a younger man. He had enjoyed pleasuring them, but he had never felt the desire to protect and cherish a woman. It was a bit unnerving, and, he reflected ruefully, the circumstances were god-awful. He wasn't aware that he was frowning, until he realized that Rayna's trusting smile had faded and she had lowered her eyes once again.

"What troubles you, *cara*?"

His voice sounded gentle, and Rayna, awash with uncertainty, raised her head and blurted out, "I . . . please, you must forgive me!"

"For believing me capricious?"

"Oh no! The other evening, when—"

"For breaking my poor jaw?"

"Well, yes. I had no chance to apologize to you last night."

"I suppose you had ample provocation," he said lightly.

She refused to smile, and gave her head a slight shake.

"Would you like to strike me again?"

"There is more," she exclaimed, for all the world like a child bent on confessing every sin.

"Ah, a dark secret that will make me blush?"

She gave him a darkling look and said gruffly, "I have never before kissed a man, other than my father and brothers, of course. You must believe me very . . . improper."

He wanted to laugh, but wisely did not. "I thought I was the one who kissed you."

"No, you only . . . well, that is to say, you only started to! You mustn't take the blame for what happened, truly. Perhaps I am a loose creature." He was still smiling down at her, and she frowned and straightened her shoulders. "I struck you," she said, her chin jutting up defiantly, "because you pushed me away from you, because you didn't . . . want to kiss me."

The smile fell from Adam's lips. "You are being silly, Rayna, even something of a fool."

"I am not a fool," she said, her voice indignant. "It is unkind of you to insult me and mock me."

"Your eyes are as green as the leaves on this rosebush when you are angry. But you mustn't be so eager to assume all these supposed sins, Rayna. Allow me my share, if you please! I pushed you away because I did not want to compromise you in any way. We were at the royal palace, after all."

He saw a blush spread over her cheeks. "That is what Arabella told me."

"She is occasionally quite acute."

"She also told me I was wise to speak to you privately."

"I don't know how wise it is, *cara*.'" Of all the times to be courting, with his sister the matchmaker!

He didn't want to be. At the thought, he straightened, staring beyond Rayna.

"At Arabella's home in Genoa," Rayna said, looking into his eyes, "there are exquisite gardens. And in the gardens are marble statues of naked gods and goddesses. I thought the male statues truly beautiful, despite what my father said. But you, marchese, you are the most beautiful man I have ever seen."

"Even with my pirate's black beard?" He tried to keep his voice light, but it sounded husky, even to his own ears.

Rayna raised her hand and lightly touched her fingertips to his thick bearded jaw. "Yes," she said simply.

She is too young and innocent, Adam told himself, forcing himself to pull away from her tantalizing fingers, and she is only infatuated, for the first time in her life. But he did not want to believe it.

"Come," he said roughly, "let us sit down." He took her arm firmly and guided her to a narrow marble bench beneath a rose bower.

She sat beside him primly, her hands folded like a schoolgirl's in her lap. "I know you are from Sicily. Tell me about your home. Do you have brothers and sisters?"

"Yes," Adam said, "I have one sister. She is near your age, a year or two older perhaps." It was a bit of the truth, he told himself.

"Is she married?"

"No. She is as fickle as I am."

"Come, marchese," Rayna teased him, "I would

not call you an old man precisely! You have not been fickle overly long."

Adam lightly stroked his fingers over her palm. "It may be that you are right," he said.

"Do you plan to stay in Naples?"

"Yes, for a short time," he said, smiling, his teeth shining white against his tanned face and black beard. "My father married when he was in his thirties. I believe that I shall wed sooner."

"You have found the woman you wish to wed, marchese?"

He looked away from her for a moment, wondering why the devil he had said that. He said deliberately, as if he were coming to a decision, "I believe so. Perhaps it was fated, long ago, just as my parents were fated to be together."

"She is . . . Italian?"

"She is someone very special, Rayna."

"This girl who is special to you . . . is she pretty?"

He studied the soft lines of her face. "She is lovely," he said.

Rayna's brow furrowed in confusion. "I do not understand," she said finally.

"Are you certain you do not?"

Rayna turned to face him, and for a long moment was drawn into the depths of his beautiful eyes. "I am not a stupid child," she said. Slowly she raised her hand to stroke his bearded jaw. He caught her wrist and bore it back to her lap.

"No, but you are very young and have been protected by your family."

Her jaw jutted out aggressively, much to his

amusement. "That, marchese, is perhaps true. However, if I met a gentleman I wanted, I doubt my inexperience would last out the year."

He knew he should keep his tongue behind his teeth, but he asked her, "Have you met the gentleman you want, *petite*?"

"Yes," she said without hesitation.

Adam rose suddenly, finding it unbearable to be so close to her.

Rayna drew back from him. "I cannot seem to please you," she whispered. "I only say the truth, and you reject it." She looked away from him, trying to draw her pride together. "You believe I speak this way to many gentlemen?"

"No," he said gently. "Will you believe me when I tell you that I have never before desired a young lady of quality?"

"I do not believe you are a scoundrel, marchese. Nor do I believe that you would . . . toy with me."

"If the truth be told, Rayna, I should not want anything to do with you."

"Why? Because I am English? Because I am not witty or . . . clever?"

"No, because this is not the time or the place. There is much about me you do not know, Rayna, much I cannot tell you. Perhaps I should not have come tonight, but, you see, I am not much at writing letters, and I have no penchant at all for poetry." He paced several steps in front of her and paused. "I suppose you could say that I want to court a lady, but as I said, it is impossible for me to do so now. There are others involved. It would not be particularly wise for me to continue seeing this lady until all has been resolved. But I would not want her to believe that I do not care about her."

Rayna traced her fingertip along the edge of the marble bench in rapt concentration. "This lady," she said softly, "could you not tell her what you are involved with? Perhaps she would understand."

"I cannot tell her. As I said, this lady was raised in a very protective family. It is quite possible that her parents, say, would not wish her to become involved with me. I should not wish her to be hurt."

"I doubt not, marchese, that the lady's parents love her much. If that is the case, then I cannot imagine they would wish to make her unhappy."

"She is a gentle lady, Rayna, and I doubt she has ever before gone against her parents' wishes."

"Perhaps, marchese, she has never before had sufficient reason to do so."

"In the way of things, I believe it a daughter's duty to abide by her parents' wishes. I would not like to see her set herself against her parents, and perhaps end by being separated from those she loves."

"Daughters are possessed of some sense, after all. And if they are convinced that their future . . . happiness is in the balance, surely the final decision should be theirs."

"And what if, *cara*, the gentleman, because of his circumstances, has misled the lady?"

"I think the gentleman makes too much of his circumstances. Misleading is not, after all, lying. I am sure," Rayna continued very softly, rising to stand in front of him, "that this lady will do what she must to ensure she is not made unhappy."

"But the lady must be very certain," he said.

Rayna touched her hands to his shoulders. He drew her slowly against him, his eyes locked to hers, and lifted her chin to him. He sensed no shyness in her when he lightly kissed her soft mouth, only tentativeness. He let his tongue lightly touch hers, and felt her start in surprise, but she did not draw back. He felt her hands creep around his back, and he knew he should release her, get out of this damned garden and out of her life until he could tell her everything. Would she forgive him when she discovered that he was a fraud, that he had played her false?

He said in as calm a voice as he could muster, "I must go now, *cara.*"

Rayna blinked at him, her senses blurred at the shock of pleasure that washed through her belly. "Not yet," she said, her eyes vague with passion, and raised her parted lips to him again.

Adam felt such a shock of desire that he trembled. He clutched her to him and kissed her until she was breathless. He would have smiled at her enthusiasm had he not wanted her so desperately. He could feel her body clearly through her frock, feel her breasts pressed against his chest, her soft belly against his manhood.

"Rayna," he said on a moan, and pulled his

mouth away from her. He stiffened and looked up at the sound of Arabella's voice.

"Rayna! Where are you, my dear? It is teatime." Arabella waited a moment in the doorway, then stepped into the garden. She looked over her shoulder, expecting to see Lord Delford bearing down on her. Idiot, she called herself silently, for all had gone perfectly. Well, brother, she thought, I wonder how you have dealt with my very lovely, very innocent friend. She glanced back at the villa, waited a few more moments, then called out again, "Rayna. You must come in now."

"Drat," Rayna said succinctly. "It really is teatime. That was to be our signal, you know." She lowered her eyes a moment. "Bella didn't want to interrupt us unannounced."

Adam grinned and kissed her once again, quickly. "I must leave now."

"When will I see you again?"

He paused. "I don't know." He saw uncertainty in her eyes, and quickly added, "You must trust me, Rayna."

"All right," she said quietly.

He lightly touched his fingers to her cheek, then strode away toward the garden wall.

"I am coming, Bella," Rayna called. She felt such excitement that she thought her sharp-eyed mother would certainly notice. To her relief, her mother seemed to see nothing out of the ordinary. Rayna lifted her cup, a small smile playing about her mouth, and gave her tea all her attention.

It was lucky, Arabella thought, unable to keep

the gleam of satisfaction from her eyes, that the Lyndhursts didn't know her all that well, else they surely would have guessed that something was afoot. She couldn't wait to get Rayna alone.

"Where the devil is Gervaise?" Celestino growled, not really expecting an answer from the other members of Les Diables Blancs.

"No doubt he will arrive when it pleases him," Adam said, trying to sound unconcerned.

Vittorio Santini, a gaunt-faced young nobleman whose burning dark eyes reminded Adam of a picture he had once seen of St. Francis, straightened from his post by the fireplace. "He told me that he has a surprise for you, marchese, nothing more."

"You are new to our company," Celestino said, pulling his flowered waistcoat over his stomach. "You will find that Gervaise's surprises are always . . . pleasurable."

Adam felt his stomach lurch at the thought of taking his turn with a peasant girl. He turned to Ugo Monti, the only one of the group over thirty, married and the father of four children. "I have wondered," he said carelessly, "how the . . . our association is maintained. Gervaise has mentioned no dues to me."

"There are none," Celestino volunteered. "We have ample means of support, mind you, without a sou from our pockets."

"What?" Adam asked, smiling cynically. "Are

we expected to steal silverware from the royal banquets to pay for our activities?"

Ugo looked at the young marchese thoughtfully. "Not at all, *signore*. The comte provides all the capital we need."

"He pleasures an old bag of a mistress, and in return, she provides him with goods to sell."

Adam cocked a questioning brow at Celestino, then gazed about the room at the other members. "Is each of us required to stud rich old women?"

There was a loud guffaw, and Celestino chuckled. "I told Gervaise that you would bring good blood to our group. Actually," he continued in a confiding voice, "before Gervaise met the old witch, we did have to cough up our own funds."

"But no longer," Ugo said.

Adam brushed a piece of lint from his black coat sleeve. "The woman heard of his prowess as a lover and moved to Naples?"

"Something like that."

"I assume she is French, or does the comte make love equally well in Italian?"

Niccolo Canova paused a moment to belch behind his hand. "No, she's as Italian as the rest of us. I heard Gervaise say once that she might even be caressing the king's bulbous nose."

"As well as other things!" Celestino laughed.

Ugo raised a quieting hand. "The comte does not want his . . . liaison discussed. The woman insists upon secrecy." He shrugged. "None of us know who she is, in any case."

"She must be excessively ugly," Adam said lightly,

and turned to pour himself a snifter of brandy from the sideboard. His mind raced. He could picture a woman now, speaking to Arabella. He had seen her seated next to Ferdinando. All he needed now was her name, and this wretched charade would be over.

Adam turned at the sound of booted steps outside the drawing room. The other men rose, setting down their drinks and their playing cards. The door suddenly burst open and the Comte de la Valle entered, a cloaked figure held tightly in his arms.

"Good evening, *mes diables*," Gervaise said, his voice smug. The cloaked girl was struggling against him, but he did not appear to notice.

"Marchese," he said, "your surprise!"

He dropped the girl to her feet and pulled back the hood of her cloak.

Adam's glass shattered on the hearth. Rayna Lyndhurst stood before him, her eyes wide with terror, her hands bound and her mouth gagged with a silk handkerchief.

12

The comte dropped Rayna to her feet in view of at least eight men, all staring at her in stunned silence. She recognized many of them from the court. Her gaze caught the marchese when the glass slipped from his hand and crashed to the hearth. She wanted to run to him, but the comte held her firmly by her wrist. She kept her eyes wide on the marchese's face.

"Well, marchese," the Comte de la Valle said in a silky voice, "does my surprise please you? The little slut struck you just as she did me. Will not revenge be sweet?"

Revenge! I did nothing save protect myself!

Celestino, regaining his wits, squealed, "Are you mad, Gervaise? She is no peasant girl! Her father is Lord Delford!"

"Shut up, Tino," Gervaise said pleasantly. "She is a gift for the marchese, not for any of you louts. Well, Pietro?"

What does he mean, a gift for you, Pietro?

Adam drew a deep steadying breath and forced his eyes away from Rayna's terrified face. He said quietly, "Tino is right, Gervaise. The girl did rebuff the both of us, but we cannot use her for our pleasure. It would be madness."

"Afraid, marchese?"

Adam smiled at the comte's silky taunt. "It is true that I have no wish to have my life cut short because of this insipid little virgin. It was you, after all, who explained the queen's secret police to me. I doubt such an act would go unavenged. You are rather a fool for letting her see all of us."

"Come, Pietro, I am no fool, and you, I trust, are not a coward. To take her, after all, would prove a great deal about you to us, would it not?"

"A test, Gervaise?" Adam said quietly, his thick brow arching upward.

"You are too harsh, *mon ami!* Let us say that you have not yet done anything that would . . . tie you to us. Come, I know you want the girl, I've watched you gaze at her. And of course I want her too. But since she is your surprise, we will save her precious virginity for you." His eyes roved to Rayna's pale face, and he touched his fingertips lightly to her cheek. She whipped her head back, a muffled cry sounding through her gag. He tightened his grip about her shoulders. "I will be interested to see what color her *aristo*'s blood is," he said softly, enjoying the helpless fear in her eyes.

You must think, dammit! "How did you get her, Gervaise?" Adam hoped that he sounded bored and aloof, the role he had played with the comte since their first meeting.

"Yes, Gervaise," Ugo said, "can we expect her outraged father at any minute?"

"Actually," Gervaise said, grinning widely, "it was so easy that I wonder if the little fool is still a virgin. She was wandering about, quite alone and in her nightclothes in the garden. As if she were waiting for her lover. Is that true, little dove?" He caressed the palm of his hand lightly over her breast. "She trembles at the touch of a man. We will soon know."

I waited for you, Pietro. I wanted you to come again!

Adam felt such rage that for a moment he could not breathe. He smoothed his fisted hands and strolled over to the sideboard to pour himself another snifter of brandy. He turned slowly, took a sip of the rich amber liquid, and stifled a yawn.

"Be that as it may, comte," he said, aware they were all watching him, "as I said, I have no wish to visit the hangman's noose. She is a tidy morsel" —this said with a brief bored look at Rayna—"but she is not worth cutting my life short. I doubt any man here would disagree with me."

Niccolo Canova said thoughtfully, "The fact that she is a lady and was wandering about in her father's garden thus garbed leads to an interesting question."

"Ah," Gervaise said in a silky voice, "our sophist speaks."

"You appear to have forgotten, marchese,"

Niccolo continued, his eyes on Adam, "that the young lady has reason to keep her tongue behind her teeth. Indeed, I wonder if she would even tell her father. But think of the scandal! She would be utterly ruined. Do not doubt that such an *affaire* would follow her back to England."

"Do not forget," Gervaise said, "that we are not common *canailles*, but men of high rank, and not without influence of our own."

"It is not the scandal I am thinking of, but what her father would do to us!" Tino exclaimed, dashing his handkerchief across his forehead. "We could doubtless deny all, even, if you wish, claim that she came willingly. But what would you do, Niccolo, if you were her father?"

"Such theatrics, Tino," Gervaise said. "Niccolo is quite right. She would be a fool to tell her father. And if she did"—his voice trailed off caressingly as Rayna gasped behind the gag—"the result would be your doing. You understand me well, little dove, do you not?"

"Her father is, after all, an Englishman," Niccolo said, "with limited resources in Naples. What could he do if she told him? Send assassins? Hardly! He might even leave Naples in a rage, which would weaken England's ties to us."

"You astound me with your flawless logic, Niccolo," Gervaise said, nearly purring. "Allow me also to point out, my friends, that despite all arguments, the deed is done. She is here. We can always discuss what to do with her later."

There was no hope for it. Adam tossed down the

rest of his brandy and threw the empty glass to Tino. "Very well, Gervaise. She is mine, you say?"

"You are the new member, my randy Sicilian."

Adam bowed formally to all of them. "You may be certain that when I am through with her, she will say nothing to anyone. I will leave you now. I take my women in private and not in front of a lot of gaping fools." He took a confident step toward the comte.

"You wish to deprive your friends of their evening entertainment? Oh no, marchese. The table will do just fine for the little *arista*."

"I do not play stud for anyone's entertainment." Adam gazed about him, trying desperately to judge the mood. He lowered his eyes and brushed an invisible speck of dust from his sleeve. "She is for me, is she not, Gervaise?"

"Yes," the comte said after a moment. "But I would be certain that the deed is, in fact, done."

Adam shrugged. "Take her yourself, then. I am not interested."

The comte frowned. His gift of the young English girl was not only a test, it was also his payment to the marchese for saving his life. "Very well, Pietro," he said slowly. "You will not rut in front of us. But you will remain here." He jerked his head toward the ceiling. "Take her upstairs."

Adam felt a surge of relief.

"But first!" Gervaise jerked the cloak from her body, closed his fingers over the laced neck of her nightgown, and ripped it from her.

Rayna shrieked through the gag, struggling with

all her strength. The comte held her painfully tight.

"Lovely," he said, staring down at her naked breasts.

Adam could almost smell the lust in the other men as they stared at Rayna's nakedness. He must act quickly! "Give her to me," he said, forcing desire into his voice.

The comte swept Rayna into his arms and tossed her like a sack of potatoes to Adam. "She is yours." Gervaise laughed. "Enjoy your sport!"

"We have always shared before," Tino grumbled.

Adam didn't wait for Gervaise to change his mind. He drew Rayna possessively against his chest and strode toward the door.

"The chit is in for a rutting!"

"She will know a man, not any of you clucking roosters," Adam tossed over his shoulder, and was pleased at the shouts of laughter that followed in his wake.

Rayna began struggling against him. Adam bowed his head close to hers and whispered fiercely, "Stop it, for God's sake! Hold still! I'm not going to hurt you!"

Instantly she quieted.

Adam took the stairs two at a time. The second floor of the house was shadowy and dim, lit with but one branch of candles set on an old table in the hall. He remembered Celestino telling him that they occasionally brought women here for trysts. He saw a door partially open and strode toward it. He stepped into a small room that held but a wide bed and a commode with a basin on it. He kicked the door closed behind him and searched in vain for a lock.

Adam eased Rayna to her feet and quickly unfastened the gag over her mouth. She swallowed convulsively, her tongue swollen and dry in her mouth. He was staring down at her, his face taut and pale in the candlelight.

"What is this place?" she croaked. "What are you doing here?"

"I cannot tell you," he said as he untied her wrists. "But you must trust me, Rayna."

"Trust you!" For a moment, sharp anger overcame her fear. "I was waiting for you, marchese, in the garden! Did you guess I would be there, like a loose, panting wanton? Did you send the comte to get me?"

"Don't be a fool."

"He laughed at me, taunted me! He touched me." She clutched her hands over her gaping nightgown.

Adam wanted nothing more than to take her in his arms and soothe away her fear and her anger, but there wasn't time.

He clamped his hand over her mouth. "Listen to me, Rayna, for we haven't much time. Remember you once told me that you trusted me?"

She looked at him, her eyes dilated with fear. *You have betrayed me.*

"You must do exactly what I tell you. Do you understand?" He lifted his hand from her mouth.

"What are you going to do to me? Rape me?"

Her voice sounded oddly flat. as if she had lost something precious to her.

"We are going to pretend that I raped you. Dammit, Rayna, you must trust me!"

Her eyes fell. "I am so afraid," she whispered.

"So am I. Will you do what I tell you?" As he spoke, he chafed her wrists to ease their numbness.

"Pietro, why did the comte do this? What is he to you?"

He drew her shuddering body against him and gently kissed her temple. "No one is going to touch you, *cara*. I promise."

He prayed that his promise would not be his last, and pushed her away from him. "Now, you must do exactly what I tell you." He nodded toward the bed. His nostrils flared at the smell of sex and old sweat. "Take off your clothes and get under the blanket."

Rayna stared at him. "You want me to take off my . . . clothes?"

He took her shoulders in his hands. "Listen, Rayna, you are here to be raped, by me. We must make them think that is what is happening. Now, do as I tell you."

It was a nightmare, she thought, her fingers fumbled at her torn nightgown. She looked from the corner of her eye toward Pietro as he stripped off his clothes. She saw urgency in his movements, and quickly jerked off her gown.

Adam paid no attention to her. He heard the bed creak and the rustling of the bedclothes. He turned quickly, sat down on the edge of the bed, and pulled off his boots. He paused only a moment before standing to unbutton his breeches.

Rayna pulled the cover to her chin. For a moment she thought she was somehow outside of herself, watching a trembling girl and the man who soon would be as naked as she. *A nightmare! If only she could wake up and laugh at this!*

Her eyes met his for a moment, then fell to his naked chest. "No," she whispered. "Please, Pietro."

He paused, his fingers on the buttons of his breeches. "I am sorry, Rayna. I have no wish to shock you, but there is no choice." He quickly turned his back to her and shrugged out of his breeches.

She stared at his body, lean and olive-tinted, so different from her own. His back and thighs were banded with muscle, his waist narrow, his buttocks smooth and sculptured as if by an artist's hand.

"Stop enjoying the view," he snapped, feeling her eyes upon him.

She saw him draw a dagger. "What are you doing?" she croaked.

Adam did not reply. He lifted his leg and sliced the dagger tip along the inside of his thigh. Blood welled up.

"What have you done!"

He still kept his back to her, not wanting to embarrass her with his nakedness. "Rayna," he said over his shoulder as patiently as he could, "virgins bleed. Since you will remain a virgin, I must bleed for you. Now, pull down the cover."

She only stared at him, and he walked abruptly near to her and whisked the cover away from her. "Open your legs, quickly!"

He heard a sharp intake of breath from her, and watched her slender white thighs slowly part. He sat down beside her, wiped the blood from his thigh onto his finger, and smeared it over her. She jumped at the touch of his fingers, her eyes flying to his face.

"Hush," he said gently. He daubed a bit of blood on the sheet beneath her hips. He turned his back to her and touched more blood to his swollen manhood. Rutting bastard, he thought, staring down at himself for a moment. His head jerked up at the nearing sound of laughter and the clomping of boots.

"Rayna, scream, now!"

He uncoiled his body and lay beside her, taking her into his arms.

"Scream, dammit!"

She let out a high, wailing cry that reverberated off the walls of the small room.

"Again!"

Rayna felt tears well up in her throat, and she sobbed aloud, helplessly.

Adam heard Gervaise in the corridor and knew he would burst in at any moment. He heaved his body on top of her, clutched her face between his hands, and kissed her brutally.

She began to struggle against him, pounding her fists against his back. That was what the comte saw when he thrust open the door and strode into the room.

Tino laughed behind him.

"Well, Pietro, was the little slut a virgin?"

Adam rolled off Rayna, rose slowly, and gave the men a victorious bow.

"*Dio*, he's still hard for her!"

"I want to see for myself," Gervaise said.

Adam shot Rayna a warning with his eyes, tore back the cover, and wrenched her thighs apart.

"Ah, she bleeds red."

Rayna was sobbing quietly, her eyes closed tightly against the men who gaped at her.

"Did you tear her?"

"No," Adam said, and immediately realized it was a mistake.

"Excellent. Now she is mine. I too have a gift for you, my lady."

Rayna grabbed the covers, jerking them to her chin. "No!" she shrieked.

"You will fight me, little dove?"

"I want her, Gervaise!"

"Shut up, Tino. If she swells with child from this night, she will know that it is a . . . gift from one of the two men she herself trifled with."

Adam said very calmly, "No, Gervaise. She is mine and no one else will take her, including you. I intend to take her to my lodgings. If she swells with child, 'twill be mine."

"I will take her downstairs," Gervaise continued, as if Adam had not spoken. "I want her shamed, with all of you watching."

"If you touch her, I will kill you."

The words were so softly spoken that Rayna barely heard them.

The comte stiffened. "Kill me, *mon ami*? Surely no woman is worth haggling over."

"She was your . . . surprise for me, Gervaise. I will keep my gift. Now, get out, and take our panting friends with you."

"See here, Pietro," Celestino began, his face flushing.

"I have no wish to draw your blood, *mon ami*," the comte said slowly. "We will play cards for her."

Adam saw a glint of confidence in the comte's eyes. He breathed a sigh of relief that he had allowed the comte to win the several times they had played. He forced himself to shrug indifferently. "As you will. I have no desire to be uncivil about this."

Gervaise turned to Rayna, a complacent smile on his face. "You, little dove, will watch. Do dress, marchese."

"I will bring her downstairs with me," Adam said. He turned his back on the comte and began to pull on his trousers.

He heard a dry laugh, and the retreat of booted feet. He walked over and quietly closed the door, listening until he was certain the comte had quit the hall.

"Rayna," he said sharply, turning back to her. "Did you understand?"

"Yes," she said.

He saw tears well up in her eyes and roll unheeded down her cheeks. She was trembling violently.

He wanted to comfort her, but there was no time. He said sharply, "Cease wailing. You are an English lady, not some sniveling little ninny! Get your clothes on and remember who you are. I will get you safely out of here."

Her chin rose and her eyes glittered in anger. "You are right," she said firmly, and quickly pulled on her ripped nightgown.

Adam paused a moment and smiled at her. "I will be proud to have you as my wife."

"I have not agreed to marry you, marchese," she said sharply.

"Even after I have shed my blood for you?"

Rayna raised her eyes to his face. "I ask, marchese, that you win the card game." Her gaze fell to his dagger.

"No, Rayna, you will not do what you are thinking. I love you, no matter what happens. I want a living wife, not a dead virgin."

He sat on the bed to pull on his boots, then rose again to fasten his waistcoat. He carefully wiped the dagger on the bedcover and placed it back in his belt. "Come, *petite*."

She placed her hand in his and walked beside him from the room.

"When we get back downstairs, I want you to be disdainful. Do not show fear. From what I know of these men, it would only excite them the more. And you must show hatred for me."

"I will try. When we leave here, Pietro, I will bathe the wound on your leg. I do not want you to become ill."

"I begin to believe that you are not your father's daughter."

They look like carrion, Rayna thought, staring around at the roomful of men. The comte sat at a table shuffling a deck of cards, a glass of brandy at his elbow, looking relaxed and utterly confident. Rayna felt her knees weaken. She pulled away from Adam, her eyes glistening with hatred.

"Ugo," Gervaise said pleasantly, "you have daughters. See that our little bird stays close. I am certain you will know how to punish her if she tries to flee her cage."

"You are scum, comte," Rayna said, "and the rest of your . . . animals as well."

"Ah, I will enjoy teaching you manners," the comte said.

"I think not, Gervaise," Adam said easily, sitting down in a chair opposite him. "I have begun her lessons and I will complete them."

"Odd," the comte said thoughtfully, his eyes still on Rayna. "I did not expect the little slut to have so much spirit. Perhaps you were too gentle with her, *mon ami*."

Adam shrugged indifferently. "I prefer a woman who has some fight left. Later tonight, I will teach her pleasure, and she will beg me to take her."

"That bores you, marchese?" Celestino asked, growing more excited.

"She will doubtless please me for as long as I

want her. Then she can return to England and wed with some red-nosed squire. I've a fancy to have my son step into the fool's boots someday."

"How cold-blooded you are, *mon ami*." He fanned the cards in front of Adam. "Would you care to cut, marchese?"

Adam waved a negligent hand. "I presume there is honor among thieves."

Celestino laughed, poking Niccolo in the ribs.

Adam assumed that Gervaise would cheat, but only with the first hand. He would shuffle the deck on the next round.

"Piquet?"

Adam nodded, looking bored. He stretched his long legs diagonally from the table and leaned back in his chair.

Rayna watched the other men cluster around the table. Only Ugo stayed so close to her that she could smell the brandy on his breath. *I will kill myself if the comte wins*. She realized clearly in that moment that if he did win, the marchese would fight him. He would fight all of them, and they would kill him.

The comte took the first rubber easily, gaining over a hundred points, just as Adam expected. Adam had played conservatively, just as he had before with Gervaise. He knew the comte relied on luck and didn't calculate the odds as he should. He also knew that if the cards ran against him, he would lose, despite his skill. Adam won the next rubber, but gained only a few points. He was careful to cut after the comte's shuffle.

Gervaise stared down at his cards, then lifted his eyes toward the marchese. He was behaving as he usually did, as if he was slightly bored, as if he didn't care who won. But his eyes held something different. Gervaise's gaze passed to Ugo as he held the English girl. She was standing still as a statue, her lovely face as pale as the finest Italian marble. She had pride, he thought, something he admired.

"My quint is good, Gervaise?"

The comte brought his attention back to the game. He started, realizing that despite what he had thought, the marchese was skilled at the game. He said slowly, "Yes, it is good."

"And my tierce?"

"Yes," he gritted out, "that too is good."

When the marchese fanned out a display of high cards before him, all of them good, Gervaise knew that he faced a master.

"I believe that is the rubber, comte," Adam said easily. "Were we playing for gold, I should have enough to buy a new waistcoat. As it is, all I win from you tonight is that silly girl."

"I will pay you gold for her."

Adam arched a brow. "I think not. Before I return her to her father's house, I want to teach her pleasure. Had I not hurt her so much the first time, I vow you would not have heard her scream."

The comte's chair screeched back, and his hands clenched into fists at his sides. For an instant Adam thought he would demand a fight.

"I thank you for your present to me, Gervaise,"

he said quietly. "It is now I who owe you something . . . special."

Gervaise felt his humiliation ease. "You will show the little slut the folly of her rudeness?"

Adam rose slowly, splaying his hands on the table. "I will mark her, my friend. You may all rest assured that she will say nothing of this night."

"Very well," Gervaise said, his voice harsh. "Take her!"

Thirty minutes later, Adam dismounted from his house and pulled Rayna into his arms.

"No," he said softly, shaking his head, "not quite yet, *ma mie*, until we are inside. Naples has too many ears for my peace of mind."

Adam pulled up short at the sight of Daniele in the entrance hall.

"My lord!"

"Daniele," Adam said, "I am glad you are here. Just so," he added smoothly, seeing Daniele's aghast expression at the sight of Rayna Lyndhurst in his arms. "We have endured some excitement tonight, Daniele. If you would please check about outside for any uninvited guests. It is possible that our dear comte had us followed."

Daniele looked at his master searchingly, nodded, and slipped silently out of the front door.

Adam carried Rayna into the small parlor and set her down gently on a sofa. "I think you need a glass of brandy, Rayna," he said, walking toward the sideboard.

"Do you really believe the comte had us followed?"

Adam shrugged. "It would not be wise to underestimate him. I had believed that he trusted me completely. I was wrong."

"You will take me home?"

"Yes, but the comte would not expect it for a couple of hours yet. Here, *cara*, drink this."

The fiery liquor burned down her throat. She drew a deep breath and set down her glass. "I am much relieved that you play piquet so well, Pietro."

Adam sat beside her and began to rub her cold hands. "I have always let the comte win at cards. It tried him sorely to lose. Odd, but there is some honor in him after all."

"What were you doing there, Pietro?"

Adam sighed, knowing he could not fob her off. "I was the new member of their . . . club. They work for Napoleon, Rayna, and it was important that I be accepted as one of them."

"But why?"

"I am a spy of sorts, but not for her majesty. I have nothing to do with either Napoleon or the queen. My venture is entirely private."

"And it involves the Comte de la Valle?"

"The comte is selling to the French goods stolen from my family. I came to Naples to discover that, and the identity of the person supplying him with them. I know now that the whole matter will be resolved within days. There is more, Rayna, but I would that you wait until then. I do not believe that the comte or any of his group will attempt to harm you again, but I wish you always to be in the company of others until I tell you otherwise." He added to himself silently that he would have one of his own men watch the viscount's villa.

"You give me orders, yet you tell me nothing."

He smiled ruefully, his eyes dropping to his hands. "It is true. I ask you again, Rayna, to trust me."

"Well, I have an order for you, marchese. My father must not know about this night. Ever."

Adam looked undecided, as if he did not realize that if her father discovered what had happened, they could forget ever seeing each other again.

"Promise me," she said.

"Very well. Perhaps it is better that he not be . . . disturbed, at least for the moment."

"Please take off your breeches, marchese."

He looked taken aback, then grinned. "My valet will see to my wound, though I would prefer your gentle touch. I have made you blush again. Forgive me."

"You saw me naked," she blurted out suddenly.

"I did not look at you as would a lover. But you, *petite*, I felt your eyes burning my flesh."

"You always mock me," she complained. "When will you be my lover?" She looked startled at her own question, but it had popped from her mouth, without her mind's permission.

"When you are my wife," Adam said calmly.

She felt tears sting her eyes at his stupid masculine presumption. She wanted to yell at him that her father would never allow them to wed. "You do not know my father," she said.

"We shall see," Adam said.

The events of the evening crowded into her mind again, and she whispered, "I have never been so frightened in my life."

"Neither have I."

"You did not act frightened."

He gave her a tender smile. "I was too busy slicing up my leg."

"I am still frightened," she said, lowering her eyes to her lap.

"I shouldn't give you more brandy. I can't have you reeling about tomorrow with a royal hangover."

"Please hold me, Pietro."

He knew that he shouldn't. Even after the terror of the evening, he felt desire for her. He looked away from her. "You were very brave tonight."

"Pietro . . ."

God how he hated that name! "No, Rayna," he said firmly, leaping to his feet and putting the distance of the small parlor between them. "And stop looking at me that way. I am not made of stone!"

If I were pregnant, Pietro, my father would have to let us marry.

"I am sleepy," she said calmly.

"Good," Adam said with a sigh of relief. "I will bring you a blanket."

"Yes," she said, not looking at him, "that would be nice."

When he returned from his bedchamber with a soft blanket in his arms, Rayna was staring into the fireplace a thoughtful frown drawing her brows together. She slewed her face about to gaze at him.

"I do not feel like a virgin anymore," she said, her voice bemused. "Your blood is on my thighs."

"Would you like to bathe before you sleep?" he said carefully, unfolding the blanket.

"No." She shuddered suddenly and her eyes dimmed. "They were all staring at me. I wanted to die."

"When you see them again, as you will, at court functions, you must pretend complete indifference. I do not believe you have any more to fear from any of them, but promise me you will never be alone."

"I promise."

Adam tucked the blanket about her legs and lightly touched her cheek. "The comte was right about one thing, *petite*. You do have spirit. Will you run me through if I ever wander?"

"Yes," she said without hesitation.

"You are much like my mother," Adam said. Before she could question him, he continued quickly, "Sleep now. I will wake you when it is time to leave."

13

Arabella felt anger so great, she shook with it. And contempt. Contempt at herself. During the weeks in Naples, she had enjoyed herself thoroughly, dancing with gallant Italian noblemen, attending every royal function available, and fancying that she was the one who was engineering the growing feeling between Adam and Rayna. In reality, she had paid mere lip service to the reason why Adam was here, treating the mystery as if it were some sort of harmless puzzle to be solved. But no longer.

She shivered, thinking of what had happened to Rayna. And the contessa! She, fool that she was, had acted like an innocent lamb in the presence of that lady. Aware that Adam had turned back to her, she quickly unclenched her fists and smoothed out the ferocious frown on her forehead. She managed to say calmly enough, "I did wonder why she asked me so many questions. Lord, Adam, if the Contessa Lucianna di Rolando is the one behind all this, there has to be a reason." *And I intend to discover what it is!*

"Bella, you have the same questions as I," Adam said. He looked about the park for a moment, watching the morning sunlight stream through the thick blanket of foliage over their heads. "I haven't the foggiest notion what her motives might be. I am simply telling you what several of the comte's friends let slip to me last night. We cannot even be certain that it is she. I am sending Antonio with a letter to Father today, telling him all that has happened. He may know who this contessa is. I expect he will be in Naples with a dozen men within a week."

"Then it will all be over. I still can't believe the effrontery of the comte! What a terrible ordeal for Rayna! You may be certain, brother, that I shall take good care of her . . . now." The vehemence in her voice startled Adam.

"She was very brave, Bella, but I am concerned that her memories of what happened may affect her in an . . . unhealthy way. I would appreciate your keeping a watch on her."

"You may be certain that I shall." Arabella, eschewing games now, said directly, "Will you marry her, Adam?"

"Yes, Miss Matchmaker, I shall."

If he had given her such credit but the day before, she would have twitted him unmercifully. But not today. "That still leaves the contessa," Arabella said after a moment. "She has invited me to lunch with her at her villa."

"You will not go."

At his peremptory command, Arabella frowned up at him. "Good heavens, Adam, we obviously need more information. You cannot go to her villa, but I, an invited guest, certainly can."

"No," he said, more forcefully this time. "And that's an end to it, Bella. We will wait word from Father."

After twenty years, Arabella knew when she could cajole Adam and when she could not. She bit her lower lip over a caustic comment, and said on a sigh, "Very well, Adam. Perhaps that is the wisest course."

"You know it is," he said sharply. "If you were a man, you would know not to rush pell-mell into the enemy's camp without knowing his strength or his motives."

Ah, Arabella thought, still not looking at her brother, but a silly woman doesn't have the advantage of all your man's tactics and strategy. She nodded and flashed him a brilliant smile, not caring what he thought.

Adam observed her closely for a moment, not trusting her completely, but there was another matter on his mind. "Bella, I have set Vincenzo to watch the viscount's villa, but he is only one man. How did she seem to you this morning?"

"Quiet, I suppose, more so than usual. Lord, after what happened to her last night, I would expect her to be cowering under her bed! When I left, her mother had decided to physic her." She laughed, despite her gloomy thoughts, remembering the scene. "Rayna sent her to the rearabout, and in the most delightful fashion."

"Bella," Adam said abruptly, "I must go now. Keep close to the viscount and away from the contessa. I have a feeling that events are going to close in around us very quickly."

"You mean that we have, perhaps, stirred the pot to boiling?"

"It is odd," Adam said thoughtfully after a moment, stroking his thick beard, "but I think the pot was boiling long before we arrived in Naples. It's like a tangled skein that can be unraveled only by one set of hands."

"Whose hands, Adam?"

Adam shrugged. "It's just an odd feeling I have. I believe it is Father."

So I am to sit docilely, twiddling my thumbs, Arabella thought, all because of your wretched male intuition? She gave him her most beatific smile.

"Be careful, puss," he said, and hugged her. He touched his finger to her lips. "And take care of Rayna."

"Ah." She forced herself to laugh. "The real reason you are worried!"

Adam quirked a dark brow at her and strode away to his horse.

Rayna chatted brightly to her parents at the dinner table that evening, laughing as if she hadn't a care in the world. Arabella marveled at her, for she appeared quite sincere in her good humor.

Arabella didn't know Rayna had come to a decision, an irrevocable decision of which she was very certain. She smiled serenely at her father as he paused to sip his wine, interrupting his diatribe against foreigners in general and Italians in particular.

Arabella took the blessed opportunity to ask Lady Delford, "Did Lady Eden fill your ears with more scandalous tidbits from court, ma'am?"

"My dear," Lady Delford said, "you do not know the half of it! The woman's tongue runs on wheels!"

"It is likely," Lord Delford said, "that the conversation you suffered today, my love, was similar to the one I had in strictest confidence yesterday with the queen. The woman is obsessed, particularly now that Napoleon is demanding Acton's removal from power. She ranted and carried on until I had a vision of my handkerchief stuffed in her royal mouth!"

"Because Acton is too pro-English, sir?" Arabella asked.

"Largely," the viscount agreed. "Not that his removal will make much difference, though. Sometimes I wish that Vesuvius would erupt again and carry all of Naples into the sea. Then we could all go home, and their royal majesties could retire with due honor to Sicily."

"I doubt the *lazzaroni* would approve such a scheme, Father," Rayna observed dryly.

Edward Lyndhurst smiled lovingly at his daughter. "True, my dear. It is the oddest thing—the peasants and their unaccountable adoration for Ferdinando."

"Not so unaccountable, sir," Arabella said, laughing. "Particularly when he dresses as they do and sells fish in the market beside them, conversing, I hear, in the most colorful language."

"Perhaps," the viscount said neutrally. "Rayna, my dear, what did you do today?"

Rayna started, but only for a moment, and then smiled brightly. "Ah, naught of much, really. I practiced the piano and studied my Italian. Maria, my maid, believes me a veritable native now."

Lord Edward, who believed that English was the only useful language, merely nodded.

"I look forward to a restful evening at home," Lady Delford said to the table at large. "Thank the Lord there are no new arrivals and yet another reception at court."

"I, too, Mother," Rayna agreed placidly. "I for one am rather tired and look forward to an early bed."

"Do you feel all right?" Rayna's mother asked solicitously.

"Just a bit of a headache," Rayna said, lying fluently. She listened with but a smile as her father recounted the news in a letter from her eldest brother. Lord Delford peered at his daughter closely before finishing smoothly, "Thomas hopes to be in England in the fall. And not alone, I might add. He will bring Lord Lynton with him, Rayna, a gentleman he assures me is all that one could wish. Thomas tells me that besides being an excellent soldier—"

"—he enjoys an income of ten thousand pounds a year?"

"Certainly he is not a pauper! He is, evidently, much interested in making your acquaintance, my dear. He is Eagleton's grandson, a gentleman of great good sense whom I much admire."

Rayna's headache threatened to become markedly worse. She saw that her father was regarding her with some perplexity, and smoothed her mouth into a smile. "He sounds a paragon, Papa," she said.

"I look forward to seeing Thomas again," Arabella said gaily, drawing the viscount's attention away from Rayna. "I must convince him that the navy, particularly an assignment with Nelson, would be far more exciting than the army."

Out of civility, Lord Delford forced a pained smile. As Arabella spoke to his wife, he glanced at her fall of honey-colored hair, just like her mother's, but when she turned, it was her father's dark eyes that shone with humor and devilry at him. He said abruptly to his wife, "If you will excuse me, my love, I have some papers to review." Arabella Welles was a handful, and too damned arrogant and sure of herself for a girl. He found himself rather relieved that she wasn't his daughter, and wouldn't be his responsibility for much longer. Without her influence, it would never have occurred to Rayna to speak back to him at dinner! It brought that black-bearded young puppy Adam

Welles to mind. At least Rayna hadn't so much as mentioned him recently. He sighed, wishing they could leave Naples and all its chattering foreigners behind them.

Rayna excused herself directly after tea and locked herself in her bedchamber, there to pass several hours in ferocious pacing. After an eternity of waiting, she finally heard the clock downstairs strike eleven. It was time to leave. She thought one last time of her promise to the marchese to stay close to her father's villa, and resolutely repressed her niggling fear that the comte or one of his dreadful friends was skulking about outside the grounds.

She donned her cloak, looked back at the lumpy pillow she had placed beneath the covers in her bed, and peeked into the corridor. No one was in sight. *What will I do if Pietro isn't at his lodgings?* She refused to dwell on that thought. She willed him to be there.

There was a quarter-moon, and the night air was cool. She made her way silently to the small stable at the back of the villa. She would have to ride bareback, for she couldn't risk her mare snorting and thrashing about if she tried to saddle her. The two stableboys were in their rooms at the rear of the stables, likely already in bed. She crept inside, and her heart jumped as one of the horses whinnied at her arrival.

She shushed the stallion in a harsh whisper and pushed several cubes of sugar into his mouth before seeking out her mare. She stroked the mare's nose and quietly slipped a bridle over her head, bribing her silence with the remainder of her sugar.

She looked at every shadow as she led her mare down the graveled drive toward the road, then slipped easily onto her back. The ride to the marchese's lodgings was blessedly short. She led her mare to the small thatch-covered stable and tied her reins to a post. She crept through a maze of thick shrubbery to the front of the house and firmly grasped the brass knocker.

The thudding sound it made against the door made her jump. But there was no answer, only silence, and she banged the knocker again. Her shoulders finally slumped in defeat. She wanted to cry and at the same time curse her ill luck.

Suddenly her heart plummeted to her toes in horror. A hand covered her mouth and someone pulled her backward. At the same time, the front door opened, and Adam stood silhouetted in the dim light.

"Jesus Christ! Rayna! Vincenzo—what the devil!"

The hand over her mouth loosened, and the man said, "I followed her here, my lord. She wasn't out of my sight for an instant."

"Thank you, Vincenzo," Adam said. He saw that Rayna was perfectly white with terror. "You may go back to the villa. I will return Miss Lyndhurst."

Vincenzo released her and stepped off the front steps, quickly disappearing into the night.

Rayna saw the marchese's disbelief turn to anger. She quickly threw herself against his chest and wrapped her arms around his back.

"How can I protect you, you little fool, if you have no regard for your own safety?" Even as he spoke, his hands were molding her against him and he was kissing her temple. "Come," he said roughly, pushing her away, "you are going home!"

"I came to see you, Pietro."

"Have you lost your damned mind?" he growled at her. She merely smiled and he cursed under his breath. "Very well, come inside before someone sees you."

His hold on her arm was not gentle as he led her through the dim entrance hall to the parlor.

Without speaking to her, he quickly strode to the long windows and drew the heavy curtains. He turned slowly, schooling his anger at her. "This is nonsense, Rayna. I should beat you for your foolhardiness. What if the comte—"

She interrupted him firmly. "I was frightened of that, Pietro, but regardless, I wanted to see you."

He grinned suddenly at the stubborn set of her jaw. "Very well," he said evenly, "now you are here. What did you wish to say to me?"

"Is the cut on your thigh healing?"

He watched color flood her face at her own temerity, and smiled. "Yes," he said. "It was nothing."

"Oh?" she said, raising her chin. "You cut yourself often to protect virgins?"

"Don't be a fool," he growled at her.

"Very well," she said amicably. "Tell me, Pietro, what is the weather like in Sicily this time of year?"

He looked at her searchingly. "Rayna, what game are you playing?"

She said sweetly, "If Sicily is to be my home, should I not show interest? Surely I would be unnatural if I did not."

"Sicily is quite warm. There is practically no rain."

"Tell me, marchese," she continued thoughtfully, "what is England like—its weather, I mean?"

He regarded her beneath lowered brows. "Are you quite through, Rayna?"

"Perhaps. What I should like to know, sir, is why, when you first saw me, you spoke in the most fluent English?"

"Damn," Adam said.

"Perhaps you only curse in English, *marchese*?"

Adam sighed. "I am not a marques," he said in English, dropping all pretense. He could not but admit a feeling of relief. "Rayna, I promised your father that you would not discover who I am."

"I haven't, yet. However, if you do not tell me exactly who you are, sir, I swear that I will ask my father directly."

He smiled reluctantly. "That, I daresay, is a believable threat. Very well, Miss Lyndhurst." He proffered her an elegant bow. "May I present Viscount St. Ives. Quite an acceptable fellow, really. Since you are not quite a stranger to him, I see no impropriety in your addressing him as Adam Welles."

Rayna gaped at him, speechless. "My God!" she managed at last. "The Earl of Clare—"

"My esteemed sire."

"Arabella—"

"My less-esteemed sister. Do you wish to review the rest of my family?"

Rayna dropped abruptly to the sofa. "I do not believe it," she muttered. "It is too fantastic! And I was jealous of Bella! You . . . odious wretch! How you must have laughed at me behind my back!"

"No," Adam said, "never that, *cara*. I felt miserable because I could not tell you who I was. Arabella too."

"You could have trusted me," she said indignantly.

"I did. As I said, 'twas a promise to your father. You see, Rayna," he continued after a moment, "your father is not on particularly amicable terms with mine. Nor does your father particularly approve of me."

"But why?"

"I doubt if I know the whole story. Evidently your father was once in love with my mother—indeed, I believe they were engaged. I gather he thinks my father some sort of marauder who stole the woman he wanted. And I, I fear, am no better."

"And Father intends me for this ridiculous Lord Lynton," Rayna said under her breath. She was right to have come, she told herself.

Adam was watching her changing expressions with some foreboding. "Now that you know the truth, Rayna, I can take you home."

"You greatly resemble your father. I feel like such a ninny not to have recognized you."

"You have not seen me for six years, Rayna."
He stroked his beard. "This foliage renders me
somewhat . . . mysterious. I, on the other hand,
rememberd you as a scraggly little weed, with
flyaway hair and skinned knees, forever trying to
keep up with your brothers."

She flushed and saw him frown impatiently, as if
anxious to have her gone. She said quickly, "So
the comte is stealing from your family?"

"He is involved, certainly. I think Bella and I
have discovered who the person is who did the
actual looting. My father should be arriving within
the week. Then, my dear, I can have a talk with
your father."

"I see," she said, casting about her mind for
further conversation. She rose from the sofa, gazed
at Adam from beneath her lashes, and swayed.
"Everything is so dark," she gasped, flinging her
hands toward him. He was at her side in an instant,
his hands clutching her shoulders.

"Are you all right?" His voice was harsh in his
concern.

"I shall be better . . . soon," she whispered.
With calm forethought, she leaned against the long
length of him.

Adam felt her tremble, and set about to soothe
her. That his soothing took the form of a gentle,
exploring kiss did not seem inappropriate to him
at the moment. Her mouth felt like soft silk beneath his. When his tongue lightly caressed her
lips, she parted her own, to allow him entrance.
He whispered love words into her mouth, a tanta-

lizing mixture of Italian and English, his breath warm and sweet. She felt his large hands stroke down her back to her hips, and he lifted her, pressing her fiercely against him.

Adam felt a momentary hesitancy in her, and immediately released her. "Forgive me, love," he managed in a ragged voice. "I would not hurt you, ever." He drew a deep breath. "I will take you home now."

"What . . . what did you say?" she whispered.

"Home. I must get you home, for God's sake."

He thought he was taking advantage of her. "I . . . I still feel a bit faint," she said in a faltering voice, and slowly eased down onto the sofa.

Adam stared down at her, his hands clenched at his sides. Did she not realize that she was driving him wild? No, of course she didn't.

Rayna drew back, a small smile playing about her lips. Adam watched her slender fingers unfasten the small buttons of her bodice.

"Rayna," he said in an incredulous voice, "you haven't listened to me! What the devil are you doing?"

She continued at her task, not looking at him, until she felt the cool air touch her bare flesh. As she pushed at the lace straps of her chemise, his fingers covered her own in an iron grip.

He stared at her a long moment. "So," he said at last on a sigh. "This is why you came here to me."

"Yes," she said, smiling. "I came to seduce you." Without another word, she slipped the straps of her chemise from her shoulders and pushed it downward. He couldn't seem to take his eyes off her exquisite white flesh. He hadn't remembered how perfectly shaped her breasts were.

He tried to jump to his feet, but she grabbed his arm, and somehow—he wasn't exactly certain later how it happened—he was on the sofa, his arms around her back, and his mouth pressed against the hollow of her throat. He felt the fierce pounding of her pulse against his lips, and groaned deep in his throat.

Adam had felt desire many times, but he had never before loved a woman he desired. He was amazed at how fiercely he wanted to possess her, to make her a part of him. He wanted her, as he had wanted many women before her, but he wanted even more than that to have her desire him.

"Come," he said. He pulled her to her feet and gently lifted her in his arms. He felt her light kisses against his throat as he carried her up the narrow staircase.

Adam placed her on his bed and quickly lit the candle. Its gentle flame shadowed her face, but from where he stood he could see the excited anticipation in her eyes, like an explorer, he thought, smiling to himself, eager to chart unknown lands.

Rayna sensed a hesitancy in him again. She lowered her eyes to the remaining buttons on her gown and began busily to unfasten them, her fingers unfaltering.

He sat beside her, pausing to push a tendril of

auburn hair from her forehead, lightly kissed her lips, and rose. He paused again, his hands on his cravat, to lean down and pull the spread over her.

She was staring up at him, her eyes wide and questioning. He gently kissed the tip of her nose, and straightened to strip off the clothes. It was like the night before, when Rayna lay sprawled on the bed before him, terrified yet trusting him. He was aware now, just as he had been then, that she was watching him, her eyes on his body. He turned slowly, naked, to face her.

"I . . . didn't remember you like that," she gasped, her throat suddenly dry.

Adam cocked his head to one side, not understanding. "Like what, Rayna?"

"It is impossible," she said firmly.

His eyes followed her gaze, and he laughed. "We shall see, *cara*," He slipped under the cover beside her, and saw she was lying rigidly beside him.

"Surely I, a simple man, do not frighten you?"

"You are not a simple man, Adam Welles, you are . . . huge!"

"And you are small and beautiful, and I will fill you, Rayna, but not with pain."

"Do you promise?" she whispered. She stared up at his dark face, close above her own. His eyes were nearly black in the shadowy light.

"I promise." As he gently possessed her mouth, his body reminded him he had not enjoyed a woman since he met Rayna at the palace, long weeks before. Touching her, feeling her lithe body respond to him, made him shudder with need. He forced himself to think of her, to make her forget any pain he would bring her.

He sloughed off the cover and let his hands rove over her breasts. Her soft mouth trembled and yielded to his probing tongue, and he felt a nearly painful urge to possess her. He abruptly pulled away.

"I love for you to kiss me," she said shyly, her fingers stroking his face. "And I love your beard. It tickles."

"I am glad," he said, and buried his face against her breasts. As he gently licked her, lightly nipping her with his teeth, he felt her nipple tauten and her body arch up against his mouth. Adam drew a deep ragged breath and slipped his arm under her back. He pulled her upward against him and let his fingers rove over her silken flesh to her narrow waist. His eyes rested on the soft triangle of auburn curls, darker than her hair.

"You are so lovely, Rayna," he said, pressing his lips against her temple. As his fingers tangled in her hair, searching for her, she clutched at his shoulder. When he found her, soft and moist, she lurched upward, her fingers digging into his arm.

"I don't understand," she whispered. Her body was tensing of its own will, her flesh rippling beneath his caressing hand.

Adam kissed her mouth, forcing her back against his supporting arm.

"Please stop," she cried out suddenly, her voice

wild, yet uncertain. "I cannot bear it! Please, Adam."

"You do not have to bear it, *cara*," he said, gazing into her widened eyes. "You need only to enjoy it."

"Adam," she whispered in a question; then her body convulsed, and she cried out his name again. He muffled her cries with a kiss and before her gasping breaths eased, he parted her slender thighs and eased himself over her.

"Rayna," he commanded, "look at me."

She raised vague eyes to his face. Her body, still afire with the rippling spasms, arched upward.

"A moment of pain, love, just a moment."

She felt his fingers gently parting her, and the sensation made her tremble. He entered her slowly, pausing a moment at her taut maidenhead.

"I love you, Rayna," he said, and pushed into her.

He thrust again, tearing through her thin barrier, burying himself deep within her. He heard her cry out, a jagged moan, but his body was raging with need. He felt her tensing with pain and it brought him a measure of control. He covered her with his body, balancing himself above her on his elbows.

"Lie still," he said, and lowered his head to kiss her. He whispered into her mouth, "Is that better now, love?"

Rayna felt him deep within her. It was an odd feeling, yet comforting, as if his body had become a part of hers.

"That is better," she said. She parted her lips for him, wanting to feel his tongue again, and stroked her hands down his back. She felt him quiver at her touch, the taut muscles tensing beneath her fingers. For the first time she felt the power of her own body. When she caressed his hips, he groaned and drew back, and she tensed briefly at the dull pain it brought her.

He felt her tense beneath him, but he reared back and plunged deep, his seed exploding from his body. He was beyond words, beyond thought, held in passion so complete that he was beyond himself. His shuddering body finally stilled and he lay on top of her, covering her completely.

He kissed her gently, caressing her face between his hands, whispering love words to her. For the first time in his life, Adam thought of the children he would have with her, of all the days and nights they would share, and he smiled.

"Whoever thought I would wed Rayna Lyndhurst," he said, more to himself than to her.

"You must learn tolerance for the English, sir," she said, grinning up at him, her voice soft and sated.

He raised his hand and lightly traced her lips. "My love, I have more than enough tolerance for the English. You know, of course, that my sister is more smug than you can imagine, that we will wed. She fancies herself responsible for my passion for you."

"Imagine Bella my sister!" She frowned a moment. "I still don't understand why Bella as my best friend did not take me into her confidence about your identity. It is too bad of her!"

"She showed admirable restraint, love, perhaps for the first time in her life."

"Adam, may I speak to Arabella now? Tell her that I know who you are?"

"I suppose it can make no difference now. I don't imagine you intend to tell her also how you spent this evening?"

Rayna chuckled, "A woman should have some secrets, my lord. Besides," she added loftily, "Arabella wouldn't understand." She smiled in delight. "Now I am certain I know something Bella doesn't!"

"I wish you didn't," he said on a sigh.

"Adam, am I going to have a baby?"

"Rayna," he said, sudden insight bursting upon him, "you make me want to beat you." He rolled off her onto his back. "Do you trust me so little that you came to me because you were hopeful I would get you with child?"

"That was perhaps part of it," she said in a small voice.

He pulled her down upon her back and kissed her. "I hope you are not with child, *cara*," he said quietly. He saw that she would protest and lightly touched his fingers over her lips. "Your father will accept me, Rayna. I have told you that. There was no reason to resort to . . . blackmail."

"I did not intend to take any chances," she said primly. "And now I believe I am suitably compromised. They would call me damaged goods, would they not?"

"I do not wish us to have a seven-month child. You will be my wife, and I want no raised eyebrows."

"Yes, my lord," she said docilely.

Adam shook his head and laughed. "Here I believed you so very biddable and gentle. You have a stubborn streak, Rayna, that terrifies me." He felt her fingers tangle in the hair on his chest, and despite himself, his breathing quickened. "No," he said firmly, pulling away from her. "We are going to clean you up, *petite*, and then it's home for you."

Rayna eyed him carefully as he stood beside the bed, and smiled. "I am no longer a virgin," she announced in a cheerful voice.

"No," Adam replied, a worried frown drawing his brows together, "you are not."

14

Arabella was grimly pleased with herself. The pistol she had taken—borrowed, rather—from Lord Delford's desk was snug against her thigh, where it would stay until she returned safely from the Contessa Luciana di Rolando's villa. She would not let Adam order her about as if she were some silly chit! Her anger was still a raw force within her and she click-clicked her mare down the rutted road that led toward the hills outside of Naples. She supposed that the contessa must like to entertain her lovers in privacy.

Her thoughts veered toward Rayna and Adam, and she smiled. She knew well enough where Rayna had spent several hours of the previous night, for she had heard her tiptoe to her room and had seen Vincenzo moving quietly back to his post near the stables. She wondered briefly if Adam, in the throes of passion, whatever that was, had told Rayna who he really was. She hadn't had the chance to find out, for Rayna was still asleep in her bedchamber when Arabella had left. Rayna had, Arabella decided, shown a great deal of gumption, slipping out of the villa to go to Adam. She tilted up her chin. It was time for her to prove that she was her father's daughter, and not some dithering chit whose only worth was to stitch a straight line and flirt charmingly.

She passed several small huts, their occupants, she saw, working in the olive groves. She was beginning to think she had taken the wrong road, when she saw a villa nestled at the base of a small hill to her left. It was an elegant house, painted a dazzling white and set amid tall green cypresses. She turned her mare onto the drive that wound in circular fashion to the front of the villa. It was small and square, its balconies along the second floor overflowing with blossoming hyacinths, jasmine, carnations, and roses. She wondered cynically if the fat king had provided the contessa with this exquisite little hideaway. She reined in her mare and slid out of the saddle. An old man, his face weathered by decades of blistering Neapolitan sun, ambled toward her, nodded without speaking, and led her mare away.

Did not the contessa have other servants? she wondered, glancing about. The peaceful setting suddenly seemed chilling. Stop it, she chided herself. No harm could come to her over a simple luncheon, and besides, she had her pistol. She tossed her head and marched to the front door, her pulse quickening in her veins. Today the contessa would talk freely to her.

Arabella was shown into a small parlor by a black-gowned servant, a woman who did not look particularly Italian.

"Ah, Lady Arabella. How delightful of you to pay a lonesome old woman a visit. I was beginning to wonder if you had forgotten."

The contessa did not look like a lonesome old woman to Arabella. She was splendidly gowned in ivory satin, her black hair pulled high on her head in fashionable topknot, with curling tendrils falling down her neck. A lovely diamond necklace lay against her bosom. Arabella wondered if her father's cargoes paid for the bauble.

"It is my pleasure, contessa," Arabella said in a smooth voice, touching her fingers to the woman's outstretched hand. "You have a lovely home," she added, gazing about the cozy parlor with its creamy white furnishings. "The fireplace is most exquisite."

"Yes, I admire Italian marble. There is nothing to rival it in all the world, I think. But I forget my manners, Lady Arabella. Will you not accompany me to the dining room? Luigi has prepared us a small meal that I hope will please you."

Arabella nodded and followed the contessa from the parlor across a narrow hallway into a sunlit room filled with yellow roses.

"How lovely," Arabella said.

"Yes, it is," the contessa agreed. "I trust you like a cold shrimp-and-scallop salad, Lady Arabella." She paused a moment, then added on a pained smile, "As I get older, I find I cannot afford to indulge in heavy luncheons."

"But you are as slender as a girl," Arabella exclaimed, momentarily diverted.

Again Giovanna felt a tug of liking for the earl's daughter. "Thank you," she said, and seated herself across from her guest.

"You are enjoying your stay in Naples, madam?"

"Ah, yes," Giovanna said. "The king and queen are most kind."

She placed slight emphasis on the "king," enough for Arabella to wonder if the contessa was mocking her. She sipped the white wine placed before her, and decided it was time for her to become a bit more worldly. She gave the contessa a disconcertingly brilliant smile. "The king and queen are indeed charming. But I must tell you that I prefer some of the younger gentlemen in the court. They are much more exciting, I think."

"Oh?" Giovanna asked.

"Indeed," Arabella continued, feigning a sophistication that would have made her father and brother stare at her as if she were a raree-show. She shuddered with delicate excitement. "There is one gentleman who is ever so frightening, but withal, he makes me feel very much like a . . . woman."

Giovanna smiled. "You are drawn to dangerous young men, *signorina*?"

"Oh yes," Arabella said gaily. "The comte in particular I find terribly bewitching."

"The comte?" Giovanna repeated carefully.

"The Comte de la Valle, madam," Arabella said, lowering her voice. "He is French, you know, and so very . . . ah, *charmant*, and manly." There, contessa, Arabella thought, sipping more of the fruity wine. *Now what do you think of me?*

Giovanna felt such a surge of anger that a small shrimp fell from her fork onto the white tablecloth. *The little fool, baiting me,* she thought. She quickly recovered her poise.

"Yes," Giovanna said, smiling. "I myself find the comte to my liking. He is particularly gallant in the bedchamber."

Arabella couldn't prevent the slight quiver of shock that widened her expressive eyes.

Such a child you are, my lady, Giovanna thought, repressing a laugh.

"I would imagine so," Arabella managed after a long moment. *Get hold of yourself, you fool!*

Giovanna leaned forward. "But not so seductive a lover as some other men I have known. More wine, child?"

Arabella gladly accepted another glass, for she had the forbidding feeling that she was no longer in control of the situation. She drank deeply.

"Thank you, contessa," she said.

Giovanna sat back in her chair and gazed pensively into her wine glass. "I remember one gentleman who could make me limp with his passion. I was much younger then, as was he, of course."

"He was your husband, contessa?" Arabella asked desperately.

"No. My husband was already dead, thank the Lord."

"Oh."

"This gentleman was an English nobleman, wealthy, powerful, and exquisitely . . . manly."

"But your son, contessa. You have not told me about your son, madam, save that he is twenty-five years old." *Why is she prosing on about an English nobleman?*

Giovanna turned a ruby ring slowly about her fingers. "My son, Lady Arabella? His name is Kamal."

Arabella could not seem to keep her eyes from the glittering ring. "Kamal?" she repeated. "That is an odd name, is it not, madam?"

"His Italian name is Alessandro, as I believe I once told you. But you will meet him, my dear. Yes, you will meet him, and very soon now."

Arabella tore her gaze from the ruby. "Alexander," she said. "That is his name in English. And how will I meet him, madam? Is he coming to Naples?" Her tongue felt oddly thick in her mouth, and her fork, poised to spear a pink shrimp, seemed suddenly heavy.

She heard the contessa say, as if from a great distance, "No, my girl, he is not coming to Naples. You will journey to meet him."

"That is impossible." The words slid from her mouth, slurred even to her own ears. "I do not feel . . . quite right," she said.

"Would you care to hear more about the Englishman who was my lover, child?" Giovanna rose from her chair and leaned toward Arabella. "I wanted him, *signorina*, but he cast me aside and chose someone else."

Arabella pulled her gaze from the contessa's face. Her eyes dropped to the wineglass still held between her fingers. The wine had tasted so sweet, too sweet. "The wine . . ." she said.

"Yes, my dear, the wine. You came here to bait me into revealing myself. You see, you have succeeded."

The contessa gently pulled away Arabella's plate.

"The wine," Arabella whispered, the contessa's words drifting like brittle fall leaves through her mind. The contessa's face blurred. "Someone help me!" she cried softly. Arabella slumped forward, her arms cushioning her fall.

She heard a woman's voice. "Sleep now, my girl. Enjoy it. When you awake, you will be glad for it."

Gervaise, Comte de la Valle, fell forward over the woman, his head on the pillow beside hers. Damn her, he thought, his breathing calming. At least she could feign pleasure and not lie like a statue beneath him. He heaved himself up on his elbows and felt her squirm under his weight.

"You are always in such a hurry, *caro*." Giovanna chided him softly. "A gentleman never takes his pleasure first."

Rayna Lyndhurst's beautiful pale face rose in his mind. He pictured her body as he had seen it briefly the night Pietro raped her. She was so white and slender, so tantalizingly young. But not innocent anymore. He felt himself grow hard at the thought of having her beneath him, struggling against him, if she wished.

"Ah," he heard the contessa murmur, "I knew you would not disappoint me."

He stroked Rayna, caressed her with his mouth as he moved slowly over her. He quickened when she tightened her white thighs about his haunches, and eased his fingers between them to caress her. He heard her breathing sharpen, felt her body writhe beneath him. He opened his eyes, and the vivid image was gone. The contessa, her black hair tangled, her face contorted in her climax, lay shuddering beneath him.

Gervaise groaned his disappointment. He withdrew from the contessa and fell away from her onto his back.

He is young, Giovanna thought, and young men are selfish. But he had given her pleasure, at last. She felt satisfied, both with herself and with him.

"*Caro,*" she said, turning on her side to face him. "I am leaving Naples."

Her eyes traveled down the length of his lean body and she nearly laughed out loud at her memory of the king's paunchy belly, his nearly hairless groin and legs.

"When, contessa?" Gervaise asked at last, pulling his thoughts from Rayna Lyndhurst.

"As soon as you leave, *mon brave.*"

He wondered why she had asked him here in the early afternoon. He usually rode to her villa in the evening, under cover of darkness. "Why do you leave so quickly?"

"My . . . business is completed here," she said. "I have enjoyed our time together, Gervaise."

He frowned, for her voice sounded silky, almost mocking. He shook his head. The payment she had given him for his services wasn't enough in his mind for having made love to her several nights a week. "What is your business, contessa?" he asked abruptly. "You have never told me."

"Revenge," she said lightly, trailing her fingers over his chest.

"Revenge," he repeated blankly. He pulled away from her caressing hand and sat up. "I thought you wished to support the French, and that was your reason for—"

He froze at her tinkling laughter.

"Your arrogance, my dear young comte, is of continual amusement," Giovanna said. She appeared to eye him thoughtfully. "I do not mean to criticize, my dear comte, but your arrogance also leads you to believe that women find pleasure with you if you but toss a few soft words and thoughtless caresses. It is not the case, you know."

He shook his head angrily and snarled, "You prefer the king, *madame?* He is nearer your esteemed age!"

He was surprised that the contessa only smiled at him. "The king is very . . . earthy," she said. "He enjoys a woman's body, and not just for his own pleasure."

"You disgust me!"

"Does Arabella Welles disgust you as well, Gervaise?"

The comte twisted about to face her. "Arabella Welles? Why the devil do you mention her? I barely know the girl."

"How interesting," Giovanna murmured. "I thought she was lying to me. Of course you are not her lover."

"What did you say?"

Giovanna shrugged. "Naught of anything, really. I have made you rich," she continued, gazing at him through her lashes, "though I cannot claim to have improved your skills as a lover."

He heard mockery in her voice again. He clenched his hand into a fist, but he couldn't strike her. He knew she was guarded by at least a half-dozen men, well-hidden, to be sure, but close by.

"You have served your purpose, Gervaise," she continued, smiling at his obvious anger.

"Purpose!" He turned to her, his face flushed. "What does that mean?"

"I mean, *caro*," Giovanna said gently, "that you should consider leaving your band of . . . patriots and returning to your homeland and your emperor. It is likely that the queen's secret police will shortly discover that the rich cargoes you have been selling to your fellow countrymen were never yours to sell. They were not mine to give you, you see. You have played your role, my little man. If you do not leave Naples soon, you will find yourself rotting in chains."

Gervaise bounded to his feet. "You have used me!" he shouted down at her. "You have betrayed me!"

"Please do not act the outraged little boy, it ill suits you. You really have no choice in the matter. You see, the queen's secret police will also suspect that you are responsible for the disappearance of Arabella Welles. I am not betraying you precisely, comte. I am giving you warning." She shrugged. "If you wish to warn the other members of your dissolute club, it is up to you."

"You are crazy, you old hag!" he snarled at her. "If anyone comes for me, they will come for you within the hour!"

Giovanna looked at him pityingly. "I told you, Gervaise, I will not be here. Besides, *caro*, to implicate a simple woman is not at all gallant, and the king and I are close, you know. No, were I you, I would not attempt such a thing. I have really treated you quite well, Gervaise."

He could only stare at her, stunned. "What have you done to Arabella Welles?"

"I have sent her to Algiers, my dear comte, to Oran, to be exact. I believe she will do quite well as a slave."

Giovanna swung her legs over the bed and reached for her dressing gown. She slipped her arms into the wide brocade sleeves and sashed the belt at her waist. "As much as I enjoy your body, *caro*, I would suggest that you take your leave now."

Gervaise reached for his scattered clothes, trying desperately to think. He was aware of the contessa's eyes upon him as he dressed. When he had shrugged into his coat, he turned to face her. "You speak of revenge, Contessa. It is a two-edged sword."

He turned and strode from her bedchamber, her laughter dinning in his ears.

A placid-faced servant ushered Adam into Lord Delford's library. Lord Delford rose from his chair upon Adam's entry, his face drawn into severe lines.

"Sir?" Adam said, striding toward him. "Your man told me you wished to see me on a matter of grave importance."

"It is your sister," the viscount said without preamble. "She rode out before noon, spurning a groom, I might add, and she has not returned."

"And it is nearly five o'clock," Adam said numbly.

"A groom brought me this letter a short time ago from the Contessa di Rolando." The viscount handed Adam a folded piece of paper.

The words were stark and short, to the effect that Miss Welles had not kept her luncheon appointment. Perhaps, the contessa wrote, Miss Welles decided not to visit her, but nonetheless, she felt it her duty to inform the viscount. She closed with, "I trust Miss Welles is not indisposed. As I am leaving Naples shortly, I will be unable to further our acquaintance."

Adam made a hissing sound between his teeth.

"I have questioned the servants and my daughter, but she knew only that Arabella intended to ride today. That is all. I knew it was a mistake," the viscount continued, his face pale in his anxiety, "to bring her here. I told your father so! I have tried to protect her, but she is as disobedient and willful as her mother!"

Adam paid no further attention to the viscount's diatribe. He was trying to arrange his thoughts logically. Arabella had been taken, of that he had no doubt. He crushed the contessa's letter between his hands, admitting to himself that she had covered herself cleverly. She had guessed that Arabella must have informed someone she intended to visit her. And she was leaving Naples shortly.

Lord Delford said, "Do you know, my lord, where she might be?"

"Perhaps. I must leave you now, sir."

"How may I assist you, my lord? After all, your sister was in my care."

"It is not impossible that a message will come here. Perhaps a ransom demand, I do not know. But your dau . . . your family should be kept safe. I have my own men."

Lord Delford looked thoughtfully down at his signet ring. "My daughter will be presented at court upon our return to England. Indeed, there is a particular gentleman who . . . In any case, my lord, I do not despair of a felicitous outcome."

"Nor do I, my lord," Adam said steadily. "But we have not the time to discuss your daughter's future."

"Of course you are right. But know this, my lord: my daughter's future is in my hands."

"Your daughter is not a child, my lord, but that must wait."

Rayna quickly backed away from the library door at the sound of footsteps. She slipped into the dining room, hopeful that Adam would emerge alone. But her father walked with him to the front door to see him out. Slowly she sank onto a chair and lowered her head to her hands.

15

Arabella was overheated and her head ached from the press of guests at Lady Ranleagh's ball. The night air on the balcony cooled her and she wished she could stay there the rest of the evening. Lord Eversley was suddenly beside her, his pleasant face somehow different, his eyes glinted down at her in silent challenge.

"No!" she cried, backing away from him, but he grabbed her and pulled her toward him. His mouth covered hers, but his kiss was brutal, punishing her until she parted her lips. His tongue was thick and heavy in her mouth. She couldn't breathe. "No!" she cried out again, but he only laughed, drawing away from her for a moment. Her foot shot out, connecing with his shin. He never stopped laughing.

"Drink this wine."

He was forcing her head back, tilting the sweet wine into her mouth. She tried to scream at him to stop, but the wine choked her, and she sputtered, swallowing it in great gulps.

"I don't want the wine!"

She was moaning softly, her head throbbing. "No wine," she sobbed. Her stomach rebelled and bile rose in her throat. I can't be sick on Lady Ranleagh's balcony, she thought frantically, only to throw herself toward the railing and retch.

She fell back onto her knees, crying softly. *What is that strange creaking? It feels like I'm moving!* She forced her eyes open to the dim light. She was not on Lady Ranleagh's balcony, but lying on a rank pile of rags. She was in the hold of a ship. Suddenly memory righted itself, and she saw the contessa's gloating face above her. The contessa had drugged her wine. Nausea clogged her throat again at the smell of her sickness in the confined space of the hold. She drew up her legs and lowered her head between them, taking short, shallow breaths. As the nausea receded, she felt a pounding in her temple. She clapped her palms to the sides of her head, only to pull them away at the stiff, stringy feel of her hair. Slowly Arabella lowered her hands, and her breath caught in her throat. Her palms were a dirty brown. She jerked a handful of her hair over her breast. Like her hands, it was a filthy, a dirty mud color. Was it meant to disguise her?

She fell back against the rags. "Adam," she whispered. "I was such a fool! How will you ever find me?" She felt salty tears streak down her cheeks. The contessa's gloating voice sounded in her mind again. Kamal. The ship was taking her to the contessa's son. But why?

There was nothing to do but listen to the creaking of the ship. She didn't know how much time passed, but the hold became pitch black as the sunlight piercing through the one small porthole dimmed. She heard a sound and sat up quickly, her eyes fastened on the far wall. The hold door creaked open and the light from a lantern filled the small room. She gazed hopefully toward two rough-garbed sailors. The man holding the lamp was older, his beard streaked with gray. He was staring at her with disgust in his eyes.

"Here she be, Neddie," he said, raising the lamp higher.

"Gawd," Neddie said. "She looks like a street trollop, Abel."

"And the smell of her!"

"Who are you?" Arabella asked, her voice breaking. "What ship is this?"

Abel set the lamp down and straightened slowly, as if his back was hurting him. "We brung ye some dinner, wench." He laughed, a low, raspy sound. "It'll taste better than ye look!"

Ned grinned, showing a wide space between his front teeth. "And here I thought to have a little sport with the wench, Abel. Lawks, I wouldn't touch that one! She probably has the pox."

"This here is a lady, Neddie lad," Abel said. "A little English lass."

"Gawd," Ned said again. He scratched his head

vigorously and Arabella shuddered at the thought of the lice nested in his thatch of black hair.

" 'Tis just as well ye don't want to toss up her skirts, Neddie, 'cause she's to be left alone. Them's the orders from the captain."

"Please," Arabella pleaded, "tell me where we are bound."

"Take yer dinner, wench." Abel placed a bowl of greasy brown stew in her hands.

Arabella's stomach knotted at the vile-looking mixture. Unknowingly, she shook her head.

"Ye'd best eat, wench," Abel said, "else ye'll be dead by the time we reach Oran."

"Oran," Arabella repeated blankly. "That is a city in Algiers."

"Aye." Abel nodded, as if amused with her.

"You must take me home! My father will pay you handsomely, I promise you! Bring me your captain, please!"

"Be yer pa as ugly as ye, I wonder?" Ned said, raising his brows at the knotty question. "And iffen he ain't, he'd likely pay us to keep ye away from him."

Anger boiled up in Arabella, and without thought, she flung the bowl of stew at Ned. He yelped and jumped back, stringy pieces of meat sliding off his chest. "Ye little bitch!" he roared.

"Nay, Neddie, don't strike the wench," Abel said. "She'll not be so full of herself by tomorrow night."

"Aye," Ned spat toward her. "Tomorrow night she'll be begging for anything we give her."

"Bring me your captain!"

Abel threw back his head and laughed heartily. He suddenly reached down and grasped Arabella's chin in his hand. "Aye, wench, ye'll be as gentle as a little mouse soon."

Ned joined in his laughter. Arabella watched the two men stride toward the narrow door.

"Don't take the lamp!" she yelled after them, but Abel ignored her. The door banged closed, and she was once again in total darkness.

She heard soft scurrying sounds. She muffled a scream and drew herself up in a tight ball. There were rats so close she could hear them gnawing at the splattered stew.

Niccolo Cipolo turned up the collar of his cloak against the dark fog from the bay. He was nearly home now, to his whining wife. He hoped the brandy he had drunk would deaden his ears to her shrill voice. He thought he heard movement behind him, and paused a moment. There was nothing. He shook his head at himself and began to whistle. His whistle suddenly died in his throat.

He stared stupidly at a black-garbed figure standing squarely in his path. The figure's face was masked and he held a whip in his gloved hand.

"Who are you?" Niccolo asked in a croaking voice.

"I am looking for the Comte de la Valle," the figure replied in a cold voice, a voice cold as the dead, Niccolo thought wildly.

"I have not seen him this evening," Niccolo

said, trying to close his fingers about the hilt of his dress sword.

"No, there was no gathering this evening, was there? No chance for you, you swine, to ruin another peasant girl."

"Who are you?" Niccolo shrieked. "I know nothing!" He whipped about clumsily and ran toward the dock. Swift footsteps closed behind him, and he was spun about by his arm, caught in an iron grasp. He raised his hand to claw at the black mask covering the man's face. The next moment the man's fist had smashed into his jaw, and he fell back onto his knees, dizzy with pain.

"You miserable bastard! Where is the comte?"

Niccolo stared stupidly up at the man.

"The queen will soon know about the pack of jackals you keep company with." The raspy voice grew soft. "Your precious comte has done you in."

Niccolo couldn't move in his fear. "I do not believe you," he cried. "Gervaise would not . . ." He broke off, then blurted out, "I will tell you the other members' names if you release me!"

"A swine and a coward," the black figure said. "I will ask you but one more time. Where is the comte?"

'I do not know!" Niccolo screamed. "Who are you?" The figure merely laughed and Niccolo bounded to his feet, clutching his sword. "I will kill you!" he shouted.

The man drew his own sword and taunted him with a beckoning finger. "Come, my brave cock."

Niccolo gave a shout of anger and hurtled himself forward.

He was facing a master, he realized within moments. The man danced in front of him, mocking him. He felt the tip of the man's sword rip easily through his sleeve. He tried to back away, his eyes fastened on the sword slashing toward him. He saw a flash of silver and felt a searing pain in his belly. The man had neatly slashed through his breeches, drawing blood.

Niccolo struck out wildly, but only for a moment. The man's sword slipped through his guard and embedded itself in his shoulder. He shuddered with the pain of it, and fell to the street when the sword was jerked from his flesh.

Niccolo clutched his shoulder, and felt sticky blood seeping between his fingers. "Do not kill me," he whispered. "I know nothing."

The figure sheathed his sword and stepped back. "No, I will not bother."

Adam turned at the sound of approaching voices. "I will leave you to the queen, *signore*," he said, and slipped quietly into the darkness.

Adam stepped quickly back into the shadows and hugged the side of the house. So Daniele had been right. The fool had returned to his lodgings.

Adam heard Gervaise curse softly as he twisted his key into the lock. Slowly, bent over, Adam moved forward. The house was dark, save for the flicker of a candle flame in Gervaise's parlor. Adam straightened, strode to the door, and quietly pushed it open. The entrance was dark. He walked softly to the drawing room and stepped inside.

"Pietro!" Gervaise whirled about, his hand on his sword hilt. "You startled me, my friend. I am glad you are come. I would warn you of our danger."

Adam smiled at him. "It is not our danger, Gervaise, but yours."

The comte moved to the sideboard and poured himself a snifter of brandy. "You speak in riddles, my friend, and I have not the time for them tonight. As soon as I have gathered a few . . . mementos, I am off to France."

"So it was your greed, comte, that brought you back here. It was not wise, you know."

"No, likely not," Gervaise agreed, tossing down the brandy. "If you wish, you may accompany me. We shall fight with our emperor."

"Ah, but I am not bound for France," Adam said softly.

"The little chick holds you here? Take her with you. We can share her favors, now that you've taught her how to please a man." He shrugged. "Perhaps I shall even marry her."

"You will never touch her, Gervaise. Now, I must know the truth from you. Where is Arabella Welles?"

Gervaise set down his goblet, a fair brow arched upward. "You are most fickle, Pietro. I fear you must forget that beauty. I doubt anyone will ever see her again."

"But I must see her again, Gervaise," Adam said. "You will tell me where she is."

The comte's eyes narrowed at the hint of menace in the marchese's soft voice. "I do not have time to enjoy the evening with you, Pietro. If you want the girl, you will have to sail to Oran. She was sent to some harem there. 'Tis all I know."

Adam sucked in his breath. The Barbary pirates. It always came back to those savages. But why? "Who sent her there? The Contessa di Rolando—your mistress?"

"I have neither the time nor the inclination to tell you," Gervaise said.

Adam gently unsheathed his sword. "I suggest that you will, comte. Now."

"What is this?" Gervaise demanded. "Have you lost your wits?"

"No, comte. You see, Arabella Welles is my sister."

"Your . . . sister." The comte stood perfectly still, rage washing through him. The miserable contessa and now this man. Both had betrayed him. "You bastard," he snarled. He drew his sword, his eyes narrowed.

"No," Adam said, a grim smile on his face. "I am not the bastard. I do not seduce foolish men to betray their country. Behold, comte, an Englishman who despises your precious emperor!"

Gervaise lunged toward his pistol that lay atop a table. It was nearly in his grasp when Adam's sword sent it clattering across the floor. "Your sword, comte! Try for honor, for once in your life."

Adam stood back, at the ready, as Gervaise

pulled his sword from his sheath. *"En garde!"* the comte spat at him.

Gervaise was well-trained, but his fury dimmed his skill. Adam nimbly parried his lunges. Beads of sweat broke out on the comte's forehead. He tasted fear, cold and cramping in his belly. He cursed, executing a swift thrust he had learned from a master in France, but the Englishman neatly deflected the death blow aimed at his heart, his sword sliding along Gervaise's until they were locked together, but inches apart.

"It is the contessa, is it not, comte?"

"Aye, you scum! But it is the last thing you will ever know!"

He lurched backward, disengaging his sword. He dashed his hand across his brow to keep the sweat from his eyes. He saw that the Englishman was not pressing him, only smiling grimly.

"Come to me," Adam taunted him. "I do not chase after cowards."

Gervaise threw caution to the winds. He laughed, engaging Adam's sword in a loud clash of steel. This time the Englishman did not retreat, and Gervaise felt his strength. He felt a cold, prickling sensation in his chest. Time seemed to stop. He stared in surprise at the crimson stain that widened quickly on his white shirt. He saw his mother's gentle face contorted in pain when she died. Then he saw nothing.

"Miss Lyndhurst is here, my lord. Vincenzo brought her. She is in the library."

Adam stared at his valet, then nodded abruptly. "See that we are not disturbed," he said curtly.

"Aye, my lord."

Adam strode into the parlor, slamming the door closed behind him. Rayna whirled about to face him, the hood of her cloak falling back.

"So," he said, his voice sounding quite calm to Rayna's sensitive ears, "despite all that has happened, you come yet again."

"Not alone, Adam. I made . . . that is, Vincenzo came with me."

"Arabella is taken," he continued, disregarding her tentative defense. "I personally warned your father to keep you safe, and yet you venture out. I do not suppose you considered the fact that Vincenzo is but one man."

"I had to see you, Adam! My father would tell me nothing."

"Your father should have locked you in your room," Adam said coldly. He strode toward her, and to his utter surprise, she backed away, obvious fear in her eyes. He stretched his hands toward her. "Forgive me, love," he whispered. "I would never hurt you."

Rayna choked down the sob in her throat and hurled herself against his chest. For an instant Adam held his arms rigidly against his sides. He felt her slender body tremble, and his hands came up quickly to hold her. "Forgive me," he repeated. "It is just that so much has happened, so quickly." He smiled ruefully. "I suppose I did want to beat you."

"Please do not," Rayna said, drawing back to see his face. "Have you discovered anything about Arabella?"

"Yes. I know where she is bound and who is reponsible."

"The Comte de la Valle?"

"He was a foolish man," Adam said.

"Was?"

Adam closed his eyes for a moment, seeing the astonished look on Gervaise's face. "Yes, he is dead."

"You . . . you killed him?"

He heard fear and disbelief in her voice. Violence of any kind was unknown to her. "Yes, love. I must get you back home, Rayna. Arabella has been taken to Oran. I am leaving tomorrow morning on the *Malek*."

"But it will be dangerous, will it not?"

He said honestly, "I do not know. I will come for you when all this is done."

"Did the comte send her there?"

"No. 'Twas the Contessa di Rolando. I am certain now that my father holds the answer to her motives. You will likely see him when he arrives here. I expect he will follow on a ship after me when he learns what has happened." He shook his head. " 'Twas the oddest circumstance. Had I hired the *Malek* sooner, I would have come upon the contessa. You see, she had hired the ship some days ago, and had sent a message to the captain early this afternoon that she no longer required his ship." He paused a moment, then added more to himself than to Rayna, "She is clever. Were I she, I would travel overland northward to another port."

Rayna grew very still. "I would go with you, Adam."

Adam grinned down at her, his white teeth gleaming. "You begin to sound like Arabella, my love. No, sweetheart, you will remain here in Naples, safe with your parents."

"I will not argue with you if you kiss me."

To close her mouth and divert her mind, he did what came quite naturally to him. He grasped her chin and lowered his mouth to hers and she slid her arms around his back. He knew he would make love to her if he didn't stop. He clasped his hands about her arms, but she resisted him and moaned softly into his mouth. Suddenly all that had happened for the past days surged through his mind, the betrayal, the death. He realized he might never see her again. He fumbled with the buttons of her gown and she helped him, her own breathing urgent, her fingers clumsy.

Adam stood over her, watching the firelight play over her white body. "You are so damned beautiful," he said. He strode to the parlor door and locked it, then shed his own clothes, leaving them strewn behind him.

Adam dropped to his knees beside her. It was the trust in her wide eyes as she gazed up at him that made him slow. He stretched out beside her and gently drew her body against the length of him. To his besotted delight, Rayna raised her leg over his, drawing him closer. Adam buried his face in her throat, his lips lightly caressing her pulse. He felt suddenly afraid, afraid of the danger the coming days would bring. He could not bear the thought of losing the future, of losing Rayna and their life together through his own death. He rolled quickly on top of her, and lowered his mouth to capture hers. Rayna stiffened for an instant at the punishing strength of him, but she sensed his urgency, his need for her. She let him ravage her mouth, and when he reared over her, she willingly offered herself to him. But she was not ready for him, and his thrust brought a cry of pain from her throat.

Adam froze at her cry. "My God, Rayna," he groaned. "I am sorry." He tried to pull out of her, but she clasped her arms about his back, holding him to her.

"No, my love. It is all right, Adam. It is all right."

Something snapped inside Adam at her softly spoken words, and he thrust wildly into her, wanting to claim her, to proclaim his ownership in the most primitive way. His wild urgency filled her mind and she felt a surge of heat deep within her. She cried out again, but not with pain. She thrust up her hips to meet him, and heard her own moans of pleasure over his raspy breathing. She felt herself opening to him, felt a need within her build until she could not control her body. She felt herself hover over a precipice of nearly painful pleasure, and she cried out. He was piercing the very core of her. She surged up against him, digging her fingers into his back, clasping him to her as if she would shatter if he left her now. She suddenly felt her body tensing, and wrapped her legs around his flanks, wanting to hold him to her, but she could not seem to hold still. She arched upward, clasping his neck, beyond herself.

Adam felt the power of her climax, the wild shuddering of her body. He cried out, burying himself deep within her.

Rayna lay quietly beneath him, nearly senseless.

Adam lightly caressed the tip of her nose. "I did not mean to hurt you, *petite.*"

"I know." She shifted slightly, and Adam clasped her to him and brought her onto her side against him. "I feel so exhausted," she said softly, lightly kissing his throat.

"You should," he said, grinning down at her.

"Adam, what will you do when you reach Oran?"

"I am not yet certain," he said calmly, hoping she wouldn't see the lie in his eyes.

"There will be danger."

"Perhaps." Adam pulled her more tightly against him. "I am a tough lout, Rayna, I will have men with me. You mustn't worry." She squeezed him to her with a fierce protectiveness, like a lioness with her cub. "You will stay safe with your parents, love. I want nothing to happen to you."

"Since I have let you ravage me like a pillaging pirate, I suppose I must trust you to settle with my father."

"Excellent," he said, and leaned down to kiss her. He felt her arm snake around his neck and his kiss deepened. He felt the quickening in her and smiled against her mouth. "You will kill me," he said softly. "This time, love, we will go slowly, very slowly."

"Whatever," Rayna gasped, and tugged his mouth back down to hers.

16

Captain Risan pushed open the door of the hold and stepped in. It took him several moments to adjust to the dim light, and even longer to accustom himself to the foul air. He heard a thready voice whisper from the corner, "Who are you?"

He saw her then, a wretchedly bedraggled woman crouched against the wall. Allah, he thought, his stomach tightening, he should have allowed the girl time on deck. The way she looked, he wouldn't have had to worry about his men keeping their distance. He shook his head, wondering at the contessa's orders to keep the girl in confinement. After she had thrown the bowl of stew at one of his men, Risan had ordered them to stay away from her. Her one meal each day was set just inside the hold door. He knew only that she was a lady, Arabella Welles, by name, who had earned the enmity of Kamal's mother, and was to be made a slave to Kamal, his half-brother.

"I am Captain Risan," he said in accented English. He walked closer and stood over her, his booted feet spread. "We have arrived, girl. Are you able to stand?"

Arabella had moved in the last two days only to relieve herself. The rats left her alone if she stayed quiet. She struggled to her knees, grasped the man's outstretched hand, and pulled herself upright. She swayed against him.

"I will feed you before we go ashore," the captain said. "My orders are to deliver you alive, and you are scarce that now."

"Must I share with the rats, captain?"

"So you've still a sharp tongue, even after six days in your own company. Perhaps, girl, you would like more time by yourself."

"No," she whimpered softly. Her fingers clutched like claws at his sleeve, and she nearly collapsed against him. He smiled over her head and hauled her over his shoulder. It was a pity she was so ugly, else he would have enjoyed her, despite the contessa's orders, and tamed her spirit in a way more pleasurable to both of them. He smiled as he carried the girl to his cabin. He hadn't had a woman in over a week, and Kamal would likely give him one of his lovely concubines for the night, once he delivered this creature to him.

Arabella felt the sting of bright light against her eyelids. She blinked and opened her eyes. After nearly a week in shadowed light or complete darkness, the world of bright sun was harsh and painful. She lay very quietly for a moment, marshaling her strength. A shadow loomed over her and she stared up at a man not many years older than she. He was dark and swarthy, with wide-spaced brown eyes. The white wool shirt he wore was parted to reveal great clumps of black curly hair on his chest. His trousers were loose and sashed at his waist by a wide black leather belt. A huge dagger dangled from his waist.

"Captain Risan?" She forced herself to sit up.

"You like what you see, eh, girl?" Risan laughed.

Arabella felt a flash of anger, but firmly repressed it. She was hungry and weak and this man would feed her. "Yes," she said softly, biting her lower lip.

"Such a pity," Risan said, looking away from her filthy darkened face. The supple young body he had felt against him when he had carried her here had made his loins tighten.

"Come and eat, wench, and then it's off to the palace."

She meant to ask him what he was talking about, but the smell of roasted pheasant filled her nostrils and she quivered with hunger. He helped her to the table and sat opposite her as she ate. The pheasant was delicious, as were the steaming rice, the stewed collards, and the sweet wine. Finally sated, Arabella sat back in her chair and glanced at the man across from her beneath half-closed lids. She felt her strength returning, and her spirits rose. She picked up a small china cup of thick black coffee, and realized it was laced with brandy when it burned its way to her stomach. She gasped and coughed, but it warmed her.

"Where are we, captain?" she asked.

"In Oran. I am to deliver you personally to his highness."

"What are you talking about? What highness?" Her fear made her voice sharper than she intended.

His hand snaked out and closed about her arm. "Careful, girl," he growled. "Your master and mine, wench, his highness, Kamal El-Kader, the Bey of Oran."

Kamal, she thought, the contessa's son. She looked up at Risan and whispered brokenly, "Please do not. I am Arabella Welles. My father will pay you whatever you demand if you will but take me to Genoa."

The captain grinned. "I know who you are, wench. We'll see if my half-brother wants to keep you." He studied her face a moment. "I doubt he will. You are the ugliest female I've ever seen."

Arabella stared down at her mud-colored hands and touched her fingers to her face. What had the contessa covered her with? Her stiff, filthy hair touched her cheek and she shook it away, shuddering.

For a moment she felt the despair that had threatened to overwhelm her in the hold. *Stop it! You have been a great fool, but even fools can save themselves.* Perhaps this Kamal wasn't the villain his mother was. Perhaps.

"The tender's ready, captain."

She looked up to see a young sailor staring at her.

"Well, my lady," Risan said, standing. "Must I carry you again? If you would know the truth, I don't wish to soil my clothes."

"I am coming, captain," Arabella said docilely. She looked longingly at his dagger as she followed him along the deck, but thought better of it.

"This is Oran, my lady. Look yon."

Arabella stared toward the bustling city beyond the docks. It looked nothing like Genoa or any other town she had seen. Its close whitewashed huts were nestled under the dazzling bright afternoon sun in a narrow valley between two hills.

"You cannot see the market from here," Risan said as he steered her down the wooden gangplank, "or the treasures that may be found there. The slave auctions are held there. You, I venture to say, would bring more hoots of laughter than piastres."

"That is a warming thought," Arabella said between her teeth. She looked about the dock at the men lounging about. Adam was right, she thought. Pirates were not a romantic lot; they were loud, dirty, and brutish. She saw no women until Risan guided her onto a wide street. They stood in small groups, clustered in doorways, dressed like crows, covered from head to toe in coarse black robes. They pointed her out to each other with obvious distaste, in Arabic, she supposed.

They began an ascent through winding streets, streets so narrow that the houses touched each other, forming a vault overhead. They walked through a dark passage and emerged in an open square, where the noise was deafening. No one seemed to pay the slightest heed to them. Arabella saw merchants crouched beside their motley wares, their strings of pepper pods and dried fish hanging beside silken robes and embroidered sandals. Sacks of green henna, destined, Risan told her, to dye women's fingers and feet, were set next to huge sides of raw meat. A scent of decay exuded from the square mingled with the aroma of spices and the perfume of flowers. She saw women, different here from the ones that had huddled in the doorways. Their dark eyes were ringed with kohl above the wisps of their veils. They kept to themselves, away from the men. The Arab men all wore turbans and long black cloaks with full cut hoods.

"You are surprised at the attire of our people?" Risan asked. "The ubiquitous long cloak is called a burnoose." He cocked a dark brow at her. "You show no fear. Perhaps you need to witness a slave auction."

"No," Arabella said. "I believe I have witnessed enough."

They emerged from the bazaar at the base of the hill. "That is his highness's palace, up there," Risan said, pointing to the huge building sprawled high atop a hill above the city. "The forts below house his Turkish troops. We will ride up on donkeys. I suggest you hold on tightly."

Arabella clung to the rough saddle horn as the

donkey weaved his way upward. As they grew nearer to the palace, she could make out the figures of men patrolling the perimeter. It looked to be impregnable. She felt a knot of fear so intense she might have fallen had Captain Risan not turned in his saddle and called back to her, "Almost there, girl! I can't wait to hear what my brother has to say to you!"

Brother! Another of the contessa's sons?

Her donkey came to an abrupt halt, and as if by habit, jerked the reins from her hands. Oddly uniformed Turks surrounded them. They looked at her with sneering laughter, likely making coarse jests about her. She slid from the donkey's back and squared her shoulders. A huge gate swung open, and Risan prodded her through.

He said on a half-laugh, "Come, girl, it is time to meet your master."

She gazed over her shoulder at the glistening Mediterranean below her. It seemed as distant as Genoa, and home.

Kamal leaned against the thick embroidered pillows at his back and gazed at Señor Ancera, a Spanish merchant. The man's jaw hung slack as he watched a swaying dancing girl.

"Shall we conclude our business, *señor*?" Kamal asked softly. "Then you may have the girl for the night."

Señor Ancera nodded, his eyes still fixed on the girl. She wore only two veils now, one over her face and the other about her waist. Her chestnut hair was loose to her waist, falling in thick waves over her shoulders to caress her breasts.

The tambourines and cymbals quickened their tempo. The girl whirled closer and let the veil slip down over her smooth belly.

The Spaniard would sign over his mother to have Orna, Kamal thought, watching the man clutch at his drink. Kamal nodded to Orna, and she let her veil fall slowly from her hips. The cymbals suddenly stopped and she sank to her knees before the Spaniard, her glorious hair spread about her like a rippling fan.

Kamal clapped his hands. Orna rose to stand before him, her head bowed.

"Take off your veil," he said.

The veil fluttered to the floor, and Kamal watched the Spaniard's eyes widen in appreciation.

"Orna is quite skilled, *señor*," Kamal said dryly. "She will await you in your chamber. You will join her once we have finished." At his nod, Orna slipped once again to her knees and kissed the toe of his soft leather boot. A eunuch appeared to lift the girl to her feet and lead her away.

Señor Ancera wiped the sweat from his upper lip. "Yes," he managed, "let us conclude our business, highness."

Kamal looked over the parchment once it was signed, nodded affably to the older man, and watched him disappear through an arched doorway. The pious Spaniards were the easiest to deal with, he thought, but it gave him no sense of mastery. "Hassan," he called to his minister.

"Yes, highness."

"See that the Spaniard visits the baths."

"I will see to it the old man gets a dousing of cold water, highness."

"My thoughts exactly, Hassan. Send Orna back. I would enjoy her dancing before she spends the rest of the day and night on her back."

"The Spanish know no better," Hassan said, and bowed himself out.

Kamal nibbled at a date offered him by a slave girl and settled back, waiting for Orna to return to ease his boredom. "Do you wish anything more, master?" the girl asked softly. As Kamal turned his head, her silk-covered breast brushed against his cheek.

"No," he said abrupty at her ill-disguised attempt to gain his notice. He turned his attention to Orna, who had begun to dance before him naked, bending her ivory body to the beat of the music. She was indeed well trained, he thought objectively, some of her movements so suggestive that they captured even his eyes. When the music stopped, Orna dropped lightly to her knees.

"You may stay for now," Kamal said, motioning her beside him.

Hassan returned, a frown puckering his forehead. "Your half-brother Risan has arrived, highness, with a present for you from your mother."

Kamal grinned. "I haven't seen my randy brother in a good two months. Show him in."

The guards at the main doors stood at attention when Risan strode into the room.

Hassan stepped aside.

"My most noble master," Risan said, and bowed deeply.

"Straighten up, brother, before I have one of my guards kick you on your smirking face."

Risan laughed easily. "You may yet give that order when you see what I've delivered to you from your esteemed mother." He turned toward a guard at the door. "Bring in the wench."

Kamal watched a scraggly figure struggle futilely against the grip of his Turkish soldier. "Arabella Welles, brother." Risan roared with laughter and flung her to her knees at his brother's feet.

Kamal stared at the crumpled woman. Her hair was filthy and matted to her head. When she raised her head to him, he stared speechless at her. Her skin was streaked with dark filth, and his nostrils quivered at her stench.

"Arabella Welles?" Kamal repeated. He came gracefully to his feet. "Is this some kind of jest, Risan?"

"No, highness. Your mother sends you the wench. I bring you a letter from her."

Kamal quickly unfolded the quartered piece of paper and read: "My son, this is Arabella Welles, the daughter of my betrayer. She is a whore who has bedded many men in the court of Naples. Enjoy her, my son. I have written to her father. Though she is a worthless creature, he will feel bound to come for her."

Arabella was breathing heavily, momentarily stunned. She forced her eyes away from the man reading the letter and quickly took in the dancing girl who was wrapping thin veils about her body, and two other, even younger girls, dressed in outlandish veils, giggling behind their hands. She began to tremble. She heard a man's voice ask, not unkindly, "Can you stand up?"

Arabella pulled herself to her feet and looked straight at him. He was taller than she had first thought, clean-shaven, and deeply tanned. His hair curled about his ears, the color of ripe wheat. His blue eyes seemed out of place in this land of dark swarthy people, and at the moment, were narrowed on her face.

"Who are you?" she whispered, though she knew well who he was. But he had no look of the contessa, she thought.

Her arm was suddenly grasped from behind and twisted. "This is your master, girl, Kamal El-Kader," Risan snarled, shaking her.

Kamal saw a flicker of pain in the girl's eyes. "Let her go, brother," he said calmly. "You are the daughter of the Earl of Clare?"

"Does your honorable mother's letter not tell you so?"

"My mother's letter also tells me your morals were a blessing to many of the gentlemen at the court of Naples." He saw a flash of fury in her dark eyes, and added slowly, "She suggests you might use your talents to amuse me until your father arrives to claim you."

Arabella looked about at the barbaric luxury, then back at the man who gazed upon her with contempt in his eyes. Her voice rang out with furious calm. "You must have the morals of an animal, if you are stupid enough to believe lies from a woman who beds men young enough to be her son!"

Kamal stared at her, unaccustomed rage building in him. An animal! It was fortunate his soldiers did not speak Italian, else one might have slit her throat for her insult. He turned slowly away from her and said to Hassan, "It appears my mother makes a jest. I am supposed to enjoy myself with this slut, who believes me an animal. Allah! The wench smells as foul as she looks!"

Arabella was shaking, but not from fear. She flung her head back and shouted at the man, "I would like to see what you look like, you savage, after spending a week in the hold of a stinking ship!"

There was another moment of silence. Kamal felt shamed. She was an English noblewoman who had suffered vilely, in the name of his mother's vengeance. She was not to have been used. But she was a whore, dishonest and guileful.

"Why," he asked her quietly, "would my mother claim you for a whore if it were not true?"

"I am not a whore!" Arabella shrieked. "You filthy barbarian!" She took a step toward him, and felt her arms jerked behind her back. She was thrown to the floor. She lay there, her cheek pressed against the cool marble, stunned, hearing angry voices above her.

"Shall we slit her throat, highness?"

She heard the sound of steel being drawn from a scabbard. She closed her eyes, a brief prayer on her lips.

"Raise her to her feet, Risan," Kamal said.

"I shouldn't have fed her," Risan said angrily.

She faced him, her arms held painfully behind her back. "You are not worth the dung it would take to cover your worthless body!"

"And you appear to be a fool," Kamal said, controlling his anger.

"At least I am not the son of a whore!"

Kamal stepped toward her and without a word drew back his hand and slapped her. Her head jerked back with the force of his blow, and she would have fallen if Risan weren't holding her.

"Filthy jackal," she hissed at him, tears of anger and pain stinging her eyes. "How brave you are, striking me while I am held!"

"Release her," Kamal ordered quietly. He stared at the furious girl, and could see no fear in her dark eyes. Very slowly he drew back his hand and struck her again. It was he who prevented her fall.

"You are held only by me now, girl," he said.

"May the devil take your soul!" Arabella whispered at him.

They faced each other, Arabella pale, Kamal flushed a furious red. "You are a fool," he said softly. "I could have your filthy throat slit."

He saw a glimmer of fear in her eyes, but it was gone quickly.

"You are a perverted heathen," Arabella said, her voice calm and cold now, for she knew that she faced death. "You surround yourself with other heathens, to make you feel important. Kill me, I do not care!"

She spit in his face. As if from a great distance, Arabella heard women shrieking, and the angry rumble of men's voices.

"I will die with honor," she said, and forced her back to straighten.

Kamal slowly wiped the spittle from his cheek. He stared at the bedraggled girl, and felt a moment of reluctant admiration for her courage.

"Hassan," he said slowly, turning to his white-faced minister. "Call Raj."

"Yes, highness."

"Women have no honor," he said to her, his voice flat. "I have no intention of killing you, at least not yet." He looked down at his hand and was not surprised to see a streak of dirty brown stain on his palm. Obviously, beneath her filth, she must at least look like a lady, else what man would have bedded her?

"If you would know about whores," Arabella said, unable to stop herself, "let me tell you about your mother. It is obvious to me that her blood flows in your veins." She cast a contemptuous eye toward the cowering slave girls. "At least she tries to be somewhat discreet about her lovers."

"I suggest you close your mouth now," Kamal said, gritting his teeth. "That is, if you wish to keep your tongue."

Arabella laughed, praying she sounded scornful. "Is that what savages do, your *highness*?"

"Raj," Kamal said pleasantly, ignoring the panting girl. "You see this creature? You are known to work miracles. Return her to me tonight. At least bathe the stench off her."

"No!" Arabella shrieked. "I won't go!"

Kamal turned away from her. "Take her away," he said wearily.

Arabella's arms were yanked outward and she was dragged from the room.

"By Allah," Hassan said in a bewildered voice. "What has your mother sent you?"

"She has sent me a guttersnipe, Hassan. A guttersnipe who needs to be taught her place." *But she is innocent of her father's crimes.*

"What will you do with her, highness?"

Kamal shrugged. "If she has served the men at court, she is likely diseased."

"Your mother," he said slowly. "She has written the Earl of Clare of his daughter's capture."

"Yes," Kamal said, repressing the anger he felt toward her. Despite what the daughter was, it was not just to use her as a pawn. He turned to his half-brother. "Did you have any conversation with the girl?"

Risan shook his head. "I saw her for the first time today. Your mother ordered that she be kept in confinement." He grinned widely. "I thought her docile enough until she saw you, brother."

"There is more here," Hassan said thoughtfully, "than meets the eye."

The huge black eunuch Raj signaled for the bey's guards to release her. He said very carefully in beautiful Italian, "*Signorina*, do not fight me. It will gain you nothing."

At the gentleness of his voice, Arabella's fury died without a sputter. She said on a sob, "I want to go home. I was brought here against my will."

"I know, little one. You are Lady Arabella Welles, daughter of the Earl of Clare." He chuckled, his great belly shaking. "I have never before seen my master so enraged. He is a man who is gentle with women. I must suppose that his anger made him blind. He did not see you as I do. Now, come. You will feel much better very soon."

Arabella sniffed back her tears. She touched her fingers to her face. She fancied she could feel the sting from his palm. "Where are you taking me?"

"To the harem."

"*Harem!*" Arabella stopped in her tracks and stared at the great black man in consternation.

"You have nothing to fear," Raj said gently. "You may trust me, my lady. I will protect you."

"How do you know who I am?"

Raj looked at her closely. She was sniffing back her tears noisily, like a child. "I imagine that everyone in the palace knows who you are. Your arrival was not . . . calm. Come now."

Arabella swallowed. She had no choice but to do as she was bid, at least for the time being. She nodded. "Very well, Raj," she said, and he smiled at the dignity in her young voice.

She followed him down a long whitewashed

corridor, bare of furnishings. It led them outside through an arched doorway into a garden as beautiful as her father's at the Villa Parese, with a huge fountain at its center.

"This courtyard separates the palace from his highness's harem. There is another garden in the harem. The women spend their hours there, my lady."

They walked through the garden on a well-tended path to a high wall beyond it. Two guards stood at a doorway, both clothed only in loose white trousers, huge scimitars at their belts.

Raj nodded to them and opened the door. Arabella stepped into a world of riotous color. Large shade trees surrounded the perimeter of the garden, a long narrow pool tiled in colorful mosaic at its center. At least a dozen girls lounged about the pool, some laughing and splashing in the water. Many of them were naked, and their young bodies glistened in the dappled sun that filtered through the thick tree branches. Beyond the garden were arched doorways, leading, Arabella supposed, to private quarters.

Arabella sucked in her breath. "This is . . . barbaric."

"It is simply that you are not used to it, my lady."

Arabella heard a shriek. She turned to see the girls pointing at her, their mouths agape.

"Raj brings a witch in our midst!"

"More like an ugly crone!"

One had spoken in French, the other in Italian. Arabella pretended deafness.

Raj spoke sharply to the girls, then gently took her elbow and led her to the far end of the arched pavilion. "For the moment you will have this room, my lady."

The room was narrow and long, its walls a bare white. At its center was a small bed covered with a red silk spread. A large armoire stood in a corner next to a table with a basin of water on it. Arabella stepped into the cool room, staring blankly about her. She heard Raj clap his hands and say something in Arabic. A thin black girl appeared.

"This is Lena, my lady. She will take care of you. Now, you must take off those filthy clothes."

Arabella nodded, anxious for a bath. Lena's fingers were on the buttons when Arabella noticed that Raj was still in the room. She pulled away from the slave girl.

"You will please leave, Raj."

It was his duty to inspect any girl that came to Kamal, but he saw that the girl was near the end of her endurance. Also, she wasn't, in truth, to be part of Kamal's harem. He spoke quietly to Lena, then left the room.

The filthy gown dropped to Arabella's feet, and all her soiled underclothes.

"Do you speak Italian, Lena?"

The girl shook her head and replied in French.

"What did Raj say to you?"

"He told me to take you to the private bath, my lady." Lena sucked in her breath in surprise when the lady was naked. Her body was white as snow, in ugly contrast to her face, neck, and hands. "Who did this to you?" she whispered.

"Your master's esteemed mother," Arabella said flatly. She saw that Lena's eyes were on the nest of hair between her thighs, and she blushed.

"Your hair," Lena muttered. She drew a deep breath. "Come, my lady. It will take me hours to clean you."

She handed Arabella a robe of sheer blue silk. It was not much of a cover, but Arabella clutched it against her nonetheless, and followed Lena from her small room down the arched passage. She entered a brightly lit room that held another girl and her slave. The girl had hair as black as a moonless night, and flawless white skin. Her soft brown eyes met Arabella's. She spouted Arabic to her slave, and laughed loudly. "Do you speak Italian, witch?" the girl demanded, standing and stretching her lovely body.

"Yes," Arabella replied.

"If you are here for our master, you will have quite a wait!" She hugged her arms about her slender waist and sauntered out of the room, her slave scurrying behind her.

"That one is Elena, my lady, the master's favorite," Lena said in a low voice. "She hopes to be his wife."

"She can have the jackal with my blessing," Arabella snarled. "They likely deserve each other."

Lena shook her head, her eyes darting toward

the door. "You must have a care, my lady, about what you say."

Arabella ignored her and looked wistfully toward the clear water.

"Not yet, my lady. You are too filthy. I will bathe you first in a tub."

Arabella felt herself relaxing in the warm water. She drank a glass of sweet wine Lena handed her and lay back as the girl scrubbed her body and her hair. She did not realize she had fallen asleep until Lena shook her arm. "You can come to the pool now, my lady."

Arabella rose lazily and stepped out of the porcelain tub.

"Ah," Lena said, "that is much better."

Arabella smiled despite herself, for the girl sounded like a mother duck whose duckling wasn't hideous after all.

She walked to the edge of the tiled pool, but Lena held her back. "Not yet, my lady." She scrubbed Arabella's hair again, her agile fingers separating each strand. A fragrance of lavender rose to Arabella's nose. Lena handed Arabella a bar of scented soap. "Wash your face again. Almost all of the stain is removed."

Arabella did as she was bid, scrubbing until her face and neck felt raw. She stood still while Lena washed her off with clean warm water.

Raj watched the English girl through the glass, thinking her more beautiful than even he had suspected. Her hair, cleansed of the stain and filth, hung in a thick golden mass down her slender back. She was almost too slender, he thought as she turned to say something to Lena, her white belly flat and her ribs too prominent after her week of privation. But her breasts were high and full, buttocks rounded and shapely. Allah, she was lovely. He laughed softly to himself, imagining his master's unbelieving eyes when he gazed at his captive again.

He saw the Alexandrian, Elena, standing in the doorway, her beautiful brown eyes narrowed in disbelief, and then in ill-disguised jealousy. "You are all pink and white, like a sow," Elena spat. "The master won't like that."

Arabella looked up and eyed the girl. "Elena," she said quietly, sitting down and dangling her legs into the cool water. "I do not want your master. Your taunts are wasted on me, I assure you. I am here against my will, and your precious master will die if he tries to touch me. Do I make myself clear?"

"You are naught but a slave! My master can do with you as he pleases."

"No, he cannot, Elena. I am not a slave. Forget your jealousy."

"You give me orders, skinny cow?"

Arabella sighed. "You are boring me, Elena." With that, Arabella slipped into the pool and let the water close over her head.

Raj wanted to laugh at the myriad chagrined expressions that flitted over Elena's face. Finally she seemed to regain her control, gave an elaborate shrug, and stalked from the chamber.

Arabella forgot her embarrassment at being naked in front of another woman. She lay on her stomach and let Lena massage warm oil into her back and legs. Lena helped her turn onto her back, pulled her long hair free of the end of the table, and combed it with long, gentle strokes.

"How long have you been here, Lena?" Arabella asked.

"Me, my lady?"

Arabella frowned at the surprise in the girl's voice. "Of course, Lena."

"I was captured from my village in Ethiopia when I was a little girl. My mother was beautiful and I suppose the slave trader thought I would look like her when I grew up. But I don't. I have been here for nine years now, serving the master."

Arabella frowned at her calm matter-of-factness. She felt the girl's hands lightly caressing the oil into her belly and flushed.

"You are beautiful, my lady," Lena continued. "The master will be most pleased with you. But you must eat."

"Lena," Arabella said sternly, "I am not a slave. That animal is not my master."

Lena looked distressed. "Please, my lady, you must guard your tongue. A woman does not say such things."

Arabella laughed harshly. "Ah, I am to go to my slaughter like a docile lamb."

A shadow fell over Arabella's face and she opened her eyes to see Raj looking down at her. She gasped in shock, grabbed the linen table cover, and pulled it about her. "How dare you!"

Raj nodded to Lena and she quickly left the room.

"My lady, forgive me for embarrassing you, but our ways are . . . different. You need feel no shame in front of me."

"No man has ever seen me naked," Arabella said, her voice high and quavering, like a child's.

"You are a virgin?"

Arabella's eyes widened. "Yes," she whispered.

"I suspected as much. Later the master may have me examine you."

"What do you mean . . . examine?"

Raj spoke as if to a child. "It is my responsibility to see that any new woman who comes to his highness's harem is free of disease, my lady. And to determine if she is a virgin." At her continued puzzled expression, he said sharply, "You are not a little girl, and surely you cannot be so ignorant."

Arabella flushed scarlet when she understood. "I wish to dress now," she said, not looking at the huge man.

"I have selected clothes for you. Come."

Minutes later, the white linen cloth still wrapped about her, Arabella said flatly, "I will not wear these . . . veils!"

"Then you wish to go to his highness with the linen wrapped around you? At least these . . . veils offer you a bit more protection than a towel."

Arabella swallowed, her eyes flying to his worried face. "What do you mean . . . protection?"

"You are very beautiful, my lady," he said flatly, "and the master appreciates beautiful women."

He saw fear in the depths of her dark eyes, yet she squared her slender shoulders and said firmly, "He will not touch me, Raj."

Raj was silent for a long moment. He guessed the minute Kamal saw the English girl, with her beautiful golden hair streaming down her back, clothed only in harem trousers and jacket, he would want her. He shuddered, knowing the girl would fight him. How odd that Kamal's mother had chosen to claim this girl a whore. Perhaps she had sown the seeds of her own undoing. It was a thought worth pursuing.

He said slowly, with careful emphasis, "It will be largely up to you, my lady. You are unlike the other girls in his highness's harem. Therein lies your advantage."

He handed her the flimsy bolero, beautifully embroidered with small seed pearls, and the trousers, fashioned of transparent silk panels of varying shades of blue. He gestured toward a pair of light blue leather slippers.

"Dress yourself, and quickly. His highness wishes to dine with you."

17

Thick early-morning fog swirled across the Bay of Naples, shrouding the sails of the *Malek* in white. Adam stood on the quarterdeck, straining his eyes toward the receding shore. He felt oddly peaceful now that they were away and there was no turning back, though he knew that his own life could be forfeit for his sister's. He shook away the thought that perhaps Arabella was already dead. No, he repeated to himself again, Arabella wasn't meant to be killed, else it would already have been done in Naples. He thought of Rayna and smiled, picturing her lustrous hair tousled about her lovely face, her mouth moist from his kisses. She had smiled at him bravely when he had taken his leave of her in the garden of her father's villa, Vincenzo standing silent watch. He ran his hand through his fog-damp hair. He was tired.

"Take your rest now, my lord. There is naught else to be done."

He turned and nodded to Daniele. "A week," he said. "A week before we know what has happened to my sister."

"So you'll fret and worry instead of—"

"All right," Adam said, raising his hand in mock defeat.

"The captain has given you his first mate's cabin. It's small but comfortable. You'll not be disturbed there."

"I will spend enough time in that cursed cabin," Adam said. "For now, I'll take my rest on deck." He eased down on a loop of thick rope and rested his head on his arms, but he did not sleep until Naples was far distant.

"My lord."

Adam shook himself awake and raised his head to Captain Alvarez, a tall lean man whose bald head was covered with an outmoded white wig.

"You've slept the day through, my lord. I thought you would like to refresh yourself before we dine."

Adam rubbed the stiff muscles at the back of his neck and rose. He shivered, and realized the sun was setting and the chill evening air was permeating his clothes. "I will join you in an hour, sir," he said. He stared upward at the billowing sails. "We have a good wind."

"The *Malek* is a fine ship. If the winds hold we will make port in Oran before you grow tired of my ugly face." He laughed at his own jest and patted his wig. "Perhaps before you catch the lice that live on my head."

Adam smiled, thinking sourly that the captain could afford to be affable, with all the gold he had pried out of him to divert his ship to Oran. He made his way from the quarterdeck, as comfortable on board the swaying ship as on land, just as was his mother. The *Malek* was a three-masted Spanish trading vessel, its hold full of Italian goods bound for Cádiz. And under tribute. Adam suspected the captain had intended to dock in the harbor of Oran in any case, but he had been in too much of a hurry to bargain with him, lice or no lice. He wondered how much the contessa had offered him.

He made his way down the companionway to his cabin, quickly adjusting to the rhythm of the ship belowdeck. When he opened the door, his eyes narrowed with irritation and suspicion. A small boy was climbing out of his trunk.

"What the devil are you doing?" he demanded, slamming the door and striding into the cabin.

The small figure spun around, one leg still in his trunk, and Adam found himself staring at Rayna Lyndhurst. She was dressed in loose brown trousers, white shirt, and cinnamon jacket, her hair tucked up under a brown work cap.

Adam slapped his hand to his forehead. "My God, I don't believe it!"

Rayna calmly stepped free of the trunk. "If I had known," she said tartly, "that you would spend the day on deck, I would not have had to stay buried in that wretched trunk! It was most uncomfortable, and I had to be very quiet when your valet came in a while ago." She pointed to the hipbath in a corner of the small cabin, steaming water rising out of it.

All the warm, loving thoughts he had squandered on her on deck fled his mind. He felt such anger at her that he could not speak. And instead of being sheepish or pleading with him to forgive her for this outrageous act, she was carping at him!

"You make a charming boy," he said finally with a sneer.

"Yes, don't I?" Rayna said, turning about to show him the fit of her trousers over her slender thighs and hips. "I stole the clothes from the gardener's youngest son." Shut up, she told herself, before he begins to roar like a lion! She had cursed her folly throughout the long day, but oddly enough, Adam's entrance had brought back her confidence. He looked as if he were thinking of beating her, and all she wanted to do was throw herself in his arms and bury her face against his chest.

"May I ask, madam," Adam said, taking a step back, "how you contrived to get on board this vessel?"

Rayna forced herself to shrug with brazen indifference. "Ah, 'twas easy. No one pays the least attention to a skinny boy. I was fortunate, though," she continued, her hazel eyes twinkling up at him. "I overheard the captain tell one of his men that the English lord would take over his first mate's cabin. I simply slipped into this room, saw your trunk, and climbed in." She turned and walked to the small table, providing him with a fine view of her trousered hips, and poured herself a glass of wine. "I was worried, however," she said, "that you could discover me sooner, and possibly convince the captain to return to Naples. So despite my discomfort, I thank you, my lord, for remaining abovedeck." She grinned impishly at him and proffered him a deep bow.

"And your father," he said, wanting to know the full of it before he stripped down those trousers and thrashed her. "I do not suppose you informed him of your plans?"

"That," Rayna confessed, sipping daintily at the wine, "bothered me not a little, let me tell you! I fear he will be most upset with me when he reads my letter. I suppose he has already read it," she continued, frowning into the glass. "Yes, most upset."

Adam thought she did not appear at all overwrought at her father's likely apoplexy.

"If he disowns me, will you still marry me, Adam? Without a dowry?"

"You may no longer be alive once I am finished with you," he said savagely.

She ignored his ill humor and remarked to the cabin at large, "I have not been seasick at all. I was worried about that, you know. Perhaps I will make something of a sailor after all." She gave him a charming smile. "I am terribly hungry. My stomach has been growling ferociously for the past several hours."

"If you eat, madam, it will be standing up!"

"Ah, but there are chairs, my lord." She set

down her wineglass and plopped down onto one of the heavily carved Spanish chairs. She could practically hear Adam grinding his teeth as she lifted one leg over the arm of the chair and began to swing it back and forth like a careless boy.

There was a light knock on the door and Banyon appeared. "My lord, when you are finished washing up . . ." He broke off, staring from the smiling boy to his master's furious face.

Adam strode over to Rayna and ripped off her woolen cap.

"Oh," Banyon said helplessly.

"Yes, indeed," Adam growled. Damnation! He knew now the ship could not return to Naples. Worse, he could not reveal that there was a girl aboard, staying in his cabin! "Damnation!" he said aloud. "Banyon, inform the captain that I've a touch of something vile, and bring my dinner here. Make it noble portions—the *lad* here tells me she is quite ravenous."

"Oh," Banyon said again.

"I fear, madam," he said between clenched teeth to Rayna, "that you will be spending the next week in this cabin."

"I do not mind in the least," Rayna said kindly. "Banyon, I am really very hungry."

"Yes, miss," Banyon said, his eyes only briefly leaving his master's set face.

"Banyon," Adam said, "tell Daniele about our . . . uninvited guest. As for the other men, and particularly the crew, keep the stowaway here to yourself."

"Yes, my lord." Banyon spared one pitying glance for the young lady before he slipped out of the cabin, careful to close the cabin door soundly. He had never before seen his master so furious. He remembered, a slow smile lighting his leathered face, when he had discovered a woman several years before in his master's bedroom, in his bed. Then the master had only laughed and firmly closed the bedroom door in Banyon's interested face.

Rayna gulped at the mean anger in Adam's eyes when he turned back to her. He took a purposeful step toward her, and Rayna leapt out of the chair and backed away.

"Listen to me, Adam Welles," she shouted at him, hating the quiver in her voice. "I could not let you leave Naples like some sort of avenging angel, bound for God knows what kind of danger! And I'll tell you something else. I do not believe that even you, at your most persuasive, could convince my father to let us wed, even if he knew that . . . that we are lovers! I am sorry for the worry my parents will feel, but I told them I was with you, and as safe as I could be. I . . . I told them that I love you and that we were going to . . . fetch Arabella."

"So now I can expect to see your father waiting for me on the dock at Oran, a pistol in his hand."

"No, I did not tell him where we were bound."

Adam cursed long and fluently. Rayna regarded him with some astonishment, and then stared wide-eyed when he turned away from her and calmly began to strip off his clothes. She had expected him to burn her ears at least until dinner arrived.

"What are you doing?"

"I am going to wash up and shave," Adam said, pulling his shirt over his head and tossing it on the narrow bed.

He sat down on the edge of the cot and pulled off his boots. "Perhaps," he said, not looking at her, "after a week in my company you will not wish to marry me. I can be a most demanding man, so I've been told, by a number of ladies."

He was mocking her! Rayna raised her chin and stared down her nose at him, which, she realized belatedly, was not all that impressive a gesture.

When he stood and unfastened his wide leather belt, she moved her chair closer. "Just a moment, my lord," she said. "If you are planning to parade in front of me naked, I would like to have a better view of my treat."

Adam scowled at her, his fingers stilled for a moment on his pants.

"Are you going to shave off that fierce beard?"

"No. I wish to leave something on."

His trousers dropped to the floor, and he stood before her splendidly naked. Rayna found herself staring at him pointedly. Despite herself, she said in a breathless voice, "I cannot imagine a man more beautiful than you, my lord." She dropped her face into her hands, remembering his words. "And you have known so many women! How can you want me? I am so . . . ordinary!"

Her guilelessness was as artful as the most skilled

courtesan's. No, he chided himself, he would not succumb to it. "Ordinary, Rayna? I have studied you most carefully, and have decided that you will . . . likely improve in a few more years."

Her face was a bright red, and he allowed a deep, booming laugh that made her want to strike him.

"I have found that I am particularly drawn to the soft auburn curls between your thighs," he added.

"At least I am not all dark and hairy!"

He grinned and stretched, knowing that she was staring at him, and walked slowly over to the basin. "Ah," he said as he soaped the sponge and began to rub it over his chest. He began to sing a bawdy sailor's song as he lathered his arms. The words were most explicit and he knew that Rayna's face must be flushed with embarrassment by the time the captain raised the serving maid's skirts and examined the treat she offered.

"You sound ridiculous," Rayna hissed at him. "Your voice is like a scratchy pipe."

"Shall I sing the verse for you again?" He heard her gasp, and resumed his song. When he wiped the soapy water from his eyes, Rayna was stalking toward the cabin door. "If you leave this cabin," he said, anger filling his voice, "I promise you that you'll not sit for three days."

Her slender shoulders slumped. He felt himself beginning to soften and sternly repressed it. Damned little fool! It was all he needed. Now he would likely have to deal with Lord Delford coming after him with his five sons, all of them after his hide! What the devil would he do with her once they arrived in Oran? Angrily he grabbed a thick towel and began to dry himself.

Their dinner arrived after Adam had shrugged into a change of clothes. It consisted indeed of noble portions of roast chicken, boiled potatoes, and green peas.

"If you drink any more wine, you will be vilely ill," Adam said as Rayna downed what was left of her third glass of wine.

She snapped the glass onto the tabletop. "Adam," she said after a moment, "I know that you are angry with me, but—"

"That, madam, is not the half of it!"

"—but I could not stay in Naples pretending to my parents that I cared naught about anything, and knowing that I would not be with you to protect you."

"Protect me! Good Lord, Rayna, *you* protect *me*?"

She raised her chin. "Who do you think would restrain you if you wished to do something stupidly male and—"

"There we are in disagreement!"

"—and if you would but cease to interrupt me—"

"You have given me the right, madam, to do any damned thing I want to do with you!"

"—and cease acting like a bully, then we could—"

"You are lucky. I hear Banyon."

Silence reigned as Banyon, his eyes darting first to his scowling master and then to the scarlet-faced young lady, cleared away the dishes. "It looks to be a lovely evening," he said, closely examining the chicken bones.

Adam scraped back his chair. "I believe I will see for myself. Madam, you will stay here. Is that clear?"

Rayna did not look at him, only nodded.

"I'll bring you some fresh water, miss," Banyon said when Adam had slammed out of the cabin. "Leave your clothes and I'll freshen them for you."

"Thank you, Banon."

Rayna washed quickly, with one eye on the cabin door. She had no choice but to don one of Adam's cambric shirts. She pulled a blanket from the cot, lay down on the floor, covered herself with it to her nose, and waited.

At least he hadn't yet beaten her, nor had he instructed the captain to return to Naples. She thought about her parents, and her conscience smote her anew. She wondered, a tear trickling down her cheek, if they would ever forgive her. Would Adam forgive her? The spirited Arabella, she knew, would have done just as she did, without a second thought. Arabella was braver than she. Well, she thought stoutly, I will not cower and whine to him. Did he really want her to be submissive and docile? Did he want his wife to be so different from his sister? Adam walked into the cabin at that moment. Rayna raised herself on her elbow and spat at him, "You can go to the devil, Adam Welles!"

Adam raised a thick brow. "I, madam? I assure

you, the devil has no need for the likes of me. Perhaps he would prefer disobedient young girls who have more hair than wit."

As he spoke, he took in the loose auburn hair, thick and lustrous, that framed her small face. And his cambric shirt.

"What are you doing on the floor?"

Rayna blinked at the sudden roughness in his voice. "Where else should I be?" she asked, wrapping her arms unconsciously over the blanket.

"You should first be hauled over my lap."

"You wouldn't!"

Adam strode over to her, bent down, and hauled her to her feet. She struggled against him, but he dragged her to the cot and pulled her onto her stomach over his knees. The cambric shirt shifted upward, baring her white thighs.

"Rayna," he said between gritted teeth, "what you've done is unpardonable, and I've waited to do this until my anger cooled. God knows what Arabella is going through, and now I must concern myself with what to do with you. The captain will be sailing nowhere near a port where I may leave you. You will never, my girl, ever again disobey me!"

Her jerked up the shirt and brought the flat of his hand down on her buttocks. "Do you understand me?"

"You . . . bastard!"

He brought his hand down again and she felt tears start in her eyes. She tried to rear up, but it was no use. "Do you understand me?" he repeated as his hand came down again.

"I will do what I believe is right," she sobbed, her voice muffled by the bedcovers.

He raised his hand, but froze at seeing the raised imprint of his fingers on her white buttocks. He lowered his hand and gently caressed the spot to ease away its sting. She lay perfectly still at his touch, no longer resisting him.

He gently turned her over and cradled her in his arms. "I love you," he said, kissing her temple. "But I will beat you again if you ever do something so stupid."

"And what if you do something stupid?"

"Your sharp tongue will be punishment enough!"

"I doubt that," she muttered.

"How is your bottom?" he asked, resting his large hand lightly on her bare leg.

"It stings."

"Ah. I will endeavor to find a remedy." He unfastened the draw string on the cambric shirt and lifted it over her head.

Rayna felt her nipples tighten under his gaze and a wave of embarrassed color washed over her face. "I thought you said that I need improvement," she said in a breathless voice.

He eased her down into the crook of his arm and laid his other hand gently down on her belly. "Perhaps I spoke too quickly."

He cupped his hand over the torrent of auburn curls, his fingers lightly stroking her. She gasped as his mouth came down to claim hers, and he felt her slender body arching upward.

"I shall have to duel with everyone of your damned brothers," he whispered with a smile into her mouth.

"Please forgive me," Rayna said softly, burrowing her body over the length of his. "But, Adam, I had to do it! I had to!"

"I will consider it," he said, tightening his arms around her back. "I trust you do not snore."

18

Kamal slowly rolled the parchment into a tight ring, tied a black ribbon around it, and handed it to Hassan.

"You seem preoccupied, highness."

"Yes, old friend. I just received word from a friend in France that the French and the English will shortly be at each other's throats again. The Treaty of Amiens is no more."

Hassan shrugged and gazed briefly at the parchment. "Did you write to the dey of this?"

"Yes. Undoubtedly he will hold a celebration."

"It does mean that the English will be distracted, protecting their puny island from the French emperor."

Kamal looked up at Ali, who stood in the open doorway waiting to gain his master's attention.

"What is it, Ali?" he asked impatiently.

"Raj approaches, highness, with the English girl."

Kamal smiled ruefully at Hassan. "At least she should no longer offend the nose."

He heard Hassan draw in his breath and turned slowly. Standing close to the huge eunuch was the most exquisite girl Kamal had ever seen, all golden and ivory with eyes so dark they appeared almost black.

Kamal stared at her, knowing full well who she was, but asking nonetheless, "Well, Raj, where is she?"

"Lady Arabella Welles, your highness," said Raj, and gently pushed Arabella forward.

"Ah," Kamal said slowly. He could not prevent himself studying her. In the soft candlelight her hair looked like spun gold. It flowed long and silky down her back, held off her forehead by a simple gold embroidered band. She was dressed in the Turkish fashion, and the gossamer veils did nothing to hide her exquisite form. He finally met her eyes and smiled reluctantly, for she was staring at him as closely as he was her.

Arabella stood stiffly, her hands fisted at her sides. She would not show fear; she must not. She studied the man lounged on the soft cushions before her. She had not remarked earlier how very fine-looking he was. Not that it mattered. He was her enemy, the son of the vicious contessa. She heard Raj say, "It was walnut stain, highness, doubtless used to protect her on her voyage here. She is again as she was."

A beautiful whore, Kamal thought, wishing perhaps that she weren't so lovely. He could picture her dressed in her European finery, drawing men to her. He wondered if she would try to seduce him to gain her ends.

Hassan said, "She does not wear a veil, Raj, nor does she kneel to his highness."

Arabella felt a quiver of anger, and her fists clenched harder. She felt Raj's soft fingers lightly touch her arm. "Lady Arabella is not Muslim," he said.

She drew herself up straighter, narrowing her dark eyes at the old man, who was regarding her speculatively.

"Still . . ." Hassan said, taken aback by the fury in those dark eyes.

"I do not kneel to animals," Arabella said in a loud, clear voice, "even though they pretend royalty."

"I see that you could do nothing about her tongue, Raj," Kamal said. He uncoiled his powerful body to stand in front of her. She raised her eyes to his face and regarded him with open contempt. So, he thought, she was still bent upon her insults. He had planned to treat her as a European lady, to speak to her gently and try to explain why she was here. Evidently, as a Muslim, he was not worthy of her favors. It angered him. Without warning, his hand shot out and wound about a thick mass of hair. Slowly he wrapped it about his hand, drawing her toward him.

"Kneel before your master," he ordered pleasantly.

"Go to hell," Arabella said, gritting her teeth against the pain in her scalp.

Kamal released her hair suddenly and hooked his leg behind hers, throwing her forward. Arabella fell on her knees, momentarily stunned by his quickness. She growled in fury and tried to jump up, only to feel his hands on her shoulders, keeping her down.

"That is where a slave and a woman belongs," Kamal said. "You will stay there until I give you leave to rise."

Raj stared at Kamal in consternation. Never had he treated any woman thus. He knew too that Arabella wouldn't submit, and he feared for her life. He opened his mouth, but he wasn't in time. Arabella thrust out her hands and shoved at Kamal's legs with all her strength. He staggered backward, but kept his balance.

"Highness!" Raj said, quickly moving in front of the girl.

Arabella leapt to her feet and turned to run, but she got no farther than the door. Raj held her arm firmly. "No, little one," he said sternly.

"You protect the little slut?" Kamal raised a mocking brow. Her eyes darted to his face and he saw fury in their depths. "Leave us," he said abruptly. "I wish to dine now, and the . . . slave will keep me company. Perhaps she can even be taught manners."

Raj heard the low hiss of her breath and said quietly, "Take care, my lady. You might consider . . . conciliation. His highness is as much European as he is Muslim."

She blinked at him in surprise until she remembered that his mother was indeed European. "I will try," she said stiffly.

Why is he protecting her? Kamal wondered silently. They were quickly left alone. He saw her glance dart about the chamber, and he did not have to be told that she was searching for a way to escape.

"Sit down," he said briefly, pointing to the cushions set in front of the low sandalwood table. For a moment he thought she would refuse, but she tossed her head, shrugged indifferently, and eased herself down to the cushions. He rang a small golden bell beside him, and three young Nubian boys entered, each carrying covered silver dishes.

Kamal gazed at the girl opposite him from beneath lowered lids. She was paying him no attention, her eyes fixed on her plate, but her rigid body gave her away—that, and her heaving breasts. He allowed the boys to serve them, then nodded his head for them to leave.

"It is baked mutton in curry and fennel. Eat."

Arabella shook her head. "No," she said. "I am not hungry."

He said slowly, his voice very precise, "If you were in the presence of any other man in this country, you would now be dead, your body thrown to the dogs."

"What is the matter?" she asked him in an equally precise voice. "You have no dogs for your barbaric sport?"

"Ah, certainly I have. But for you, little slut, I

would have my soldiers take you. You would doubtless, however, find that quite enjoyable."

The words were scarce out of his mouth when he felt the grains of rice strike his face. She was staring at him, her face perfectly white. She dropped her spoon to the table.

Slowly Kanal wiped his face. "You will eat your dinner now."

She shook her head, mute.

"If you do not eat, I will have your clothes taken from you. A woman without clothes, I have found, is very vulnerable."

Her expressive eyes widened, and he was pleased to see her hand tremble as she picked up her fork.

"I am pleased that you can be . . . conciliating."

Arabella shot him a look that promised retribution, but he only smiled. Why, he wondered, as he forked down a bite of lamb, was he baiting her? Where had his calm logic fled?

Though the lamb was tasty and tender, Arabella could swallow only a couple of bites. She was too aware of the man so close to her. She accepted a piece of pita bread he handed her, and nibbled it around the edge. She supposed it too was good, but it curdled with her fear and tasted like paste in her throat. She sipped at her wine, then set the goblet down.

"I want to know why I am here," she said.

"You are here to be my slave," Kamal said easily. She stiffened, just as he knew she would, squaring her slender shoulders. "You look like my slave," he continued, his eyes lingering intimately on her breasts, "and I will teach you to respect and please me, your master."

To his surprise, Arabella smiled, an enchanting smile that brought forth dimples on either side of her mouth. "Pray stop being an ass," she said. "Although I find your rhetoric somewhat amusing, I grow bored with you. I asked you why I am here. I expect an answer."

He made a noise that sounded suspiciously like a hiss to Arabella, but when she met his eyes, they were expressionless. He lifted his goblet and slowly sipped the sweet red Cypriot wine.

"My mother—the contessa—she told you nothing?"

Arabella shook her head, deciding she wouldn't tell him what she did know. See if the pirate was capable of truth.

Kamal shrugged and speared another square of lamb on his fork. "There is no reason for you not to know. You are out of the game, so to speak." He started to add that he had never wanted her involved in his mother's vengeance, but her ill-disguised contempt for him held him silent. He continued in an expressionless voice, "Twenty-six years ago, my mother, the Genoese Contessa Giovanna Giusti, was captured by my father, Khar El-Din, along with your father's half-brother, Cesare Bellini. Your mother evidently paid a great deal of money to my father to keep the contessa and to kill her husband's half-brother."

"My mother! That is a ridiculous lie!"

Kamal arched a thick brow. "If you persist in

wagging your shrewish tongue, I will tell you no more."

Arabella bit down on her lower lip. "Very well, I will listen to you."

Kamal smiled at her with satisfaction. "I see that you are capable of manners. The reason my mother was sold to my father was that your mother—an English harlot—wanted the wealth and position the Earl of Clare could doubtless offer her. Once she was pregnant, your father did indeed wed her, and did nothing to save my mother. She bore me within a year of her captivity. She has waited long for revenge for the evil done to her."

Arabella wanted to shriek at him that it was ridiculous, all of it, but she held her temper.

She drew a deep breath and said slowly, "My father has always told me that the corsairs were honorable. He paid tribute to your father, Khar El-Din, and your half-brother Hamil, yet you" —her voice frayed with contempt—"you looted and burned two of my father's ships and killed all his men. Your notion of revenge is chilling."

"The revenge, my lady," he said, "will be the capture of your esteemed parents and their disposition as slaves in Constantinople."

Arabella could only stare at him; then she threw back her head and laughed deeply. "You credulous fool! Your mother, *your highness*, is a vicious harridan, a liar, and the mistress of an evil Frenchman and of the king!"

Kamal felt his face grow red with fury. "Do you want the flesh flayed off your back?"

"Ah, the honorable gentleman now makes his savage threats! You and your mother are two of a kind, both of you dishonorable animals!"

No one had ever spoken thus to Kamal and he could only stare at her. Did she not understand that he could break her slender throat with one hand?

"You are afraid to hear the truth?" she taunted him softly.

"The truth, my lady? That you are indeed your mother's daughter? A fact I have little trouble in believing now that I have met you."

Arabella held to her control. "I repeat, *your highness*, are you afraid to hear the truth?"

Kamal waved a negligent hand. "Proceed with your tale."

Arabella's brow puckered in thought. "I do not know anything about your mother, nor has my father ever mentioned a half-brother. He met my mother in England. She was to wed another man, but fell in love with my father instead. She was anything but a harlot. Indeed, she was an eighteen-year-old girl, the daughter of an English baron. Your mother's story of my father bringing her to Genoa, unmarried, is ridiculous. My mother is a lady, and my father a gentleman." She paused a moment, sensing that he was listening to her. She leaned toward him, her eyes intent and serious upon his face. "My mother could have no reason to rid herself of your mother. She was my father's wife! Perhaps there was jealousy on your mother's part. I do not know. But you must believe me. My parents are honorable people. They would be incapable of perpetrating such a deed as your mother claims."

"I see," Kamal said quietly. "How, then, my lady, did my mother arrive in Algiers? Her own free will? She sold herself?"

"I do not know."

"And what was the name of the English gentleman your . . . honorable mother was supposed to have married?"

"A childhood friend, a viscount," Arabella said. "I know little else." A memory, vague and misty from Arabella's earliest years, rose unbidden in her mind, a memory of her mother's old nurse teasing her mother about her father's ruthlessness in taking what he wanted. "Aye," she could hear the woman saying, "he'd take you again, my pet, and devil take the consequences!" Arabella shook away the senseless memory, aware that Kamal was speaking.

"It is likely that you are truly ignorant of what happened. Are you so certain that your mother did not play your father's whore until he finally married her?"

"That is impossible. My mother is a lady."

"You spin amusing tales, my lady," he said softly, "but they have no substance. It is time for you to change your thinking, just as you have changed your clothes."

"I have no intention of changing my thinking." Arabella stared at him, her fork clattering to her plate. She said slowly, "I asked you why I was sent here. I am bait, am I not? I am to lure my father here?"

He nodded and looked away for a moment, unable to bear the anguish in her eyes.

"I will not allow that," Arabella said calmly. "You will have to kill me first."

"Kill you? Pride sits ill on a woman's shoulders. Consider yourself a slave—my slave. I am your master and you will obey me."

"Master!" she scoffed. "I would as lief call a jackal master! And what would you now, *master*, force me, as would an animal?"

"Why should it matter?" he asked coldly. "You gave your body willingly enough to all the foppish gentlemen in Naples."

"That is another of your mother's lies."

"If it is a lie, it could be easily disproved, could it not?"

Arabella shrank back, unable to help herself. "No," she whispered, her hands covering her breasts in a protective gesture.

"If I did not know of the harlot's blood flowing through your lovely body, I would be much moved by your virgin's performance. As it is, I only hope that you are not diseased."

She stared at him, not comprehending.

"Cease your playacting!" he roared at her.

"Oh," she said suddenly, remembering Adam's words. "You mean the pox."

He blinked. "Yes," he gritted at her, "the pox."

"What is it?"

"Enough!" He stretched out his long legs toward her. "Come, slave, and remove my boots. I grow tired of both your foolish pride and your lies."

"The only thing I would remove is your black heart!" She grabbed the knife and scrambled to her feet.

Kamal did not move. He looked at her eyes and saw naked fear, despite her show of bravado. He rose slowly, unwilling to frighten her more. "Give me the knife," he said, and held out his hand toward her.

Arabella shook her head, beyond words.

He frowned at someone behind her and shook his head. Arabella whirled about to face her new foe. In the next instant, her wrist was held in a punishing grip and the knife flew from her fingers to the carpet. He had tricked her so very easily. Tears of frustration at her stupid failure streamed down her cheeks. The grip on her wrist eased.

"Now you become the soft, pleading woman," he said. "I will go easy with you, if you prettily beg my pardon and admit to your lies."

He could not see her face, for her head was bowed. "You search for gentle words, my lady?" He slid his hands up her arms, drawing her closer to him. "I am accounted a good lover, and since you are no blushing innocent, I expect you to do more than spread your lovely thighs for me. It will pass the time until your father arrives."

Oddly, Arabella remembered teasing Adam about lovemaking. So long ago, it seemed, the two of them arguing in the gardens at the Villa Parese.

So curious she had been about men, and what men and women did with each other when they were alone and in love. But this wasn't love. This was terror. To die, she thought, without having ever known what love was . . . She felt his fingers tangling in her hair. He was an animal. She shuddered and heard him laugh softly. A cry of pure rage broke from her throat.

She flung herself at him, striking her fists at his face, kicking at his legs. She felt his arm go around her, choking off her breath, but still she fought him. She kicked him in the shin and his hold eased.

Her fingers closed about her heavy silver wine goblet and she brought it against his head with all her strength. She heard the satisfying thud. In the next instant she was on her back on the carpet.

Kamal shook away the pain from his temple. He held himself away from her, knowing if he touched her he would likely break her neck. She was staring up at him, and he knew that she expected to die, that she had known he would kill her when she attacked him. Her jacket was ripped and he saw the soft white flesh of her breast. He also saw the marks from his fingers on her upper arms. She bruises easily, he thought.

He took a step toward her.

"Stop! Stay away from me!" Arabella scrambled among the cushions her back was pressed against the wall.

No woman had ever fought him; indeed, with many European women, he had sometimes felt as though he were the one being used for their pleasure. Why did this girl fight him when she had given her favors so freely to other men?

It angered him beyond reason. He moved so quickly that Arabella's screams were stuck in her throat. He pulled her to her feet and threw her over his shoulder, impervious to the blows she rained on his back.

He moved his fingers intimately over her buttocks, knowing that to her it was the most effective punishment. She writhed and squirmed, but to no avail. He carried her into his bedchamber and dumped her unceremoniously onto the floor.

"You act like an ill-broken mare," he said, standing above her. "I will treat you like one." He pulled off the leather belt at his waist, seized her hands, and bound them together.

He retrieved another leather belt, tied it to the one about her wrists, and jerked her toward the bed. She was screaming at him in English, a whore's curses, he thought, not slowing.

He secured the length of the belt to the bedpost and stepped back from her. She lay on her back, her arms drawn upward.

He started to tell her that she would spend the night on the floor, but held himself silent. Let her wonder.

Arabella watched him shrug off the white shirt. When his hands went to the buttons on his white trousers, she closed her eyes. And waited. She heard his boots hit the floor. Her body was tense with fear. She tugged at the belt wrapped around her wrists, but could not ease them. She felt his presence very near her, but would not look at him.

Kamal checked to see that the belts were secure. He started to touch her, but pulled back his hand. Her hair fell about her face and down her back in a torrent of golden silk. He wished she were not so lovely.

Arabella heard the bed give under his weight. She opened her eyes, but could see nothing, for the chamber was dark. She passed the next hour tugging at the leather with her teeth, half her attention on the man in the bed.

Finally she fell into an exhausted sleep. She did not hear him rise, nor did she feel the weight of the blanket he tossed over her.

19

"Wake up, lady!"

Arabella felt a hand on her shoulder and jerked upright, a cry of pain on her lips because of her numb wrists. She stared into the black eyes of a young man she had seen the previous night. She looked frantically around for Kamal, but the chamber was empty save for the two of them.

"Who are you?" she whispered as he unfastened her bonds.

"Ali, lady. My master said to release you and take you back to the harem."

Arabella rubbed her aching wrists and slowly rose to her feet. "Where is your master?"

"With his soldiers. He enjoys training with them." Ali studied the girl who had spent the night tied to his master's bed. The welts on her wrists were black and purple.

"I hope," Arabella said, "that someone runs a sword through him."

Ali drew back, pity for her replaced by anger.

"A worthless woman does not speak of his highness like that. You are lucky he didn't kill you."

Arabella sighed. "I am too valuable to be so lightly discarded," she said. And she realized that it was true. If she were dead, the contessa and her son would have no bait to lure her father to Algiers. She knew too that her father would verify that she still lived before he came. Then come he would.

"No woman is that valuable," Ali said.

"I am hungry," Arabella said.

Raj stood at the gate to the harem, waiting for her. He spoke quietly to Ali in Arabic, then dismissed the boy. "Come, my lady," he said. "Lena will bind your wrists."

Arabella followed the huge eunuch into the harem garden. It was still early in the morning and few of Kamal's concubines were up and about. Those who were, stared at her and whispered to each other behind their hands.

"How many girls does that lascivious jackal keep prisoner here?"

"There are twenty girls presently in his highness's harem," Raj replied calmly, not pretending to misunderstand her.

Arabella wondered for one insane moment if she could get all the girls together and foment a revolt. She laughed aloud at the thought.

"His highness did not touch you," Raj said, eyeing her.

"No," Arabella said shortly. "I would not allow him to."

Raj shook his bald head. "If he had wished to

take you, my lady, there would be no one to stop him. You least of all."

"I . . . angered him."

"And it got you nothing, save bruised and numb wrists."

Arabella tried to shrug indifferently. "He cannot kill me," she said. "You know that he cannot. My father is not a fool."

"No, your father is anything but a fool, my lady."

Arabella looked at him sharply. "You know my father?"

"No, but I have seen him, and you, my lady, with your black eyes and eyebrows, have the look of him." He saw that she would question him further and said abruptly, "No, my lady. I encourage you to accept your fate. There is nothing else you can do."

My fate. Was her fate to be raped by that animal Kamal? To lie in his bed until he had her father? And her mother?

Arabella looked up to see Lena, her brow furrowed with concern.

"See to your mistress," Raj said, and left them.

Lena rubbed Arabella's wrists with a soothing cream and bandaged them, clucking over her while she ate her breakfast of soft, flat pita bread, fresh oranges, and pomegranate juice. She spent the next hours in the bath, and her hair was again washed, her body massaged with a jasmine cream. She was scarce aware of the chattering Lena or the harem girls who drew close to see her. Did Adam know what had happened to her? If he did know, what would he do? She shot a deadly smile toward a beautiful oleander tree. She hoped he would draw and quarter the contessa.

After a lunch of cold shrimp and rice, Lena left her alone to nap. To Arabella's surprise, sleep came quickly, but her dreams were violent and steeped in darkness.

She awoke heavy-eyed and frightened. She forced herself to leave her small chamber and stroll into the harem garden. The fragrance from the flowers soothed her somewhat, and she lay down in the sun near the pool.

"Well, daughter of a witch," a sharp voice said.

Arabella opened her eyes and smiled up at Elena.

"I hear you are such a bitch that the master tied you to his bed."

"That is correct," Arabella agreed.

"He will ask for me tonight, and you will stay in your chamber and rot!"

"I hope that he will ask for you, Elena. I would like to be left to rot."

Elena eyed the English girl in frustration. Would nothing pierce her white hide? She could not believe that the girl did not want the master. Every girl in the harem wanted to gain his attention. "Where did you learn to speak Italian?" she demanded. "You are English."

"I grew up in Genoa. At least, I spent about half of each year there."

"Ah," Elena said suddenly, her beautiful mouth curving into a vicious smile. "I understand you now, English cow! You know that the master can have any woman he wishes. You are only pretending that you do not want him!"

"Elena," Arabella said patiently, sitting up, "do you not want to be free? Do you not want to make your own decisions? Decide your own fate?"

"What do you mean?" Elena asked, her voice heavy with suspicion.

"I mean that no one—man or woman—should be forced to serve another. It is not right." Arabella looked around at the beautiful gardens and the graceful arched building. A calm, serene prison, but a prison nonetheless. "This is your world. It is quite small, you know. And it is even guarded."

"You are crazy," Elena said. "When the master takes me to wive, I will have you killed." She turned on her heel and walked away.

Arabella stared after her for a moment, then lay back and closed her eyes against the afternoon sun.

"You must forgive Elena," came a gentle voice. "If she has not Kamal, she has nothing."

Arabella opened her eyes. The woman who had spoken stood above her, her belly swollen mightily with child. Kamal's child? "Who are you?"

"I am Lella. I wished to speak to the woman who managed to anger Kamal." She spoke in very slow, precise Italian.

Arabella swung her legs over the edge of the chaise and sat up. "Please sit down. It is hot and your burden is heavy."

Lella nodded and eased herself down beside Arabella. "You are English, child?"

"Child?" Arabella smiled. "You are scarce older than I."

"I am nearly twenty-five, and carrying this babe makes me feel like a graceless old woman."

Arabella shook her head. "You are beautiful," she said sincerely. Lella's thick dark brown hair glistened with amber light, and her heart-shaped face was classical in its perfection. Her gray eyes were warm and intelligent.

"I had thought you would be kind. Is it true that you angered Kamal so that he tied you to his bed?"

"I was relieved to be tied to his bed and not be in it!" Arabella said tartly. She paused, then tilted her chin upward. "I am sorry if you carry his child and are perhaps fond of him, but—"

Lella gurgled with laughter. "Yes, I am fond of him," she said at last, clasping her hands over her huge belly. "It is not his child I carry."

Arabella frowned at her.

"Kamal is my brother-in-law," Lella said. "My husband was Hamil." Her voice broke on his name, and she whispered, "He did not even know I was with child when he . . . died."

"I am sorry. Forgive me for wounding you. It is just that I do not know what to do, and my helplessness makes me a witch."

Lella patted her hand. "You are not a witch. Indeed, 'twas a witch who sent you here. Kamal's mother is a woman who knows only bitterness and hate. Kamal is not like her."

"Ha!" Arabella snorted. "He has treated me with contempt, taunted me, called me a liar and a harlot, accused my parents of the most ridiculous crimes, and you tell me he is not like his mother!"

"My, I would like to have seen that," Lella said, admiration in her voice. "Kamal is usually so kind, particularly to women, and so exquisitely calm. What did you say to him to spend your night tied to his bed?"

"Perhaps I was not wise . . . but he angered me so. I called him an animal, a barbarian, a savage—"

Lella held up her hand in horror. "No more! My dear child, you are fortunate not to be dead!"

Arabella shrugged. "As to that, he cannot kill me. I am bait, and bait must be live to be useful. And if my anger keeps him from ravishing me, I shall become a demon from hell."

"But I have heard that you . . . well, that you are no maid."

"Another of his mother's lies. Lella, is there anything you can do to help me?"

"No, child, I am truly sorry. Were it not for Kamal, I would even now be shut away, or worse, sold months ago. Carrying Hamil's child made me particularly vulnerable to his enemies. But Kamal would not allow his mother to treat me with other than honor. Perhaps you can speak to him . . . more reasonably, convince him of your innocence, at least. If you ceased to antagonize him, were perhaps kind, he would likely listen to you."

It was on the tip of Arabella's tongue to tell Lella that she would as soon be kind to the devil himself, but an idea came to her, one so simple, one so final, that she could not disregard it. She accepted it, knowing there was no other way. Suddenly she felt calm and serene. "Perhaps you are right, Lella," she said at last.

Lella gazed at her doubtfully, disliking the cold calmness in her voice. She said slowly, not realizing that she was planting seeds of action in Arabella's mind, "As I said, Kamal is not a vicious man. Indeed, you are so lovely, he could not long be angered if you behaved more like . . . well . . . like a . . ."

"A soft, submissive woman?"

"Yes. You are, after all, a woman."

"And women play roles, do they not?"

"I am not certain what you mean. My Italian is not so fluent as yours."

"It matters not. Oh dear, here comes Elena again. Has she nothing else to do besides attack me?"

"She fears you." Lella rose ponderously. "We will speak again, child. I will take care of Elena, at least for now."

Arabella watched Lella drew Elena into conversation, and true to her word, the two women disappeared into her chamber.

Kamal stood naked as Ali sluiced him with cool water. He flexed his tired muscles and tried to focus his thoughts on anything but the English girl. He had lain awake for hours listening to her breathing the previous night, wondering what the hell he was going to do with her. Actually, he really did not have to do anything with her, simply wait until her father came for her; but at that thought, his loins tightened in protest. He wanted her; he wanted her to cease fighting him and cease lying. He wanted her to look at him with desire, not fear or hatred.

"What did you say, Ali?" he asked, realizing that he wasn't listening.

"I wondered, master, if you wished Orna to dance for you this evening?"

"No . . . yes." Kamal smiled to himself. Orna would dance for him and for the stubborn English girl. "And, Ali, tell Raj that I want the English girl again tonight."

Arabella was waiting for Raj to come with a summons from Kamal; indeed, she was looking forward to it. When he appeared, a worried frown on his fleshy face, she smiled, a soft smile.

"His highness wishes your company this evening," he said.

Arabella lowered her head. "As he wishes," she said.

"I have brought you new clothes."

"That is very kind of you, Raj. May I see them?"

Arabella fingered the gossamer trousers and the yellow jacket. There were matching yellow leather slippers. "They are beautiful."

Raj frowned, but said smoothly, "I selected the colors. You will look lovely."

Arabella said softly, "Yes, you chose well. I thank you."

"Are you . . . well, my lady?"

"Yes, of course." She allowed a deep sigh and stared beyond his massive shoulder toward a point unseen. "I have been thinking much today. You told me to accept my fate. Perhaps that is what I have done."

"You wish to be with his highness?"

"Why not? Lella told me he is not a barbarian. If I am more understanding, perhaps he will be also." Her proud young voice rang with sincerity.

"His highness will be . . . surprised."

"But pleased, Raj?" she asked eagerly. "Will he be pleased?"

"Undoubtedly," the eunuch said dryly.

He left her then to dress. When he returned for her, she was standing in the doorway gazing out over the garden. She looked utterly beautiful, her golden hair flowing free down her back, her slender form outlined clearly through the trousers.

"Do you still feel as you did, my lady?"

She smiled slowly, but her eyes were infinitely sad. "Yes, certainly. It is just that . . ." She raised her hand in a small gesture, then dropped it to her side.

"What troubles you, my lady?"

Arabella looked down at herself. "I am used to showing myself to advantage, Raj."

He eyed her full breasts straining against the

soft material. "I see no flaw in your beauty, my lady."

"It is probably nothing," she said. "I just wish for a jewel, a brooch perhaps to make me more elegant."

He had not thought her vain, nor had he believed her capable of thinking herself anything less than a great lady, no matter her circumstance or costume.

"I should feel more . . . confident in myself had I something to wear that reminded me of happier times."

Still he remained uncertain, until she raised liquid eyes to his face. No one, he thought, could remain indifferent to those fathomless eyes. The master would be pleased were the girl to smile. Raj nodded. "I will bring you something. Wait here."

Arabella nodded, a cleansing smile brightening her face.

"So," Elena said, stepping out of the shadows, "you play games to be with the master."

Arabella stiffened, but she said nothing.

"He will tire of you, and quickly. You are cold and he will find no warmth between your skinny legs!"

"You are probably right," Arabella said, her pulse slowing. "Perhaps his highness will desire something quite different after tonight."

Elena snarled in frustration, and beat a hasty retreat when Raj approached.

"This should brighten your spirits, my lady," he

said, and to Arabella's utter chagrin, he slipped a sapphire-and-diamond necklace over her head. She wanted to laugh aloud and howl at the same time at the failure of her plan. She tried to tell herself that a brooch clasp probably wouldn't have been strong enough for the task. She managed a weak smile. "It is beautiful, Raj. I thank you."

He nodded. "Come, my lady."

She followed him silently, thinking furiously. She had to do something! Raj's chambers. She gazed at him through her lashes, waiting until they had nearly reached the harem gates.

"Raj?"

He turned somewhat impatiently to face her. "My lady?"

"I must . . . that is, I have to . . ." She managed a flush of embarrassment and lowered her head.

"I see," he said, smiling slightly. "I will await you here, my lady."

Arabella dashed back toward the harem suites. Before she veered away from her own small room, she glanced back toward Raj. To her profound relief, he was in close conversation with one of the girls. She slipped into the outer chamber that Raj used for his sitting room. She saw a small writing desk and hurried toward it.

She rejoined Raj some minutes later, schooling her face into a passive expression.

She followed him docilely from the harem compound to the palace. The air was warm and perfumed from the profusion of flowers. A full moon lit the night sky. She felt her heart begin to thud as they neared Kamal's chambers. Please, she prayed silently, give me strength to do what I must!

She heard music as they neared, barbaric sounds, she thought, stiffening.

Kamal reclined on cushions, his eyes on a dancing girl. He was dressed in pristine white, a wide crimson leather belt at his waist. His head was bare and his streaked wheat-colored hair gleamed in the candlelight. He raised his eyes from the dancing girl when he saw Arabella. He saw no anger on her beautiful face. She looked calm, accepting.

He frowned as he said crisply, "Here, girl. We will enjoy the entertainment while we dine."

Arabella briefly met Raj's eyes, and her own held a hint of . . . apology? "Thank you, Raj," she said, and quickly left his side.

She lowered herself onto the cushions beside Kamal.

To her chagrin, her stomach grumbled, and she blushed.

Kamal smiled at her bowed head. "Here, you may eat while you watch Orna."

She accepted the flaky pastry filled with small chunks of lamb, peppers, and rice. It was delicious and gone quickly.

"You are too thin. Here, have another."

She ate the second slowly, her eyes on the dancing girl. The music increased in volume and tempo. The girl was covered from head to toe in

sheer silk veils. As she whirled about to the sound
of the clashing cymbals, one of the veils floated to
the floor. For a moment Arabella felt herself drawn
into the frenetic, savage music and the movements
of the dancer. The veils billowed around her slender body. Arabella gulped. The girl would soon be
naked!

"Does Orna's performance please you?" Kamal
asked, watching her widened eyes.

"It is . . . most unusual."

"Do you dance?"

"Not like that."

"Ah, yes. The minuet, the cotillion. They are
enjoyable enough, I suppose."

Orna was whirling faster and faster, dipping
backward, then tossing her long brown hair. The
last veil fell to the floor, but still she moved to the
music, now slow and sensuous. She moved closer
to Kamal, the small cymbals fastened to her fingers beating a primitive rhythm. She was so close,
Arabella could see the sheen of sweat on her smooth
belly. She leaned back, thrusting her hips forward.
Arabella's wine goblet trembled in her hand and
wine fell to the white cloth.

Kamal nodded and the music stopped. "She is
most talented, is she not?" he asked, looking at
Arabella's whitened face.

Arabella was too embarrassed to reply. The girl
hadn't moved and was so close that Arabella could
see clearly the damp profusion of brown curls
between her thighs.

"I think you would look equally lovely in such a . . . position."

He was baiting her, she thought, and forced herself to keep quiet. She picked up another pastry and slowly bit into it, as if it were the only object that interested her.

Kamal laughed softly, and clapped his hands. The girl, to Arabella's immense fury, fell forward on her knees and kissed Kamal's boot. It took all her fortitude not to fling the wine in his face.

He nodded and the girl backed from the chamber. The musicians had already faded away. They were alone.

Kamal began to eat. "You are silent, Arabella," he said.

"More pensive, perhaps, highness."

"Pensive? Were you not well-treated today?"

"Oh yes! I suppose I was . . . lonely."

Kamal frowned ferociously at her bowed head. He could not see her face, for her silky hair fell like a veil, obscuring it. "Lonely?" he questioned, leaning closer toward her.

She raised soft, brilliant eyes. "I am but a woman, highness. My happiness cannot be found within myself. I am fashioned differently."

He felt a perverse stab of disappointment. She was behaving just as he had hoped she would: docile, pliant, and submissive to him. "You are fashioned for my love, Arabella. You are fashioned to receive me as my scabbard does my sword."

She colored charmingly, and he lightly touched his fingers to her bare arm. She did not draw away. "Do you want to receive me, Arabella? As a man and as your master?"

"You will not hurt me?" she asked softly.

"Hurt you, my little flower? There is only brief pain, and that only when a woman is a maid. After, there is only pleasure. Have you not found that to be true?"

She nodded, her eyes on his strong fingers. They were rough against her soft skin.

"Ah, I see you make no more protestations. I am pleased." But he wasn't pleased. He knew a moment of fierce anger. The girl was like the rest, perhaps only more intelligent. She had toyed with him until she had gained his interest. Now he could have her. He was annoyed that he had been such a fool. Allah, he could have taken her the night before and she would have readily yielded to him. It had been all a sham.

"Stand up," he ordered harshly.

Arabella locked her trembling knees and rose to stand above him. She felt his eyes traveling over her body, thoroughly and intimately. She caught her lower lip in her teeth.

"Take off your clothes."

Her eyes flew to his face. His blue eyes studied her, and she felt for a brief moment that he could see into her mind. She quickly lowered her head. "Will you not help me . . . master?"

He laughed, and the sound made her flinch. He thought he had won, and he was enjoying her humiliation. She stood quietly, not daring to look again into his penetrating eyes.

Kamal rose gracefully. He clasped his hands about her shoulders and slowly drew her to him. "Kiss me, Arabella," he said.

She raised her face and rose to her tiptoes. She felt his mouth lightly touch hers. He tasted sweet, of oranges and wine. She felt his tongue softly glide over her lips, then gently probe until hers parted. To her shock, Arabella felt a surge of tingling warmth deep within her belly. No, her mind cried, and she stiffened. He tightened his hold on her and she felt his hands moving upward from her waist, over her bare ribs to her breasts. The only feeling she knew now was raw fear. His mouth was punishing now, and she hated his tongue probing into her.

"Please," she whispered, and pulled back.

Kamal studied her flushed face. "What bothers you, little flower?" He had felt her reaction to him and sought to bend her completely to his will.

"I . . . I wish to feel your flesh against mine."

He felt a surge of lust at her words, but remnants of reason warred in his mind. "Why have you changed toward me?"

"I desire you. Do you not want me?"

"Yes," he said thickly, and quickly untied the leather sash at his waist. His white shirt quickly followed, and he faced her, naked to the waist.

Arabella probed at the small buttons on her jacket. She felt his hands on her breasts, caressing her nipples through the soft cloth. Her hand slipped slowly to the band of her harem trousers. Slowly, very slowly, forcing herself to lean against him, she grasped the slender dagger.

"Savage! Animal!" she shrieked at him. She raised the dagger, clutching it in her fisted hand, and struck at him. He jerked away so quickly that the sharp point sliced across his shoulder and did not plunge deeply into his flesh. Arabella gazed a moment at the long jagged cut, oozing blood, furious with herself that she had not thrust it deep into his heart.

Kamal lurched back and stared at her. He was tempted to laugh at himself, for he had been naught but a fool, a gullible fool. He felt his blood streaking down his chest. He had no further time for thought, for she lunged at him again. He struck her outstretched arm and she staggered backward.

"I'll kill you, you bastard!" She was crouched forward, moving closer toward him, the dagger held tightly in her hand. "I'll kill you!"

She rushed him and he quickly sidestepped. He caught her wrist, feeling the delicate bones crunching beneath his fingers. She was crying, and screaming at him in frustration. He tightened his grip until the dagger flew from her hand to the floor.

They faced each other, panting.

Tears of rage streamed down Arabella's face. She threw herself at him, pounding her fists against his chest, kicking out at his legs.

He pulled her tightly against him and she felt his blood seep through her jacket to her skin. He grabbed a handful of hair and pulled her head back.

He stared down into her distraught face and laughed.

"I hope your blood is poisoned," she spat at him. "Next time my aim will be true!"

He tightened his hold on her, knowing that he was crushing her ribs, but she made no sound, no plea.

"There will be no next time, my lady." He considered taking her now, ripping off her clothes and throwing her to the floor. He saw his blood smeared over her breast, and laughed again at his own stupidity. He grasped her arm and dragged her into his bedchamber. He looked only briefly at her bruised wrists before binding them. She squirmed and writhed against him, cursing him, but he finished tying her. He stood over her, staring down at her crumpled figure.

"Sleep well, little flower," he said, and turned to walk away. Her yells of rage followed him.

Arabella's breathing slowly calmed. She had not harmed him greatly, and for a moment she wondered if, in her heart, she had wanted her aim to be true. Was she so weak that she was unwilling to sacrifice herself to save her parents? Had she killed him, her death would have been assured. She lowered her head against her arms and cried softly. Would Raj be punished since it was his dagger she had taken? She did not want the big eunuch to suffer for her.

The time stretched endlessly, and the lone candle guttered. Still she stared toward the doorway, wondering what Kamal was doing. She shivered.

Would he return and rape her, and perhaps, after he had finished with her, give her to his soldiers? Suddenly she laughed, a harsh, grating sound. So very foolish she had been, so full of vain bravado! She could have remained safe, even in Naples, if she hadn't been such a silly fool, certain of her own ability to take care of herself.

She saw Kamal silhouetted in the doorway. There were no soldiers with him. She forced her breathing to calm.

"I know you are not asleep, Arabella," he said. He strode over to her and sat on the edge of his bed, staring down at her.

She said nothing.

"Are you so afraid of me that you pretend sleep?"

Fool! she yelled silently at herself, but could not prevent snapping back at him, "I am not afraid of such as you!"

"No," he said slowly, "I do not think you are." She saw him flex his white-bandaged shoulder. "But perhaps you should be."

"It doesn't matter," she said, raising her face to his. "I hope that your pain is great."

To her surprise, he laughed. He leaned toward her and grasped her chin in his hand. Before she could jerk away from him, he kissed her hard on her mouth, then released her.

"Now you are afraid, are you not?"

"No," she said, but her voice shook. She was completely helpless, and she knew it. To her unutterable relief, he stretched out on his bed and turned on his side, away from her.

"Please do not hurt Raj," she said after a while. "He did not know what I intended."

"He has already been tortured and hung," came the calm response.

"No! You could not be such a barbarian!"

"Hold your tongue, else I'll stuff your mouth with cotton."

Her voice broke on an anguished sob.

He listened to her cries dissolve into hiccups. He said nothing more, and let the laudanum his physician had given him pull him into a deep sleep.

20

The Earl of Clare waited patiently for Viscount Delford to finish his furious tirade before gracefully flicking open his snuff box with his left hand and inhaling his favorite sort of Spanish Bran. He appeared to reserve all his concentration for the task.

"Perhaps you did not hear me, my lord," the viscount said, gritting his teeth and striding around his desk.

"I did hear you quite clearly, my dear Edward," the earl said calmly. "In truth, one remark most assuredly held my full attention. I believe your exact words were 'Your damned scoundrel of a son has run off with my daughter.' Do I have that correct?"

"You know you do," the viscount said, restraining his temper. "For God's sake, my lord, where has he taken her?"

"I cannot imagine my son abducting a young lady of quality. Surely it is most unlike him."

There was a mocking gleam in the earl's eyes that the viscount chose to ignore.

"My silly daughter imagines herself in love with your son. I realize now that he must have told her who he is."

"Ah," the earl said. "I begin to understand. Is it that your daughter ran off with my son, my lord?"

"He should have brought her back, damn him!"

"Not, my dear Edward, if she stowed aboard his ship, which undoubtedly she did. Most enterprising of her." For a moment he met the viscount's smoldering eyes with a limpid gaze. "I would not have expected such . . . dashing behavior from one of your offspring. I only wish Adam had restrained his chivalrous ambitions and awaited my arrival."

"Dammit, Clare, where are they? Not in Naples, Lord knows, I've searched everywhere."

"It's likely they're nearing Oran. How my gallant son plans to rescue his sister is quite beyond my simple wits."

"Oran!" The viscount paled visibly. "My God, that's in Algiers! It is a stronghold for the Barbary pirates."

"Exactly," the earl agreed.

"How do you know? Surely you can be mistaken."

"No, unfortunately. Adam left one of his men here to tell me where he was bound. From what Vincenzo told me, it is clear to me he did not know your daughter would be joining him. But that hardly matters now. It occurred to me that Adam might offer himself in exchange for his sister as . . . bait. He will not do so now. He must protect your daughter."

"You do not seem terribly concerned, my lord," the viscount sneered.

"Do I not? I assure you, my lord, I am most concerned. You see, I now know who engineered this fantastic scheme, and why. But I also know my daughter is relatively safe. She is not the object of the game. I am. I am sailing to Oran on the morrow. I will contrive to bring your daughter safely back to you, Edward."

"I am coming with you."

The earl cocked a thick black brow.

"You heard me, Clare. It is my daughter who might be brutalized by those savages."

"Impossible," the earl said curtly. "My son would never allow her to be taken. But I suppose you must come," he added on a sigh. "Incidentally, my dear Edward, what is your daughter's name? My lamentable memory—I confess to have forgotten."

"Rayna," the viscount snapped.

"Thank you. Adam is not lost to all sense of propriety. We shall both dance at their wedding, Edward."

"He will not wed her! I have told them both that!"

"How very Shakespearean of you," the earl said gently, a glint of humor in his eyes. "Recollect your youth, my dear Edward."

The viscount reddened.

"Just so," the earl said softly.

Arabella stirred at the sound of a gentle voice saying her name and an insistent shake on her shoulder. She opened her eyes and blinked. "Lena?"

"Yes, my lady. I have brought your breakfast."

She was in her own small room. "I do not understand," she said.

"His highness carried you here early, at dawn."

She looked down dispassionately at her bruised wrists as she said quietly, "I will need some more of your ointment, Lena." She frowned, thinking of Kamal carrying her back to the harem. Had she hurt him so little that he could bear her weight?

"You fought him again," Lena said in a sad, matter-of-fact voice.

"Yes," Arabella whispered, her thoughts on Raj, the man who had been kind to her, the man she had witlessly betrayed. Tortured and killed—no, murdered—all because of her! She dropped her face into her hands and sobbed softly.

"My lady! What is this?"

Arabella raised her tear-streaked face to see Raj standing in the doorway, his wide brow furrowed with worry.

"Y-you are alive!" Arabella stuttered, as relief flooded over her. "Oh, thank God! I thought . . . Kamal said that you were dead because you allowed me to . . ." She broke off, realizing that Kamal's lie had been her punishment.

"Of course I am alive," Raj said, sitting down beside her on the narrow bed. "His highness is not an unfair man. What you did was most foolish, my lady."

"I failed," she said flatly. "That is more tragic than foolish, I think."

"You speak nonsense. His highness told me that if he punished me, he would have to punish himself as well for being a gullible fool." He paused a moment, studying Arabella's ravaged face, waving to Lena to leave them. He handed Arabella a peeled orange and watched her take an absent bite.

"Do not make the mistake of thinking his highness soft, my lady. He has, shall we say, made allowances for what you did. But he will not forget."

Arabella wiped orange juice from her chin. "I hope he will remember, and leave me alone," she said in a dull voice.

"He told me of your . . . playacting. It is odd, but I believe that your show of submissiveness angered him more than your attempt to kill him."

"Perhaps I should tell Elena that!"

"No, you mistake me, my lady," Raj said patiently. "He has been told you are a harlot. Your courage did not fit with his image. When you pretended last night to succumb to him, he was again convinced that your brave front was naught but a trick." Raj sighed. "Allah only knows what he will do now."

"Allah and the devil!"

"You have challenged him and made him look the fool. He is not a man to be taken lightly, my lady."

Arabella felt tears blur her eyes. She gazed up at Raj and whispered brokenly, "What am I to do? He will allow his wicked mother to murder my parents! I must stop him!"

"Even if your own life is forfeit?"

"Yes."

"I will leave you now, my lady." He rose slowly to stare thoughtfully down at her. "You are not a restful woman, Lady Arabella."

Arabella was in no mood to be baited by Elena and her small group of cohorts. After her bath, she returned to her small chamber and sat on the edge of her bed, staring at the whitewashed wall. How much longer did she have? she wondered. A week perhaps, no more. And Adam—did he yet know where she was? Even if he did know where she was, she thought dismally, he had no chance of rescuing her.

"Lady Arabella."

She raised dull eyes to Lella.

"May I visit you for a while?"

"If you wish."

Lella sat awkwardly beside her. "I admire your courage," she said after a moment.

"If I were truly courageous, I would have killed him. I think perhaps I knew I would die if my aim were true. I am more a coward."

"No, you are no coward." Lella folded her hands over the mound of her belly. "You know, child, I feel as though I am responsible. It was I who told you to be more conciliating, more submissive."

"No," Arabella said firmly. "It was my idea, and you will not take any blame. Besides," she added bitterly, "he is quite all right. 'tis merely a scratch on his shoulder."

"You are fortunate, Lady Arabella, that it is Kamal who rules."

Arabella cocked a disbelieving brow at her and snorted.

"Nay," Lella continued, smiling at the unlady-like sound, " 'tis true. Hamil, my husband, I love . . . loved him dearly, but he was a Muslim, his beliefs rigid. Had you defied him, he would have treated you very differently. I do not mean to say that he was not a merciful man, it is just that—"

"Women rank somewhat above dogs," Arabella interrupted acidly. "Ah, Lella, how do you stand to be a prisoner in this place!"

"No, you must attend me, child. Muslim men love their women, truly, but they believe that women are fashioned to be the mothers of their sons, that women are weak creatures and need their protection. They could not conceive of a woman who wants to step out of her slippers and act as they would act. I tell you this so that you will understand how unusually Kamal has behaved toward you. It is doubtless because of the years he spent in Europe."

"Kamal truly lived in Europe?"

"Indeed. He returned to Oran but seven months ago when his half-brother died. He is a good ruler, but I do not believe it is what he truly wants. His sense of duty, his honor, if you will, compels him to carry out his responsibilities to the Dey of Algiers. Nor do I think him particularly happy. He is more European than Muslim, you see, and the two cultures war within him."

"If he is so much tied to Europe, then how can he bear to treat women as he does? Locked up as prisoners, used for his pleasure."

Lella smiled. "I did not say that Kamal was stupid, child. He knows and accepts the Muslim way. As the Bey of Oran, he must conform to Muslim law and Muslim tradition. That includes his harem. He must pleasure himself with his women; if he did not, those he rules would question not only his leadership but also his commitment to this way of life. Do you understand? It is his duty, and Kamal would never shirk his duty."

"I do not want to understand," Arabella said finally, her voice flatly heavy. "I must hate him, and I must somehow save my parents from his cruelty."

"It is not his cruelty, child, but his mother's. Again, his honor dictates that he avenge her."

"But you say he is not stupid! You know what she is like, Lella! How can he be so blind?"

"Lady Arabella, she is his mother! Do not you defend your parents with every breath you take? Also, he does not know her. He was taken from her at a very young age and raised by men and his father, as is the custom. When he was sixteen, Hamil and Kamal's mother convinced Khar El-Din that he should be educated in Europe. Their be-lief was that he would learn the ways of the Europeans and thus aid Hamil when he came to power."

Somehow, Arabella thought, turning over what Lella told her in her mind, somehow I must reach him. I must make him understand! Lella's voice broke into her reverie. "Do you know that he refuses to take a wife? To his mother's fury, he has announced that if I birth a son, the child will be his heir."

Arabella felt a surge of hope. Perhaps if she spoke to him as she would to a European, he would come to trust her, believe what she told him. On the heels of that wishful thought, she realized that he would believe she was but playing another role with him. Was there nothing she could do? She wanted to be alone, to think. "Lella, you are most kind to me, and all I do is argue with you. You must be tired with the burden of your child."

Lella gave her a twinkling smile and rose clumsily to her feet. "Dear child, whatever you decide to do next, please take care. Kamal can be pushed only so far. He must retain the respect of his people to be an effective ruler. If you need me, you have but to send Lena to me." With those words, she was gone.

Arabella rose and stretched. How was she to save her parents? Surely Kamal would be wary of her now. She hung her head, staring at the toes of her red leather slippers, admitting to herself that she had not wanted to kill him. 'Twas his mother who deserved punishment, not him. What then was she to do?

She strolled out into the harem garden. She gazed at the beautiful young girls who were kept here for his pleasure. She heard their chatter, felt the power of their presence. *His pleasure!* She halted, frozen in her tracks. He had wanted her; she realized that now, but he hadn't forced her. She had only herself, her body, to bargain with. She felt but a moment of fear at the thought of being naked and vulnerable to him. She tossed her head, her brow furrowed in pain. She would bear it; she must bear it. Her willingness in his bed in trade for her parents' safety.

She paused, suddenly apprehensive. She was a virgin; but she was, after all, twenty years old. Was it possible that she no longer had a maidenhead? If not, could a man tell if a woman had never before been with another man? What if he still believed her a wanton after he had sated himself with her body? What if he laughed at her bargain after he had taken what he wanted? Arabella started at a rippling of pain. She stared down at her palms, at the deep scratches her fingernails had made, in her anxiety. How did one go about seducing a man?

The afternoon stretched endlessly before her. She returned to her small chamber and lay on the bed staring at the ceiling. When Raj appeared in the open doorway and informed her that Kamal wished to see her, she felt a surge of profound relief.

"Very well," she said, swinging her legs over the side of her bed.

He frowned at her. "I pray you will not attempt any more foolishness, Lady Arabella."

"No," she said calmly, "I will do naught to hurt him." *Only I will be hurt by this night.*

21

Hamil stood on the quarterdeck of his *xebec*, his legs spread, his hands on his hips. There was a grim smile on his face as he watched the *Malek* draw closer. He could picture the confusion and helpless fury of the captain. He, Hamil El-Mokrani, Bey of Oran, knew better than anyone that the *Malek* was under tribute.

"Raise the white flag, Boroll," he said to his captain, "though I strongly doubt the captain will believe our good intentions."

"At least he isn't fool enough to fire on us."

Hamil's dark eyes glittered in anticipation as the *xebec* drew alongside the merchant ship. He heard the harsh grating of the grappling hooks and felt the deck tilt beneath his feet as the *xebec* scraped against the *Malek*'s hull, and Boroll and his men scrambled aboard her, their scimitars drawn at the ready. The crew of the *Malek* offered no resistance. Their captain was no fool, Hamil thought. Quickly his sailors were herded into a single line across the quarterdeck.

Hamil saw no woman. He strode to the railing and leapt gracefully onto the *Malek*'s deck. A thin man wearing an outlandish wig sped toward him.

"Sir!" The man wheezed in his fear. "We are under tribute! Why do you stop us?"

"You are Captain Alvarez?" Hamil asked.

"Aye, and we journey first to Oran and then to Cádiz. I know the bey, sir, and he will not approve what you have done!"

Hamil smiled. "Well, then, Alvarez, greet the Bey of Oran, for he stands before you."

Captain Alvarez's eyes widened. "Highness," he croaked. "You are dead! It is your half-brother Kamal who holds rule."

"Hardly dead. You look well, Alvarez."

"How . . . how may I serve you, highness?"

Hamil gazed again down the line of sailors. "Bring up your passengers, Alvarez. I have . . . business with one of them."

"I have but one passenger, highness. Lord St. Ives, an Englishman."

"Bring me this lord," Hamil said harshly.

Adam strode forward, leaving Rayna in Daniele's substantial shadow. "I am Lord St. Ives," he said.

Hamil frowned. The bearded man standing before him looked somehow familiar. "What is your given name?"

"Adam Welles."

"Ah," Hamil said. "Your father is the Earl of Clare."

Adam bowed slightly. "I understood also that you were dead, highness. Drowned in a storm. You are Hamil?"

"Yes," Hamil said curtly. He turned abruptly away from him and demanded of the captain, "I am looking for a woman. I was told she was to be a passenger on the *Malek*. Where is she, man? Tell me now, else I'll have my men sack your precious ship."

"The contessa," Adam said slowly. "You search for the contessa."

Hamil whirled about at Adam's words. "What do you know of the bitch?"

"I searched for her too, highness, in Naples. Unfortunately, as Captain Alvarez will confirm, although she did hire the ship, she never appeared to take her to Oran. I do not know where she has gone. Perhaps northward to leave from another port."

Hamil stood silent, deep in thought. "You are alone, Lord St. Ives?" he asked finally.

"No, I have two men and my . . . cabin boy with me."

"Your destination is Oran?"

"Yes."

Hamil turned to Alvarez. "Lord St. Ives and his men will accompany me. You may take your leave, captain, but you will not dock at Oran. I believe you and I have much to discuss," he continued, turning to Adam. "I will deliver you safe to Oran. My oath on it." He stretched out his hand and Adam grasped it.

"May I say, highness," Adam said, "I am glad that you live."

"No more glad than I," Hamil said.

A silent slave lighted the candles in Hamil's cabin. Hamil waited until the man had finished his task, then nodded dismissal to him.

"We are in private now, my lord. Be seated and we will talk. Your cabin boy, send him away."

Rayna gave a tiny gasp and moved closer to Adam.

"I ask that he stay, highness," Adam said steadily.

Hamil smiled, and gazed thoughtfully at Rayna. "He is a very pretty boy," he said. "Perhaps you would like to sell him to me? I have a good friend who has a liking for . . . well-favored boys. No ugly whiskers to mar his pretty face. Yes, I will buy him from you."

"I must decline, highness," Adam said politely. "He may be pretty, but his temper is capricious. He is disobedient and impertinent, and would bring no pleasure to this man you speak of. Indeed, he would likely whiten his hair within a month."

"I am certain," Hamil said, lowering his eyes as he brushed away a fleck of dust from his white sleeve, "that my friend could make him more . . . conciliatory. Such a foul-tempered youth as you describe, my lord, is in need of the whip. It would soon enough still his tongue. Once he is tamed, my friend would doubtless treat him well."

Adam gritted his teeth. He felt Rayna's fingers plucking fearfully at his sleeve. "The boy, despite his looks, is no plaything for a pederast, highness. I should dislike seeing him forced to play the part."

"Ah," Hamil said, his eyes still lowered. "So he prefers girls, does he?"

"Highness," Adam said, "I wish the lad to remain in my service. He is my obligation and my responsibility. Now, if you please, we have much to discuss."

"Certainly," Hamil said easily. He motioned to the cushions that surrounded a low, round sandalwood table. "Be seated, my lord. As to the boy, it will be as you wish. But his clothes offend me. As a sign of my friendship to you, I will have him better garbed."

"No!"

Hamil smiled at the high-pitched shriek. "I had thought the boy older, my lord, yet his voice has not yet deepened. And I believe you are right. Your servant dares to speak when he should be silent."

Hamil shrugged, turning away. "Be seated," he said again. He poured two goblets of wine and offered one to Adam.

Adam took the goblet and eased down onto the cushions, motioning Rayna to sit behind him. He said without preamble, "Highness, the contessa has had my sister abducted and sent to Oran. I do not know why. I do know that three of our ships were taken this year by the Barbary pirates, and it was she who was selling the cargoes in Naples.

But it has done me little good to discover that. My sister is taken. Who, highness, is this contessa?"

"None of your ships were taken until after my presumed death," Hamil said, more as a statement than a question.

"That is true."

"This contessa, my lord, is the mother of my half-brother Kamal, the man who now rules Oran."

Surprise held Adam silent for some moments. He said finally, "But she is Italian!"

"Indeed. She was sent to my father, Khar El-Din, some twenty-six years ago from Genoa, by your father. She is the Contessa Giovanna Giusti."

Adam felt Rayna stiffen in surprise behind him. "My father," he repeated slowly. "I felt he would know her motive. But why, highness? Why would my father send a woman into captivity?"

"I was very young at the time," Hamil said. "I do recall my father mentioning that she was involved in an intrigue against your father's wife." He frowned with concentration. "I remember that my father received a chest of gold in payment from your father."

"All these years, Adam," Rayna said suddenly, sitting forward, "she has waited to revenge herself on your father!"

"Indeed, *signorina*," Hamil said. "Why do you not remove that ridiculous wool cap? A slave cannot drink wine in his master's presence, but a young lady most certainly can."

Rayna gasped, her hands flying to her cap.

"I suppose," Adam said, a black brow cocked at

Hamil, "that you have known for some time that my cabin boy was not what he purported to be."

"I am not blind, my lord. Even in those clothes . . . well, just to see her walk . . ." He laughed deeply. "Forgive me, *signorina*, but I have had little to amuse me these last months."

Adam smiled at Rayna and pulled off her cap. Her auburn hair cascaded down her back. "This, highness, is Rayna Lyndhurst, my affianced wife."

"I am charmed, *signorina*." He poured her a goblet of wine and handed it to her.

Her cheeks were flushed and her hand trembled as she accepted the wine. "I am . . . mortified," she said.

"Besides being disobedient," Adam said dryly, "she believes that I cannot conduct my own affairs without her protection. She stowed away aboard the *Malek*. When I discovered her, 'twas too late to turn back to Naples."

"I have another friend, my lord," Hamil said, "who has a fondness for white-skinned women with red hair. Perhaps you would like to—"

Adam burst into laughter, covering Rayna's horrified gasp. "I will keep her," he said finally. "I believe she is correct. It is revenge the contessa seeks."

"To hear a woman speak wisely is refreshing," Hamil said.

Adam smiled, but his thoughts were elsewhere. "I was right, then. My sister is to be bait. Bait for my father."

"Yes, 'twould appear so."

"Why, highness, have you not returned to Oran to reclaim your throne?"

Hamil stared thoughtfully into his goblet of wine. "My half-brother Kamal," he said. "I have always held great fondness for him. I do not know if he is involved in this treachery with his mother. I wish to be certain before I proceed." He raised dark eyes to Adam. "My wife is in Oran, in the palace harem. She still lives—that I know. I will do nothing to place her in danger." He added, his voice brightening with pride, "She carries my child."

Rayna broke the brief silence. "If the contessa sent Arabella to her son, it does not bode well for his innocence."

"No," Hamil said, "it does not."

"And the contessa will most assuredly return to Oran," Adam said.

"Of a certainty she will."

"Will Kamal harm Arabella?" Rayna asked.

The men's eyes met across the table. Hamil said slowly, "It is true that my brother carries the blood of the corsairs, but he was educated in Europe. I cannot imagine he would . . . harm a gentle, well-bred lady."

Adam cursed. "My sister, unfortunately, is about as gentle as a desert storm, a . . ."

"A sirocco," Hamil supplied. Again he met Adam's worried gaze. "I understand your feelings about your sister, my lord, but you must understand mine. I had hoped to capture the contessa and wring the truth from her. That failing, I must, some way, manage to see my half-brother alone, without warning, and learn the truth. If he is part of his mother's treachery, I cannot risk my wife's safety." He rose gracefully from the cushions. "I will leave you now, my friends. I must tell my captain to set course for Oran."

Hamil strode from the cabin, leaving Adam to gaze abstractedly at Rayna.

"Perhaps," Rayna said hopefully, "Arabella will be too frightened to . . . anger this Kamal."

"What is likely is that I shall have to kill him," Adam said.

Kamal flexed his shoulder and winced at the pain the movement brought him. He tried to shake away the image of Arabella's face, streaked with tears of frustration at her failure to kill him. It came to him again that she had hesitated before she struck. What kind of woman was she? He was, he decided, seven kinds of a fool to see her again.

She looked proud, almost defiantly calm, when she stepped into his chamber. Her glorious hair flowed down her back nearly to her narrow waist. Her dark eyes gazed at him, velvet black, like midnight. He felt a stirring in his loins as his eyes fell to her breasts. She stood silently, saying nothing, enduring his scrutiny.

"Come," he said in an oddly hoarse voice. "I wish to speak with you."

Arabella glanced at the food set upon the table and felt her throat tighten. She nodded mutely and eased down on the soft cushions.

A slight Nubian slave boy poured wine into her

goblet. She downed it quickly, hoping it would ease her fear and increase her resolution. Her goblet was quickly filled again. She raised her eyes to Kamal's face as she sipped the sweet wine.

"I trust you wear no hidden weapons tonight," he said.

"No. Would it matter if I had?"

He gave her a twisted smile, watching her gulp down some more of her wine. "It is I who should be wary of you," he said quietly. "I do not know what it is you expect me to do to you, but you needn't drink yourself into a stupor."

"Why not?" she said baldly.

"I have never forced a woman. I have no intention of starting now."

She could not help herself, and the words flowed from her mouth unbidden. "No, but then again, a slave would have no say in the matter, would she?" *Fool! Why do you bait him?*

He said easily, "You are right, of course. But I have never used a woman, even one of my slaves, harshly."

Arabella gazed at him from beneath her lashes, relief flowing through her that she hadn't angered him. She found herself for the first time seeing him as a man, seeing him as the man who would likely take her innocence. She felt a small frisson streak through her. Before, she had recognized dispassionately that he was as striking as a Viking warrior, his hair bronze and gold, his eyes a brilliant blue. His body was powerful, emanating strength. She had pictured his naked torso, the muscles rippling across his chest, even as she had struck at him the night before. But her thoughts then had been to destroy him, the enemy.

Now he was a flesh-and-blood man. She observed his high cheekbones, his straight nose, his squared, clean-shaven jaw.

"Do you like what you see, Arabella?"

She started at his amused voice, and her eyes locked to his for an instant before she dropped them to her lap. She said honestly, without weighing her words, "I had not seen you as a man before."

"And you do now?"

"It is difficult not to," she said tartly, nervous at the sudden caressing quality of his voice. "You are large and the room is small."

"I see," he said. He leaned back against the pillows, his eyes narrowing on her face. "There is no knife, and the fork is dull-pronged. If it is your plan to lull me, it will do you no good. And I might be tempted to break your beautiful neck if you attack me again."

Unconsciously Arabella's fingers went to her throat. "No," she said quietly, "I will not try to harm you again." She raised her eyes to his face and tilted her chin upward. "I discovered that I am not a murderer."

"I consider myself fortunate that you have some qualms, my dear. Odd, but you look like a queen when you raise your chin. A very cold queen."

She shivered at the ill-veiled sarcasm in his voice. "Please, I do not wish to fight with you. I wish only to make you understand, to make you believe that my parents are not what you have been told."

Kamal raised his wine goblet and sipped at the sweet liquid, all the while his eyes narrowed on her pale face. "I am listening," he said.

"Lella told me that you lived for many years in Europe, that you are not like other . . . Muslim men, that you are . . . kind."

"Ah, my sweet Lella." He chuckled. "Did you despise her for her defense of me?"

"Perhaps," Arabella said honestly. "At least I disbelieved her. You have not been kind to me."

"Would you have been kind to a wild creature who called you vicious names and hurled more insults than my soldiers have scimitars?"

"You mock me," Arabella said in a taut voice. "You had not been held alone in the dark hold of a ship for a week with naught but rats for companions!" She added bitterly, "I suppose I should thank your mother for making me look like a crone, else I would certainly have been raped by all your honorable men."

"Yes," Kamal said thoughtfully. "She did show some mercy, did she not? I wonder why. She has been most single-minded in pursuit of her revenge."

Arabella leaned forward to plead with him, but before she could open her mouth, he continued in a mocking voice. "Likely she didn't want to take the chance that you would become diseased, and thus harm me. But then, of course, she could not be certain that all your . . . dalliance at the court had not resulted in the same thing."

She stiffened, jerking back. She drew her hands into her lap, and noticed blankly that they were drawn into tight fists. She felt suddenly helpless, beyond her depth with this man.

Kamal frowned at the tear-veiled pain he saw in her eyes. "Why do you draw away at the simple truth?" he asked harshly. "Why do you continue to act like the innocent maid? My God, woman, if you wish me to listen to you, you will cease this nonsense!"

Arabella choked back tears of frustration and dashed her hand across her eyes. It was an oddly childish gesture, and Kamal felt an instant of compassion for her. No, he thought, honest with himself, it was tenderness he felt, and it alarmed him.

"I should not have had you brought to me tonight," he said.

"No! I mean that I . . . wanted to see you."

She seemed so damned transparent, so guileless. He shook his head, his shoulder reminding him that her guile could fool a saint.

"Why? To plead with me? To charm me into giving in to you?"

"I am not charming, at least with you," she said, and he flinched at the open candor in her voice, the shining innocence in her beautiful eyes.

She was digressing, losing herself in a morass of counterthrusts that would gain her nothing, she thought desperately. She drew a deep breath, and her chin tilted upward unconsciously. "I do not mean to anger you." She shrugged helplessly. "It is just that I do not know what to do."

"What do you want to do, Arabella?"

He watched her eyes widen and her tongue caress her lower lip. It was a sublimely sensual gesture, and he felt his body leap in response. He drew back, knowing it was but another ploy, but toward what end? Faint color crept over her pale cheeks.

"Do you want to bed me? Compare me, the savage barbarian, to your other conquests?"

To his utter surprise, she did not fling angry words at him. She bowed her head in silent submission. His loins tightened and he felt his pulse begin to race. Even as he damned her silently for her effect on him, he rose gracefully to tower over her.

"Come, Arabella," he said, his mouth twisting into a mocking smile. "I wish also to compare you to my other . . . women."

She raised her pale face to his. Again her tongue moved unconsciously over her lower lip. Her mouth felt dry with fear. She whispered, "You will not hurt me?"

"Hurt you? I would not hurt you even if that is what pleased you."

Her eyes went blank at his words.

Damn her! When would she cease acting! He stretched out his hand to her. For a moment Arabella gazed at his hand, at his strong fingers, their blunt tips. Bronze hairs covered the back of his hand, and she shuddered at the image of his hands on her body, caressing her, knowing her.

She closed her eyes a moment, drawing strength from herself. She had naught but her body, and her body would be all of her that he would possess. He would not touch her feelings, her soul. Slowly she rose to her knees and raised her hand to his. She felt his warmth closing over her as he drew her to her feet.

"Your hand is cold, Arabella," he said, pulling her gently against him.

"I am sorry," she said softly, her eyes upon the strong column of his throat. She felt his arms close around her back, and she shivered.

He held her, lightly stroking his hands down her back. He felt her quiver but knew it was not from desire, not yet. "Give over, Arabella," he murmured against her temple. "I will give you pleasure. It is what you desire, is it not?"

His arms slid over her hips and in a swift graceful movement he lifted her into his arms.

"Your shoulder," she gasped.

"I shall survive."

She forced herself to wind her arms around his neck and lay her face against his shoulder.

Kamal smiled grimly. She was soft and giving now. He eased her down upon his bed and released her. "You are made for pleasure," he said, his voice deep and raspy as his eyes roved over her body.

"I do not understand this pleasure you speak of," Arabella whispered.

"Do you not?" he grated at her. Why did she continue to lie to him? He stepped back, unfastened the leather belt at his waist, and drew off his white shirt. The white bandage on his shoulder contrasted with the bronze of his flesh.

"I am sorry I hurt you," Arabella said, raising her hand to touch him.

Kamal drew back, then sat on the edge of the bed to pull off his boots. When he rose he was wearing only his trousers. His hands were on the buttons when he chanced to look down at her. He saw fear and embarrassment in her eyes. Did she dislike naked men? He shook his head, suddenly angry with her, and stripped off his trousers. He straightened slowly and watched her eyes fall down his body.

Arabella felt herself go cold at the sight of him. He was more beautiful than any of the statues in the Parese gardens, and more frightening. The golden hair that was sprinkled over his chest narrowed to a straight line down his flat belly, then bushed out at his groin. His manhood was swollen, thrust out from his groin, and she could not imagine how he could enter her body without rending her.

She gasped, unaware that Kamal was standing quietly watching her reaction to his naked body.

He sat down beside her, and she tried to pull away, but he pressed her onto her back. She could feel the heat of him. He clamped his arms on either side of her, holding her immobile.

"Arabella," he whispered softly, and lowered his head.

She breathed in the scent of him, sweet and musky, a heady male smell that made her blink in surprise. She felt his mouth lightly touch her forehead, her eyelids, her nose.

"Touch me, Arabella," he murmured against her lips, his voice a ragged whisper.

Slowly she raised her hands and rested them on his chest. She could feel the steady pounding of his heart beneath her palm. He felt so warm, his flesh smooth over the powerful muscles. Suddenly she felt his tongue gently probing against her closed mouth and she stiffened. His hand moved to stroke her throat, then upward to caress her chin. "Open your mouth," he commanded softly. "I want to taste you."

She obeyed him.

It was an invasion, relentless but oddly exciting. He probed her mouth, touching her tongue, until she was gasping for breath.

He raised his head and smiled down at her. He ran his fingers along the line of her jaw, back to circle her ears and pull the hair from her face. He looked thoughtful as he smoothed her hair on the pillow, forming a cloud of gold about her face. "Let us try again," he said. He lowered his face and this time she didn't start at the familiar touch of his firm mouth. She parted her lips this time without instruction from him and felt a jolt of warmth surge in her belly at the touch of his tongue. He said softly, his warm breath filling her mouth, "Think of my manhood thrusting into you as my tongue does into your mouth."

She quivered at his words, half in fear and half in excitement.

"You cannot," she whispered. "You are too large. You will hurt me." She felt his body shudder at her words. He stretched beside her, and she felt his manhood pressed against her thigh, huge and threatening. "No," she nearly cried, "you cannot!"

"Hush," he said. "I am as other men. You know I will not hurt you."

Kamal rose upon his elbow to look down at her. She lay very still, her eyes dark as midnight upon his face, deep and questioning.

"Your coloring is fascinating," he said, stroking his fingertip lightly over her dark eyebrows. "Golden hair, ivory flesh, and eyes as dark as a man's deepest secrets."

Slowly his fingers roved down her throat to unfasten the small line of buttons on the flimsy jacket. She raised her hand as if to stop him, then let it fall again to her side.

"I am afraid," she whispered, gazing up into his eyes.

"Have your other men hurt you? You may be certain that I shall not."

"You don't understand," she began, only to draw in a sharp breath at the touch of warm air against her bare flesh. She turned her face inward to his chest, a defensive gesture to hide her embarrassment. She heard his quick intake of breath, and knew that he was staring at her breasts, naked to his eyes.

"You are beautiful," he said, and his voice seemed to come from a great distance. She felt his hand gently cup her breast, and she jumped. "No, little flower, let me enjoy you." She stilled, closing her eyes, as if it would blind his vision as well. She gasped when he gently rubbed his palm over her nipple. She felt the strange sensation of her breasts swelling, her nipples growing taut and hard at his touch.

"I do not know what—" She felt his mouth close over her, his lips gently tugging at her, his teeth nipping at her flesh, making her shudder, deep, gulping breaths tearing from her throat. He slipped his arm beneath her, arching her back upward to caress her more deeply.

Kamal felt her resistance warring with the tentative urging of her body. He raised his head and rained soft kisses on her face as his hands caressed her breasts. To Arabella's surprise, she heard herself moan softly. Her eyes flew open and she saw a gleam of triumph in his eyes.

"Please," she whispered, "do not shame me."

He laughed softly, and she felt embarrassment hold her rigid. She wanted to strike out at him, and at the same time, her body was trembling, turning toward him. She did not understand herself; she felt her control slipping, her mind becoming vague, her stormy thoughts dissolving.

"I do not want this . . . I do not want you," she gasped, shoving her hands against her chest.

"Do not lie to yourself," he said, his hand sliding over her ribs down to her belly. "I believe for the first time you are being honest with me." She began to squirm against him as his fingers pulled at the thin leather belt about her waist.

"No," she pleaded, her voice sounding oddly hoarse.

The belt was gone and she felt the trousers sliding down her hips. She bucked against him, terrified, her hands flailing against his chest. He held her firm, throwing a powerful leg over hers to hold her still.

"I will go gently with you. Do not fear me, Arabella. Hush . . . lie still." His hand lay quietly in the hollow of her belly. She felt the heat of it searing her, but the ache she had thought building in her abdomen was lower. She tried to bring her thighs together, but his leg kept them slightly apart.

He brought his hand up to hold her face still. He kissed her again, deeply, and when her mouth opened, she accepted his possession. He sensed it too, and lazily his hand slid down over her breasts, fondling them in turn, then lower, to rest again upon her stomach.

"Do not be angry, Arabella. Your body accepts me. In but a moment you will moan again, softly, into my mouth." But even as he spoke, he found himself wondering at her seeming inexperience. Her fingers clutched at his chest and shoulders tentatively, as if she did not know what would please him.

His hand slid lower, but she didn't moan, rather she gasped aloud at the feel of his fingers gently tangling in her soft curls, probing until they found her.

"Ah," he murmured, deep satisfaction in his voice, "you are hot and moist, ready for me."

Arabella squirmed, only to find that her hips were thrusting upward against his caressing fingers. "You cannot touch me there," she gasped. "Please, you must not—"

"Your lovers have been so remiss? That is the very essence of your womanness, Arabella. You are pushing against my fingers. Do you not enjoy my touch?"

"No," she moaned, and heard him laugh softly at her lie. Arabella didn't understand what was happening to her. There were sharp, almost painful surges of sensation that made her legs stiffen, a swirling of need deep within her that brought sharp gasps from her throat. The urgent need receded as his fingers left her, and she wanted to cry aloud for him to touch her again. She felt him gently exploring her, lightly stroking her inner thighs, touching her intimately. She reared up against him when he slipped two fingers inside her, and she heard him draw in his breath.

"You are so small," he said hoarsely. "I can feel you stretching for my fingers." He eased out of her and teased her soft flesh before slipping but one finger inside her.

She tried to pull away from his probing finger, but he held her still, and gently began to caress her rhythmically with his thumb. She felt her moistness, felt the urgent need to give herself over to him. She fought herself, fought against losing herself in this man and giving him power over her. She shook her head, tangling her hair about her face, but her hands tugged at his arms, moved wildly over him to knead the muscles in his back.

"Please . . . ahh . . . I cannot bear it!" She felt his fingers as white-hot pleasure, burning into her until she was gasping hoarsely.

"You are so responsive, so filled with passion," he murmured against her mouth. "Tell me you want me, Arabella."

She gazed at him with wild, vague eyes. "I don't know . . . please, help me."

He closed his mouth over hers again, possessing her, the symbolic thrusting of his tongue driving him wild with his own need. He wanted to claim her with his mouth, but something held him back. There was a disturbing innocence about her that he did not understand, and he sensed that she would draw away from him were he to caress her as he wished to. He deepened the pressure of his finger, and saw the darkening passion in her eyes, felt her hips urgent against him.

"Do you want me to give you release, Arabella?" he asked her quietly.

"I feel as though I am dying," she gasped. He lifted his fingers an instant and she cried out as though in pain. She felt her body as liquid, molten sensation, and when he began to caress and stroke her again, she could not control the shimmering surges of pleasure that ripped through her. Her fingers dug into his shoulders, tangled in his thick hair. Then she was beyond herself, swirling in pure sensation.

Kamal felt the intensity of her climax, and he kissed her, smothering her cries of pleasure in his mouth. He raised his head and she arched upward, her breathing coming in short, panting gasps.

"Arabella," he whispered. "I can't wait any longer." He thrust his finger deeply into her, easing her for his entrance. She was so tight, so very small. He felt her muscles convulse, and he fought for control as he reared over her. He felt her tense at his probing finger, and realized vaguely that he was hurting her. But that was not possible. Then suddenly his finger butted against her maidenhead.

He froze, all feeling suspended. Very carefully he withdrew his finger and eased himself down on top of her. He cupped her face between his hands. "Arabella," he commanded hoarsely, "look at me!"

She opened her eyes and he saw tears swimming in their depths.

"I'm sorry," she whispered. "What have I done to anger you?"

He drew a deep, calming breath. Many things became clear to him in that instant. She was offering herself to him because of her parents, not because she wanted to pleasure herself with another man. No wonder her fear and embarrassment at seeing him naked, at feeling his man's body against hers.

He cursed softly in Arabic, and rolled off her, over onto his back, trying to still the raging need of his body.

"I do not understand," Arabella said, her voice shaking.

"You are a virgin, damn you!"

She smiled sadly at the taut frustration of his voice. Slowly she placed her hand on his chest and felt the pounding of his heart.

"Don't touch me, if you wish to remain a virgin!"

Her hand stilled. If he didn't take her, she would have nothing to bargain with. She had lost her innocence all because he hadn't believed her. And, she knew, it was too late now; he had shattered her, had plunged her into the depths of feelings that she had never known existed. She felt tears streak down her cheeks, and tasted their saltiness as she licked her lips. The unbelievable passion she had felt was fading, but she knew she had given him nothing. His pleasure was found, she assumed, in thrusting himself into her body. Oddly, she quivered at the thought. Slowly, as if she were watching someone else, she stroked her hand down his chest to his belly. She felt him shuddering, felt his eyes upon her face.

"Arabella?"

She knew he was asking her, knew that he wouldn't force her.

"Please, Kamal," she whispered. She leaned over him and kissed him on his mouth. Her fingers found him, and tentatively, innocently, she touched him. The feel of him both alarmed and excited her. A man, so different from her.

He gave almost a growl, lurching up and tossing her upon her back. She felt her thighs parted, felt him probing against her. She stiffened, waiting for the pain. Suddenly he seemed to gain control of himself. He entered her slowly, then stopped.

"I will try not to hurt you."

Ha paused, watching her closely. When her eyes cleared, he gently eased more deeply into her until he was pressing against her maidenhead. "Arabella." His voice was a sharp command and she looked deep into his eyes.

He thrust forward suddenly, tearing through the thin barrier. She screamed and tried to throw him off her. Her fingernails digging into his arms brought him a measure of reason. "Hush," he said softly. "Hold still. We will wait a moment until you become used to me and there is no more pain."

He thought he would lose all control when he saw the blind terror leave her eyes, and she whispered, as if in surprise, "I feel as though you are burning me. The pain is lessening."

He closed his eyes, not wanting her to see the naked feelings in his. He felt her arms twine about his neck and she began to relax beneath him. She had absorbed the sensation of him. Slowly he eased more deeply. She tensed in pain, and he stilled immediately, waiting.

"Do you know how you feel to me, Arabella?"

he whispered into her mouth. "How warm you are? How tightly you are holding me inside you?"

"The way I feel . . . it pleases you?" she asked. She moved slightly beneath him, inadvertently drawing him deeper inside her.

"I cannot!" he gasped. He groaned, throwing his head back, and Arabella felt her body explode in pain as he thrust his full length into her. He was surging inside her, beyond himself. Vaguely, through the pain, she realized that if he felt as she had at the height of her pleasure, he would not, could not stop himself. She hugged him to her, biting her lips to keep the cries of pain to herself. She felt him suddenly tense over her; then she felt him flooding her, filling her with his seed.

His head was beside hers on the pillow. She could feel the fierce pounding of his heart against her breast. The tremors that had shaken his body began to subside and he quieted. It suddenly occurred to her that she now understood passion. She felt him raise himself slowly on his elbows and gaze down into her face.

"I am sorry I hurt you."

She studied his face solemnly. "The first part was . . . nice," she whispered shyly. "But you are so large. I do not like the pain."

Kamal smiled at her innocence. "Arabella, the next time I enter you, there will be no pain. All will be pleasure, you will see."

She looked at him, surprise on her face. "You are no longer so huge."

"Alas," he gently mocked her, "I am but a weak

man, and I must have a few minutes to replenish my strength. A man is only large when he is aroused."

"Oh," she said, absorbing this bit of information. Then she smiled up at him impishly. "I am a strong woman, and I do not need time to replenish anything!"

"That is true, but I will give you a little time to ease the soreness you must feel now."

"Yes," she said slowly, her eyes narrowing on his face. She read the questions in his eyes, and turned her face inward, against his shoulder. She began shaking at the intimacy they had shared.

"Arabella?"

His voice was gentle, and she felt his hand smoothing back the tangled hair from her face. "You were inside of my body," she gasped. "I never before imagined . . ." Her voice trailed off.

Surprisingly, he didn't push her to continue. He moved slowly from her body and rose to stand beside the bed. She looked up at him questioningly, and rose to her elbows. His voice stopped her.

"Lie still."

He brought a soft cloth and a basin of water, and sat down beside her. "I will clean the blood from you."

"No! I cannot . . . it isn't proper."

He laughed, a deep, rich sound that made her writhe in embarrassment. "Nothing we have done is proper, my lady. Now, close your mouth and your eyes and lie still."

She felt the damp cloth move between her thighs, and grew rigid.

Kamal frowned at the splotches of blood smeared on her thighs, remembering her cries of pain. Gently he bathed her, then pressed the wet cloth against her to ease her soreness. He knew he must talk to her, but his eyes traveled over her slender body, and no words came to his mind. Her legs were beautifully shaped, long and straight and temptingly curved. He felt himself growing full of desire at the sight of the damp profusion of curls covering her woman's mound. He leaned over her, unable to help himself, and gently began to caress her.

At the touch of his mouth, Arabella jumped, gasping in shock. "You cannot! Please, Kamal!" she cried, her fingers tugging at his hair.

He heard the confused outrage in her voice, and slowly left her, drawing himself up to lie beside her. "In time, Arabella," he said softly, drawing her against him, "in a little while, I will love you as you are meant to be loved."

"I do not understand," she began, and he kissed her lightly, stilling her words.

"My mouth will give you greater pleasure than my fingers, and your pleasure, Arabella, gives me pleasure."

"Oh," she muttered, embarrassed color deepening on her cheeks.

He pressed his fingertips against her lips. "Hush. Sleep now."

He gently held her against him, stroking his

hand down her back to calm her and soothe her. Arabella sighed deeply, and nestled closer to him, unwilling at the moment to question what had happened to her.

22

Arabella kept her eyes tightly closed, even as she arched upward to deepen the pressure of his caressing tongue against her breast.

"I know you are awake, Arabella," she heard him say, laughter lurking in his voice. "Your body won't let you hide from me any longer."

"I am embarrassed," she admitted, her eyes still firmly closed.

"I know, but it will pass quickly." His hand moved over her ribs and waist to knead the softness of her belly.

She still fought to hold herself aloof, but his fingers moved lower and she couldn't swallow the gasp of sharp pleasure that tore from her throat.

"Oh! Damn you!"

Her eyes flew open and it took her a few moments to make out his face above hers in the darkness. "It is still night," she said stupidly.

"To my everlasting gratitude," he said, grinning at her flushed face.

Arabella knew she should talk to him, make it clear to him that she came to him only because of her parents. She had to bargain with him. She had to . . . She moaned and she vaguely heard him draw in his breath at the sound.

He moved on top of her, and she felt the heat of his body, felt his manhood throbbing against her closed thighs. "Arabella," he said softly, and she parted her lips to him. She stroked her hands down his broad back, pausing but a moment before her fingers kneaded the firm muscles of his buttocks.

She felt his hard thighs press against hers, easing her legs open, until he lay shuddering with need between them. She knew but a moment of stabbing fear before he drew her with him into a world of dazzling sensation. She whispered his name, and felt his tongue probe in her mouth, as if to taste the sound of his name on her lips.

She sighed deeply, and he felt her surrender. The sweetness of it made him wild with desire to possess her, to make her cry out his name at the moment of her climax.

When he moved down her body, he felt her tense but a moment, then she was open to him, her hips arching upward to meet his mouth. The delicate softness of her, the heat of her moist flesh, made him tremble with pleasure. He felt her hands digging into his shoulders, and the innocence of her touch made him slow, taking exquisite care with her so she would know the full sweetness he could give her. She was making rasping sounds deep in her throat, and he felt her legs stiffen as she neared her release.

He left her, and without pause moved over her and eased himself into her, and was drawn into the dark warmth of her body. He pulled her close to him and kissed her deeply. He felt her stretching to hold him, but he could feel no tensing of pain, no resistance in her. Slowly, with extreme care, he pushed his full length into her. He raised himself until his belly was pressed against hers, heightening her pleasure, and he began to move slowly.

"Is there any pain?" he asked her softly, watching the shadows on her face.

Arabella could find no words. She shook her head against his throat, her arms clutching his back. When he eased his hand between them to caress her, she lurched upward, moaning her pleasure.

He felt her muscles squeezing him, felt her stiffen beneath him. The feeling was infinitely satisfying, and he let himself take his own pleasure, her cries mixing with his deep moans.

"We're sweating."

He raised his head to smile into her dazed eyes. "Yes," he said. Just the sound of her voice made him want her again. He shook his head, wondering at himself. He felt a surge of protectiveness so powerful that he sucked in his breath. "No," he said.

"No what?"

He started, unaware that he had spoken aloud. He didn't reply, feeling her sliding away from him into sleep. He rolled onto his back, bringing her with him, and pulled up the light cover over them.

The gentle pink sunlight of dawn flickered into the chamber. Arabella stirred, felt Kamal's arms tighten about her, and snuggled against him.

But sleep didn't come again. She breathed in the salty male scent of him, and recoiled at the intense satisfaction it brought her. She did not move, afraid of waking him. She didn't know how she would face him in the light of day, seeing in his eyes his triumph over her.

Oddly enough, it wasn't her offering of herself that brought her shame. Indeed, she felt oddly philosophical about the loss of her virginity. She would do it again, if it would save her parents. No, she thought miserably, it was her own passion, feelings unknown to her until Kamal, that made her writhe now in shame. She was a lady; surely a lady wasn't supposed to feel so *consumed*, so very wanton.

Arabella drew a deep, shuddering breath. Twice she had given herself to him. Twice. He had known her for a virgin. Surely now he had good reason to question the story his mother had told him. She felt him turn more closely against her in his sleep, and she stiffened. Slowly she tried to pull away from him. She felt a nagging soreness between her thighs, and it occurred to her for the first time that she had lost what her husband—that vague, myste-

rious man who was somewhere in her future—would
expect on their wedding night. She stuffed her fist
against her mouth, against the soft cry that threatened to escape.

"Arabella?"

Quickly she turned her face away, unable to
face him. She felt his warm breath against her
temple. "No," she grated, "do not touch me!"

Kamal came fully awake. He could not recall
ever having felt so complete, so very satisfied before,
until her voice broke through.

"What is the matter?" he asked softly, his fingers tangling through her hair and gently kneading
the back of her neck. He heard her swallow a sob
and raised himself on one elbow over her.

"Arabella, look at me."

She turned her face toward him, and he saw the
desolation in her eyes. "I must talk to you," she
said, and her eyes fell.

He felt a cold knot begin to grow in his belly,
and anger at himself, at her, at the miserable
situation that had forced them together. He laid
his hand lightly on her breast, and was pleased to
see the pink nipple lose its velvet softness and
begin to tauten.

"No!" she shrieked, jerking away. "You cannot
touch me, not again!" She rolled to the side of the
wide bed and came up to her knees, drawing the
cover upward to hide her nakedness.

"I see," Kamal said, his voice tightly controlled.
"What you mean is that I cannot touch you until I
have agreed to your terms."

Had she been so wretchedly obvious? She got a grip on herself and forced her eyes to his face. It was impassive, and she did not know what was in his mind. "Yes," she said more steadily. "What I did, I did for my parents. Surely now you cannot carry through your mother's revenge."

"Why not?" His voice lashed her like a snaking whip.

She felt the force of his anger, but refused to back down. She raised her chin defiantly and gave him stare for stare. "You know that she lied to you, at least about me."

"Yes," he said, hurting her now with his mocking gaze. "You were a virgin. Look at the sheet. It is stained with your virgin's blood."

Inadvertently her eyes fell to the dark splotches against the white sheet, and she recoiled. "Please," she said, "you must stop this insane plot." She lowered her eyes and ran her tongue over her lower lip. It was a sensual gesture, and Kamal found his loins tightening at the thought of her tongue touching his.

"So," he said finally, sitting up, oblivious of his nakedness, "you sold your body like a common whore."

Did a common whore feel such pleasure? she wondered blankly. "I . . . I wished to bargain with you, and I had naught else."

He understood her, and although he would never admit it, he admired her courage, admired her for the irrevocable step she had taken. Still, to hear her speak so coldly about bargaining with him with her body roused fury in him. "A woman's weapon," he mocked her. "How very naturally you came by your talent."

"What do you mean?"

"Perhaps," he said softly, "my mother was not so very wrong about you, my lady. Perhaps she observed you teasing gentlemen, and came to a not unreasonable conclusion. You showed me . . . great promise, Arabella. In the past, have you allowed the gentlemen who desired you to go only so far? Perhaps caress you and fondle you? Did you play with them, but not allow them to possess you?"

"No!" The import of his words infuriated her. "Only one man tried to kiss me before, and I kicked him!"

"But your passion, my dear. I could caress you right now and soon, very soon, I know you would yield to me yet again."

"Damn you," she hissed at him. "You will not touch me again! I will not allow it! I felt nothing for you, do you hear? Nothing!"

He knew of course that she was lying, but it angered him so that he wanted only to wound her. "So it was all an act?"

"Yes!"

Kamal reached out, grasped her upper arm, and jerked her toward him. "Listen well, Arabella. What I decide to do about your parents has nothing to do with what occurred between us last night. I can have you whenever it pleases me." His voice dropped to a harsh growl. "You are my slave, my high-and-mighty lady, here for my pleasure. If I wished to spread your lovely thighs right now, I could do so."

She threw back her head and said with deadly calm, "If you do, I will fight you. I will not . . . act again to make you feel the marvelous lover!" She felt his fingers tighten painfully on her arm and thought vaguely that she would bear bruises. "Are you such a savage that you must prove to me that you are the stronger?"

He threw her arm away from him. He uncoiled his powerful body and rose from the bed to stare down at her. "It would appear you are the fool, my lady. How could you expect honor from a savage? Why did you not attempt to seal your bargain before you lost your maidenhead?"

She stared at him dumbly.

"You no longer have anything . . . unusual to offer, Arabella."

"I hate you," she cried hoarsely. "You have no honor. I was a fool ever to believe that I could expect anything from you but an animal's savagery!"

Kamal turned quickly away from her and rang the bell beside his bed. "When next you decide to use pretense to gain your ends, my lady, take care who your victim is. Not all men are weak fools to be manipulated by a woman."

Ali appeared in the doorway.

Kamal did not look at her, merely waved his arm toward her. "Assist the lady back to the harem,

Ali, though I doubt she can successfully use her wiles on Raj."

Arabella wanted to cry, to yell, to hurl herself at him and make him suffer for his cruelty. God, what a fool she had been! All for naught . . . all for naught. She grasped the sheet around her and rose from the bed.

"You will pay for your dishonor, you miserable barbarian!" She ignored Ali's gasp and marched from Kamal's chamber, her chin high, the white sheet trailing after her.

Kamal threw himself back down on the bed and pillowed his head on his crossed arms. Had she truly expected him to yield to her wishes, besotted by her beauty and her body? He realized that her actions had been clumsily innocent and free of guile. She had not had the experience to bind him to her, to make her demands so that he could gracefully succumb to her. She was a woman of extremes, he thought, and she knew no middle ground. His eyes fell to the bloodstains on the sheet. He had been a fool to take her. Indeed, when he had realized she was a virgin, he had not wanted to harm her. It had been she who had seduced him, all for her own ends. He dismissed from his mind his own angry words hurled at her, and slowly allowed his fury at her to build as he remembered her harsh insults.

Lella found Arabella curled up like a hurt child on her narrow bed. She knew, as did every other woman in Kamal's harem, that Arabella had spent the night in Kamal's bed. She had also heard of her return just after dawn, not in Kamal's company, but in Ali's.

"It gained you nothing," she said flatly.

Arabella quivered at her stark words. "No," she said finally, still burrowed against the wall, "it gained me less than nothing."

"So what will you do? Stay hidden from the world and mourn the loss of your virginity? That is a coward's way."

Arabella turned slowly, stung by Lella's harsh words. "I would that you leave me alone," she said dully, refusing to look at the other woman.

"Why? So you can sulk in private? How, Arabella, could you have been such a fool?"

Tears glistened in Arabella's eyes, and she angrily dashed them away with the back of her hand. "I was a woman—he made me so, and thus, I suppose, a fool. A weak, pliable fool until morning brought me reason. Then it was too late and I had not the talent to bargain with him."

"I gather you angered him?"

"I have but to open my mouth, and he is angered. I have not the wit, as I said, to pretend, to say honeyed things, and gain my way."

Lella closed her fingers about Arabella's hand. "Well, it will do you no good to remain in hiding. Elena is busy proclaiming in that smug way of hers that Kamal was displeased with you. Surely you do not wish—" Lella broke off. "You startled me, Raj!" She smiled at the eunuch, who stood in the open doorway. "What is the matter? Why do you look so grim?"

Raj drew a deep breath. "His highness," he said slowly, his eyes upon Arabella, "has decided on his revenge."

Arabella felt a lump of fear in her throat. She could find no words, and only stared at him.

"What do you mean, Raj?" Lella asked.

"His highness has ordered me to have all his women present for his . . . inspection. He has informed me that he wishes to select his mate for this night."

"But he has never done that before!" Lella exclaimed, pulling herself clumsily to her feet.

"No," Raj said slowly, "he hasn't. I can only assume that what passed between Lady Arabella and him last night has brought this to pass."

"He is a barbarian," Arabella spat. "It is disgusting!"

"No, it is your punishment, my lady," Raj said.

"Punishment!" She shot a hard look at Lella. "He is a savage, no matter what you say. I will not be a part of this, Raj. I care not what he does!"

Raj slowly plucked a speck of lint from the wide sleeve of his blue robe. "His highness expected that you would refuse, my lady. He informed me that you would be present, even if I had to have you bound and dragged before him."

"Does he have the conceit to believe that I care if he selects a woman for his bed as a man would select a mare to ride?"

"I do not know what is in his mind, my lady."

Lella said gently, "You will not refuse, Arabella. You will face him, but not in bonds."

Arabella stared down at her twisting hands. "I suppose," she said finally, her voice infinitely weary, "that if I do not have honor and pride, I have nothing. If you would excuse me now, I wish to prepare myself."

Raj wished he could comfort her, say something to ease the pain he saw in her vivid eyes, but he didn't know what Kamal intended. When Raj had come before him, Kamal had appeared very calm, but his instructions were issued in such a cold voice that Raj could feel his anger simmering just beneath the surface. He realized that he didn't want to know what Arabella had done to evoke such rage in him. He watched her as she ran her fingers through her disheveled hair.

He started at the sound of her voice. "Do not worry that I will act anything but the bored observer, Raj. Whatever it is he intends, I will not be drawn."

"I hope your intentions become fact, my lady."

23

We are all like sweets in a confectioner's shop, Arabella thought, lined up in our prettiest wrappings to entice the buyer. Only here there was no buyer, there was simply the master who owned all the dainty morsels set before him. The girls were giggling, preening in front of each other, smoothing their soft trousers over their hips. More like an endless feast, Arabella thought, now that she knew what it was men wanted of women. She flushed deeply at the thought, and brought her fisted hands up to cover her eyes. But she still saw herself panting like any loose creature, beyond herself, aching for him to pleasure her. She saw him clearly, his man's body all hard planes and sharp angles, his flesh smooth and furred, covering the sinewy muscle.

"I hate him," she said, and drew back, realizing that she had spoken aloud; the young girl standing near to her was glancing at her, her head cocked in question. The girl's belly was beginning to swell

with child. Arabella swallowed her moan of distress.
Would a babe be her unwanted punishment for
the previous night? She could feel again the hurtling of his seed deep in her body. A man's gift to
a woman, or a man's curse.

The afternoon sun was beginning to slant downward, bright slashes of light knifing through the
oleanders. Arabella drew herself apart and sat upon
a narrow marble bench. She heard Elena's bright
voice and her laughter. The girl probably was
quite nice, she admitted, when she was not around
her.

Arabella was lost in her own misery until she
was drawn by the sounds of approaching men. The
huge doors to the harem were flung open and
three Turkish soldiers, brightly garbed in their
crimson-and-white uniforms, flanked Kamal as he
walked slowly into the harem garden. Behind him
walked an old man whom she had seen before but
did not know. She watched Raj approach Kamal
and bow deeply before him.

Bowing before a swine, she thought, tensing at
the sight of him. He was dressed in pristine white.
His shirt was full-sleeved and opened in the front
to show a chain of gold, an odd medallion hanging
from it. His waist was banded by a scarlet silk belt
from which hung a curved dagger, its ivory handle
covered with jewels. Unlike English gentlemen's,
his trousers were cut full, tucked into black leather
boots that hugged his muscular calves. He looked
powerful and forbidding, despite the slight smile
on his lips. His thick golden hair was brushed

neatly, but Arabella was jolted by the memory of tangling her fingers through it, enjoying its softness and the tempting curls that hugged his ears. His blue eyes were cold and slightly narrowed against the harsh rays of sunlight. She could feel him searching among the women, searching her out. She wanted to shrink away, to hide beneath the marble bench, but she would not allow herself to show him how she feared him.

Slowly she rose, and for an instant across the distance their eyes locked. She reached out and plucked a rose from the bush beside her. Slowly she held the rose in front of her and began to pluck off its petals, one by one, until it was naught but a naked bud. Then she dropped it and ground it beneath her heel.

Kamal felt anger at her for her symbolic act. Was he to take the blame for her calculated folly? He said in a calm and clear voice, "Raj, display my women to their best advantage. I wish to inspect them now."

Arabella ground her teeth in fury at his words. A woman to him was naught but a toy, an object to be enjoyed at his leisure and tossed aside when he grew bored. Or, a woman who angered him was to be humiliated before he tossed her aside.

Raj was lining the girls up in front of the arched entry columns. Lella sat on a cushioned bench near to the rippling pool, seemingly unmoved by the silently awed girls now standing straight for their master's inspection.

Kamal moved forward, but stopped beside her. "You are well, my sister?"

"Aye," Lella said softly. " 'Twill not be long now, Kamal. If I do not birth the babe soon, he will come from my body speaking to me of all his woes."

He smiled, but Lella knew it was an abstracted smile. "Kamal . . ."

He brought his eyes back to rest questioningly on her upturned face.

"Why do you do this?"

The smile never left his face. "I remember Hamil chiding me—before he met you, Lella—that the master must know the women in his harem. He would say that the eunuchs occasionally slipped in a pearl of great beauty."

"Ah," Lella said.

"Stay away from her, Lella," he said suddenly, his voice harsh. "She is not what you believe her to be."

Lella studied his face before saying calmly, "Unfortunately, my brother, she is exactly what she appears: young, innocent, desperate for her parents . . . and foolish."

He shrugged and his lips tightened into a taut line. Lella watched him approach the women, and wondered yet again what he intended.

Arabella slipped behind a lovely Turkish girl with inky black hair, thankfully, taller than she. And waited. When he reached her, he ignored her and turned sharply to stand before the women.

When he spoke, Arabella started, for his voice

was gentle, as if he were addressing a group of well-behaved children.

"You are all lovely," he said, his eyes caressing them individually. "And you make my choice more difficult than a man can stand." He clapped his hands, and his servant Ali stepped forward and began to distribute small presents to each of the girls. There were cries of delight and excited murmurs of gratitude. Arabella shrank back as Ali approached. He looked at her, his dark eyes hooded, and passed her by.

Is this your punishment, you savage beast? she wondered, wishing he would look at her so she could show him her disdain. You do not pay me like you do the others for being your whore?

Kamal stepped back and casually stroked his jaw, as if in deep thought. Finally he said, "I wish Elena to be with me this night. I have missed her grace and her beauty and her gentle presence."

Elena tossed her head, a smile of triumph curving her beautiful lips upward.

Kamal's voice rang out. "I have suffered the graceless attentions of a girl from that faraway island of England. She is fit only to adorn a chamber, for her coldness would freeze a man's desire."

He looked at Arabella as he spoke, but she didn't move a muscle. She simply gazed through him as if he did not exist. Damn her, he thought to himself. "I desire a woman who is warm and yielding to me," he continued coldly, "a woman I can . . . trust."

Arabella drew in her breath in fury at his words, but still she held herself perfectly still. He would soon cease his taunts and his lies and take his leave. She had but to remain calm and withdrawn from him.

Kamal wished he could shake her until her head lolled on her beautiful neck. He would even welcome her curses, her insults, for then he would know that she was not indifferent to him.

He stood for a moment longer before his women, then turned sharply on his heel.

He heard Elena snicker behind him. He paused a moment as her voice, heavy with triumph, hissed, "Daughter of a sow! Cold English bitch! I told you the master would see through you!"

Arabella looked into Elena's brilliant eyes, now alight with the pleasure of her victory. She felt her body growing rigid, but when she spoke, her voice was light with laughter and disdain. "It is true, Elena, I have not the wit to play the whore. Perhaps if you perform as your master wishes, he will pay you with another gift, as men do for their whores."

"Lying slut! You are jealous because the master chose me!" Elena did a small dancing step in front of her. "I knew, skinny witch, that the master would find you lacking! You are no woman! You are naught but a cold passionless shell!"

Cold and passionless! God, the lunacy of that accusation! Kamal thought bitterly.

"Well, cold bitch? Haven't you anything to say now?"

Very calmly Arabella stepped toward Elena and slapped her hard with her open palm against her cheek. Elena gasped as her head rocked on her neck. "You have the mind of a child," Arabella said very softly, "and the manners of a trollop."

"Bitch!" Elena cried, and threw herself at Arabella.

Arabella had never slapped another human being in all her twenty years. Her hand stung; she had no time for thought, for Elena had grabbed masses of her hair and was pulling it painfully. Something broke inside Arabella. With a speed she did not know she possessed, she launched herself at Elena, her hands grasping the girl by her throat. Elena screeched in fury at the suddenness of the attack, but she was no coward, and the thought of humiliating her rival before Kamal was sweetness to her. She clawed at Arabella's hair, pulling her head back until Arabella released her throat.

Kamal whirled about and stared for an instant, openmouthed, at the two women. He ignored the cries from the other women, and plunged forward to grab Arabella away from Elena. He shouted to one of his soldiers to hold Elena. He tightened his hold on Arabella's arms, surprised at her strength. "Stop it!" he grated. "Hold still, damn you!"

Suddenly Arabella leaned limply against him, all fight gone from her. "That is better," he said, shaking her slightly. He eased his hold on her, intent upon turning her about to face him.

She moved so quickly he was stunned. He felt her hand slam into his belly, and the force of her blow made him double forward. He grabbed for her, only to feel her knee crash into his groin with all the strength of her fury. He lurched downward, falling to his knees.

The idyllic harem garden was a pandemonium. Cries of the women filled the air. Arabella felt her arms pulled behind her until she moaned in pain. Two Turkish soldiers were jerking at her until she thought her arms would be pulled from their sockets.

She saw the flash of a silver blade above her, and closed her eyes against the pain she knew she would endure. To die because she lost her head . . . to die for naught . . .

"Stop!"

Her eyes flew open and she saw Kamal rise painfully to his feet. They stared at each other, and she smiled, thrusting her chin upward in mute defiance.

Kamal felt Hassan's hand on his arm. "Are you all right, highness? By Allah, the girl is mad!"

"I am well enough," Kamal said, drawing several slow, deep breaths to ease the pain in his groin.

"Our laws are precise, highness. Any man who strikes a bey must die."

Kamal said slowly, willing his mind to obey him, "She is no man."

Hassan drew back. "That is true, highness. Our laws have never considered that a woman would attack her master."

Lella's voice rang out, sharp with fear, "No,

Kamal, please, you must not kill her! She does not know our ways . . . she did not mean—"

"I meant it," Arabella spat. "Do not try to defend me, Lella!"

"Kill her!" Elena panted. "Kill the bitch!"

Kamal heard the furious arguments raging around him. God, what an utter fool he had been! He had pushed her too far and now she would pay for his petty revenge.

"Highness," Hassan said quietly, "you must punish the girl. If you do not, your guards will quickly spread the story that the Bey of Oran was brought to his knees by a woman. You must do something!"

"But it was my fault," Kamal said quietly.

"No matter, highness. You cannot let this pass. I know that you cannot kill her. The whip, highness, let it be lashes from the whip. 'Twill break her proud spirit and show all that you are no weak man."

"Kamal, no!" Lella tugged at his sleeve.

Kamal raised his head and again looked at Arabella. She was staring not at him, but through him. He prayed to God and Allah for inspiration, but none came. He knew he had no choice. He raised his hand for quiet. "The English girl will suffer ten lashes. Tie her to the column₄"

"Eiee!" Elena cried. "The whip! Flay the flesh from the bitch's back!"

"Animal," Arabella said softly, her eyes cold upon Kamal's face. She saw something in his eyes. Regret? "I hate you," she said dully, and turned away from him. The two soldiers dragged her to an arched column. There were potted plants hanging from hooks embedded in the marble. One of the soldiers ripped off the lower of the plants. Arabella realized what they would do and began to struggle impotently against the man who held her. He said something sharply in Arabic and jerked her hands toward him. He tied her wrists together with a leather strap, then stretched her arms upward to fasten the leather into the hook, drawing her to her toes.

She closed her eyes a moment, fear flooding her. Just as she had never before struck another, neither had she ever been harmed. She hung against the column, helpless, impotent. Fool, she screamed silently at herself, ten times a fool! She jerked when she felt a man's hands tearing away the thin jacket, leaving her naked to the waist. She felt the coldness of the marble against her heaving breasts. Plead with him, damn you! She shook her head violently at her own thought, pressing her cheek against the column. She gritted her teeth, waiting.

Kamal thought furiously but could find no plausible excuse for releasing her. He heard the snap of the whip and flinched, feeling the brutal leather striking his own flesh.

"You cannot release her, highness," Hassan said, seeing his master's indecision. "I am sorry, but it is your . . . duty."

Kamal shook off Hassan's hand. He called to the soldier who plied the whip, and spoke to him softly. "Do not free your strength on her, Lam.

Spare her as much pain as you can. I do not want her scarred."

The man, Lam, looked at his master for a long moment, then nodded. He had never before beaten a woman, and the thought of plying his vicious whip on the beautiful creature, hearing her scream, watching her writhe to escape the pain, brought him no pleasure.

Kamal felt sweat bead his forehead as he watched Lam nearing Arabella.

"Please, Kamal, do not do this!"

He stared into Lella's anguished face. "I have no choice," he said. He watched Lam pull Arabella's long hair from her back and fling it over her shoulder. He winced at the sight of the slender expanse of flesh, so soft, so exquisite, like creamy ivory.

Lam stood back from her and slowly raised the whip.

Arabella held her breath, waiting for his first blow. Oh, Father, she prayed silently, do not let me shame myself!

She heard the soft hiss and jumped, more in surprise than in pain, as the whip came down across her back.

She was surrounded by fearful, strained silence, the only sound her own harsh breathing. She wondered crazily if the man whipping her could smell her fear. Suddenly the whip cracked through the air and curled around her back to her ribs. She lurched with the pain, seeing brilliant flashes of light before her eyes. Again and again the whip seared her and she felt the wet of her own blood. The pain was tearing at her, rendering her mindless. She pulled impotently at her bonds, jerking away from the whip.

Lam watched helplessly as the whip struck her breasts, drawing blood. He was controlling his mighty strength, but it was not enough. The girl was not tough-skinned like the men he had punished. But she made no cry.

"You play with the bitch!" Elena cried. "Mark her for the miserable slave she is!"

Arabella sagged against the column, all fight gone. It was all she could do to prevent herself from screaming. The pain . . . oh God, never had she dreamed of agony so all-consuming. A soft whimper tore from her throat when the whip came down again.

From a great distance she heard Kamal's voice, ragged, pained. "Enough! Stop, Lam, it is enough!"

He couldn't bear it any longer. Two more lashes and he would have thrown himself at Lam.

"But, highness—"

"Be silent, Hassan," he said. He was at her side in but a moment, wincing at the raw welts across her ivory back. Blood trickled down over her trousers.

He walked around the column to see her face. Arabella felt his presence, just as she had heard his voice. Slowly she opened her eyes and stared up at him. His lips formed her name.

She pursed her dry lips and spit at him, full in the face. "Jackal," she whispered. The simple action brought her immense, crawling pain that overpowered her. She gave a soft cry and collapsed against the column, blessed darkness claiming her.

"Raj," Kamal called. "Cut her down and care for her."

"Yes, highness," Raj said with careful calm. Never before had he seen Kamal so angry, or now, so anguished.

Kamal stared at her pale face for a moment longer, then whirled about, calling his men together to leave the harem. He paused a moment, seeing Elena walking toward Arabella, her hands clenched into fists. "Raj," he called out. "Do not let anyone near her. You are responsible for her care. You alone."

Elena stopped in her tracks. She wasn't stupid. Kamal wanted the English girl, no matter what she had done. She felt a lump of misery in her belly. What hold did the proud bitch have on him that she, Elena, could not break? She tossed her head and wheeled about.

Kamal walked slowly, like an old man, back to his quarters in the palace. How, he thought, can a man's pride bring him so low? She had guile, damn her, but not enough to ply him with soft phrases, to make him believe that she could not live without him, to gently guide him toward what she wanted to achieve. And now she hung beaten and unconscious, all because of him. He didn't blame Elena. She was a child, with a child's rage and a child's gloating triumph. But he was a man, and a damned fool.

"Highness."

"Leave me, Hassan," he said wearily.

"Lam told me she would not be scarred. He said he treated her as gently as he could."

"I know. But she is a woman, not a battle-hardened man."

"A woman who attacked you, highness."

"I have lost her," Kamal said, amazed at his simple words. He stared almost uncomprehending at Hassan.

Hassan felt a knot in his throat. "You never found her," he said slowly. "She is not one of us, highness. She was never yours to keep."

"She was a virgin, until I took her."

Hassan blinked. "But your mother . . . The letter . . ."

Kamal gave him a twisted, cold smile. "Yes," he said softly, "my mother. No man had touched Arabella, but I was too stupid to realize her innocence until . . . until it was too late."

"What will you do, highness, when the Earl of Clare comes to claim her?"

"With her or with her father? By Allah, Hassan, I feel like an actor in a play, and I do not know my lines." He paused a moment, rubbing his palm over his forehead. "I would see the earl's captain, Sordello. Have him brought to me."

Sordello, though treated kindly enough over the past weeks of his captivity, felt a frisson of fear when the guards came for him. The slave market, he thought. I will be gelded and sold on the slave block. The guards were gruffly silent, but they did not hurt him.

He was guided into an awesomely beautiful chamber, its furnishings opulent crimson and gold, the tapestries on the walls of exquisite woven cloth. They were Italian, he realized numbly.

"Sit down, captain."

Sordello gazed at the man who had taken him. Slowly, trying to still his trembling legs, he eased himself down on the fat cushions across from him.

"Would you care for wine, captain?"

Sordello shook his head.

"Come, captain," Kamal said gently, "I will drink with you. There is no poison, I assure you."

Sordello gulped down the sweet red wine.

"Have you been treated well, captain?"

"Yes."

Kamal eased back, and Sordello was struck by his barbaric splendor. He was reminded of pictures he had seen as a child, of the ancient pashas, fierce-looking men. But this man was young, and seemingly kind, at least to him.

"How long have you sailed with the Earl of Clare?"

Sordello stared at Kamal, wondering if his question was simply an amusement or if what he said would determine his fate. He cleared his throat. "The earl allowed me to be a cabin boy when I was but ten years old."

"And what is your age, captain?"

"Thirty-five. I have captained my own vessel these past five years."

"Then you have known the Lady Arabella since she was born."

"Yes," Sordello said nervously.

"When you were a boy, did you know the earl?"

Sordello nodded. "I was his gate boy, but he knew I wished to be at sea."

"Did you know the earl's half-brother?"

Sordello started. "The earl's half-brother?" he repeated dumbly. "I remember him, yes. He died when I was very young."

Kamal had prayed that the captain would tell him that there had been no half-brother. But that, at least, then, had been no fabrication. "How did he die?"

"I do not know. There were many things happening then. My master, the Earl of Clare, had brought his countess to Genoa, but 'twas not well between them for some time."

"Was she his countess, his wife, when she arrived in Genoa?"

"I do not believe she was. I also remember that she fought with him, but always he treated her gently."

Kamal looked thoughtfully into his wine goblet. Another truth. Did Arabella lie to him, or did she not know? "Tell me about this half-brother."

"His name was Cesare Bellini, if I recall correctly. I was but a child. He was a foppish young man, but pleasant enough, I suppose. Why do you question me like this?"

Kamal waved away his question. "Do you also recall a Genoese contessa, Giovanna Giusti?"

Sordello gazed at him warily. "Vaguely. I saw her several times in Genoa."

"Was she to have wed the Earl of Clare?"

Sordello started, and shook his head in confusion. " 'Twould have been impossible. 'Twas his lady he wanted for wife. No one else. He nearly lost her. I remember his rage, like a demon possessed him."

Kamal sat forward. "What do you mean, captain?"

"I know little of it, only that Joseph, my friend, was with her and they were taken by bandits. Joseph was killed and the lady badly hurt. 'Twas an awful time."

Kamal realized that Sordello was speaking from his child's memories. What child could understand treachery? It was becoming a puzzle, Kamal thought, and only the earl and his mother knew the true placement of the pieces. But he had heard at least two damning truths from a man who had no reason to lie. "Tell me about the Lady Arabella, captain."

Sordello smiled, despite his nagging fear. "Ah, such a lively little sprite. Not a bone of fear in her body. The earl, her father, spoiled her shamefully, I suppose, but it didn't change her. So bright she is. I remember her telling her father that she had no wish to marry until she found a man like him or her brother." Sordello came to an abrupt skittering halt. "Why do you ask about the lady?"

"She is here," Kamal said calmly.

Sordello jerked up to his knees.

"Calm yourself, captain. The lady is quite well,

I assure you." *Liar! If she is broken, 'tis your doing!*

"But why?"

It was on the tip of Kamal's tongue to tell Sordello of the earl's treachery, but he knew well enough that the man owed his loyalty to the Earl of Clare. He would say nothing against his master; indeed, if he could, he would invent tales to protect him.

Kamal had gleaned all the truth he could. He rose gracefully to his feet. "You will not be here for much longer, captain. I thank you for speaking with me." He nodded toward the guards who stood at the entrance of the chamber.

He stood silently, watching the captain leave between his two guards. *A lively little sprite.* Kamal felt his belly knot. God, what had he done?

Kamal stood over Arabella, watching Raj gently massage a white ointment into her back.

"It will heal her, highness, and draw out the pain. In two or three days she will be fine again."

He looked at her raw back, then remembered her writhing about and the whip striking the front of her. "Her breasts?"

"The whip did not split her flesh."

Kamal saw flecks of blood in her hair. He lifted the stiffened hair and began to rub off the blood.

"I will keep her drugged," Raj said, eyeing Kamal, "at least for another day. She must keep quiet and rest, to heal."

Kamal nodded. "Turn her over a moment, Raj."

Raj clasped her shoulders and gently eased her

up. Kamal gazed at the thin red line that cut the underside of her left breast and higher on the right, barely missing her nipple. Very gently he ran his fingertip along the red slash, remembering the feel of her in his mouth, remembering how she had cried softly and arched her back to draw him closer. He dropped his hand.

"I will stay with her for a while," he said.

"As you will, highness." Raj eased Arabella onto her stomach again, straightened, and stretched his back. "You do not wish Elena this evening?"

Kamal gave a short bark of laughter. "No. I have decided to arrange a marriage for her. Say nothing to her until I have all the details worked out."

"You are most generous, highness," Raj said dryly, but Kamal did not hear him. He gently picked up Arabella's hand and began to stroke it lightly.

24

Hamil hunkered closer to the small fire and stretched his hands toward the flame. The night air was chilly, surprisingly so, Rayna thought, after the scorching day. There was a tension in Adam, a tension so palpable she wondered how he could act so very calm, so very patient while Hamil settled himself comfortably on a blanket opposite them. Adam knew as well as she that Hamil had news of Oran and Arabella. She picked up her cup of thick Turkish coffee and slowly sipped the potent brew.

"What have you learned, Hamil?" Adam asked quietly, breaking the silence.

Hamil did not reply for a moment, pondering whether to speak the truth to the woman's brother.

"Arabella is well, is she not?" Adam's voice, in his concern, was sharper than he intended.

"Yes," Hamil said finally. "She is . . . well."

But he had forgotten the sharp-eyed Rayna.

"Come, Hamil," she said. "What has happened to her?"

Hamil quirked an eyebrow at Adam, remarking as he did, "Are you certain you don't wish to sell the girl? She is far too perceptive for a female." He sighed deeply. Adam's concern for his sister, so clear in his searching eyes, made further jests die in his throat. "Very well. Your sister was whipped."

"What?" Adam roared, springing to his feet.

"Beaten?" Rayna repeated blankly. "Why, Hamil?"

He shrugged. "Sit down, my lord. She will be quite all right. You told me she is proud and as tame as a sirocco, but it seems that she attacked Kamal in the harem, and in front of his guards. Instead of killing her, as he would have been expected to do, he merely had her whipped."

"I'll kill the bastard," Adam said tensely, his hands locked into fists at his sides.

Hamil did not add that he had also learned his wife was expecting their child at any time. For a moment he forgot Lady Arabella Welles, dwelling on his joy at the news. Both he and Lella had believed she was barren, but he had not set another above her. He loved her too much.

"Why," Rayna asked, her hand on Adam's arm, "did Arabella do such a thing?"

Hamil regretfully let go of his pleasant thoughts and turned to the lovely young girl who was looking so seriously at him. He said starkly to Adam, "Kamal has bedded your sister, my lord. My man did not learn all the details, but it appears she fought him, insulted him, and even tried to kill him once before. All to save her parents, I would guess. But she must have gone to his bed willingly. My half-brother would never force a woman, even one as provoking as your sister."

Adam's face was pale in the gentle firelight. "He has much to answer for, Hamil," he said, more calmly now.

"Yes," Hamil said quietly. "It would appear so." He frowned a moment in deep thought. "There is more here, I think. Evidently Kamal also stopped the whipping, and afterward he stayed with her."

"Perhaps," Adam said harshly, "he feared she would die. Without her, he would have no bait."

"I do not think so," Hamil said. He turned suddenly at a slight noise near their campfire. "Quickly, Rayna," he said, "put on your cap. No one save my captain, Boroll, knows that you are a woman. Not all of my men are trustworthy, and I do not wish to have to fear for your safety."

Rayna looked furtively about and quickly stuffed her hair under the cap.

"Always stay close to me or to Lord St. Ives," Hamil continued, "until this business is done. Some of the men owe no particular loyalty to me. And I must admit that you would be a temptation to any man."

"As is my sister," Adam said more to himself than to Rayna or Hamil. "She will not stir from my side," he continued to Hamil. He rose suddenly and began to pace about the fire. "We must face your brother now, Hamil. I cannot allow my sister to endure more torment."

"Not yet, my lord. Not yet. His mother, the contessa, has not arrived. More important, it is impossible for me to enter the palace and see Kamal secretly. There are more guards and slaves around him than you can imagine."

"Dammit!" Adam snarled. "Your spy managed well enough to get into the palace. I cannot wait longer, not knowing what will happen to her!"

"My lord," Hamil said, "your sister can do nothing outrageous for a time. She is still recovering in her bed, and quite safe at the moment. We must wait. Stop your pacing, Adam," he chided, but his voice was more gentle.

"Wait for what?" Adam snapped. "Wait until my father arrives? Wait until Kamal murders my sister?"

"No. We wait for Kamal to leave his palace. He is known to go into Oran, among the people. I will move quickly when he does."

The air was charged with violence, and Rayna quickly said, "Your half-brother Kamal. You paint him one minute with a treacherous brush, Hamil, and the next as an honorable man."

"I suppose it is true," Hamil sighed. "I am torn by doubts. I would have sworn upon everything I hold precious that he never coveted my power or my position. He was educated in Europe, you see, and I wondered if he would ever return to live in Oran. I doubt that he is much a Muslim now, though it is his duty to be so, and that worries me, for how can a man who does not truly believe in the Muslim ways rule effectively? At least he has Hassan."

"Who is Hassan?" Rayna asked.

"My minister, now Kamal's, I trust. A wily old fox who would gladly give his life to see justice done and to keep power in the hands of my father's sons."

"How often have you seen your half-brother, Hamil?" Adam asked, seating himself again beside Rayna.

Hamil shrugged. "He visited Oran rarely in the past nine years. I grew to know him best, I think, through his letters. I learned much of the European mind from him, for, you see, he thinks like you, my lord. He sees more than is in my purview in Oran. He understands Napoleon and he understands the English hatred and fear of him. He is an . . . intelligent man."

"Perhaps," Adam said suddenly, "I could see him. Privately."

"No," Hamil said sharply. "All that would result from such a meeting would be your capture." Seeing that Adam would continue to argue with him, he said coldly, "I cannot be responsible for Rayna's safety. I have waited many months, my lord, thought and planned. I regret your sister's involvement, but it does not change what I must do."

Rayna said suddenly, "You know, Adam, that Arabella would never give herself to a man she does not care for."

Adam said wearily, "She doubtless gave herself, my love, to bargain for my parents' safety."

"I did not think of that," Rayna said, staring into the dying fire.

Hamil laughed. "Perhaps that was one of your sister's motives, my lord. But know this. Kamal is a handsome man, well-formed, and young. Women have been offering themselves willingly to him since he was a lad." In answer to Rayna's unspoken question, he added with a crooked grin, "He does not look dark and fierce like me or your lord, Rayna, He is golden as the sun, with eyes the color of the Mediterranean."

"Oh," Rayna said in a stunned voice. "Goodness," she added as her mind sorted through the various implications.

Adam cursed. He tried to imagine his sister succumbing to a man out of passion, but failed. She had never cared for a man in all her twenty years, and many of the gentlemen buzzing around her had been handsome and quite polished. But he couldn't imagine her bending to a man who was her enemy, a man who threatened her parents. No, she would have given herself to Kamal only to bargain for their parents' safety. But she has no experience, he thought, no guile. His fear for her sharpened, for she knew no middle ground. He cursed again. "We are so near to Oran," he growled. "It does not sit well with me to sit about like a dithering fool."

"Nonetheless," Hamil said, steel in his voice, "you will do as I bid, my lord." He rose and dusted off his white trousers. "And if you are tempted to go against my orders, remember your red-haired sprite here. Tomorrow we will learn more. I bid you good night."

Rayna was fiercely glad that she was Adam's responsibility. He would do nothing foolish with her in his charge. "Please, Adam," she said softly. "Hamil is no fool."

"I know he is not," Adam said tersely, "but it does not alter how I feel." He pictured Arabella lying beneath Kamal, and he saw red.

Rayna sought to distract him, and quickly rose to wind her arms about his waist. "All will be well, my lord," she whispered. "You will see." She rose on her tiptoes to kiss him. She felt his resistance, then the undeniable rise of passion.

He made love to her gently, slowly, watching her closely as she reached her climax. Was he treating Rayna, he wondered, as he prayed Kamal had treated Arabella? His fury at the man he had never seen washed over him once again, and he took his own pleasure quickly, violently.

Rayna sighed softly, and clutched her arms around Adam's back when he made to leave her.

"Love," he whispered softly against her temple, "the ground is hard. I don't want to crush you. Let me go."

But she didn't. She knew that he was again thinking about Arabella. She said softly, "Adam, you have left me."

He brought his attention back to her, and smiled ruefully. "Unfortunately," he said dryly, "a man's thoughts, if they wander, result in the rest of him wandering also."

"I will forgive you this time, my lord." She let him ease off her and roll to his back. When he pulled her against him, she pressed her cheek to his shoulder and rested her leg over his belly.

"It won't be much longer, Adam. I am afraid too. Not just for Arabella, but for our parents. You know my father will not sit idle in Naples."

"No, he won't. Likely my father has seen him. Lord only knows what they will do."

"Perhaps," she said quietly, "my father will be more amenable to reason when I see him again."

"You have that much faith in my sire?"

"Perhaps I have more faith in your virility, my lord."

"You little wretch! Dammit, Rayna . . ." He broke off, knowing that if his child were growing in her womb, he had only himself to blame. And he had continued to make love to her. He couldn't seem to help himself, no matter the arguments to the contrary.

At least, Rayna thought thankfully, his thoughts were absorbed in different matters. "Where will we go on our wedding trip?" she asked.

"To Greece, if it pleases you. We will take the Cassandra and sail the Aegean."

"It pleases me, my lord. It pleases me much."

She felt him tense, though he said nothing. "Adam . . . ?" she asked softly.

"Do not worry, Rayna," he said, his voice tinged with anger, "I will not do anything foolish."

"Father, she is beautiful! She is named *Fearless!* Just like Mother's sailboat. Ah, to be on the sea is to be free!" She unfurled the mast, laughing as the rising wind tore through her hair. The sunlight was so bright, she had to squint and shade her eyes with her hand.

It was dark, dense darkness shrouding her pain. "Oh God, she is dead and I killed her! The fence was too high for her. Father, Diana was so proud, and I killed her!" Tears splashed down her cheeks, her sorrow mixing with the pain from her broken ribs. She heard a gentle voice speaking to her, easing through the darkness.

"Papa? Please forgive me, Papa."

She felt gentle hands lightly stroking her hair back from her forehead. "I forgive you," the gentle voice said. "You must think only of getting well now. Do you understand, *cara?*"

"Yes, Papa. *Why did she have to die?*"

"It's all right, sweetheart. No, you mustn't move. Lie still. Drink this and you will sleep."

She did as she was bid. She felt his hands on her shoulders holding her up while the rim of the goblet touched her lips. How odd that her back felt seared with pain when it was her ribs she had broken. She was lying on her stomach.

Suddenly the darkness was closing in on her, and she cried, "Don't leave me, Papa! Don't leave me!"

"I won't leave you. I promise."

She felt strong fingers close over her hand, and she sighed deeply, calm now. She drifted back into a bottomless sleep where there was no light and no dreams.

Kamal gently disengaged his hand and sat back in his chair. She believed him her father, a man who obviously loved his child. Ah, Arabella, what have you done to me? You are as willful as an untamed colt, as unpredictable as the desert wind, and I am drawn to you as a moth to a bright flame. Your beauty makes me tremble even as your foolish pride makes me want to thrash you. And now I have hurt you, and if you did not hate me before, you will now. I have lost you, yet never possessed you, save for that night when I tasted your beauty, savored your innocence, felt you cling to me in the discovery of your woman's passion.

"What in God's name am I to do?"

He did not realize he had spoken aloud until he heard Raj's voice breaking into his reverie. "I do not know, highness. You are fatigued. I will stay with her now, if it is your wish."

"She drank more of the drug."

"She will sleep for many hours now, highness."

Kamal raised troubled eyes to the eunuch. "She dreams and speaks. She thought me her father."

"Then I shall be her father as well, if she again speaks."

Kamal felt weariness seep into his bones. Slowly he rose and closed his fingers about Raj's arm. "Call me if she worsens."

"Yes, highness."

Raj watched Kamal walk wearily from Arabella's small chamber. He smiled sadly. Life was a simple matter for a Muslim, with a law for every situation, but for a man like Kamal, Raj could foresee only the pain of unhappiness, for the Englishwoman would leave, and if Kamal harmed her father, her hatred would live with him for all his years. He started at the sound of Kamal's tired voice. "If she awakens, Raj, do not send for me, and do not tell her that I was here." A rueful smile twisted his lips. "I wish her to get well, and the sight of me would likely make her relapse."

Raj nodded. It was true, and nothing could change it.

"Oh, Lella, surely your baby must come soon!"

"It is my fervent plea to Allah each hour. I told Kamal . . ."

She broke off, seeing Arabella's face twist in anger.

"Does your back pain you still?" she asked.

Arabella shifted slightly against the soft pillows. "No, there is nearly no pain now. But I am bored, Lella. Two days I have sat about doing nothing save . . . think."

"You must rest to regain your strength."

"For what reason?" Arabella asked in a bitter voice. "So that Kamal may again humiliate me? Perhaps force me to his bed? Call me a harlot and a liar?"

Lella sighed. "Oh my," she gasped suddenly, hugging her arms about her great belly.

"What is it?" Arabella pushed herself upright, her eyes wide upon Lella's astonished face.

"The baby. I think my time has come."

Arabella made to rise. "I will help you, Lella."

"Lie still! I will have the midwife fetched. You will stay here and pray that I bear a son."

Lella rose with pained awkwardness while Arabella watched her helplessly. "I will pray, Lella," she called after her.

Arabella forced herself to relax against the soft pillows. She prayed and she thought. Occasionally she tensed at the faraway sound of breathless screams. Would it be her own screams she heard in the future? Her own screams to bring forth Kamal's child? She shuddered, wanting only to repress her images of him. He had you beaten, you fool! He is your enemy; he must be your enemy! She moaned softly, but not from pain. Indeed, even as she swung her legs over the side of the bed, she felt only a tightness in her back. She had refused Raj's drug that morning, preferring a clear head to the fuzzy vagueness that had woven haunting dreams. The remembered dreams became vivid to her now, and suddenly she realized that in them her father had spoken to her, had calmed her and stroked her.

It had been Kamal.

"No," she cried softly, and lowered her face to her hands. She heard footsteps nearing her chamber and quickly lay again on her back and closed her eyes.

"Lady Arabella?"

"Raj," she said. "How is Lella?"

"She is fine."

"I have heard her screams."

"Birthing is a painful process. It will be many hours yet. I have brought you food and a special drink."

She started to reject the drink but thought better of it. No, better to play docile and drowsy. Better to pretend. Lella was giving birth; surely there would be excitement and perhaps carelessness. Perhaps she would be able to slip away. Freedom.

Arabella saw that she was right as the afternoon dragged on. Raj was with Lella, and most of the harem girls talked in small clusters near Lella's chambers. She dressed in a loose silk robe, pulled on blue leather slippers, brushed the tangles from her hair, and tied it back with a bit of ribbon.

She walked slowly about the gardens, her eyes straying to the high walls and the double gates. There was a tall willow tree whose branches fell over the side of the far wall. Arabella stared at it, not for its beauty, but for its potential as a means of escape. Slowly she began to smile. Did the ridiculous men believe the girls in the harem too weak to climb a tree and escape their clutches? There was likely a guard on the other side of the wall, but to Arabella that was just as she wished it. She had no illusions about a woman escaping from Oran, but a man would have a chance.

She realized with awful truth that she had no money. But Raj must have money—that, or jewels—in his chambers.

Arabella heard another scream. Oh, Lella, please

be all right. You are my only friend here. She realized she was digging her fingernails into her palms. She wanted to go to Lella, but she knew Raj expected her to be asleep from the drug he had given her. Slowly she made her way back to her chamber, there to pace and plan and worry about Lella.

It was near to nine o'clock at night. There was but a sliver of moon in the sky as Arabella stealthily left her chamber. Everyone was still with Lella, including Lena, who had brought Arabella her supper and then left her soon thereafter, telling her not to worry, that Lella was holding her own and the babe would be birthed soon.

It had been child's play, Arabella thought, a grim smile on her face, to steal a small bag of gold coins from Raj's chambers. She fastened the leather pouch at her waist and patted her braided hair, wound tightly about her head.

She slipped through the garden like a silent shadow and made her way to the willow tree. Ah, Lella, she thought as she carefully climbed among the branches, you have given me my chance for freedom. She smiled, thinking about the wadded clothes and pillows she had formed in her shape on the bed. With any luck at all, no one would know she had escaped until morning.

Arabella paused at the top of the wall, staring over the side. There was one man who was patrolling the perimeter, and he looked anything but alert. She sent another silent plea heavenward, holding herself perfectly still until the guard was at least twenty yards away from her. She studied the rocky ground below, then wriggled down on the wall until her feet were dangling. She let go and landed lightly on the ground. There was no sound from the guard. She quickly selected a rock and drew back against the wall, waiting for the guard to come.

He was a young man, and not overly large, Arabella saw with relief, and he was whistling a lighthearted tune. Well, I am sorry, she told him silently, but you are going to have a great headache.

He saw her in the same instant the rock was slamming toward his head. He grunted in astonishment, then crumpled to the rocky ground.

Arabella paused but an instant before pulling off his clothes. He was wearing a flowing burnoose over his uniform, none too clean, but of great value to Arabella, for it would hide her hair and every unmasculine curve of her body. Once garbed in his clothes, she straightened over him and softly cursed. She had nothing with which to bind him. She shrugged philosophically and dragged him into the shadow of the wall.

"Sleep a long time," she said softly, then turned and began to make her way down the treacherous slope toward Oran and the harbor.

"Highness, your sister-in-law has given birth to a son!"

Kamal was alert immediately, a wide smile on his face. "Excellent, Ali. Is Lella all right?"

"Yes, highness. It is after midnight—do you still wish to see her?"

"Indeed, just for a moment."

Kamal dressed quickly and made his way to the harem, Ali at his heels. He found Lella looking pale and exhausted, her son bundled in her arms.

"Well, my sister"—he smiled down at her—"you have given Hamil a son, and me a nephew."

"He is perfect, Kamal, and the image of his father."

"I would have expected no less of you, Lella." He sat beside her and pulled back the linen cover from his nephew's face. "Ah, he does not have all his father's beauty, praise Allah!"

Lella's smile suddenly saddened and tears formed in her eyes. She turned her face away, but Kamal gently touched his fingers to her jaw. "I understand, Lella. I loved him too, you know."

"Yes," she gulped after a moment, "I know. Kamal, why did it happen? He was as much at home on a ship as on land. How could he have fallen overboard?"

He held her and her son, his own pain clutching at his heart while her tears fell on his neck. "Sometimes," he said, "I think we are here to be taunted, to play the fool for some force that we do not understand. There is no escape from our own miseries. All is duty, honor to rules that we did not make. All is acceptance."

"Must you give her up, Kamal?"

His arms tightened about her, then eased. Gently

he lowered her onto her pillow and straightened. He looked tired and beaten.

"I am sorry," she said softly.

"Do not be, Lella." He gazed about Lella's chamber, a twisted smile curving his mouth. "Can you honestly see Arabella content in my harem? She would tear it apart stone by stone, and me with it. You are tired, sweet sister. Sleep now. I will see you and my perfect nephew in the morning."

He kissed her gently on her pale cheek, then rose. "It is nearly mid—" His voice broke off at the loud shouts coming from outside.

"What the devil!"

Raj, his face drawn and his bulk shaking from exertion, rushed into the chamber. "Highness! She is gone! The guard on the eastern wall was found unconscious, stripped of his clothes!"

Kamal felt his blood run cold. He heard a muffled shriek from Lella, but didn't turn his eyes from Raj. Very calmly he said, "Bring me the guard, quickly."

He was in Arabella's chamber, the bundle of clothes she had formed beneath the covers lying unregarded in his hands, when the guard, clothed only in a loincloth, stumbled before him.

His first thought was that with a man's clothes she would have some protection. "Tell me what happened," he said tersely.

"I seek a ship bound for Genoa." Arabella murmured the words again and again, trying to lower her voice to the gruffness of a man's. Sweat beaded

on her forehead, from fear and exertion. The peril-
ous climb down the steep hill from the palace to
the city had left her muscles aching and her breath
short.

The city looked ghostly under the sliver of moon,
and the eerie silence made her heart pound so
loud she feared discovery at any moment. She
winced with each step she took, for the guard's
boots were too large and had rubbed her heels
raw.

The closer she came to the harbor, the more her
fear grew. An unarmed man alone would as easily
be the victim of robbers as would a woman. She
clung to the shadows, doggedly refusing to give in
to her fear.

The shadows became men—pirates or simple
fishermen, Arabella didn't know. She heard them
laughing and talking in Arabic. She walked on
toward a three-masted ship, her head down, con-
centrating on nothing more than her next step.

Almost there. She heard men call out to her,
but she only shook her head, as if she were on an
errand of grave importance. She heard a group of
men closing behind her but she was too afraid to
turn to face them. She waved toward the ship. A
deep voice that came out of a nightmare rang out
behind her, in fluent Italian,

"Hey, you there, hold! What do you want with
my ship?"

It was Captain Risan.

She closed her eyes against his voice. *Run,
escape!* She lunged away from the dock, back to-

ward the narrow, dark streets. She heard his voice again, raised high, cursing her. The boots dragged up and down over her heels, slowing her and making her grit her teeth in pain.

He was so close she could hear him breathing. She felt a hand come down on her shoulder, and reeled from the impact. She turned, her hand balled into a fist, and struck out at him. He growled in fury, and shoved her, hooking his booted foot behind her legs. Arabella sprawled to her back in the dirt, Risan slamming down over her. She struggled beneath him, swinging her fists at his face, but he grabbed her wrists and pulled them down against her belly.

She saw his fist above her face, and closed her eyes against the pain, but nothing happened.

"By the beard of the Prophet!" he said. " 'Tis naught but a boy!"

She blinked up at his surprised face. "Let me go!" she growled, trying to heave him off her. "I mean you no harm! I did nothing!"

Four men were standing over her, laughing and pointing. She couldn't understand what they were saying. She twisted suddenly, but it only brought Risan forward, his face but inches above her own.

She heard a sharp intake of breath. She dredged up the foulest language she had ever heard and spat it at him.

He stiffened, his eyes never leaving her face. Suddenly his dark eyes glistened. Slowly he lowered his hand to her breast.

"No, my little lad," he chided her softly as she

writhed beneath him. "By Allah." He ripped the burnoose from her head.

"Please," she whispered, her eyes fastened upon Risan's face, unaware of the stunned silence around them. "Let me go."

"It is you," he said. "And I believed you ugly as a camel wallowing in a dung heap." He eased off her, clasped her wrists more tightly, and pulled her to her feet. He had no fear that she would escape, for his men surrounded her. He grinned, his white teeth flashing in the near-darkness, and proffered her a deep bow. "Lady Arabella," he said, laughter lurking in his voice. "Were you seeking me, my lady, or are you a gift from Allah?"

"I have money. Please, captain, you must help me get away from here. I will pay you well." She was babbling, but could not stop. "I must return to Genoa. At least show me a ship bound for Italy, please!"

Risan motioned to one of the men and spoke a few sharp words. Arabella felt her arms pulled behind her back. She struggled, then stilled, knowing it would gain her naught. She shrank back against the man as Risan reached his hand to her hair. The man thrust his hips against her, laughing as he did so.

"Hold still, my lady," Risan said, "else you will inflame my men." She gnawed her lower lip between her teeth and stared at him. She felt his fingers touch her hair, then slowly begin to unwind the thick braid around her head. "Please, don't," she whispered.

"If only I had known," he said, as if to himself, "I might not have sailed so quickly to Oran." He lifted a mass of hair and brought it to his face. She watched him rub it against his cheek. "I do not think I want to know how you managed to escape my half-brother. I will even pretend that I do not notice you are wearing the uniform of his guards."

"You will . . . help me?"

"Let us say, *cara*, that I will not be so careless with you as my brother was. After I have my fill of you, perhaps I will free you, perhaps I will return you to Kamal. You will be one of the few women to have knowledge of both of us."

"*No!*" All her hopes, all her confidence, all shattered. She gave a sharp cry of agony at her failure. She felt Risan's hand touch her face and she forgot everything. She kicked out at him, shrieking in fury, and drove her elbows into the stomach of the man who held her. She heard a grunt of pain but the man didn't loose his hold on her arms. She saw Risan's face contort with anger. "I should take you right here," he hissed at her, "in the dirt and filth, with my men holding you down." Suddenly he whirled about. Arabella raised dazed eyes. A half-dozen men on horseback were bearing down on them, Kamal at their head. Her heart leapt at the sight of him. He looked other-worldly in the dark night, his white burnoose flowing out behind him.

Kamal leapt off his stallion's back, relief flooding through his body at the sight of Arabella.

"I believe you lost something, brother," Risan said, bowing deeply.

"Release her," Kamal said in a flat cold voice. She was staring at him, her hair flowing about her pale face, her eyes wide with uncertainty.

"I found her, Kamal," Risan continued. "I will pay you for her."

Kamal held out his hand, and Arabella, without a thought of anything except that he was there and she wanted to cry with relief at the sight of him, took three steps toward him and pressed herself against his side. He felt a great tremor run through her body.

"You will be rewarded, Risan, for finding my . . . property." Her gratitude did not last long, he thought, feeling her stiffen at his words. "I would pay you with the money she carries, but unfortunately it is stolen."

Without another word, Kamal swung up onto his horse's back. For a long moment he merely stared down at Arabella. Then he gave her his hand and pulled her up in front of him. His stallion, Timar, snorted at the extra weight, dancing sideways until he heard his master's voice quieting him. "Put on the burnoose. It is chilly where we are going."

Arabella did as she was told, wondering at the odd flatness of his voice. Anger, rage, she could better understand.

"Where are you taking me?" she asked after she had wrapped herself completely in the full white burnoose.

"Be silent," Kamal said. He turned in his saddle and rapped orders in Arabic to the men behind him.

Puzzled, Arabella watched the town of Oran and the harbor recede in the distance. They were riding inland, toward a range of mountains.

The horse lengthened his stride as they reached open ground, and Arabella felt Kamal's arms tighten about her waist. She turned slightly, fatigue washing over her in great waves, and rested her head against his chest.

25

Arabella snuggled closer, not wanting to leave the safety of her dreams, but his voice came again, his warm breath touching her temple. "Wake up, Arabella. You can sleep again, soon."

"Kamal?"

His arms tightened about her. "Put your arms about my neck and hang on."

She did as she was bid, aware that his stallion was quiet now. "Where are we?"

He did not reply until he had dismounted. "We're at our camp."

She raised her head from his shoulder and blinked at the activity. "It's still night," she said as he eased her to the ground.

"Yes. You slept for but an hour. Sit here until our tent is ready."

Arabella sank to the rocky ground, wrapped the heavy burnoose more securely about her against the cold, and stared around her. They were on a flat stretch of ground at the base of rolling hills. One of the men was building a fire; another was lighting lamps and setting them at intervals around the area. She recognized Ali working with yet another man to erect a tent. She heard the snorting of horses and watched Kamal pull the saddle from his stallion and lead him into a small fenced-in area. What camp? she wondered. Why had Kamal brought her here? And where was "here"? She looked up at the sky, black as velvet, studded with stars that looked like sparkling diamonds. Everything was so quiet. It was as if they were the only humans on earth.

"Come."

She looked up to see Kamal standing over her, his hand outstretched. She studied his set face in the flickering firelight.

"Where?" she asked baldly, unconsciously shrinking back from him.

He leaned down and grasped her under the arms and jerked her to her feet. "I have a lot to say to you, my lady," he said coldly, "and not in my men's hearing."

He was like a stranger in the long flowing white robe and hood that was secured to his head with corded leather bands. The boots slid off her heels and she moaned softly at the pain.

"I have not hurt you," he growled, shaking her arm. "What is the matter?"

"My feet hurt," she said, not looking at him.

Kamal looked down at her booted feet, then shouted something in Arabic to one of the men.

She took another step before Kamal, cursing softly, lifted her into his arms. He carried her into a tent and sat her down on a cushion. Arabella blinked at the opulent surroundings. The tent wasn't large, but its slender poles held the tent ceiling above Kamal's head. Animal furs were spread as a bed; thick carpets covered the rocky ground; a brazier of coals burned brightly against the night chill.

"I suggest, my lady, that you keep your tongue between your teeth. I am in no mood for your arrogance. Now, let's get those boots off and see what you've managed to do to your feet."

Arabella gritted her teeth and raised her leg. She felt tears sting her eyes as the leather scraped over her raw heel.

"You are nothing less than a fool," Kamal said after he had pulled off her other boot. Her heels were raw and bleeding. He turned and left the tent, to return a few moments later with a basin of water and a cloth.

A small, strangled cry escaped her lips when he pressed the wet cloth to her heels. His lips were a thin line; otherwise, he paid her no heed. When he set her feet in the basin of water, Arabella rose off the pillows with a yelp of pain.

"Sit still," he said, clamping his hands on her shoulders. After a moment, he rose, and again left her.

Arabella stared ahead of her, seeing nothing. This is ridiculous, she thought, trying to turn her mind from the stinging pain. Sitting here like an idiot with my feet soaking in water, with a man who would just as soon wring my neck as look at me. She tugged off the burnoose and flung it away from her.

The sight that greeted Kamal upon his return was almost comic, and an unwilling smile curved his mouth. Arabella was disheveled, tendrils of hair curling haphazardly about her face, garbed in an overly large uniform that made her appear a child playing grown-up. The smile left his lips when he saw the water was tinged red.

"Lie down," he said sharply.

"Why?" Arabella demanded, feeling suddenly very vulnerable. I am alone with him in the middle of nowhere and he is furious, she thought.

"What a pity," he said, ignoring her, "that you could not find a guard who wore a smaller-size boot." He lifted her feet from the basin and pressed her backward. He sat down beside her, drawing her feet onto his lap. Very gently he daubed a healing ointment onto the raw flesh, then wrapped both her feet in clean white cloths. "There," he said inconsequentially, not looking at her.

Arabella ran her tongue over her suddenly dry lips. "What do you intend to do with me, Kamal?" She hated the tentative, weak sound of her voice. He raised his head and noted her pallor and the shadows of exhaustion beneath her widened eyes.

"What you did, Arabella," he said at last, his voice low and controlled, "was so incredibly stupid that, had I not known you, I would have laughed at the story of a woman dressed as a man traipsing alone to the harbor of Oran. Did you honestly

believe that you could board a ship and sail blithely
to Genoa?"

She knew he was right, knew that her despera-
tion had led her to commit an act that was sheer
folly, but his calm recital of her impulsive act
stiffened her resolve. "Did you expect me to docilely await the arrival of my father? Greet him
dressed in heathen veils, and watch you condemn
him for an act of which he is innocent?" Just
speaking the words brought her to the end of her
endurance and she jumped to her feet, her hands
fisted on her hips. "Just what do you intend now,
master? Another beating to make you feel strong
and powerful? I wish you had not come. What is
another rape? Perhaps your brother would have
been kind enough to kill me once he was through!"

Kamal felt a pulse pound in his temple. He
uncoiled his powerful body and rose to face her.

"I don't care what you do to me!" she shrieked
at him. "I hate you!"

He seized her arms and shook her until her
head lolled forward. She didn't have the strength
to fight him and when he drew her against him,
she laid her head against his shoulder, whispering
brokenly, "I hate you . . . I hate you."

He felt her flinch when his hands caressed her
back, and he cursed softly.

"Is Lella all right?"

He blinked, his hands quieting. "Yes, she does
well. She bore a son, the image of his father."

"Then she is happy."

"Yes." He gently pushed her away and began to unfasten her shirt.

"You plan another rape?" she spat at him, holding herself rigid.

His hands stilled. He cupped her chin in his palm and forced her face upward to meet his gaze. "Rape, Arabella? Have you managed to twist what happened that night between us, as you have twisted other things? As I recall, you wanted me as much as I wanted you. Do you not remember how yielding you were, how moist and warm your body was for me? You can pretend many things, Arabella, but not the quivering of passion I felt when I was deep inside you."

"Stop it! I will not listen to you! It was nothing, I tell you, I only—"

He closed off her frantic words with his mouth. The feel of her against him released all the fury he had felt, all the fear that had gnawed at him. He held her head, forcing her to accept the punishment of his kiss. He forced her lips to part and thrust his tongue into her mouth, knowing he was savaging her, bruising her soft lips. Suddenly his anger dissolved in his need for her. He eased his pressure, now gently seducing her with his tongue. He kissed her mouth, her closed eyes, the tip of her nose. He slipped his hand between them and let his fingers caress her belly. He felt her resistance disappear as his fingers pressed lower, teasing her, probing gently at her.

"No," Arabella moaned softly, but her body was straining against him. She felt his palm pressing lightly against her, rotating slowly, tantalizingly, and she could not seem to call up a shred of resistance.

"You are moving against me, *cara*," he said softly into her mouth. "I want to touch you, caress you, Arabella, feel you open yourself to me. I want to taste your sweetness."

"No," she cried softly yet again. Her ragged breath caught in her throat when his hand left her. Then he lifted her, pressing her belly against his hard manhood. "Please," she whispered, "don't make me feel this way. Please . . ."

"Feel how much I want you, Arabella," he said, molding her soft hips against him. "I want to be deep inside you, make you part of me, bind us together."

He let her slide back down his body, then gently pressed her back against his arm. He kissed her deeply while his hand stroked over her breasts.

She felt ripples of pleasure course through her, but the ache was lower, pounding at her, making her writhe against him for relief. He slipped his thigh between her legs and pressed upward. She cried out, unable to help herself. She moved against him wildly, so beyond herself that she wasn't aware that he was pulling off her shirt until she felt the cool air on her breasts. She felt the heat from his body and wanted him naked against her. Desperately she fumbled with his belt. She felt dazed and helpless and frantic. She was tugging at his clothes, vaguely aware that his powerful body was quivering at her touch.

Kamal released her, closing his eyes an instant to get control of himself. Quickly he pulled off her men's clothes, and the sight of her, naked, trembling, her breasts heaving, nearly undid him. He jerked her up into his arms and carried her to the pile of soft furs that was his bed. He gently laid her upon her back, but she wouldn't release him. She was arching up to him, her hands tugging at his neck to pull him down to her.

"Just a moment, love," he whispered.

"I cannot bear it," she cried against his throat. "Please . . ."

He ripped off his clothes. Pulling off his boots brought him a measure of reason, and when he was naked, he held himself back, lying beside her but not yet touching her.

"You are so beautiful," he said, his eyes following his hand as it stroked over her full breasts. He paused a moment, cupping her breast, feeling the erratic pounding of her heart. He wanted to go slowly with her, but realized that she wouldn't allow it. When he touched her, probing gently with his fingers between her slender thighs, she cried out, arching upward.

Kamal moved on top of her. Her arms were wildly searching down his back to his buttocks, pounding him, her nails scratching him in her frenzy. He balanced himself on his elbows, arching his back so that his manhood was hard and demanding between her thighs. Slowly he moved against her, not entering her, watching her eyes darken.

"Tell me you want me, Arabella," he commanded.

"I . . . want . . ." Her words stuck in her throat and she thrust her hands between them to clutch at him. But he pulled back and rose to his knees between her thighs. Slowly he lowered his head and began to nibble and kiss her belly. Her soft cries, her frantic hands clutching at his shoulders, tangling in his thick hair, made him tremble with desire. He lifted her hips, and to his immense pleasure, she parted her thighs wide, offering herself to him. He nuzzled her and teased her with his tongue until he felt her stiffen. Quickly he parted her and thrust his full length into her small moist body. He covered her, thrusting his tongue into her mouth just as his manhood was thrusting deep inside her.

"Wrap your legs around me," he said into her mouth. Her lithe movement brought him deeper and he felt his control dissolving. But she was beyond him, so wildly caught up in the swirling passion that he ceased to be apart from her. She felt as though she were merging with him and the image was as blinding as the sun. She was crying aloud, and he covered her mouth with his, capturing the dazzling sounds that came from deep within her. He rode her and she met his every thrust, wanting more, until her body began to convulse with the nearly painful pleasure and she was plummeting, merging into him, consuming him, possessing him. He felt her final cry, the immense shuddering of her body, and released the hold he had on himself.

"I can feel you," she gasped when he tensed above her and poured himself into her.

Kamal felt as though his very soul had been torn from his body. He fell on top of her, and she took his full weight, clutching at his back to bring him even closer. He raised his head and looked into her eyes. "You are mine, Arabella," he said softly. He lifted his hand and gently pushed back damp tendrils of hair from her forehead. "Now and always. You are mine."

Arabella did not emerge from the aftermath of her pleasure. His words floated gently over her mind, and she smiled and closed her eyes, replete and exhausted.

Kamal pulled away from her, his eyes never leaving her sleeping face. Nothing was decided, save that he could not let her go. He closed his eyes a moment, unwilling to admit to the vagaries of fate that had brought him a woman he could not have. He remembered her back and gently turned her onto her stomach. The welts had faded, leaving faint red lines. His fingers slowly traced over the marks, as if willing them to disappear. What in God's name was he to do?

Slowly, careful not to awaken her, Kamal turned her toward him and gathered her in his arms. He felt her stir and press more closely against him. He pulled a soft wool cover over them, wondering as he did so if when she awoke she would jerk away from him with loathing, denying again the passion that had passed between them.

Arabella awoke slowly, a muted groan coming from her throat. She was lying on her side, one leg bent upward, the other straight. She felt his hands stroking her hips, his fingers curving around her buttocks to touch and caress the soft flesh between her thighs. She caught her breath when she felt him press closer, his manhood easing slowly into her.

His hands were gently kneading her belly, drawing her downward to take more of him into her. "No," she gasped, fully awake now.

"Hush, love," he murmured, his lips caressing her shoulder. His hands moved upward to fondle her breasts, and as always with him, she felt her resistance fading. Without conscious thought, she squirmed her hips against him, drawing him deeper. But even as her passion mounted, she was aware of what she was doing, aware that he was robbing her of her will, her determination. Tears stung her eyes, falling unheeded down her cheeks even as her body sought his rhythm.

Kamal eased out of her and gently turned her onto her back. He pressed her thighs open and entered her once again. He felt her muscles tighten around him and he gave a low animal moan and thrust deep. He sought out her mouth, plunging his tongue into her warmth. He tasted her salty tears, and jerked back as if she had struck him.

"Arabella," he said. He touched his fingertips to her wet cheek and she opened her eyes. "Why are you crying?"

"Please," she whispered, "let me go. Please don't do this to me."

"I am not hurting you, *cara*, I am giving you pleasure. There is no place for your tears between us."

"I don't want you to make me feel this way." As if giving lie to her words, her hips pressed upward.

She felt his shuddering over her, felt his member throbbing deep inside her. "Arabella," he gritted, "hold still, or I will leave you, and I have no wish to." She turned her face away, wondering blankly how she could cry at the same time her body was demanding that he not leave her.

She felt his lips caress the line of her jaw. "I am doing nothing to you but what you wish," he said softly. "I will leave you if you do not want me."

She swallowed a salty tear. "I don't want you. I hate you . . . I hate myself."

In the next instant her body was cold and bare to the cool dawn air. She felt bereft, alone and empty. She jerked upright and stared at him. He was lying on his back, his arms pillowing his head. He was magnificent, she thought, her eyes wandering down his powerful body. She wanted to weave her fingers in the tight blond curls on his chest. She drew a deep breath, and scrambled to the edge of the thick furs.

"We will talk," he said quietly. He could see her trying to gain control of herself. She clutched at the cover and drew it over her. She could feel the churning desire deep within her belly and wanted to scream at him for making her lose herself to him. She kept her eyes lowered, unwilling to look at him. He knew he had won, knew that she wanted him, yet he had left her, alone and vulnerable, her body aching. He had merely been toying with her, demonstrating his mastery over her.

Arabella drew a deep, shuddering breath. "You are cruel," she said at last.

Kamal's thick brows drew together. "You would accuse me of forcing you again?" he said in a coldly mocking voice.

"No," she said slowly, her fingers fretting with the wool cover, "but you delight in making me forget who I am and what I am. You make me hate myself for being so . . ."

"Passionate?"

She quivered at the stark word, then drew herself up. "Why have you brought me here?"

"There are naught but unhappy memories for you at my palace. I wanted to show you some of my country, make you understand . . ." He broke off, unwilling to lie, and unwilling to tell her that he wanted her to love him, to care for him as he did for her. "I want you to know me as some man other than the Bey of Oran. Alessandro, perhaps."

"It does not matter what you call yourself," she said, forcing the final words from her throat. "The man Alessandro does not own people. He does not own women." She dashed her palm across her eyes, an oddly childish gesture. "You still keep me your prisoner; you still plan to harm my parents. I hate you and I will do everything in my power to escape you. I will not be one of your pliant women to loll at your feet and seek your favors."

He felt his belly churn in frustrated anger. "It is just as well that you no longer seek my favor, my lady. You are no longer a virgin and your value is greatly diminished. Your lovely body is mine for the taking, without any false bargaining."

"You savage!" She flung herself at him, her fists flailing at his chest. He caught her easily, drawing her arms above her head. He slammed a leg over hers, holding her immobile. "You can spit at me all you want, my lady, but within a remarkably short time, you know I could have you begging me to take you."

"That is a lie!"

"Is it? What a pity that you are so inexperienced, unlike my other women. They, at least, know how to pleasure a man; they are not selfish in their passion, as are you. They are not ignorant little girls."

Humiliation at his cruel words washed over her, leaving her shaking with fury. "I hate you!" she yelled. She struggled impotently against him.

"You are becoming boring in your conversations, Arabella," he said, mocking her.

She slipped one hand free and struck him as hard as she could on the jaw.

He grunted more in surprise than in pain, grabbed her arm, and slammed his body down on top of her. Still she struggled, her body heaving and writhing beneath him. Finally, exhausted, she stilled. He clasped her wrists in one hand over her head and gently caressed her face with his other hand. "You cannot win, Arabella. Do not fight me. Give me your . . . loyalty."

She felt his manhood huge and hot against her belly, and she closed her eyes tightly against his intent gaze. "I will give you nothing but my hatred," she whispered, gritting her teeth.

She heard his hissing breath. "Then let me give you a true reason for your hatred," he snarled. He reared up, pulling her thighs apart, and plunged into her unwilling body. He did not touch her, ignored her pounding fists and her cries of rage and pain. He grasped her hips and drew her upward to impale her completely. Still it was not punishment enough. He captured her legs and drew them over his shoulders and rose to his knees. He knew he was hurting her, but even as he wanted to hurl himself away from her and beg her forgiveness, he heard her crying her hatred of him. She screamed when he thrust brutally. He spilled his seed into her, then jerked out of her as if he could not bear to touch her.

She didn't cry; she was beyond tears. Her body burned. Slowly, painfully, she drew her knees up and buried her face in her arms. She felt degraded, used. Suddenly she started shivering from a cold that came from deep inside her. She did not look at Kamal; she rose painfully and began to pull on her men's clothes.

"You will not escape me again, Arabella," his cold voice said behind her. "I told you, you cannot win against me."

She ignored him. She looked at the boots but knew that she could not bear to pull them on. She straightened and looked down at him. "I am leaving, Kamal," she said.

"My men will stop you before you take one step beyond this tent."

"I owe you nothing now, Kamal," she said in an emotionless voice.

She heard his taunting laugh. She pulled the burnoose about her, raising the hood over her hair and fastening the corded leather about her head. Slowly she turned to face him. "I bid you farewell."

"Come back to bed, Arabella. It is only dawn. Do not make me have to come after you. If I do, I will tie you down."

"You can go to hell," she said in a very precise voice. She whirled about and kicked the brazier of live coals against the tent flap. Flames billowed up in an instant.

Arabella dived through the opening, a scream on her lips as she breathed in the cold morning air.

"Quickly!" she yelled. "The master is within! There is fire!"

In an instant the small camp was in confusion. The men rushed toward the tent, none of them paying her the least attention. He would be all right, she told herself, looking back over her shoulder at the burning tent.

She chose Kamal's stallion, Timar, and jabbed the bridle bit into his mouth. She grasped his flowing mane and swung up onto his broad back. She forced the stallion to plunge at the other horses, and soon all of them were running wildly away from the camp. But she couldn't help herself, and looked back to see Kamal standing in front of the tent, staring after her.

26

Arabella pushed
Timar until his coat was glistening with sweat.
They were deep in the hills now, going north, she
prayed, toward the sea. She drew Timar to a halt
on a rocky rise and stared back. Nothing. No one.
I am free, she thought, flinging her head back. I
am free! *And Kamal is unharmed*.

"Stop it", she hissed aloud at herself. She leaned
forward and patted Timar's thick neck. She smiled
suddenly, picturing how she must appear: barefoot,
dressed like a man, scraggly tendrils of hair fram-
ing her face, and smelly as the stallion.

The sun was high overhead now, and there was
no water in sight. There were scrubby trees about,
and patches of wildflowers and shrubs. Surely, she
thought, there must be water somewhere. It was
not, after all, the desert. She refused to dwell on
the fact that she had no food and no weapon. I will
reach the sea before nightfall, she told herself over
and over, as if reciting a litany. She click-clicked

Timar forward, higher into the hills. The land was savagely beautiful, the air fresh and cool. She heard animals but saw none.

She drew Timar up at the edge of a boulder-edged cliff and stared down into the narrow valley below. It was barren and looked bone dry, and there was no path downward. She stared about her with mounting frustration. North was straight ahead, a sheer drop to the valley below. She turned the stallion east.

The trees became thicker, the ground softer, but still she saw no water. Timar was heaving and she forgot her own swollen tongue at the stallion's plight. She slid off his back and tethered him to a skinny-branched tree. She sank down to the ground, leaned back against the trunk, and closed her eyes. The land is as savage as its people, she thought, and I will die here, alone.

Don't be a coward! She forced her eyes upward and saw that the sun was slanting westward. Were there wild animals? She shivered, remembering the strange animal sounds she had heard throughout the long day. She closed her eyes and pressed her face against her arms. She saw Kamal standing in front of the burning tent, dressed only in his white trousers, looking after her as his men raced after the horses. She had been too far distant to see the expression on his face. Was it anger? Contempt? She shook her head and struggled to her feet. What did it matter what he thought? She felt a wave of dizziness from hunger.

Suddenly all thoughts of food and water fled her

mind. There came a loud roar through the trees. Lions roared, she realized stupidly, and lions ate people! Timar snorted and pulled against his tethered reins, his eyes rolling in fear.

"Kamal . . ." Arabella started at the sound of her own voice, raspy from thirst, saying his name. She knew she could not survive in this brutal country. Life suddenly seemed very precious, and at the nearing roar of the lion, very fragile.

"We are going back," she said, and swung up on Timar's back. She could feel the stallion quivering in fear and she gave him his head, letting him set his own pace back from whence they had come.

For an instant Arabella couldn't believe her eyes. She blinked, but the small pool of water was still there. There were animal tracks around its edges, so the water must be safe. She slipped off Timar's back and led him to the water. She waited until he had drunk his fill, then fell on her knees to cup the cool water in her hands. She splashed the water over her face, reveling in the taste and feel of it. Finally she rose and looked around her. There were clumps of bushes around the pool, and behind her, harsh barren rocks, lying loose, as if broken off from the sheer cliff above them. She thought briefly of spending the night there, but her belly growled in protest. There was still light, perhaps several more hours. Time to reach Kamal. She was starting toward Timar when the lion's roar seemed to reverberate off the rocks. The stallion reared in fright, tossing his great head. "No!" Arabella screamed, but she was too late. Timar wheeled about and broke into a mad gallop away from her. She saw a shadow of movement toward the rocks. She stared, paralyzed, at the huge lion poised atop a flat boulder. It was a female, she thought vaguely, and the females did the killing for the males. Slowly she began to back away in the direction Timar had fled. The lion snorted and tossed her head. Arabella broke into a run, but fear made her look back. The lion seemed a statue; then suddenly it launched into the air. She screamed as her bare foot struck a rock, and crumpled to the ground, her eyes closed.

She heard the loud crack of a gun and a terrible screaming sound, and whirled around, knowing the beast would be on her. The lion seemed suspended in air; then it was twisting, blood spurting from its throat. It fell to the ground not three yards from Arabella, dead, a bullet through its brain. Arabella stared at the lion. Slowly she raised her head and saw Kamal, the gun still in his hands, standing silently watching her, near the edge of the pool. She ran her tongue over her suddenly dry lips. Time stood still and yet he made no move toward her. A strangled cry escaped her lips and she was running, oblivious of the sharp rocks cutting her bare feet, running until, with a cry, she launched herself at him.

Kamal threw the gun to the ground and caught her against him. She was sobbing and clutching at him as if to assure herself that it was really he. He ripped off the burnoose and stroked his hands through her filthy hair.

"Hush," he whispered against her ear. "It is all right now."

Arabella sniffed loudly and whispered against his throat. "I was coming back to you."

"I know."

"You saved me."

"Yes."

"But I stole your horse."

"I let you."

Arabella drew back, staring up at him. "I don't understand."

Kamal let loose a shrill whistle. To Arabella's surprise, Timar soon appeared behind them.

"Why?"

He pulled her against him again. "I had intended to find you much sooner, but Timar's tracks were difficult to follow through the rocks, and he could not hear my whistle. I told you, *cara*, I want us to have time together, alone."

"You don't want to . . . thrash me?"

"Perhaps, a bit. But first we must see to your needs. Are you hungry?"

"Oh yes!"

"You're dirtier than an urchin. How about a bath first?"

"I'm sorry I burned down your tent."

Kamal smiled ruefully at her. "One would think I would no longer underestimate your inventiveness. Make me a promise, sweetheart." He cupped her dirty face in his hands and lightly kissed the tip of her nose. "Promise me you will stay with me, else you will age me beyond my years."

A gentle shudder coursed through her and she nuzzled her face against his hands. "I promise."

"You've scared at least five years off me since I met you." He gave a strained chuckle. "I suppose I should be thankful you're not as dirty as you were upon your initial delivery to me." He released her, albeit unwillingly. "Why don't you bathe while we've still daylight? I'll set up camp and make us some dinner."

She nodded, feeling suddenly shy. She saw the lion from the corner of her eye and shuddered at the remembered terror. "No," he said softly, "it's all right. I'll take care of the lion."

Arabella managed a smile and walked gingerly toward the pool. She sat down at the edge and unwrapped the bandages from her bruised feet. "You are a mess, my girl," she said.

"Indeed, but the soap will help."

Kamal handed her a bar of scented soap and a clean towel, and left her.

Close to an hour later, Arabella, scrubbed clean from head to toe, appeared in the small camp, the towel wrapped securely about her, and stared. Kamal was hunkered next to a fire, turning a skewered rabbit over the flames; the horses were tethered some feet away; the lion was not in view, much to her relief, and a small tent stood close by.

At her gasp, he raised his head and smiled at her. "Did you believe me useless, Arabella?"

She shook her head and pulled the towel more tightly to her.

He rose, and she found herself suddenly shy.

She took a step back. He frowned. "Don't be afraid of me, *cara*."

"I'm not afraid of anyone," she said, stiffening.

"And don't ever lie to me. Your nose turns red." He didn't give her a chance to reply. "I've brought you some clothes and a comb for your hair. Come to the fire. After saving your beautiful hide, I don't want you to catch a chill."

He handed her a soft velvet robe with long full sleeves. "I promise not to look," he said, grinning at her.

"Did you plan all this?" she asked, taking the robe from him.

"Not precisely *this*," he said, waving his hand around the small camp. He turned his back and Arabella quickly shed the towel and pulled on the robe. She felt ill-at-ease and vulnerable. "I won't wear those ridiculous veils again."

He smiled at the challenge in her voice. "No," he said only turning to face her. "The blue velvet is lovely. Sit beside the fire and dry your hair."

He had placed wool blankets on the rocky ground. "What if it rains?" she asked, goading him, as she sat cross-legged.

"If it rains, I will lay you beneath me to keep you dry."

She flushed a dull red, and for the first time since Kamal had met her, she was silent. Then, "Where is the lion?" she asked finally, accepting some of the rabbit. "Is it not dangerous to leave the carcass close to us? Will not other animals want it?"

"I have taken care of it," Kamal said. "Have some more rabbit." He wasn't about to tell her that he had sent his men, with the lion's carcass, back to the other camp. "Why were you coming back, *cara?*"

She felt the warm flush suffuse her face, both at his endearment and at his question. "I had no water, no food, and no weapons," she said. "I am not entirely stupid."

"You execute your escapes with dash, *cara,* but once you are away, things go awry."

"I said I was not entirely stupid."

"I am sorry I forced you."

Her head jerked up at his softly spoken words. She remembered the painful thrusting, the humiliation of being at his mercy.

"You have the talent, Arabella, of bringing out the extremes in me," he continued when her silence stretched long. "Will you forgive me?"

"I . . . You hurt me."

"I know. 'Twas not well done of me."

"Not just my body, but my . . . spirit."

He gently removed the rabbit bone from between her fingers and tossed it away. She did not flinch at his nearness, and he drew a deep breath and stared toward the spitting fire. It was dark now, and the stars overhead glittered down like sparkling diamonds.

"When I was a boy," Kamal said finally, "I saw my father rape a woman he had captured on a raid. It was as if he had ceased being a man and had become a raging animal. The other men laughed and cheered my father, for the woman was Spanish, and thus an infidel and of no count. Hamil did not laugh. It was he who pulled me away. He told me that a man should not prove himself by hurting another who is weaker, even though it be but a woman. I had forgotten that incident until after I forced you. I felt like the savage you have several times accused me of being. Your bravado, *cara*," he added on a wry smile, "and your damned stubbornness made me forget."

"Do not blame me, sir, if your veneer of civilization peels off like the skin on an orange!"

He laughed. "No," he said. "In the future, when you anger me, I shall kiss you and caress you until you are soft and yielding to me. Ah, you blush again, Arabella. It pleases me that no other man will ever know the depths of your passion, and rest assured that I shall never let you forget it!"

The future. She realized suddenly that she wanted a future with this man, and she felt her mind shy away from all the reasons why it could not be so. Instead she said, "It is so beautiful here. Savage and untamed. I felt so alone and frightened all day."

"And now?"

She drew a deep breath. "Now," she said, smiling, "I feel safe and warm and . . . well-fed."

Kamal looked about their primitive camp with a rueful grin. "You are easy to please, *cara*. I must remember that."

She knew she should ask him what he now intended, but she did not want to sever the bond between them. There would be time enough tomorrow. "I have known you but a week," she said.

"Surely it has been at least a year," he said, gently mocking her. He eased down beside her, stretching his long legs toward the fire. "Life here is different," he said after a moment. "It has been difficult for me to adjust, even though I spent my childhood years trained as a Muslim."

"Lella told me that you lived in Europe. I do not understand."

"You forget that my mother is Italian, Arabella. She wanted her son to be educated in Italy, and Hamil, my elder half-brother, helped her to convince my father. I spent ten years in Rome and Florence. In that, *cara*, we are lucky."

"What do you mean?"

He did not reply immediately, but rather rose and fetched a thick wool blanket from the tent. He spread it out beside the fire, then sat down cross-legged. "Will you bring your blanket and join me? It is getting cooler and we should share our warmth."

Arabella eased down beside him, her profile to him. Her hair was dry now and flowed down her back in a cascade of soft honey. She felt him staring at her and quickly turned to face him. "You did not answer my question, Kamal."

He lifted his hand and began wrapping a thick tress of her hair around his hand. "When my mother first told me of the treachery of your parents—no, do not interrupt me as yet—I asked her if there were children. I told her that you and your brother were innocent of any wrong and should not be harmed. When I first realized who you were, it was my intention to treat you as an English lady." He gently touched his fingertips to her chin and brought her about to face him. "But you were so damned insulting, and there was, of course, my mother's letter claiming you were nothing better than a whore. I suppose I thought a young lady who had undergone what you had should be fainting or crumpling in hysterics, or pleading with me. To hear myself cursed as a savage, a barbarian, and an animal . . . well, as I said before, *cara*, you provoke me to extremes."

Arabella frowned at him a moment. "I have never fainted or succumbed to hysterics in my life."

He wrapped her hair about his fist, drawing her closer. He lightly kissed her lips. "I have always admired strength and courage, but I never expected to find such traits in a woman. Nor," he added softly, "did I expect such passion."

She flushed slightly, but did not move away from him. "Nor did I," she said, and he laughed softly at her honesty. "Did you know many European women?"

"Yes, certainly. Italy was my home for ten years. I grew to manhood there, with many ladies willing to instruct me in pleasurable pastimes. Understand, Arabella, when I returned to Oran to assume my half-brother's duties, I had to conform to what was expected by my people and the Dey of Algiers."

"Lella said that. She also told me that she did not believe you were happy here."

"All of us do what we must. There has been much between us, Arabella, yet not enough. It was my intention to humiliate you, you know."

She cocked her head in question. "Which time?"

"The afternoon I ordered you whipped. I had no choice, yet I knew I was the one to blame, not Elena, who has the unbridled passions of a child, and certainly not you. You bore my venom longer than I would have, had I been you." He smiled slightly. "Of course, your well-placed blow to my manhood was a painful reminder of your anger for several hours."

"You make me sound like some sort of Amazon, with nerves of iron. 'Tis not true, Kamal. I had not the courage to accept my own death to save my parents. When I attacked you with the dagger, my hand wavered. Your death would have meant mine, and I was too afraid to accept it. Even today, I realized I did not want to die, that life was too precious. I am very much a coward."

"No, *cara*, you are not a coward. You are vibrant and full of life; 'twould be cowardly to force your own death. You will not be scarred," he added, touching his fingertips lightly to her back.

"You stayed with me, did you not?"

He looked at her full in her face and gently traced his fingertips over her arched brows. "Yes," he said, "I stayed with you until you were fully aware. I left you, fearing that your hatred of me would make you more ill. I have found that I cannot bear to be away from you. When the guard was discovered last night and I realized what you had done, I knew such fear for you that I wanted to howl my anger at myself." He watched her thick dark lashes sweep downward to hide her expression from him. Slowly he leaned forward and kissed her soft mouth, a gentle kiss, undemanding. He felt her start of surprise; then her lips parted. He allowed himself the deep pleasure of her mouth, then drew back. He saw disappointment in her dark eyes and smiled.

"No, *cara*. I hurt you and you are still likely sore. I do not want to cause you any more pain."

"It is the oddest thing," Arabella said, her voice sounding husky to her own ears, "but when you touch me and kiss me, I want nothing more than for you to continue. And you always know just what to do."

"Just the sound of your voice makes me want to love you, to make you cry out with pleasure."

"But I don't know what to do! You must be disappointed in me."

"Arabella," he said firmly, pulling away from her, "I do not wish to discuss this anymore. I am not made of stone."

"Then why did you kiss me?" she demanded, staring him down.

"Because you are here and you are beautiful and I love you."

His words fell between them like a sharp clap of thunder. Arabella's breath caught in her throat and she could only gaze at him. She was aware that her heart was pumping furiously, and she swallowed convulsively. "Oh," she said.

Kamal rose gracefully to his feet, his face averted. Damn you for a fool, he cursed himself. But the words had slipped out. He said abruptly, "It is late and you must be tired from your busy day. Come, let us sleep."

But sleep was the furthest thing from Arabella's mind. She watched him stride to the small tent and pull back the flap, his harsh-toned words still echoing in her mind. She sprinkled sand on the dying fire, picked up the blankets and walked slowly to the small tent. It was dark within. "Kamal . . ."

"Yes?"

"I brought the blankets."

"Good. It gets cold in the hills. We will need them."

She stood quietly for a long moment, her eyes adjusting to the dark. She could make out his outline; he was lying on his back, his head pillowed on his arms. Time seemed to slow. She was aware only of him, his flat, emotionless voice, and of her pounding heart. He was trying to protect her, she knew, from herself and from his feelings, feelings he believed exclusive to him.

"Kamal?"

"Yes?" He sounded impatient with her, almost angry.

"I would rather have you than the blanket."

Why was she pushing him, damn her! He jerked himself up on his elbow, wishing he could see her face clearly. "I would suggest that you lie down and go to sleep."

"Very well." She eased down close to him, but not touching. She pulled the blanket over her. He could hear her breathing, and he forced himself to turn on his side, away from her. Then she spoke again. "Do you really love me?"

"No, dammit! I tell all my women that—it is what they want to hear!"

There was absolute silence. A muscle jumped in his jaw at the sound of her broken sobbing.

"By Allah," he grated, "do you wish to strip all honor from me?"

"No," she whispered, her voice liquid with her tears.

"Stop crying!"

"I . . . I can't."

"You claimed you never fainted or became hysterical!"

"I am not hysterical," she cried, sobbing louder.

He cursed fluently in Arabic and drew her roughly against him. "Hush. Please, *cara*. I cannot bear to hear you cry." He did not immediately realize that he was stroking her hair, placing light kisses on her temple. She turned her head and his kisses fell on her cheek and her mouth. He tasted her salty tears. "No, love," he murmured into her mouth, his hands stroking down her back, "do not cry."

"All right," Arabella said, sniffing. He smiled into the darkness, then fell tautly silent as she touched her fingers to his face, gently caressing the line of his jaw. "Please, Kamal, love me."

"I don't want to hurt you!"

"I am hurting now."

It seemed perfectly natural for him to slip his hand inside the robe and stroke her breasts. She arched up against him and pulled his head down. The touch of her soft lips and her tautening nipples made him frantic with need for her.

"Tell me what to do. I want to please you as you do me."

"To feel you moving against me, to hear you moan, to taste you is the greatest pleasure you can give."

She didn't believe him, and to prove it, she slipped her hand between them and stroked down his belly. She felt him suck in his breath, and she smiled into the darkness. "You are not naked," she whispered, her fingers fiddling with the buttons on his trousers. He gave a harsh groan and quickly shed them. When he drew her to him again, he thought he would burst with desire. She was as naked as he and so softly warm that he trembled. "Can I touch you as you do me? Would that give you pleasure?"

"Yes," he said.

"I love your body. You are so different from me."

"Thank God and Allah." He forgot his attempt at humor when he felt her fingers touch him, tentatively at first; then, as she felt his enthusiastic response, her hand closed about him, lightly caressing him. He moaned softly and thrust his hips forward. He clasped her hand and pulled her away from him.

"I will leave you if you continue."

"Ah," said Arabella wisely. "I do not want that."

He laughed and pulled her against him, pressing her legs apart with his thigh. "Do you not, my lady?"

He felt her trust in the absolute giving of herself to him. He rubbed his cheek for a moment against her taut nipple, watching his hand lie in the valley of her belly.

"Please kiss me," she said.

He raised his head. "Where, *cara*?" He could feel her flushing and added on a chuckle, "Is your nose turning red?"

"I like you to kiss me . . . everywhere."

"In this, Arabella, we will never be in disagreement."

His mouth tantalized her, creating a rhythm that made her want to cry out in frenzy as the pulsing warmth grew and raged in her belly.

"You are so responsive, Arabella, so giving and open to me."

"Please, Kamal," she moaned. Her fingers clutched at his hair, urging him.

"Yes," he said.

She cried out, feeling her mind filled with naught but him and the pleasure he was giving her. Her body shattered and she was hurled beyond herself, yet bound to him, soaring, her gasping cries filling the silence.

They lay locked together, kissing each other softly, languidly.

"Arabella?" The sound of his voice brought her back to reality, and she nuzzled her mouth against his throat. "Did you mean what you said?" he asked.

"Yes."

His body tightened a moment; then she could see the outline of his smile. "Do you remember what you said?"

"I want you . . . deeper."

He squeezed her ribs until she yelped.

"I love you," she whispered. At her simple words, she felt a great weight slip from her mind. "I love you."

He clasped his arms around her and rolled onto his back, bringing her on top of him. "I will never let you forget it, madam," he said, and kissed her.

"Kamal," she said after he allowed her to catch her breath, "why do you love me?"

"Because you're a witch and have cast a spell on me."

She was silent for a long moment. Finally she said tightly, "I do not think I am always a nice person."

"True. But you are also never boring."

"Oh!" She moved over him sensuously and was delighted to feel him growing hard yet again against her belly. "I will make you suffer, sir, if you do not tell me the truth!"

His hands roved through her hair and downward to caress her hips. "Because you're so damned honest," he said at last. "And so loyal."

Arabella buried her face in his throat. "What are we going to do?" she whispered, and he heard her voice break.

"We will talk about it in the morning," he said firmly, and gently continued to stroke her back.

Kamal poked a piece of pita bread into Arabella's smiling mouth and lightly kissed the tip of her nose.

"It's stale!"

"If you, *cara*, would let me out of your arms long enough, I could do some hunting."

Arabella sighed, her brow furrowed in deep thought. "No," she said at last, "I would rather be hungry for food than for you."

"Shameless hussy. You will kill me before I am thirty."

She gave him a wide, smug smile. "I am a woman now," she said, immensely pleased with herself. "I am twenty, you know, Kamal. I was beginning to think that I was cold, that I would never find a man who would make me feel such . . . marvelous feelings."

Kamal leaned over and began to nibble her throat.

"That is not marvelous," she giggled, "but 'tis a

beginning!" She threw her arms about him, knocking him off balance, and they fell together, Arabella sprawled on top of him. She moved over him sensuously, reveling in the taut hardness of his body beneath her.

"How could you ever have believed yourself cold?"

Arabella raised her head from his shoulder. "Well, there was only one gentleman who kissed me, and I didn't like it at all. In fact, I kicked him in the shin."

"I would have preferred the shin to where you kicked me!"

Her lashes swept downward, hiding her eyes. "I am sorry. I was so afraid, and you made me so angry."

He gently stroked her thick hair from her face, winding long tendrils about her small ears. "Arabella, will you give me your loyalty?"

She tensed at his deadly serious tone, unable to answer him. She pictured her parents, Adam, and Kamal's mother. "How can I?" she cried, trying to pull away from him.

He held her tightly. "I will not let you go, so stop fighting me." She stilled, but he knew that the outside world had finally intruded, and it must be dealt with. "I will do nothing to harm you, Arabella. Do you believe that?"

"But if you harm my parents, you harm me!"

"I know. Will you trust me to put a stop to all the madness?"

"Do you now believe my parents are innocent?"

His hands tightened a moment about her back, then resumed their gentle caressing. "If I believe them innocent, I condemn my mother as a vicious liar." He sighed deeply wishing they could ignore, at least for another day and night, the reality that awaited them. He kissed her passionlessly, and set her away from him. He felt the fatalism that was inbred in his culture, beginning to seep into his mind, paralyzing him. "Dammit!" he said, pounding his fist against his open palm. He rose swiftly to his feet and gazed down at Arabella. He saw uncertainty and fear in her wide eyes. Instantly he dropped to his haunches and drew her against him. "I love you, and I want to be with you forever. It will be so, Arabella, I promise you."

Would wanting something to be true make it so? Arabella wondered, snuggling against him.

By tacit agreement, they did not discuss the future for the remainder of the day. Kamal hunted, bringing back a rabbit for their dinner. They bathed together in the small clear pool, their enjoyment in each other taking on a nearly frantic quality. When they lay together that night in the tent, sated and languid, Kamal whispered against her temple, "You are giving and open to me."

"Yes," she said softly. "How else should I be when you wrap me in sunshine?"

"A witch poet," he said. He pulled her robe away from her and lightly rested his palm on her flat stomach. He splayed his fingers and touched her pelvic bones. He felt a jolt of fear, picturing her belly swollen with child. She seemed so narrow. "Are you built like your mother?"

His middle fingers were so close to touching her where she had begun to ache, that for a moment she could not make sense of his question.

"Are you?" he repeated.

"Yes, I suppose so."

"Did she have difficulty birthing you or your brother?"

"I remember, long ago, hearing my old nurse, Becky, talking to my mother about being lucky in her husband. She said that he had stayed with her and helped her birth my brother. Why do you ask?" His fingers were absently tangling in her hair.

"I don't want to hurt you," Kamal said.

"You are hurting me now," Arabella said, pulling him closer to her.

He smiled reluctantly, drawn from his frightening thoughts. "Do you know," he said, watching her eyes, "that I was trained in the art of lovemaking?"

"You were . . . wh-what?" she stammered, blinking up at him.

"At the ripe old age of thirteen, an old woman, probably about your age, *cara*, introduced me to the marvels of my body and a woman's body." His fingers lightly touched her. "Here," he continued in a soft voice, "she taught me was a woman's essence. Here is softness, warmth, and a woman's release. She taught me how to stroke and caress both with my fingers and my mouth, to control my own desire until the woman had reached her climax."

Arabella was mesmerized by his words. "But that seems so . . . calculated," she gasped.

"*Then* it was, I suppose," he continued, a smile of satisfaction on his face at the convulsive movement of her hips against his fingers. "She observed me with other women to ensure that I followed her instructions. It was a bit unnerving. I remember one young girl who liked me, and probably felt sorry for me. In any case, she began moaning and carrying on before I scarce had a chance to begin. I thought myself the most brilliant lover in the land. Ada, my teacher, on the other hand, nearly fell over a chair laughing. Yes, most unnerving for a thirteen-year-old boy."

"If you ever, for the rest of your life, touch another woman," she said, clutching his upper arms, "I will not . . . ahh . . . be responsible for . . . oh God . . . my actions!"

She heard him laugh as the nearly painful sensations mounted, driving her into rippling spasms of pleasure. She was still trembling, her heart pounding erratically, when he gently entered her, and covered her with his body. "I love you," he said, and began to thrust slowly in and out of her, teasing her, caressing her again until she was throbbing with need.

She could only moan, clutching him to her with all her strength. In those moments, there was nothing save them, their world bounded by sensation and their love for each other.

Arabella whispered, "I do not hear your teacher laughing."

"Master!"

Kamal grinned at Ali, giving him a jaunty salute before he helped Arabella dismount.

She stood beside the stallion for a moment, staring about the camp. All signs of the burned tent had been obliterated, for which she was thankful, and another had been erected. She saw the lion skin, and shot Kamal a questioning look beneath lowered brows, but he was speaking to one of his men and did not notice.

It was close to noon, and Arabella, her stomach growling, was relieved to see food spread upon a cloth near the small fire. She was again wearing her men's clothes and thus sat cross-legged near the food and began to munch on an orange, enjoying the sweet taste.

"Here are lamb and bread," Ali said, handing her a plate.

Arabella thanked him solemnly, then gave him a dimpled smile.

Ali wondered at this woman with her golden hair and her spirit that made him shudder. A woman should not behave as this one did, but his master loved her. Ali had seen it in his eyes.

"You will marry the master?" he asked, squatting down beside her.

"Yes," Arabella said without hesitation.

"You have driven my master nearly wild," he said. "It is good that he has finally tamed you."

Arabella ceased chewing on the tasty lamb and cocked a dark brow. "Tamed?" she asked carefully, an inexplicable frisson making her shiver.

Ali shrugged. "He is the master and he will have what he wishes. I am pleased that Elena will not be his first wife. She is a bitch, that one. I suppose if a man wishes spirited sons, he must breed them off a spirited woman."

The lamb fell unheeded to Arabella's plate. The world was intruding. She felt a rush of nausea and swallowed convulsively. "First wife," she repeated stupidly, feeling numb and cold despite the warm sun beating down. "Breed? That sounds like two animals!"

Ali regarded her with some surprise. "It is our way," he explained as if to a dull child. "Women are made to breed and birth men's sons. Allah knows that a man cannot be happy with but one wife. The master, after he satisfies himself with you, will doubtless take three more wives. He will want many sons to follow after him."

Arabella lurched to her feet, the food from her plate splattering to the ground. She looked wildly around her, wanting only to hide and bear her pain in private. Fool! Kamal's first wife! She laughed aloud, shocked at the raw agony of the sound.

"Arabella?"

It was Kamal. The master. The man who had tamed her. The man who wanted her for his first wife.

She turned distraught eyes toward him and slowly began to back away from him. "I will not do it!"

she shrieked at him. "I will not be but one of your women, Kamal! May the devil take all of you savages!"

Kamal stared at her, stunned. He started toward her, only to draw up at the shouts from his men. He whirled about to see swirls of dust in the distance, heralding the coming of a number of men. There were no hostile tribes this close to Oran, but he would take no chances. "Arabella, get into the tent and stay there! Now!"

Arabella felt her blood curdle with fear. Robbers? More men like Risan? There were only a half-dozen men here with them. Many more were riding toward them, possibly twenty. She looked toward Kamal, watching him numbly as he caught a wickedly curved scimitar from one of his men and pulled his dagger from his belt. Did he expect her to hide, to watch him die? Kamal shouted at her again, waving the deadly scimitar toward the tent.

She needed a weapon, anything. She dashed into the tent, frantically searching. She found a dagger lying on a pile of furs. She heard the shouts of men now, nearly at the camp. She pulled back the tent flap and gazed out. Kamal and his few men stood together, but the riders were spreading out, surrounding them. Three men were riding directly toward Kamal, their faces swathed in *kufiyahs*.

She stole up to stand directly behind Kamal, unaware that her hair was unbound and streaming down her back. Suddenly one of the men shouted and pointed at her. She felt her blood freeze.

Kamal whipped about and their eyes locked for a long moment.

"No," Arabella said, moving closer to him. "If we die, it will be together."

To her absolute astonishment, the man shouted again, and it was her name that rang out.

"Arabella!"

Her dagger clattered to the ground. "Adam! Kamal, 'tis my brother, Adam!"

She ran forward before Kamal could stop her. The three men pulled their steaming horses to a halt, whipping up clouds of dust. Adam leapt from his horse and caught her to him.

"My God! Are you all right?" His eyes were examining her anxiously as he awaited her answer. Arabella was laughing and hugging him, oblivious of the men who stood stock-still about them.

"Oh yes, Adam, I am in fine fettle! How are you here? Come, you must meet Kamal."

Adam pulled off his *kufiyah*, stared down at his beautiful sister, and threw back his head in deep laughter. "You amaze me, Bella. I should have known that you would be anything but dead or abused."

Kamal looked at the handsome black-haired man who was Arabella's brother. He knows her as well as I do, he thought, and he understands her. Slowly he walked toward them.

"Kamal."

He stopped abruptly, and turned very slowly

toward the man astride a huge black stallion. He felt gooseflesh rise on his arms.

The man gracefully dismounted and stood a moment watching him.

"Have you no greeting for your brother?" Hamil slowly pulled off his *kufiyah*, his eyes on his brother's face.

Arabella turned in Adam's arms to watch the two men staring at each other. "His half-brother Hamil?" she whispered.

"Aye," Adam said. "He is my friend."

Slowly, the shock fading from Kamal's mind, he smiled at his half-brother and said, "You have a son. Now he is no longer *my* heir."

Hamil had pictured this meeting many times in his mind. Kamal's first words dissolved his final niggling doubts. He gave a great shout and held out his arms. The brothers embraced, slapping each other on the back, talking at the same time.

They fell apart and studied each other.

"I see that death has painted your hair with a streak of silver, Hamil. I imagine it was not my prayers that saved you, but rather your own stubbornness."

"And you, brother—have you bankrupted my coffers?"

"You have returned just in time to prevent me from doing so!"

"Lella. She is well?"

"Well, but terribly sad. Your son is beautiful, Hamil."

"Life," Hamil said with a great heaving breath,

"is most odd. You see, I have brought the woman's brother to take her off your hands. He assured me that no man could intimidate her. She is a hellion and too proud to be but a woman."

"That," Kamal said, turning to smile at Arabella, "is true. Come, my brother, and pay attention to my . . . future wife."

"Wife! By God, little brother, you have the woman eating out of your hands in a mere week?"

Arabella, hearing Hamil's words, did not stiffen; rather she smiled widely. "Adam," she said, "what did you tell Hamil?"

"Only the truth, Bella, only the truth. What is this Kamal said about a wife?"

"I want to meet Hamil," Arabella said, all possibilities now clear to her. Kamal would no longer be ruler of Oran. He was free. But what if he did not want to leave? She shook herself. Her life had taken so many bizarre turns in the past week that one more made her thoughts dance about in confusion.

"Lady Arabella, I believe," Hamil said, studying her beautiful face. There was a dirt smudge on her cheek and her men's clothes were wrinkled, too big, and somewhat the worse for wear.

She met his gaze unflinchingly. "I have heard much of you from Kamal. You look very fierce."

Hamil shook his head, a smile hovering around his mouth. "Your servant, my lady," he said, and bowed before her. It was only then that he became aware of the murmur of voices from Kamal's men. He turned and raised his hand. "I am returned to the land of my father," he said. "We will rejoice together before we return to Oran."

"Kamal," Arabella said, tugging at his sleeve, "this is my brother, Adam. He looks fierce also."

The two young men eyed each other. Adam said carefully to his sister, "You wish to wed with this man, Bella?"

"Certainly," Arabella said, tilting her chin upward. "You would too, Adam, if you were a woman."

"Perhaps not, *cara*," Kamal said with a twisted smile. "I think that you are blind, thankfully so."

Adam looked into his sister's eyes and realized that she was no longer the same girl he had known in Naples. She had changed; she was a woman. What the hell, he thought, would his father do? He cleared his throat. "I have another surprise for you, Bella." He turned and waved to a small figure astride a horse. "Come here, Rayna."

"Rayna!" Arabella gasped, and began to laugh. "Oh, Kamal, my brother has finally met his match! Rayna, my shy Rayna!"

"Ha!" Adam said. "She has been nothing but trouble since I met her. She stowed on board with me to come and save you, little sister."

The two girls clasped each other, each laughing and crying while the men watched them with amused tolerance.

"Women," Hamil said, shaking his head.

Rayna, like Arabella, was dressed in men's clothes. "I was so scared for you, Bella," Rayna said, stroking her friend's arms. "Adam kept telling me that you would be all right."

"And you, Rayna, you left your father's house?"

"Yes. I fear he will be furious with me." She did not sound at all concerned and Arabella shook her head in wonderment.

Hamil turned to his brother. "We must talk, Kamal. There is much I have to tell you and much that must be decided."

Kamal nodded and motioned toward a clump of oleanders some feet away. He heard the girl Rayna say to Arabella, "He looks like a Viking, Bella! So handsome!"

"That is not all," Arabella said, smiling wickedly.

"The woman, Lady Arabella," Hamil said thoughtfully as they walked together, "you truly wish to have her?"

"Yes," Kamal said. "And you, brother, have now given her to me?"

Hamil nodded. They would speak more about it later. But now . . .

They sat cross-legged beneath a skinny-branched oleander.

"Tell me what happened, Hamil," Kamal said quietly.

He listened to his half-brother speak calmly of the storm, of the men who tried to murder him, of Antonio and Ria and his months on Sardinia. "When I was strong enough, I made my way to Cagliari. I discovered that you had returned to Algiers and taken my place." He paused a moment, staring toward the men who were now staking the horses and enlarging the camp. "I did not want to believe that you, my brother, had been the one who betrayed me. It took me but a month to discover who the . . . person was."

Kamal became very still. Slowly, pain and inevitability heavy in his voice, he said, "My mother."

"Yes. I am saddened."

"She will probably return to Oran shortly." He paused a moment. "My mother sent me Arabella."

Hamil nodded. "Lord St. Ives, Adam Welles, has told me much. I fear, Kamal, that your mother has created a fabric of lies that we may never entirely unravel."

"Why? Why, Hamil, did she do this?"

Hamil heard the suffering in his brother's voice, and sought to excuse her, for Kamal's sake. "She knew great bitterness in my father's harem. Her mind is not like a Muslim woman's. She must have hated her imprisonment and our father."

"And the Earl of Clare? Is he the villain she has painted to me?"

"Tell me what she told you. It is a piece of the puzzle Adam Welles could not provide." Hamil listened intently, then said quietly, "Her disappointment twisted her. I do not know how she came to my father. I was but a small boy then and was not in his confidence. But the Earl of Clare . . ." He paused a moment, then said quickly, "He is a man, not a coward. Were he to kill, he would do it outright, not skulk about on his belly, weaving vicious plots. I suppose there is much of him in his son, Adam, and he is an honorable man."

"It is the same with his daughter."

"Have you taken her to your bed?"

"Yes, and I will take her to wive. She is bright as the sun, as proud as an untamed gazelle, and loyal. Shall I tell you what she has done to me since I met her but a week ago?"

When the brothers returned to the camp, Hamil was still grinning over Arabella's actions. "Her brother, Adam," Hamil said, "has likewise been taken by a slip of a girl. The earl will be greeted by a double surprise."

"Yes," Kamal said, wondering what now awaited him, "he will indeed."

"I believe, Kamal, that I am content with my Lella and . . . my son."

28

Arabella gazed at Hamil intently for a moment, then asked, "Why did you not return directly to the palace when you arrived in Oran?"

A woman without a veil, a woman who looked a man straight in the eyes. Like Ria, Hamil thought, and smiled. "I had to know if Kamal had anything to do with my betrayal. One of my men discovered he had left the city with you. I was relieved, for I wanted to speak to him privately."

"That is reasonable," Arabella said, and Hamil, who wouldn't have thought to ask a woman if she agreed with him or not, shook his head, bemused. She turned slightly in her saddle and smiled toward Rayna, who was in shy conversation with Kamal. "Kamal is hurt," she continued. "I knew that his mother was a . . . well, not a very nice person, but how could I expect him to believe me? You know, it is odd. Even though she drugged me and had me sent here, there were times when I thought she actually liked me."

Hamil, who hadn't the vaguest idea of how to deal with Kamal's mother, merely nodded. He had found himself hoping that she would have heard he was not dead, and disappeared.

"Lella loves you," Arabella said unexpectedly, jerking Hamil from his twisting thoughts. "And she was my friend. You are very lucky, Hamil."

"Yes," he said, "I am."

"Do you have . . . other wives?"

"Yes, one other, but she died in childbirth. Lella is my only wife now."

"But you keep many women in your harem, and use them, all in front of Lella."

Hamil strove for patience. "It is our way," he said. At her look of disapproval, he said sharply, "Men have needs that one woman cannot—"

"Bosh! That is ridiculous!" She turned sharply in her saddle and glared at him, Hamil- El-Mokrani, the Bey of Oran. "How can a man ever justify hurting his wife by taking other women to his bed, especially when his wife loves him with all her heart? It is cruel and selfish."

"Lella," he said stiffly, "understands and accepts what she is. She is not outspoken and rude like European women."

"I do not understand," Arabella said, cocking a brow at him, "why it is that Lella, your wife, cannot also have a harem filled with handsome young men. After all"—she shrugged elaborately—

"women do have needs, you know, and you are but one man."

Hamil stared at her. The thought of Lella in another man's arms made him nearly blind with rage.

"Do not be angry with me," Arabella said kindly, reaching over and patting his sleeve. "Kamal told me once that most Muslim men would throw me to the dogs for my sharp tongue. But," she added seriously, "if I were a man, and lucky enough to have Lella, I shouldn't want anyone else."

"You, my lady," Hamil said, "will drive my brother insane!"

"Oh no," Arabella said sweetly, "Kamal does not need to prove his manhood by flaunting dozens of other women in front of my nose."

"Kamal!" Hamil shouted over his shoulder. "Come and remove this woman before I am forced to teach her manners!"

Arabella laughed gaily. "If by manners you mean blank submission, I doubt that even you could succeed, Hamil! Poor Lella!" Hamil heard her bright laughter as she wheeled her horse about to join Kamal. Outrageous female, he thought, shaking his head. A woman with a harem! But the thought of Lella, hurt because she shared him with other women, gave him pause.

"Few survive a battle of wits with my sister," Adam said, reining in beside Hamil. "Even, I see, the great Bey of Oran. Is your hide still intact?"

"Your father did Kamal a great disservice," Hamil said. "A woman should understand that—"

"Ah," Adam said, laughing, interrupting him, "she did poke a few holes in your hide!"

"She had the ignorant effrontery to suggest that women shoud have harems filled with handsome young men!"

Adam could think of no response, he was laughing so hard. He sobered quickly enough when their cavalcade reached Oran. Hamil had removed his *kufiyah* so that his people would recognize him. Adam gave his place to Kamal so that the two brothers rode side by side up the narrow path to the palace.

"I hope," Kamal said dryly, "that old Hassan will not collapse at the sight of you, my brother."

"I only hope he will want me back after these months with you!"

"He has suggested upon occasion that I have shown more wisdom than he had expected."

They reined in at the fort. Hamil and Kamal met with the Turkish captain, then rejoined the others and continued to the palace. Kamal's face was a set mask at the news the captain had given them.

"Brother," Hamil said, replacing his *kufiyah*, "I believe it best that you greet your mother as the Bey of Oran." At Kamal's startled look, he covered his brother's hand with his own and said softly, "Let me remain dead for a while. I know it saddens you, but for your peace, she must admit to what she has done. Perhaps," he added, not really believing his own words, "she now regrets her actions."

Kamal nodded, and Hamil left him alone while he spoke to the others.

Hamil watched the obeisances made to Kamal by his Turkish soldiers at the palace. He hung back with Adam and Rayna, pulling his *kufiyah* farther down over his brow.

"You found her!" Hassan bore down on Kamal and Arabella, beaming at Kamal. It was but an excuse. He whispered hurriedly to Kamal, "Your mother arrived yesterday. She was told by Raj that you had the woman beaten. She was most pleased."

Kamal merely nodded and strode forward, Arabella at his side, into, ironically to Kamal, the Hall of Justice. His mother, gowned not as a Muslim woman but as a European, stood beside his great chair. Her black hair looked glossy and was artfully piled about her face in small ringlets. Kamal felt sick at the sight of her joyous, triumphant expression.

"My son!" Giovanna gracefully stood on her toes to hug her son's shoulders and kiss him lightly on his cheek. She was not aware that Kamal did not return her greeting, for her eyes fell upon Arabella, looking for all the world like a dirty waif. But she still had those proud eyes, Giovanna thought. Kamal had not broken her pride.

"Raj told me, my son, that the girl escaped you after you had her beaten. I see you found her."

"Yes," Kamal said. "I found her."

He wanted to pull his mother into his private suite, to hide her shame and his, but Hamil would not be able to follow. He gazed at his brother from the corner of his eye, standing at the back of the hall, his head slightly lowered.

"Well, Lady Arabella," Giovanna said, her lips in a mocking smile, "have you enjoyed my son?"

Arabella smiled at her. "Actually, he is not as polished a lover as all my others, contessa. The gentlemen at the court of Naples"—she gave a delightful little shudder—"particularly the comte, were so gallant, so . . . civilized."

"You lie!" Giovanna snarled at her. "You were a virgin! I protected you against violation so that you would come to my son undiseased."

"Then why did you write to me that she was a slut, Mother?"

Giovanna drew up at the sound of her son's calm voice. Too calm. She drew in her breath, and her gentle smile caressed his face. "So that you would use her, my son, use her as I was used. So that she would experience what her parents forced me to experience."

"I had thought, Mother," Kamal continued in the same calm voice, "that we agreed that the children of the Earl and Countess of Clare were not to be involved."

"I had no choice," Giovanna said, her eyes dimming with regret. "The earl was too cowardly to come to Naples as I had hoped. His daughter . . ."

She broke off as Hassan gestured to Kamal. She glared at the old man, but Kamal turned to him and listened to his soft speech. Kamal straightened and turned back to his mother. "It seems, madam," he said, "that you will have your wish. The Earl of Clare has come to Oran and awaits outside."

Giovanna closed her eyes as joy swept through her. Nearly twenty-six years had passed. And now he was her prisoner, he who had spurned her! Would he look his years, be old and bent, his face wizened and ugly with age? Would he recognize her? She touched her fingers to her face, feeling the lines that indented her flesh. Better to savor the revenge that was now hers, and not the old flare of desire that had made her ache for him.

Anthony Welles, the Earl of Clare, paused in the entrance, gazing about the large chamber. His eyes fell upon his daughter, and he felt a reluctant smile curve his mouth at the proud tilt of her head and the calm expression on her lovely face. Adam had assured him but moments ago that Arabella was unharmed, but his anxiety had not vanished until he saw her. He hoped that Edward Lyndhurst, speechless upon seeing Rayna clothed like a boy and standing in the curve of Adam's arm, would not errupt until this business was done.

Giovanna's breath caught at the sight of him. Age had touched him, but not as she would have expected. He was still tall and upright, his shoulders wide, his body lean. His once-black hair was streaked with white, but his dark eyes as they touched her face were as vibrant as they had always been. Soon, she thought, he would be pleading with her to save his precious daughter. How she would delight in telling him that her son had taken Arabella's valuable virginity, treated her as he would any slave, and beaten her. How she would enjoy his humiliation, his rage, his helplessness!

The earl nodded to his daughter, staying her with his hand, and walked toward Giovanna.

"You have finally come," Giovanna said, hating herself at the sudden breathless quality in her voice.

"As you see, Giovanna," the earl said, and negligently brushed a fleck of dust from his immaculate blue sleeve.

"And your countess." She spat the word. "Did she willingly send you to your punishment alone?"

To her chagrin, the earl raised his eyes and gave her a wry smile. "Actually, Giovanna, my *wife* would now be at my side, despite my wishes, but she had the misfortune to badly sprain her ankle." He heard Arabella gasp behind him but did not turn. "You have seen my daughter, Giovanna. Her face must give you the memory of Cassandra's beauty."

"She will come!" Giovanna shouted, pain and hate ripping through her. "Were it not for her, you would have wed me!"

"Do you really believe that, Giovanna?" the earl asked pleasantly. "I fear, contessa, that your character now shows on your face."

Giovanna's hands flew to her cheeks, and she felt herself choking at his mocking words. "My son has rutted your daughter, my lord! Rutted her as a stallion ruts a mare! She is ruined!"

The earl's expression did not alter. Slowly he

turned to face his daughter. "Are you ruined, my dear?"

"No, Papa," Arabella said softly. "I am not ruined. It is true, I promise you."

The earl's face gave nothing away. "Giovanna," he said slowly, turning back to her, "did you not tell your son that you and my half-brother tried to have Cassandra killed? That she was brutally raped and would have died had I not saved her in time? Did you not tell him that I had broken with you long before I brought Cassandra to Genoa, that I no longer wanted you as my mistress? Did you not tell him that Khar El-Din captured you and my half-brother for the ten-thousand-pound reward I promised for the villains?"

"It is not true!" Giovanna shrieked. "You lie, my lord. You lie to save yourself and your precious daughter!"

"Why would I lie, Giovanna? You have paid for your crime, and the years have dulled my vengeance toward you."

"No! It is my vengeance!" She flung her arm toward her son. "Kill him, Kamal! He lies as he has always lied! Kill him and his miserable daughter!"

"Mother," Kamal said, pain dimming his eyes, "Hamil is alive."

Giovanna stared at her son. "No," she whispered, her eyes blank upon his face. "He cannot be! I was promised . . ."

He gazed at her hopefully, even as her treachery poured from her mouth. "Mother," he said, "it is true then."

Arabella felt sorrow wash through her at the sight of Kamal's set face. She wanted to go to him, to comfort him, but she stood still as he continued in a leaden voice. "He survived your plot to kill him." He turned slowly, like an old man, and called to Hamil, "My brother . . . the time for truth has come."

Giovanna felt her throat close at the sight of Hamil, vigorous and strong, his appearance changed only by the wide white streak through his black hair. She felt numb, frozen, her eyes locked on the man for whose death she had paid so dearly. A man who had never done her ill.

"No," she whimpered.

"Ah, Giovanna," the earl said, "what has your hatred brought you to? You had so much in Genoa. You could have wed another, enjoyed a full and happy life."

Arabella felt a surge of pity for the trembling woman, despite all she had done. She had listened to her father's calm recital of the crimes Giovanna had committed. It seemed impossible that such things had occurred, and to her mother. Kamal now wore a shuttered look, and her heart ached for him. Slowly she walked to his side and closed her hand over his.

"Do not touch him, you slut!"

Arabella had no time to move. Giovanna's hand struck her hard, and she felt her lip split.

Kamal gave a low feral snarl and caught Arabella against him, holding her tightly to keep himself from striking his mother.

"She has bewitched you," Giovanna shrieked at Kamal, "just as her mother did him! She is a doxy, a whore, just like her mother!"

Hamil saw his half-brother's face contort with pain and rage. Allah, he should have had her killed! He should have spared Kamal. He stepped forward, but was stopped by the earl, who said in a coldly dispassionate voice, "Giovanna, can you not admit to yourself that the images you have created from the past are not true? Must you now destroy your son with your hatred for me?"

Giovanna stared at the man who had haunted her dreams for so many years, the man she had desired above all others. "I loved you," she whispered. "You cast me off."

"Then it was I whom you should have tried to kill instead of Cassandra. She was innocent, Giovanna."

"She was your slut, not your wife! She followed you from England; it was she who kept you from me! If the *bravi* had killed her, you would have returned to me!"

The earl met his son's eyes across the hall. He heard Arabella say softly, "Father?" He had prayed that neither of his children would ever learn what had happened so many years before. Now, he realized, there was no hope for it. He felt the waves of tension sweeping about him like eddies in a whirlpool. He saw Rayna Lyndhurst in the circle of Adam's arm, her father standing still as a stone beside them.

"Giovanna," he said, his voice clear and calm,

for he was speaking not only to her but also to Rayna and his children, "I told you Cassandra was innocent. She is more innocent that you know. It was I who forced her to accompany me to Genoa. I stole her from the man she was to have married, Edward Lyndhurst, but a day before her wedding." He ignored Rayna's gasp of surprise, continuing, "I wanted to wed her, but it was she who refused me. She was my prisoner, Giovanna, at my villa. It was many months before she came to return my love. Let me ask you, Giovanna. Would you have tried to kill her had she been my wife?"

Giovanna knew he spoke the truth. Memories, so many memories. Cesare, the earl's half-brother, telling her that the English girl behaved like no man's mistress he had ever met. She had been so young, so golden, so proud. Her eyes sought Arabella. Young and golden and proud, like her mother.

"You have caused much misery and grief, Giovanna," the earl said, watching her closely. "You have hurt many innocent people, including your own son. It must cease."

"You left me with Khar El-Din," she snarled at him, leaning heavily against her son's chair, the chair from which he dispensed justice to his people each week. "You knew he held me. Damn you, you knew!"

"Yes," the earl said. "I knew, for he wrote to me to claim his reward. I left you with him, Giovanna, because I wanted my wife to know no more fear. I have answered my own question for you, I believe.

Had I arranged for you to return to Genoa, you would not have rested until you had killed my wife."

The truth of his words hung in the silent air, but the earl felt no sense of triumph, only an ineffable sadness for the misery of it all, the waste.

"Madam," Hamil said, "I am the Bey of Oran, and you are subject to my judgment. Because you are the mother of my half-brother, I will not have you killed. You will take the veil of your religion, madam. Perhaps in the years to come you will regret what you have done. If you do not, it will not matter, for we will be safe from your schemes." He turned to Hassan. "Escort her to Raj. Tomorrow she will travel to Sicily."

Kamal said quietly, "No, my brother. I shall escort her to Raj." He gazed at Arabella as if memorizing her face, then took his mother's arm and led her from the room.

Hamil said to the earl, "You shall be repaid for the ships and goods she had taken. I am sorry that so many men lost their lives. My brother was guilty only to the extent that he believed his mother, and vowed as a dutiful son to carry out her vengeance. He is an honorable man, my lord."

"I understand, highness," the earl said, his gaze going briefly to his daughter.

"Now I wish to see my wife and my son. Hassan, see to our guests' comfort."

"Papa," Arabella said, and flung herself into his arms. He hugged her tightly to him, his eyes closing for a brief moment.

"You smell like a horse," he said, holding her away from him.

She grinned up at him. "You should have smelled me and seen me when I arrived here! But it is all right, Papa," she added hurriedly. "Kamal is not like her." She lowered her lashes a moment. "His name is Alessandro. I . . . I love him, Papa."

The earl tried not to be shaken at her words. "So certain, Bella?"

"Yes," she said in her clear sweet voice.

"Life is never what one expects, is it?" he remarked, more to himself than to her.

"No," Arabella said, "it isn't. Papa, did you truly abduct Mother? The day before her wedding?"

The earl's smile was rueful. "Yes, my dear. I wanted your mother, had wanted her for several years. I took her. She fought me, escaped me, nearly got herself and me killed before she decided to keep me. She is a valiant woman, Bella, and you are much like her."

"But how could she not love you immediately?" Arabella asked in a wondering voice.

"Your faith in me is warming. I was, however, rather ruthless, you know. She was a gently nurtured young lady, and she thought she loved Edward Lyndhurst."

"Then I am right to love Kamal," she said with alarming certainty. "He too was ruthless."

"I am not certain," the earl said dryly, "if that is a trait I much appreciate in a man involved with my daughter."

"Well," she said blithely, "I was valiant too,

Papa, and since I didn't already love someone, it didn't take me long at all to decide I wanted Kamal. Not too long," she amended, flushing a bit.

"I see Lord Delford looking quite purposefully at me, my dear. We will discuss this . . . ruthlessness later."

"No wonder Lord Delford would like to send all of us to perdition!"

"I have spent six long days with Edward Lyndhurst," the earl said. "Let us hope that he is resigned to having Adam as his son-in-law. He became quite drunk one evening." The earl shook his head in amusement. "He was positively jovial. Most enlightening."

"You mean he became human?" Arabella asked, awed.

"Absolutely. Well, Adam, Rayna, you are both fit, though like Bella, you are in need of a bath."

"Father," Adam said firmly, "I am going to marry Rayna."

Lord Delford cast a bland glance at the earl. "You know, my lord, Rayna is my daughter."

"I had forgotten how like her mother she was. You are to be congratulated, Adam. Well, child, do you want my son?"

"With all my heart, my lord."

The earl paused a moment, and his brow furrowed. "I am not certain that it is a match I approve. After all, Delford, you have scarce behaved toward my son in an . . . approving manner."

"Clare . . ." the viscount said through gritted teeth.

"I believe you even called my son a scoundrel. Scarcely a term that a father could appreciate."

"He will change his mind, sir, when he gets to know Adam," Rayna said with great seriousness, her hazel eyes fastened on the earl's face.

"Do you really believe so, my dear?" The earl feigned a deep sigh. "I do not know. Perhaps, Delford, you can convince me that your daughter will content my son."

"Your jest wears thin, my lord!" the viscount said.

"Perhaps you are right," the earl said. "Why don't we send our children away and share a bottle of wine?"

Arabella giggled, then quickly coughed into her hands. "I'm sorry," she said. "Yes, I would like a bath. Poor Hassan, he looks like a worried aunt, surrounded by all these foreigners. Rayna, I'll take you to the harem."

"Harem!"

"She will join you in a moment, sister," Adam said drawing Rayna's hand through his arm.

"I suppose," Arabella said, eyeing the two of them with a complaisant expression, "that you want to kiss her and tell her all sorts of nonsense."

"Indeed," Adam drawled. "Now that I can forget about you, my dear, all my attention can shift to this little nuisance."

"Nuisance!" Rayna cried. "Arabella, don't believe him. Had it not been for me, I am certain he would have done something unbelievably foolish."

"Like dress yourself in harem trousers and take my place, brother?"

Adam flung up his hands in mock defeat. "All right, enough from both of you. Rayna, I swear you are no longer a nuisance. Father, Lord Delford, if you don't mind, Rayna and I will stroll for a few minutes in the gardens."

The viscount looked as though he would protest, but the earl gently nudged him in the ribs and led him away.

"Well, thank heaven, it's all over," Rayna said.

"And all of us are in one piece." Adam smiled down at Rayna and teased her gently, "It would appear that I was right to have faith in my sire's ability to bring your father around."

"True," she said placidly. "As yet, I am not certain about your virility."

"I imagine our wedding trip in the Aegean will settle that question."

"I trust so," Rayna said demurely.

"Little baggage! Have you ever seen the *Cassandra*?"

Rayna shook her head, then sighed. "No, and my father is likely to have a fit when he discovers how we're going to spend our wedding trip. He will say it's only a bloody boat, totally unsafe, with but strips of wood between us and drowning."

"Maybe we should guard it as a secret. Or, since it seems that your father and my mother were closer than we imagined, we should leave it to her to convince your father."

"Doubtful," Rayna said thoughtfully. "You know, perhaps Father is too fixed on his dislike of the sea. I have decided to give you a chance to prove to me it's safe," she added handsomely. "Do not forget, Adam, that I wasn't seasick once aboard the *Malek* or Hamil's *xebec*."

"If you continue to be such a good sailor, I shall have to impress you into the navy. Perhaps you could serve with Nelson."

"Wouldn't my brothers have a fit!" She giggled. "Imagine, all of them in the army. Now, my lord, if you will excuse me, I will join Arabella in the harem."

Adam kissed her lightly on the lips and watched her follow one of the slaves to the harem. When he rejoined his father and the viscount, he heard Lyndhurst say, "I don't like it, Clare. A harem! It's ridiculous. You are certain they will be all right?"

"They will be surrounded only by women, my dear Edward," the earl said. "Certainly safer than with the men they've decided to wed."

"Father . . ." Adam said, his eyes narrowing.

"Ah," the earl said blandly, "here is Kamal. Perhaps you would like to accompany him, my son. I will become acquainted with him later."

"Father," Adam said softly, "Kamal is not what he appears. He was educated in Europe."

The earl merely nodded.

"I had no idea," the viscount said slowly, once

they were alone again, "that Cassie had been harmed. She never told me."

"No. It has been many years now, yet every once in a while she still dreams of it."

The viscount accepted a glass of wine from a silent slave, and raised it in toast to the earl. "Perhaps," he said slowly, "I should forgive, finally, all that happened so long ago. The woman Giovanna—her hatred is chilling."

"I should be pleased if you would, Edward. It would be an excellent idea, I think, given that we shall be like to share many grandchildren in the future."

"Not in the too near future, I hope," the viscount said, but there was a crooked smile on his face.

"My sentiments exactly," the earl agreed.

"Giovanna's son, Kamal—what will become of him? I gather that he is innocent of his mother's deeds."

"I am not certain," the earl said. "Arabella wishes him for a husband." At the viscount's widened eyes, the earl added, "Yes, it is a problem, is it not?"

"You could not allow it! The man is a foreigner, a Muslim!"

"At this point, I don't know what he is. If he is as honorable as Hamil said, I fear that it will be he who will refuse Arabella. When Hassan returns, allow him to show you to a chamber, Edward. I think I shall speak to the young man."

Not long thereafter, Ali bowed the foreign gentleman into his master's private bathing room. Kamal had just emerged from his bath. He stood naked at the edge of the pool, his thoughts clearly elsewhere, even when Ali spoke to him. "Highness," Ali repeated.

The earl studied the young man. He was tall, well-formed, a handsome man, but that, the earl knew, was of little importance. He carried most of his father's features, save they were refined, purified. His body looked taut, pain emanating from him.

"What is it you want, Ali? And do not call me 'highness' anymore."

"One of the foreign gentlemen to see you."

Kamal turned around, then stood very still, his eyes locked on the earl. Very slowly he wrapped a towel about his waist and nodded dismissal to his servant.

"Your daughter lied to you, my lord," he said. "She is not as she was."

"My exuberant daughter is no longer a virgin?"

"No, she is not."

"Well, you still live, Kamal, so you must please her."

A reluctant smile creased Kamal's cheeks. He touched the healing wound on his shoulder. "She is unlike any other woman I have ever known."

"My son tells me you were educated in Europe?"

"Yes. I had not thought to return to Oran until the supposed death of Hamil. Then I had no choice."

"No, I suppose not. Duty is a stern taskmaster, I have always found. Pride is another."

Kamal turned away from him, his jaw clenching. "Your daughter must wed a man of her own rank, an Englishman, a man whose honor is unquestioned."

"My daughter refused such a paragon. It is you she wants. I have found that when Bella makes up her mind, an earthquake would have no effect. Do you not love my daughter? Do you wish to live as a Muslim and remain in Oran?"

"I wish you to take your daughter back to where she belongs."

"You know," the earl said gently, "you cannot be blamed for your mother's deeds. Her bitterness does not touch you. What is more important is that you must not blame yourself."

Kamal waved away his words. He said very calmly, "I want Arabella's happiness. I would appreciate it, my lord, if you would take her back to Genoa as soon as possible."

"She will not understand."

"She will do as you and I bid her."

"Damnation!" Adam said. "What are you going to do, Father?"

"I will do as Kamal wishes. We are all leaving on the morrow, aboard the *Cassandra*. Captain Sordello, as you can well imagine, is dizzy with relief at our arrival and his freedom. Yes, we will leave tomorrow, and then we shall see."

"Where is my sister now?"

"With Hamil and Lella, admiring their son."

"I have told your fierce husband, Lella," Arabella was saying, "how sad you were without him. Now, if only he will see reason, all will be well."

"Reason, Arabella?" Lella asked, puzzled.

"I suggest, my lady," Hamil said sternly, "that you keep your idiotic opinions to yourself, else I shall call my brother to remove you."

"We will hope," Arabella said, disregarding him, "that your son has more of his uncle in him, Lella. Look how he is clutching my finger."

"He is his father's son and he is trying to break it!" Hamil growled.

"Arabella, what have you done to put my husband so out of temper with you?"

"I simply told him," Arabella said in great innocence, her eyes wide, "that if he is to keep a harem, you should have one also."

Lella blinked at her, then began to laugh, a joyous sound that made Hamil's heart swell. "Ah, my husband," she said, still gasping with laughter, "I have seen a very handsome young soldier. Unlike you, he has no streak of white hair on his head."

"Lella!" He turned narrowed eyes toward Arabella. "Now that you have stirred the hornet's nest, I suggest you go torment my poor brother!"

Arabella merely smiled, and hugged the black-haired baby once again. "That," she said, "is an excellent idea!" She walked jauntily from Lella's chamber. Still smiling, she strode to her old room and rang for Lena.

Kamal stood alone in his chamber, a glass of brandy in his hand. He quickly downed it, feeling its warmth all the way to his belly. But it could not erase his mother's twisted face from his mind. She had said nothing further until he had delivered her into Raj's care. To Kamal's surprise, she had raised her face to the eunuch and said quietly, "You have won, have you not?"

"No," Kamal said now to his silent chamber. "No one has won, I least of all."

If only, he thought, he had known Arabella's father, none of this would have occurred. He felt a lurching pain even as he thought of the man's understanding. The earl's dark eyes, so like Arabella's, had but added to his pain. Tomorrow she would be gone from his life, and he would never see her again.

He struck his fist against the wall, but his inner pain was so great that he scarcely noticed.

"Master."

He turned to face Ali, knowing that the boy knew what had happened, just as everyone in the palace now probably knew.

"Leave me," he said.

"His highness wishes that you and he dine with the foreigners, master. We must hurry."

To face Arabella once more. For a brief moment he pictured her beneath him, her hands kneading the muscles of his back, her soft body open to him. He could practically taste the sweetness of her, feel her breathless moans of pleasure reaching deep within him, igniting his own desire, until he thought he would explode with it. And her bravery. A woman to swell a man's heart with pride. A woman who would wed a man other than himself, and bear his children, not Kamal's.

"Master, you must go."

His dazed eyes peered through Ali. "Yes," he said finally.

"Hassan is beside himself," Ali said, grinning. "He is running to and fro, praising the return of Hamil, yet wishing that the both of you could rule. What will you do now, master?"

Kamal said nothing while Ali pulled his shirt over his head.

Ali continued irrepressibly, "Will you wed with the beautiful English lady? You will likely have to beat her, master. Her tongue is too sharp and would make a man's rod soft. Ah, but what children you will make, master! Golden and proud, all of them!"

"There will be no children," Kamal said harshly. "Give me my belt, Ali!"

Ali, cowed by Kamal's ill humor, did as he was bade.

Once dressed, Kamal looked a moment about his chamber. "Have all my things removed, Ali. My brother will wish everything to be as it was." He did not wait for his servant's reply, but strode from his chamber. He stood quietly in the doorway of the banquet hall for several moments, watching all the people who had changed his life. All save his mother were there. Lella sat beside Hamil, her smile so radiant that it would have shamed the sun. The girl Rayna was dressed in a European gown, her lovely hair piled high on her head. His eyes went from Adam to the earl, and he recognized them as strong men, honorable men. He found himself tautly searching for Arabella. She was not present. He wondered, a stab of pain searing through him, if she had refused to be present. Did she now despise him? Well, he thought, it is what you want, you fool!

"My brother," Hamil called out, waving to him. "Bring your handsome devil's face here. My Lella commands it!"

Kamal nodded, and seated himself beside his half-brother. He felt stiff, unnatural, as if it were another man peering through his eyes.

The earl toyed with his goblet of wine, wondering how Giovanna and Khar El-Din had produced such a magnificent son. He understood the young man's pain, but knew, for the moment at least, there was nothing he could do about it. There was a sudden silence around the low table, and he looked up toward the arched doorway. His jaw dropped. Arabella, garbed in shimmering yellow harem trousers and jacket, her sunlit hair long and flowing down her back, smiled a small, quite wicked smile, her eyes upon Kamal.

She walked gracefully forward, her eyes never leaving his face. Slowly she sank to her knees before him and touched her lips to his boot. Her hair cascaded about her, touching the thick carpet.

Kamal flinched as if struck. "Get up!" he roared.

Arabella raised her head and searched his face. She cocked her head to one side in question, the gentle woman's smile never leaving her lips. "Yes, my lord," she said in a beguiling voice. "If that is your wish." She turned to smile impishly at Hamil. "Is not a mere woman to show her loyalty and respect to her master?"

"Indeed," Hamil laughed, "but not, I vow, in front of your father! You may kiss my brother's boots in private, my lady!"

"Sit down," Kamal said in a furious whisper, "and cease your nonsense."

"Yes, my lord," she said docilely, her eyes still twinkling.

"Arabella," Rayna said in awed tones, "you look so . . . different."

"I've a mind to see you thus clothed, my love," Adam observed. "But first I must see to having my boots polished."

The earl watched his daughter's eyes searching Kamal's set face. There was such longing in her fine eyes that he winced. He knew deep within him that, like him, she would love but once. Perhaps, he thought, she could convince Kamal that his mother's shame did not touch him.

"You are silent, Kamal," Arabella said softly.

He ignored her for the moment, nodding toward the slave boys to serve the dinner. "There is much on my mind," he said tersely.

"I . . . I am sorry about your mother, Kamal. Perhaps we will visit her in the future, if it is your wish."

"No," he said. "It is not my wish."

Arabella frowned at his profile. Not once had he even looked at her since she had seated herself beside him. She wondered if she had embarrassed him with her clothes and her dramatic gesture. He seemed angry, remote, and she did not understand. The spiced lamb tasted like ashes in her mouth. She looked toward her father. "How did mother sprain her ankle, sir?"

"How else?" the earl said, smiling. "On her sailboat, of course. She tripped on the dock. Still, I nearly had to tie her down to keep her from coming with me."

Adam laughed, and lightly squeezed Rayna's hand. "So that is what I have to look forward to, my love? Tying you down to keep you safe and sound? I fear, Father, that my little dove has finally shown herself to be a hawk."

Lella said to Hamil, "Do you wish me to leave, my love, so I will not be influenced to rebellion?"

"I will simply keep your belly filled with child and your mind filled with me."

Kamal flinched. God, how he wished for the dinner to end. He felt like a wounded animal who wanted only to skulk away and tend his pain in private. He felt himself go pale when Hamil raised his wine goblet and said in a hearty voice, "Although my esteemed brother has returned his throne to me, I vow that he will not repine. He has gained a woman who, if he treats her as a man must a willful wife, will bring him great happiness. Keep her on her knees, my brother, but I warn you to keep your mistresses a secret from her, else she'll bring you low!"

Kamal uncoiled his powerful body and rose. He looked toward the earl. "Lady Arabella will leave on the morrow with her father. She will return to the life to which she was raised."

He heard Arabella gasp, but did not turn toward her. He strode from the chamber.

"My dear," Lella said, grasping Arabella's wrist. "You must give him time."

"No!"

"Arabella," the earl said sharply, "leave it be!"

She turned pained eyes to her father. "You knew, did you not? You knew that he no longer wanted me!"

She rose clumsily and rushed from the chamber, heedless of the babble of voices behind her. She paused in the palace garden and breathed in the clean evening air. He was being noble, damn him, she thought. She leaned over the wall and saw Kamal striding away from the palace, down the winding road to the fort.

The fragile leather slippers were not made for running, but Arabella ignored the sharp rocks and dashed after him. The soldiers made no move to stop her. "Kamal!"

She saw him pause as if struck. He turned slowly. "Go back, Arabella. I have no wish to see you again."

Cleansing anger washed through her. "Then talk to me, you coward! Do not run from me!"

"Very well," he said, and waited for her to reach

him. She was before him, her luminous eyes searching his face. Her silken hair fell over her shoulders like soft, flowing honey. His fingers itched to touch her, but he stood stiffly, saying nothing.

"I . . . I do not understand," Arabella said. "What have I done to displease you?"

He stepped back as she reached out her hands to him. "You have done nothing."

"Then why are you behaving like this? I thought that you would be pleased. Hamil is returned; you are free. You are free to be with me."

"No," he said. "I am not free."

"You speak in riddles, Kamal. Please, tell me what troubles you."

He drew a deep breath, knowing that she would continue to argue with him if he told her the truth. She could not understand his shame, his dishonor. In a very calm, emotionless voice he said, "I much enjoyed my time with you, my lady. But it is over."

Arabella stared at him, her thoughts tumbling over themselves in confusion. "You cannot mean it," she said at last. "You make it sound as though I was naught but a diversion to relieve your boredom."

"What else?" He shrugged, and turned away from her to look out over the Mediterranean, shimmering under the white moon.

"No," she whispered.

"I enjoyed taking your virginity, but your skills do not compare with those of my other women."

"Why are you saying these things?" She wouldn't

cry, though she felt her body shuddering with pain at his cruel words. "I love you."

"It will pass," he said.

"But you told me you loved me!"

"A man will say many things when he desires a woman in his bed. But remember what those words gave me. A willing, yielding woman to writhe beneath me. I vowed I would break you to my hand, and I succeeded . . . too well. You are now no different from my other women, spiritless and docile, and utterly submissive."

She sucked in her breath, her pain blending with unreasoning fury. She drew back her hand and slapped him with all her strength. His head snapped back with the force of her blow, but his arms remained rigidly at his sides.

Arabella whirled about and raced back up the road to the palace, low, animal moans breaking from her throat.

Kamal watched her fleeing from him, fleeing from his life. Slowly, as if in a dream, he turned and continued to walk stiffly toward the fort.

29

Villa Parese, Genoa, 1803

Arabella hiked up her skirts and stepped from her sailboat onto the dock. The day was warm and the old muslin dress, more gray than blue from many washings, clung damply to her back. She felt tendrils of hair curling haphazardly about her face, and impatiently tucked them behind her ears. Her mother would tease her about catching no trout for their dinner, but she hadn't so much as lowered her fishing pole into the calm waters of the lake. Why wouldn't the pain go away? she wondered. Is this what she had to look forward to? The crushing emptiness that gave her no peace?

Two months. Two months since she had returned to Genoa, to the Villa Parese. It seemed more like a decade. At least she no longer had to smile and play the role of the happy sister. Adam and Rayna had been married a month before and were now sailing in the Aegean on their wedding trip. Rayna's parents had shortly thereafter returned to England. How odd it had felt to watch Viscount Delford with her mother, knowing now what had really happened. To believe that if her own father had not stolen her mother away, she could have been the viscount's daughter. What would it be like, she wondered, to have a man love you so much that he would abduct you from under your fiancé's nose?

She turned and stared down at her reflection in the placid water. She looked thin and drawn, her mouth a straight line with no lurking laughter in her eyes. She felt drawn to the water for a long moment, until she realized the direction of her thoughts and drew up sharply.

"Do not be a damned spineless coward," she said aloud to her reflection. She hurled her fishing pole into the water and watched her face dim into rippling waves.

She and her parents would be returning to England in the early fall. Hundreds of miles away from Kamal. Alessandro. Were he in England with her, he would be Alexander. She pressed her fists to her temples, wanting to blot his face from her mind, but his fierce Viking's blue eyes devoured her, caressing her thoughts, understanding her as no man had ever understood her. Yet he had not wanted her.

She felt suddenly small and defeated, empty as a husk tossed aside by a careless hand. Surprisingly, Arabella felt tears sting her eyes. She had shed no tears since that awful night in Oran. Indeed, she had felt numb, mouthing good-byes to Hamil and

Lella, numb as the *Cassandra* sailed from Oran's harbor. Oddly enough, upon their return to the Villa Parese, her home had felt alien to her; it was Oran that seemed real.

She shook herself, forcing herself to think of Kamal's harem. That had certainly been real. And Elena, far more experienced and skilled than she was. Did Kamal still take her to his bed? Did he take a different woman to his bed each night?

"You savage! You barbarian!" She shook her fist over the silent lake.

"I am pleased I am still in your thoughts, Arabella, even though you insult me."

She blinked at the softly spoken words. She was imagining things. She wanted him so badly that she even dreamed of him speaking to her.

"How long will you ignore me, Arabella?"

Slowly she turned. Kamal, dressed as finely as any European gentleman, stood on the end of the dock, gazing at her. "You cannot be real," she whispered, half-covering her eyes with her hand.

He strode toward her, the dark brown knit trousers molding to his muscular thighs. She took a shaky step backward. She heard him shout as her foot came down into empty air. She gave a yelping cry as she fell backward, and flung her arms toward him.

Kamal caught her and pulled her back onto the dock. "I have saved you from a soaking," he said. "Will that gain me something other than curses?"

"You are truly here," Arabella said, her eyes hungrily devouring him.

"Yes," he said.

"You look so very fine."

"I thank you, my lady." He grinned, his blue eyes twinkling down at her, and proffered her a mock bow. "Did you believe the savage barbarian could not clothe himself as a gentleman?"

Arabella's gaze was serious upon his face. "I was thinking of you bedding other women. Elena . . . your harem."

"Elena is now wed to a Turkish captain. As for the other women, I seem to have lost my taste for their favors." His voice dropped to a husky murmur. "The only woman I want is a stubborn hellion who makes me want to thrash her one moment and love her the next, until she moans in my arms."

"Oh." She felt suddenly shy, and fastened her eyes upon the toes of her sturdy shoes.

"I was not expecting you to still appear so slender. Indeed, you are too thin."

Arabella cocked her head to one side. "You believed I would stuff myself with food without you?"

"No, but our babe . . ." He broke off suddenly, realizing that the earl had used his honor against him. He grinned, then threw back his head and laughed deeply. "You, my love," he gasped, "are about as pregnant as I am!"

Arabella felt herself go rigid, the joy that had begun to burgeon within her withering. "You came," she said dully, "only because you thought I carried your child?"

He grew immediately serious, and said quietly,

"That I believed you pregnant gave me the excuse to come to you."

"And now will you leave again?"

"I fear if I tried, your father would have me locked up. He has been most concerned with your unhappiness."

"I am not unhappy," Arabella said with stiff perversity. "I want no man's pity. You, your highness, can take your condescending hide back to Oran and wallow in your harem!"

"But I am no longer a highness, and no longer maintain a harem. You now behold, Arabella, a simple man who owns three ships and little else, a man who indeed has very little to offer you. Not even a gentleman's title."

She ran her tongue over her suddenly dry lips.

"Without words, *cara*?" he mocked her gently. "If you will not speak to me, you might as well kiss me."

He pulled her against him and lowered his head. She felt his lips, light and undemanding, touch her mouth. She shuddered at the feel of him, his scent, his sweet taste.

"Please do not make sport of me," she whispered into his mouth.

His kiss deepened, and she felt the urgency of his need in his trembling body and his hard manhood against her belly. Her unhappiness vanished, leaving her wildly giddy. She wound her arms around his neck and pressed herself against him.

"If we continue," he growled softly, deep in his throat, "our babe will quickly become a reality."

She tugged at his thick hair, and let her tongue mingle with his until she was trembling with desire. When he lifted her hips, pressing her hard against him, she moaned softly into his mouth.

"Arabella, we must talk."

"Yes," she gasped. "Yes, we must talk."

He smiled at her tenderly. "I will take care of your baser needs once we are married, and not before."

The earl watched his daughter tug Kamal's hand, leading him into the shelter of the forest. A smile touched his lips and he turned to walk back to the villa. He imagined that his son-in-law would do quite nicely in shipping. All in all, his mild deception had worked quite well.

"I will do whatever you wish, my lord," Arabella said, and kissed Kamal's nose.

"I do remember how pleasurable it is to gain your obedience."

Arabella rubbed her cheek along his smooth jaw. "It has been two months, Kamal. It seemed like forever."

"I know, for me also. I saw my mother, Arabella, in the convent in Sicily. She was very quiet, withdrawn. I almost wished to hear her cursing, vowing vengeance."

"Have you finally forgiven yourself for what she did?"

"No, but perhaps, in time, my shame will dim. I love you, Arabella, but I was like a miserable animal in pain. I could not bear to have you witness my dishonor."

"But I am a part of you! What you feel, I feel. You must promise me never again to lock me out."

"Since you are an old woman of twenty, I suppose I must grant you some wisdom."

"Now you are teasing, and I am serious, Kamal!" She buffeted him in the stomach lightly with her fist.

"Behold a serious man," he said. "Your father and mother must wonder what we are doing. I doubt they will believe that I haven't thrown you to the ground and had my way with you."

"I really do not think it a bad idea."

"Are you certain, Arabella?"

"Certain I want you to have your way with me?"

"Witch! Certain that you wish to wed me?"

"I will follow you back to Oran dressed in harem veils if you try to escape me."

"And will you fall to your knees before me and kiss my boots?"

"Yes, master," she said, lowering her lashes so he could not see the outrageous laughter in her eyes.

"And you will allow me as many mistresses as I desire?"

"If I leave you the strength to pursue another woman, I will not cavil."

He laughed deeply, and hugged her to him.

"Kamal," she said softly, "will you mind living in England? And in Italy, of course, unless Napoleon boots us out?"

He answered her in stilted, charmingly accented English. "If my lady will keep me warm during the long winters, I will contrive to be content. I will want to visit Oran, you know," he continued, switching back to Italian.

"As will I. Kamal, I do not wish to uproot you from what you know. It would not be fair to you."

He was silent for a moment. "It is odd," he said finally, "but I felt uprooted when I returned to Oran as bey. I suppose my knit breeches fit me better than my white trousers. There will be difficulties, Bella. Much will be new to me."

"But we will share, Kamal," she said firmly. "Everything. Has Hamil slipped back into his old ways?"

"He is a Muslim, Arabella, as is Lella. But I noticed that he showed little interest in his harem. He spends most of his time with his son. Incidentally, I met your mother. She is charming. You have much the look of her."

"And here I thought she had had a boring courtship compared to mine!"

"Have you spoken to her about what you learned?"

"No. Father asked Adam and me not to."

"Perhaps it is for the best. Your father, by the way, is pleased. Never will he have to pay more guineas for tribute. And since I will join him in shipping, we are likely to become disgustingly rich."

"All right," she said agreeably. She stared up at him, her breath drawn in suddenly at the sight of his beloved face. "We had best not stay here," she said hoarsely, "else I will keep you in the woods until winter."

"I do not know how you can be so slender with such appetites."

"Only with you: a gentleman who is a Viking, a pirate, a highness, and a magnificent lover."

"This gentleman," Kamal said, gently stroking her jaw, "fully intends to plunder, pursue, and otherwise possess this lady until she has no thought of another."

"Do you promise?" she asked, touching her fingertips to his lips.

"You have my pirate's oath on it," he said.

About the Author

When best-selling Regency and historical-romance writer Catherine Coulter is not at work on a novel, she spends her time sailing, playing the piano, reading, or enjoying beautiful Marin with her husband, Anton.

Catherine Coulter is the author of the historical romances *DEVIL'S EMBRACE, CHANDRA,* and *SWEET SURRENDER* as well as of many Regency romances— *THE AUTUMN COUNTESS, THE REBEL BRIDE, LORD DEVERILL'S HEIR, LORD HARRY'S FOLLY, THE GENEROUS EARL, AN HONORABLE OFFER, AN INTIMATE DECEPTION*— all available in Signet editions.